GW01397874

Rising on Dragon Wings

Magic of Virankan, Book One

Baine Fox

BAINE FOX LLC

Dedication

For Adam, and for our children. I love you all.
Also, are you happy now, Adam? I wrote the damn book!

Acknowledgements

Christine, for keeping me focused and letting me spitball ideas at you constantly. I can't wait to see "Christine W. Henkle" at all my local booksellers when you're the next big thing!!
Thank you to everyone who read an alpha and beta draft.
Viki Luxe, thank you for ALL your formatting help, and for cracking that whip to keep me in line! (Y'all should go read her books, they're awesome!)
Romance Discord, y'all are just the best. Thanks for putting up with me.
Kayleigh of Enchanted Edits, the best editor.
Kierston of WildCraft Maps, my map is incredible, you're amazing. I would never have gotten this far without your helping in bringing Virankan to life.
Thank you.

Glossary

I WANT EVERYONE TO be able to enjoy my world as much as I do, and part of that is ensuring that there is no confusion in how I intended places and characters to be pronounced. I know we've all read at least one book with a difficult character name; we sounded it out and settled on how we thought it was, only to learn it's incorrect. Hopefully this pronunciation guide will prevent that!

I've also included races and places that are mentioned (but not directly involved) in this story, and a brief explanation of what they are.

Alyss: like Alice
Amthryn: AM-thren
Anitra: Ah-NEE-tra
Aprana: App-rah-nuh, no emphasis
Balvin Island: BAAL-vin, home to a dormant volcano and a Stoneborn mining operation. Some humans still live on the island, mostly living and working near the mine or fishing along the coast.
Beltak: BEL-tak
Bonded: short for Dragon-bonded, see below

vii

Draconid: Druh-CON-id, A special gift given to a dragon-bonded person who has gone above and beyond for the dragon race, showing great compassion, bravery, and self-sacrifice. Allows for the partial shift into a half-dragon form, humanoid body with wings, horns, and tail of a dragon. Grants the recipient additional strength, speed, and more magical power than their humanoid form.

Dragon: Four legged, two winged reptile creatures that can control wind and fire with their magic. Females have two horns that resemble a domestic goat's horns. Males have four horns, two that match the female's, and two that curl on the side of their head similar to a ram.

Dragon-bonded: A Skinshifter who is bonded to a dragon at birth. When the Vynar lays a clutch, those eggs are imbued with magic that connects the hatchling to a Skinshifter. The infant and hatchling will be born at the same moment, and be bound to each other for life. Dragon-bonded will have two animal forms, whichever animal they inherited from a parent, and a dragon form.

Eerla: EAR-la

Faladrik: Fa-LAH-drick

Fates: The four Fates are Viranka, Goddess of Creation, Eskan, Seer of Destiny, Chava, who rules over life, and Dante, who rules over death. After the creation of the world, the Fates retired to their rest far beneath the surface of the planet, and have not been seen for millenia.

Hatherus: HATH-eh-russ

Human: a race of people that did not magically evolve as much as other races did. Some humans do have magic, these are called Mages. Humans almost exclusively live on Shaesan, a far distant continent. In recent history, the human king has agreed to favorable trade terms and currently the races are at peace, but some factions fear Virankan and its magical people.

Jarn: like John or Jack, yarn with a J.

Jessamine/Minnie: Jess-a-myn/MIN-ee

Maurgen: Mar-GEN, -gen is a hard g, as in get

Narith: Nar-eth

Nightwalker: a race of people who dwell underground in the hills of central Virankan, they are unable to withstand direct sunlight and exist entirely in darkness or night. The Nightwalkers have different sub-species within their race, with varying powers, abilities, and restrictions.

Ocrans: Ock-rens

Otikul: Oh-teh-kull

Sea of Monsters: A section of ocean between Virankan, Balvin Island, and Dragon Isle that is home to many deep water creatures. Despite being so close to land, the ocean is deepest here, a fissure caused by an ancient earthquake. It is extremely dangerous to sail in these waters. Very few people attempt to cross, and even fewer succeed.

Skinshifter: a race of people that live in the plains and lower hills of Virankan, each person has an inherited animal form they can shift into at will.

Stoneborn: a race of people that prefer to live in or under the mountain region to the north. Their skin can become hard as stone when needed. Their magic is primarily centered around the elements of earth and fire, and they are the keepers of all the ancient records and legends.

Taurak: TAR-ack

Virankan: VEER-ank-en, the continent and world named for the goddess Viranka, one of the four Fates.

Vyn: Vin, the first dragon who formed a bond with a human

Vynar: VY-nar, the leader of the dragon race and the only female who can lay and hatch Bonded dragons. She mates less frequently than other females, and her mating flights are a celebrated occasion for all dragons and Bonded, called the Rising.

Wealdkin: WIELD-kin, a race of people most commonly found living in the Wildwood Forest, capital city is Amthryn. They have a wide array of nature-based magic that varies by person.

Zahite: Zah-height

Zavier: ZAY-vee-er

Zeniyah: Zen-AYE-ah

One

Zavier

A SHIVER OF EXCITEMENT raced through his draconic body as the Spire of Hatherus came into view. The imposing tower rose over the bustling city like a sentinel standing guard, complete with small dragon statues facing each cardinal direction. After two years away, the familiar sight of his bustling city filled him with immense joy. He couldn't contain the happy burst of flame that rose from his chest and erupted from his maw.

Prince Zavier Davengard, dragon Skinshifter and ambassador for his people, was used to spending months away on diplomatic errands. However, this last trip had by far been his longest stint away from home. What had begun as a simple renegotiation of trade agreements between the Skinshifters and Humans had turned violent, setting off a chain of events that kept him busy and traveling for over two years. He'd crossed the ocean and two continents several times in those two years, been to half a dozen

1

cities, and met with hundreds of dignitaries. He was more than ready for a relaxing stay at home with his family.

From far below, the bellow of dragons heralded his group's arrival. While he soared above them, his parent's dragons, Alyss and Faladrik, lay sprawled along the bank of the River Virankan, sunning themselves. The pair of dragons watched as Zavier's group of Skinshifters winged closer. Maurgen, Zavier's golden dragon partner who flew alongside him, returned their greeting with a roar of his own.

Maurgen angled his descent to land near the waiting dragons at the river, but Zavier's guard Jarn and his maroon dragon Zahite began to circle down to the city. Zavier followed Jarn toward the palace courtyard while the other guards in their party split off to land at another courtyard.

"Don't forget to tell your father about the Stoneborn offering you their princess in marriage," Maurgen teased through their mental link.

Groaning, Zavier replied, *"I'd rather not tell him. I'm honestly not sure if Father would be honored that their king would trust us with his only daughter, or furious with me for turning down a marriage, any marriage... Or worried that I offended Otikul by refusing her!"*

Zavier heard Maurgen release a long-suffering sigh. *"You're over-thinking, idiot, and you're ruining my fun. King Otikul is your friend and ally, he offered you his daughter as an alliance. He accepted your reasons for refusing."* Maurgen snorted, sending the mental image of himself settling down on the river bank. *"I just want to hear what your father says, it might be amusing."*

"Go sun yourself, you great over-sized lizard," Zavier replied, annoyed that Maurgen had gotten the better of him. He landed gently beside Jarn in the mas-

sive courtyard. Like many other places in Hatherus, the courtyard had been built to accommodate the immense size of dragons. Zavier raised the magic to shift his skin, allowing the warm flow of power to creep over his body. It started almost as a tingle in his shoulders as his wings began to disappear. As the world shifted around him, he closed his eyes. His huge dragon-form shrank down and changed, bones popping and rearranging painlessly into his humanoid shape.

His parents, King Taurak and Queen Narith, appeared at the top of the steps at the main entrance to the palace, waving eagerly. A teenage boy on the cusp of manhood pushed past them and leaped from the stairs to bolt toward Zavier.

"Branton?" he had time to say before the youth collided with him, nearly knocking him off his feet. Wrapping his arms about the boy, Zavier was unnerved to realize his "little" brother was the same height as himself. "You're going to be a giant, Brant!" Zavier chuckled.

Shoving his elder brother in the arm, Branton's cheeks flushed pink. "Not you, too! Father has been making height jokes for months!"

Laughing, Zavier draped an arm over his brother's shoulders and the pair strode toward their waiting parents. "That's what happens when you grow up, little brother; people make ridiculous comments. They did the same when I was your age. I think it's a rite of passage."

"Welcome home!" Their father, Taurak, engulfed Zavier in a warm embrace. Holding his son at arm's length, Taurak ruefully shook his head and said, "I'd nearly forgotten what you look like!"

Zavier snorted as Narith pushed her husband aside, eagerly welcoming her son with a kiss on his cheek. "How can you possibly forget what he looks like, Taurak? He is the spitting image of you, just like his brothers. How are you, dearest? Have you eaten?"

Her constant mothering had been annoying when he was last home, Zavier mused, but now he found it a comforting reminder of her love. Smiling, he nodded. "I'm perfectly well, and yes, we ate a few hours ago. I'd like to give my verbal report now, if we could."

"Come along then," Taurak said, gesturing up the stairs for his wife to go ahead of him. "Your mother and I have a council dinner meeting tonight, but tomorrow night the family can eat together. Caddoc has also been called back."

As they entered the foyer and turned down the hallway that led to his father's study, Zavier wondered if his elder brother would actually come home. The last he had heard, Caddoc was in Lockhill with a pair of Nightwalker women 'entertaining' him, but that had been at least a month ago.

His father's office and study felt and looked the same as it had the last time he'd been home. An ancient wooden desk sat in front of a wide bay window with a well worn wing-back chair behind it. Across the room, a group of sofas and armchairs circled a brazier, currently unlit on this warm spring day. Books and scrolls lined one wall beside a door that led to his father's private library. Sinking into his favorite armchair, Zavier waited for his family to arrange themselves before launching into his report of the past two years.

They knew all of it already, of course. He'd sent detailed reports back bi-monthly, sometimes more, along with personal letters for each member of his family. Every time he thought he'd completed negotiations, yet another issue arose and he'd had to

4

start over. Most recently, there had been a skirmish between two Nightwalker factions near the Stoneborn border that had spilled over the territory lines and disrupted mining operations. Mediating between the other races took delicate skill, especially with the hot-tempered Stoneborn and the coldly calculating Nightwalkers.

"And finally, King Otikul of the Stoneborn is excited to offer a dozen of his finest craftsmen and miners to us in exchange for an equal number of our farmers. They have already cleared several acres in a valley near Nagrain that has good sun. They are hoping to increase their farming productivity with our help."

Pensive, Taurak asked, "Do you feel that the trade is fair? How long would this exchange last?"

"The farmers would stay for at least two seasons, through the harvest. We'd want to ensure the Stoneborn are confident in their farming before our people return home. I do think we're getting the better end of the deal," Zavier replied frankly. "We should offer to send not just farmers, but men who are familiar with the mountains and how to farm in those valleys. Particularly ones able to use their animal skins to help clear, plow, and gather. Aprana has several families that have experience with those mountains."

Smiling with pride at her son, Narith added, "Eerla would also have people with knowledge of rough farming conditions. I agree with Zavier's assessment."

Taurak nodded. "I do as well. I'll draft a response and have it sent to Otikul at once, and send word to the Elders of Aprana and Eerla about borrowing some of their younger men. Well done, Zavier."

"When you write to Otikul, be gracious. He offered me his daughter's hand in marriage before I left," the prince replied, his voice almost sheepish.

"That is rather impressive, he values his daughter far above anything else in his kingdom," Narith chirped, but Taurak frowned.

"I hope he wasn't offended by your refusal?"

"Not at all, I could tell he was sincere in the offer, but knew we would refuse," Zavier said as he readjusted in his seat. "He wants a stronger tie to the other races. One of his younger sons is courting a Wealdkin woman. We should keep his daughter in mind if we have someone close to us in need of a bride."

He noticed his parents exchanging a quick glance, but before he could inquire about the look, Branton asked another question. He let the thought fade away and the family spoke for another hour about more trivial matters, simply enjoying their time together. All too soon they separated for the evening, with Narith reminding Taurak that they couldn't postpone the council members again, as they had canceled the night before in order to go flying.

Zavier and Branton watched their parents leave the study arm in arm. Leaning across the sofa to nudge his little brother, Zavier asked, "How are your magic lessons going? Your last letter said you were struggling."

Branton heaved a dramatic sigh. "The Elders won't let me do anything fun, they've got me reading books non-stop to learn the theory of magic."

"Ahh, yes, I remember those books. I would sneak off to practice in the caves by myself with Maurgen as my lookout."

Eagerly, Branton scooted himself to the edge of the sofa and leaned in closer, as if they were conspiring or sharing secrets. "I've been practicing in my room, but that's better! I can summon both fire and air so far, but not very well."

"It sounds like you're doing great then, I was older than you before I could summon both and as you know, I'm still not very good at it," Zavier chuckled.

"Why is that?" Branton asked hesitantly.

"Why am I not very good at magic?"

"Yeah."

Zavier felt a stab of regret that he had missed so much of his little brother's life while he was traveling. They hadn't had a lot of bonding time, not since Brant had been quite little. He promised himself he would remedy that while he was home as he formed a reply.

"I'm really not sure. The power is there, it's just weak. I can do little things like a fireball or a small breeze, but that's about all. The healers who have looked at me all said I was perfectly fine, so I guess I just have weak magic. It's not uncommon for dragon-bonded to not be very powerful," Zavier explained, leaning back in his seat and crossing his arms behind his head.

"Yeah, but you're a prince, *and* dragon-bonded. That's supposed to make you even stronger than most, isn't it?" Brant questioned. "That's what the Elders said about you."

Sighing, Zavier dropped his arms. "In theory, yes, it should, since I have what the Elders call a 'double gift.' We inherit the dragon shifting ability from Father, but I also bonded Maurgen when I was born, so I ought to be twice as powerful. But I'm not." Zavier shrugged, shaking his head ruefully. "I'm not worried about my magic. I'm well trained in most weapons, plus, when you can skin-shift into a giant dragon, who needs magic?"

7

The brothers shared a laugh at Zavier's accurate logic. They began swapping stories of their magical lessons, physical training and combat, and how tough their Uncle Beltak was about aerial defense. While Branton recounted an aerial training lesson of several months ago, Zavier traced his thumb across the long scar that ran along his jaw.

Yes, Uncle Beltak would take aerial defense quite seriously. It had been about fifteen years since Zavier and his elder brother Caddoc had fought above the city, coming close to killing each other. That had been one of the few times they had refused to obey their father's order to not fight each other. Afterwords, Zavier had forbidden the healers from mending the long slash to his jaw when they healed the rest of him. He wanted a physical reminder to not be as selfish as his brother, and to serve his people to the best of his abilities.

Two

Minnie

"JESSAMINE?" SHE COULD HEAR the quavering voice of her mother calling her from the garden where she had left her ten minutes ago. Minnie sighed at the bowl of biscuit dough and brushed flour from her hands. Exasperated in equal parts by the distraction from her work, and her mother's insistence on using her full name, she covered the bowl with a towel and left the kitchen.

"Yes, Mama, I'm here," she replied, hurrying down the hall and out the back door. Typically she could leave her mother happily playing in the dirt long enough that Minnie could get dinner started, but today had been a rough day for them both.

"Jessamine, I don't know where…" Rosemary Hernshaw, kneeling in the garden, held up her trembling hands with confusion etched into the lines of her face.

"We're in the garden, Mama. You said you needed to pull weeds around the herbs today. Do you want to go inside?" Minnie crouched beside her mother, resting a gentle hand on her shoulder. She could feel a fine tremor run down her mother's body.

"Weeds?" Rosemary lowered her hands, looking around the carefully planted herb garden. "Oh, yes, weeds. That's right. No, leave me here. I'm alright now. Thank you, dear."

"I'll be right inside, Mama," Minnie said, standing. She watched for another minute as her mother knelt back over the row of thyme, diligently pulling weeds out and piling them beside her.

Sighing, Minnie returned to the kitchen. She stirred the stew, and used her magic to mentally smother the fire down to a smolder to keep it warm. Her father and sister would return soon for lunch and she still needed to finish making biscuits. She washed her hands and got back to work.

Minnie was placing biscuits on the baking sheet when she heard her mother calling her again. She hurried to place the last two biscuits and move the tray to the oven before retracing her steps to the back garden.

Her mother had left the rows of thyme. Glancing about, Minnie saw her tottering with uneven steps toward the back gate.

"Mama, where are you going?" Minnie called, swiftly catching up to her and taking her arm to assist her.

"Apples, dear. We should have apples," Rosemary chided, as if it were the most obvious answer.

"Mama, there are no apples right now, it's still spring. Come, let's go inside and get you washed up, Daddy and Juni will be home soon."

Coaxing her the entire way, Minnie got her mother turned around, and they slowly hobbled back to the house. As they neared the steps, Rosemary leaned heavily on Minnie, until she was not quite carrying her mother through the door, down the short hallway and into the bathing room.

"Wash your hands and face, Mama, while I go check on the biscuits," Minnie instructed, and hustled back to the kitchen just in time to pull the biscuits from the oven before they burned. She spilled them into a carved wooden bowl and draped a towel over top. She heard the back door open and close again, and assumed her father was home from his morning fishing and her sister home from school.

Thomas Hernshaw, close-cropped dark hair damp from the sea, entered the kitchen with his wife on his sun-weathered arm. He guided her slow steps with infinite more patience than Minnie was feeling. She smiled her gratitude at him, and pulled out her mother's padded chair for her.

"I found her wandering toward the back door," Thomas said, lowering Rosemary into the chair. Minnie could see from Rosemary's face that she was no longer present with them, her mind had wandered away from her again.

"It's been one of her rougher days," Minnie whispered, carrying the stew pot to the table. Her younger sister Juniper appeared in the doorway from the hall, smiling a sheepish apology for her tardiness.

"Mama rearranged the bathing room, I tidied it all away after I washed up," Juniper said, slipping into her chair and taking a biscuit from the bowl her father was holding out to her.

"Thanks, Juni, she's had no focus all day. I've struggled to get any work done around the house," Minnie explained, ladling stew into their bowls.

The little family ate quietly, Minnie alternating with her father to spoon stew into her mother's mouth around their own bites. When they had finished the meal, Juniper stood.

"Minnie, I'll stay with Mama this afternoon. You haven't had a break or been to see Elder Lirance in over a week," the young girl said, brushing her silvery hair away from her face.

"Really? That would be wonderful, but are you sure you don't mind?" Minnie asked, concern warring with excitement.

"Go on, shoo," Juniper said, waving her off. "I'll take care of everything."

Minnie met her father's eyes and he nodded toward a bundle of worn nets in the corner, indicating he would be at the house to assist if needed. Juniper was more than capable, but she was only fourteen, and their mother was having a particularly difficult day. But with Thomas there as well, Minnie could go out for the afternoon and not feel too guilty for going.

She eagerly ran to her room, changed her flour-covered clothes, and re-plaited her unruly hair. The last thing she did was grab the small stack of books she had borrowed from Elder at her last visit. Within moments, she was hurrying to the stone walk that led to the village from their little cottage on the hill.

Ocrans was a quaint little village located on the cliffs above the Sea of Monsters. A rough switchback road led to the ocean where a handful of dedicated men harbored boats and kept fishing equipment, including her father. The village center divided the small town into quarters, businesses with apartments over them lining the streets.

On the outskirts closest to the cliff edge lived Lirance, the village's dragon-bonded Elder. Curled up behind the house, basking in the afternoon sunlight, lay the massive brown dragon Horth, Elder's Bonded partner. Horth had his eyes closed, heavy, horned head resting on his taloned front paws. His leathery hide showed hints of grey around the muzzle, and his four long, curved horns were yellowing with age.

Minnie had spent much of her youth with other dragon-bonded children in this small cottage, learning magic and their history from Elder Lirance. His magic was, as he described it, 'mediocre at best' but he was an incredible teacher and historian.

Minnie opened the gate to the back garden, expecting to see Lirance sitting in one of the rocking chairs overlooking the ocean. The seats were empty, however. Horth lifted one eyelid, giving her a baleful look from his cat-like yellow eye.

"Greetings, little Draconid. He is inside, having a nap. He should wake soon, if you wish to stay and talk with me for a while," the sonorous voice rumbled through her mind.

"Are you sure? I don't wish to disturb your nap," Minnie began, but the dragon snorted and lifted his head.

"I was hardly napping," he scoffed. He adjusted his front paws, nearly the size of her entire body, re-crossing them to rest his head upon. *"Sit, stay a while. Did you finish the books Lirance lent you?"*

Minnie adjusted her usual rocking chair to be in his line of sight and sat, tucking her legs under her. "I did, they were fascinating. I really liked this one." She held up one of the leatherbound books for him to see the title, though she wasn't actually sure if a dragon could read or not. "It's *'Anatomy of a Dragon,'* I had no idea you had four lungs!"

"Have you never healed a dragon, then?" Horth asked with a chuckle.

"No, I haven't, I guess we've never had a dragon be injured while in Ocrans. I usually see dragon-bonded bringing deliveries, and if they need healing, they're in their humanoid form!"

The pair discussed the books she had been assigned to read, Horth explaining that he had gleaned his knowledge from Lirance's mind, until the Elder awoke from his nap. He shuffled into the garden not long after Minnie arrived, looking sheepish that he had been caught asleep.

"Good afternoon, young Minnie," he said as he settled his thin frame into the chair.

"Good afternoon Elder, I've come to return the books I borrowed," she said, placing the stack on the small table between them.

"Thank you, you may choose others before you go. I have one on royal protocols I think you should read," the old man replied, patting the books fondly.

"Royal protocol? Why would I need to know any of that?" she scoffed, a mirthless chuckle escaping her. She had no need to learn protocol when she was unlikely to ever leave the village. As long as her mother was ill, she would have to stay and care for her.

He wagged a finger at her. "You are dragon-bonded, you should always know the proper and polite way to greet royalty, or any visiting dignitary."

She scowled, but didn't argue further. Everything he suggested she read was fascinating, so she had learned to trust his instincts. Rumor in the village said that Lirance had prophetic dreams and visions, but she had never been brave enough to ask him if that were true. It just seemed too personal to ask, since he had never volunteered the information.

A young man approached from around the corner of the house, following the same path Minnie had taken. "I'm sorry to interrupt, Elder, I've a delivery for you from Hatherus," he said. He wore an embroidered badge of service on his tunic indicating he was part of the dragon-bonded messenger system.

"Ahh, thank you, Trevor," Elder said, taking the wrapped package from him. "Would you like a drink before you leave?"

Trevor shook his head, "Thank you, sir, but no thank you, I'll have my meal at the inn before heading on to my next town. Do you have anything for me to take back?"

"Not this time, but when you come by next week I'll have a few letters for you to bring to friends in various towns. Go get some rest now, before you fly off again."

Trevor bowed to Elder Lirance and Horth, and smiled politely at Minnie before he turned and walked away. That was the pattern of most dragon-bonded interactions in Ocrans, she thought ruefully. They came, they delivered, they left. Sometimes one would stay for a night or two, but most were eager to escape the sleepy little town. Currently the only Bonded who lived in Ocrans other than herself and Elder Lirance were two children, the others had all left upon reaching adulthood.

"I have a few more books for you to borrow set out inside, and of course you're welcome to anything on the shelves. Now tell me, how have you been since we last spoke?" Elder asked. He had unwrapped his package, tucked a scroll of parchment into his pocket, and set the two books aside.

Minnie chewed her lower lip, hesitating to complain. "Another one of the villagers asked me why I was still here, and why I don't have a dragon. She said it wasn't natural, and I should have left with the others."

15

"She's ignorant, don't let her get to you," Lirance said at once, waving away the woman's comments.

"I don't expect everyone to know every detail, of course, but you'd think it would be common knowledge by now, with how often they ask me. Mama is ill, I have to care for her."

Lirance nodded, reaching over to pat her hand. "It's quite admirable of you to give up your time to care for her, no one should fault you for that."

"It's not that..." Minnie squirmed in her seat. "The village is constantly asking me to use my magic for them, especially to heal them, and I don't mind, truly. It's my duty to use my gifts to help others, but it does bother me when they ask for help, then complain that I am unusual for not having a dragon."

Looking a little uncomfortable, Lirance didn't answer, but Horth snorted a jet of warm air over them. *"You are unusual, but that is not a bad thing, little one. You have more power in your little finger than most dragon-bonded could dream of. For unknown reasons, your dragon never came, but that does not make you any less a dragon-bonded. Circumstances in your life prevent you from leaving like the others did. That is not your fault."*

No, it wasn't her fault, but it still made her feel more ostracized. She was unlike the villagers, but she was unlike the other dragon-bonded. It was a very lonely existence. For as long as she could remember she had dreamed of seeing the places described in her books. Exploring the Stone Mountains, getting lost in the Wildwood Forest, meeting people of other races, even flying across the deadly Sea of Monsters to the Human continent of Shaesan. Traditionally a dragon-bonded left home when their dragon came to claim them, usually as a teenager or young adult. Minnie was twenty-six

16

years old, if it hadn't happened by now, it wasn't going to happen at all.

She'd asked Elder once, why she was the only dragon-bonded alive without a dragon. He'd evaded the question before finally admitting that he had no idea why. He'd made inquiries with the dragons, but they'd refused to tell him anything. When her invitation to the capital didn't arrive on her eighteenth birthday like the other dragon-bonded, she'd assumed it was because she was dragonless. Who wants a dragon-bonded with no dragon, her mother had said once when she found Minnie crying. It had become one of her favorite things to scream at Minnie when she was in one of her rages.

Horth had explained that Minnie's dragon was uniquely powerful, much like Minnie herself, and might be taking longer to learn how to control her magic. But that had been a long time ago, and still she was alone. Minnie was too afraid to ask again. What if her dragon just didn't want to be with Minnie? What if she wasn't good enough for the dragon?

Later that afternoon, as she picked out books from the shelves inside the cottage, the conversation replayed in her mind. She couldn't possibly leave home, even if she did have a dragon. Juniper was only fourteen years old, still in school, and she was almost as talented as their mother had been with the herbs in the apothecary shop. If Minnie left, Juniper would have to care for their mother, and she couldn't make her sister give up her life. She had to stay.

No matter how much she secretly wanted to leave.

Three

Zavier

A S TWILIGHT FELL ACROSS the city, Branton excused himself to an evening lesson. Zavier
moved across the room to sit at his father's large
desk. Turning the chair to face the windows, he
absorbed the view of the city and the Spire of
Hatherus, which rose hundreds of feet over the
other buildings. From here he couldn't make out
the market stalls or any people, but he could
see the night market lanterns being lit. Along the
Spire's winding road were dozens of merchant stalls,
restaurants, artisans selling handmade wares, mer-
cenaries offering their services, and so much more.

Behind him the door opened and Zavier turned
to see Jarn approaching. He'd changed from his
usual guard's uniform of leather to a more relaxed
short-sleeved vest over bare chest, but his sword and
a dagger were still sheathed on his belt. The guard
had been assigned to Zavier over ten years ago as
his head of security and had traveled with him con-

stantly. Although they'd been awkward around each other at first, they'd eventually formed a personal friendship as well as a professional one.

"Done for the night?" Zavier asked.

"Yeah, and heading into the city to find a woman, and some drinks, hopefully not in that order. You should come," Jarn added, dropping into the seat beside the desk.

"Me? I'd be recognized, and that wouldn't be any fun for you. Remember Osmara?" They'd tried drinking in a tavern in the Wildwood Forest border town and been recognized almost at once. Citizens had crowded around to ask him for favors, or to plead their case to the Wealdkin high council. Jarn and another guard had to escort Zavier out and back to their lodgings.

"You've been gone two years, and we didn't make a big fuss about returning. You don't even look the same with how long your hair is now," Jarn pointed out.

Zavier nodded, "That's true..."

"You've complained often enough that you don't get to experience normal life, this is one of those normal things: men having a drink after a long business trip."

Yes, he had complained about that. He spent most of his time with his 'prince face' on, he rarely got to be just Zavier.

He smiled. "Alright, I'll go."

"Good! Maybe we can find you a lovely woman to warm your bed, too," Jarn teased, pumping a fist in the air.

Standing, Zavier shook his head. "I agreed to a drink, don't get greedy!"

The pair left the study, following the hall to a side exit of the palace and down the path, skirting the training field. Within a few minutes they were in the city itself, surrounded by people eager to get home for their dinners, or off to their local tavern. Zavier had never been in the city without some fanfare, or at least half a dozen armed guards, just in case. There had never been any violence in Hatherus toward the royal family, at least not in living memory, so the guards usually just performed crowd control.

Zavier had often lamented that he couldn't just watch, or interact with his people like others do and relished this opportunity. Jarn had been right, he was overlooked when people weren't expecting to see their prince. He had never before been invisible within his city, or any city, and able to see the real unguarded truth of his people. His father had once said the same, adding that it was difficult to understand their populace from their position when they hadn't experienced what the people had. He'd had loud arguments with the council who wanted to forbid the royals from mingling, claiming the people wanted to look up to the family. There was nothing different about the royal family except their animal forms, and how they had earned their status.

Jarn led him to a quaint pub on a busy side street. The pub sat between an art gallery and a restaurant, with small tables scattered around a patio. A faded but still legible sign over the door proclaimed it to be the Golden Dragon Tavern. Inside, the pub was well lit, with men and women clustered around gaming tables or sitting to a meal and drink. Jarn indicated an empty table in the back before flagging down a barmaid and requesting drinks and some food.

As he tucked himself into the corner seat, Zavier heard snippets of a conversation nearby. Jarn sat across from him, his head cocked in a question.

Holding a finger to his lips to indicate silence, Zavier nodded toward the group of men one table over.

"— returned today from up north, saw them land at the palace this afternoon," said a man with graying hair. "There was no fanfare or announcement, but it's impossible to mistake the size of Maurgen. There was another gold dragon too that could only be the prince."

"Good, the elder prince hasn't been doing a very good job lately. I requested an audience with him and was turned away!" Exclaimed a fair-haired man with ruddy, sun-damaged skin. "Thankfully, a servant told Queen Narith, and she summoned me to apologize and offer to help me. I didn't want to bother her or King Taurak with my trifling matters, but I'm sure glad she offered."

"I've been turned away by Prince Caddoc too, he said to petition the council if we needed help. As if the council don't take months to get back to a man! None of 'em have any idea what it's like for us, and we have it far better than smaller towns!" This from the youngest, who had a bandage wrapped awkwardly around his upper arm.

Jarn and Zavier exchanged looks. All the royals were supposed to be approachable by their people, despite the council insisting otherwise. Even Branton, at only sixteen years old, spent hours every week in a meeting room at the palace where people could speak to him. Caddoc refusing to meet with their citizens was a flagrant disregard for his responsibility as one of the princes of their territory.

The gray-haired man spoke again. "Like you, I don't like to bother the king and queen, and when I needed a word, they were in Amthryn. I petitioned the council and they gave me a brush off, telling me I should have planned better. As if I could plan the flooding we had last spring! I needed a healer for my grandbaby, she'd had a fever that wouldn't come down, and we couldn't afford the healers fee. I requested five silver coins, and promised to pay with interest after the harvest, but the council declined."

"What did you do?" asked the youngest man.

"I planned to go home and sell whatever valuables we could, anything to help my son afford the healer. Young Prince Branton saw me leaving, said he'd overheard and wanted to help. He brought their family healer and had her well by the next day. No charge! Then he came out with some of his guards and they helped us all bring in the harvest and prepare the fields for the next planting."

"He's a good one," the fair-skinned man said, lifting his mug. "He and Prince Zavier are like their father. I remember him coming to help in the fields when I was a lad, and my Da says his father did the same."

"It's true," said the eldest, nodding. "I've never had a complaint with any royal until Prince Caddoc turned me away, and the council too."

"I went to them about a healer too, I was fixing a wall outside my house and cut myself on an old nail," said the youngest, tugging on his bandage. "I couldn't afford the healer fee, and the council sent me away, so my neighbor patched me up and gave me some herbs."

Another round of drinks arrived at their table, and conversation changed from the royal family to the likely weather in the coming weeks. Zavier and Jarn stared at each other, both unsure what to say. Finally, Jarn cleared his throat.

"Well, that was..."

"Enlightening," Zavier finished. He lifted his mug and gulped down half the contents, wiping his mouth with an almost feral growl. Branton had mentioned Caddoc's recent slacking in his letters, but this was unacceptable. If the citizens were too afraid to tell his father, Zavier certainly wasn't.

"You'll tell him?" Jarn asked after a sip of his own drink.

"Of course. It's not just irresponsible, but potentially dangerous. What if that man had died from an infected arm? The family might have been unable to tend their fields or feed themselves. I've had plenty of issues with my brother's behavior, but I can't allow him to neglect our people that way."

Nodding, Jarn smiled. "Glad to hear you say so. Now, put it from your mind for a little while, we came out so you could be yourself, not... you know what," he said with a wink, tapping his forehead to indicate the circlet Zavier wore when he was officially working.

Jarn changed the subject and kept Zavier talking for several hours, even getting him to laugh a few times. They'd gone through several rounds of beer and just ordered a second round of whiskey when two women approached their table.

"The tables are full, do you mind if we share?" one asked, indicating to the two empty seats at their table. A quick glance around confirmed that indeed, the tavern was completely full.

"Uh, yeah, sure," Zavier agreed, scooting his chair a bit to one side. Jarn also agreed, and moved to the seat directly next to Zavier.

"Thanks, we appreciate it," the woman replied. She sat opposite Zavier, toasting them with her mug. Her friend sat as well, but did not say anything. She had her eyes downcast, staring into her glass, though Zavier noticed she flicked her eyes up a few times to look at each of them.

"We came out to celebrate, she's just graduated from the healer's school with top marks!" exclaimed the chatty woman, nudging her friend and lifting her glass in a toast. The shy one smiled faintly.

"Congratulations," the men replied together.

"Thank you," was the whispered reply.

Jarn asked a few questions, engaging the woman in an animated conversation while Zavier and the recent graduate sipped their drinks. After a few moments, the girl lifted her head to meet his gaze with her remarkably pale blue eyes.

"She made me come out tonight," she smiled, her voice barely above a whisper.

Returning her smile, Zavier nodded toward Jarn. "He made me come, too."

"I'm Shayla," she held out her hand to shake his.

"I'm…" He hesitated, debating to himself if he should hide his name. Deciding to trust that Jarn was right and he would go unrecognized, he clasped her hand, saying, "Zavier, I'm Zavier."

"It's lovely to meet you. What brings you two out tonight?"

Relieved that she didn't appear to recognize him, Zavier replied, "Oh, just a bit of relaxing. We've been traveling for a while, and I'd promised him a drink once we got back home."

"Traveling sounds amazing," Shayla gushed, leaning toward him eagerly and placing a hand on his forearm. "I'm from Calding, I'd never been outside the village until I came to Hatherus. Where have you been?"

He told her about their most recent trip to Nagrain, focusing on the underground city and the mountains around it instead of the politics that had taken up most of his time. He was giving her a description of the massive forge in the deepest level at the heart of the city when he felt her hand run along his thigh. Certain it was just an accident, he ignored it and continued on.

Shayla asked questions and made comments, but her hand never left his thigh. She inched it higher as they spoke, until she was leaning across the table and her hand was damn near on his groin. Frantically, Zavier wondered what he should do. He was no blushing virgin, but he'd never been one for the casual encounter like his brother was, particularly because his brother was so casual with his encounters. Women tended to approach Zavier wanting something only the prince could give them, and as a man he found it off-putting and vaguely insulting, so he'd grown distrustful and hesitant. It had been almost a decade since any woman had approached him without a secret agenda.

"Shut down that obnoxious brain of yours, and go with it," Maurgen suggested in his mind. A brief thought showed Zavier that the dragon was curled on the riverbank with the other dragons currently in the city.

"What, and take her back to the palace? No thanks," he replied snidely.

Maurgen snorted. *"Suggest going to her apartment. If she attended the healer's school and was from another town, she must have lodgings nearby."*

"What about Jarn?"

"What about him? Has it been so long that you've forgotten how to be with a woman and need a babysitter? You're a big boy, and no one knows you're here. You have your sword, don't you? Quit being a wussy."

Thinking that his dragon was entirely too rational, Zavier placed his hand over Shayla's. He didn't move hers away, but it did prevent her from getting any closer to vital parts of him. As if on cue, his cock twitched in his trousers. Dragon-bonded, especially the men, tended toward a high sex drive, and it had been quite a while since he'd had release with anyone but his own hand.

Their silence was just getting to the awkwardly long stage, so he cleared his throat and blurted the first question he could think of. "What made you want to be a healer?"

Shayla's fingers flexed under his hand, digging nails into his thigh. "It seemed like a good career path. Now that I'm certified I can apprentice for a year to get some hands-on experience. Then I'll be able to set myself up in any town I want, since we always need good healers."

"Yes, we do..." he agreed, thinking again of the men they had overheard earlier.

"Listen..." Shayla said, glancing at her friend, who had moved so close to Jarn she was nearly sitting in his lap. "Do you... would you want to walk me home? We can talk where it's quieter, and I have a bottle of whiskey that I haven't opened yet."

"Go with her. You complain of being lonely, don't miss your chance at some companionship."

Zavier sat for a moment, debating, but finally nodded. Fishing in his pocket for the roll of leather he kept his coins in, he dropped a couple on the table by Jarn, giving the guard a meaningful wink.

"I'll see you tomorrow," Zavier told him with a small mock salute.

"Be careful," Jarn replied with a tilt of his head. Zavier nodded, thinking of the assassination attempts made against him in Shaesan less than two years ago. But Maurgen was right; Zavier was armed. Plus, Maurgen was nearby. If any trouble arose he and the other dragons would know almost instantly.

Shayla took his hand and led him out the door, across the little street and down an alleyway. She clung to his arm as she walked, her skin cool to the touch, and he wondered what animal-skin she was. As a dragon shifter he rarely felt the effects of too much alcohol, but he knew the other Skin-shifter species weren't quite as lucky. He hoped she wasn't too affected by alcohol.

Zavier let his free hand hover near his sheathed dagger, just in case, but allowed himself to be led through the city streets without resistance. The tavern wasn't very far from the healer's school so it only took them a few minutes to make the journey. A three story building that housed single apart-ments for students sat situated beside the school, and this is where she led him. Hand in hand they climbed the stairs to the top floor, Shayla giggling as she tripped on a shoe left on the landing.

"Sorry, some of them aren't very tidy," she said, breathless with laughter. "Most of them are out tonight, my room is down here." Leading him to the third door down the hallway, she pushed it open and stood back to let him in. The small room was clean, books stacked on a desk to one side, and a bed just barely large enough for two beside an open window.

Shayla closed the door, then launched herself at him, kissing him fiercely. Stepping back, he allowed her to press him into the wall, his hands resting on her hips. Desire rose within him, and he wondered exactly how long it had been since he'd last been with a woman. Before Maurgen could berate him for not paying attention, he jerked his thoughts back to the woman in his arms. He felt Maurgen mentally pull farther away, attempting to give what privacy he could.

Running his hands up her back, Zavier opened his mouth to deepen the kiss, only for her to pull away from him. She pressed her face into his chest, her hands sliding down to his waist. Her entire body had gone stiff. He dropped his hands to his sides, wondering if he had gone too far. She lifted her face to his again, nibbling his neck and licking along his lower lip before kissing him. He once again moved his hands along her back.

She squirmed and stepped away, breaking the kiss. Feeling like he had misunderstood something, he pulled back.

"Is everything alright? Should I leave?" he asked, not wanting her to feel pressure.

"No, don't go!" she exclaimed, turning back to him and pressing herself into his chest with her arms wrapped around his neck. Now thoroughly confused, he waited.

"I wanted to ask you something, but didn't want to ask so publicly," she whispered. One of her hands traced a line down his neck.

"Ask me something?" he repeated, feeling dull-witted around his lust.

"Yes... you see, I recognized you. The students were made to memorize portraits of the royal family, so when I saw you at the tavern, I insisted we go to your table."

Zavier's stomach twisted on itself. Unwrapping her hands from his neck, he stepped away from her. She continued, speaking rapidly.

"I am supposed to apprentice with a healer for a year, but they assigned me to the healer in Calding! They want me to go right back home where I'll be stuck forever. If you can put in a good word for me, I could apprentice here in Hatherus. Please, I can't go back to that town or those people! I'm meant for more!"

"So you brought me here to do what, seduce me and ask for a favor?" Zavier asked, edging around her and toward the door. At least this one had shown her motives before actually sleeping with him. His body felt hot, he knew his face had reddened with his anger and embarrassment.

"I have to get a better apprenticeship, without it I won't be able to charge my real worth!" She grabbed his arm to hold him in place, but he shook her off.

"Your real worth?" he repeated, turning back to face her.

"I know I'm a good healer, but the dean seems to hate me—"

"Perhaps she dislikes you because she sees the same thing in you that I now see," Zavier snapped, his hand on the doorknob.

Shayla threw herself against the door, desperately grabbing for his hands. "Please, you liked me in the tavern. I'll suck you off, sleep with you, I'll do anything to get you to help me! I need this!"

Shaking his head, Zavier took her by the arm and dragged her gently to her bed. She seemed to think he was giving in because she reached awkwardly for his belt buckle. He pushed her hands away and sat her down on the edge of the bed.

"If you wanted to whore yourself for a favor, you should have tried my elder brother. Sleep it off," he sighed, crossing the room again to the door.

"I am not a whore!" Shayla screamed, standing.

"Only because I've turned you down," he snapped. "A woman so unscrupulous as to attempt this is clearly not worthy of the healer's certificate. I'll be sure to let the dean of the school know what kind of woman they've certified."

He left, slamming the door shut on her reply. He didn't even walk down the stairs; he spotted an open doorway at the end of the hallway that led to a balcony. Just as he heard the door opening behind him and Shayla's angry footsteps approaching, Zavier leaped off the balcony. As he began to fall he pulled the magic from his body and let it engulf him, summoning his half-dragon Draconid form. Wings sprouted from his shoulder blades with a mighty gust of air. Even his wingbeats sounded angry as he rose over the city.

"I don't think that went well," Maurgen said, hesitant. His voice sounded faint, buried as it was behind the layers of shielding Maurgen had built for their privacy.

"Nope, not one bit."

"Shall we leave for a few days? That forest you like is only a few hours from here."

Confusion, fury, and lust roared through Zavier's mind and body to the point where he wasn't sure what he wanted to do. He'd trusted a woman, and once again, she'd let him down. They always did, and that is why he'd all but given up on meeting someone.

Sighing, he replied, *"I'd love to, but Mother would be furious if I disappeared again so soon. Let's just fly for a few hours, then head home."*

Four

Minnie

T HE SUN HUNG LOW over the ocean horizon when Minnie made herself leave the little garden. She'd delayed as long as she could since her father was home to get dinner going, enjoying her time quietly reading and occasionally asking questions. Minnie waved as the bonded pair adjusted themselves to watch the sun set, their personal nightly ritual. She was almost to the stone path that led to her family home when she heard her name being called by a panicked female voice.

"Minnie, there you are— I was afraid I wouldn't find you." Sophia, one of the few people in the village she might actually call a friend, ran up to her panting for breath.

"What's going on, Soph?"

"Old Tobias fell out of his hayloft, they think he's broken his back, please come—" but even as she spoke Minnie had started running. The two women raced down the road to his farm, following the shouts ahead of them.

"Here she is! Back up, everyone back up now, give her room!" Various men spoke together around them, their voices overlapping and blending. As Minnie approached she took quick note of the circle of men standing before the faded wooden barn. Above their heads, the open door to the hayloft still swung on creaking hinges. She absorbed these inconsequential details as they skidded to a stop on the hard packed dirt road.

Minnie shoved her stack of books at Sophia and fell to her knees beside the injured man, golden light covering her hands. She traced the air over his body from head to toe, closing her eyes to reduce distraction. Images of the inside of his body filled her mind as she passed her hands over him. There was a fracture in the top of his skull and his spine was compressed, it was a miracle of the highest caliber that he was alive at all.

Minnie took a deep breath and pushed the golden power from her hands into his body. She had tried to explain this process to several people but no one had understood exactly what it was or how she did it. The power wrapped itself around the broken vertebrae and mended them, smoothing the tightened muscles, filling in cracks and reconnecting severed nerves. There were audible snaps and cracks from the man's body and he released a vicious scream as everything knit back together in seconds. She saw damage to his heart, a weakened vessel that had burst, probably what had caused his fall. The final thing she healed was the gash in his head and the fractured skull bone, as well as reducing the swelling in his brain. She slumped with relief as Tobias opened his eyes, sore but completely healed.

"You... I..." Tobias looked around in confusion, his eyes traveling from Minnie and Sophia sitting side by side to the men surrounding them, then up to the open door of the hayloft above them. "I was tossing straw down, my chest hurt, then I lost my balance. Last thing I remember was trying to grab the door..."

"We saw you grab your chest, then you fell," said a young boy clutching his father's shirt.

The boy's father nodded, adding, "We were just walking up to see if you needed help with the fields. Thank the Fates we did..."

"Indeed, thank you all. And you, Minnie, Sophia, thank you."

"It was, nothing, Tobias," Minnie panted, still winded from the run. Healing never tired her. She always felt exhilarated feeling the power course through her hands and watching the chaos of injury smooth itself out.

"It's everything to me, young lady. I am in your debt. Without you my children would be orphans right now." Minnie fought not to cringe. She had been unable to save his wife and child during childbirth, the babe had already passed by the time she arrived and the blood loss the mother had suffered had been too much for her body to handle. Despite Minnie's efforts to stop the bleeding and heal her body from the traumatic birth, her heart had given out and Minnie had been unable to restart it with magic.

The men around them pushed in to help Tobias to his feet. Sophia pulled Minnie up and wrapped an arm around her waist to keep her standing. "Come on, let's get you home to rest."

The two women turned to walk away but were stopped by the father of the young boy. "Miss, that was amazing. Are you alright?"

"Yes, I'll be fine, just need a little rest. Thank you for asking," Minnie replied, suddenly eager to get away from the onlookers.

"Can I help you get home?"

"Thank you sir, but I've got her, I'll get her home safely. You stay and help with Old Tobias," Sophia firmly refused, nudging Minnie to start walking again. They weren't stopped again, and they had made their way slowly back to the edge of town before Sophia spoke again. "That was incredible, Min. I'll never understand how you do that."

Minnie gave a small smile. "Not many people do, myself included. Old Tobias must be blessed by the Fates to have even survived the fall at all, let alone the damage his heart had sustained."

The friends continued their slow walk in silence, until Minnie was able to support herself again as they neared the town center. The townspeople bustled around them, going about their daily lives without a clue someone they knew had nearly died. Minnie found that morbid, and tried to shake the thought off.

"Thanks for walking me back, Soph. I can make it home from here," she said to her friend, holding her hands out to reclaim her small bundle of books.

"Get some rest, Min. Hey, how's your mother? Do you think she'll reopen the shop any time soon?" Sophia asked, indicating the closed apothecary across the street from where they stood.

"I hope so. Her confusion has gotten worse the past few days, but she has plenty of energy. Another day or two of rest and I may take her to her workroom and see how she does. She's always remembered her recipes better than anything else."

The friends waved and parted, Minnie lost in thought as she trudged up the stone path. Several weeks ago Rosemary had taken a sudden turn for the worse, and for no apparent reason. Minnie had used her magic to scan her mother, as she had many times in the past. The damage done to her brain by a long ago injury was permanent, and long since healed. Nothing appeared to have changed to trigger the decline. It frustrated her that some things she could heal, and others she had no control over. Old Tobias wasn't the first emergency she'd been called to and had successfully saved someone who would surely die otherwise. But her mother? Rosemary had nothing Minnie could heal. All they could do was manage her as best they could.

Before she climbed the final steps to the cottage, Minnie turned to watch the last of the setting sun. Birds swooped overhead, twittering. Her chest ached as she watched them fly, the sudden need to join them so strong she sank to the ground. How long had it been since she'd been in the air? More than three weeks, certainly. Had it been a full month? She shook her head, tears welling in her eyes.

Behind her, the door opened and her father's footsteps approached. She looked up into the weatherworn face she loved so dearly, a sad smile on her lips. He sat down beside her, draping his arms over his knees.

"Watching the birds?" he asked in a soft voice.

She nodded, throat tight. He understood, she thought. "How long has it been for you?" she asked, her eyes fixed now on a group of sparrows dancing across the sky.

"Four months, five days," he said without hesitation. She snapped her head around to stare at him, incredulous. "What?" he chuckled. "I love the sea, but my people are herons. I like to fly occasionally!

35

Your mother gets upset with me, too, if she knows I've been in the air."

When Rosemary was upset, her health took a drastic turn for the worse. Minnie had tried to ask why her mother hated when they flew, why she was so afraid, but no one would answer. All her father said was it related to her accident. It was most unfortunate that all three members of Rosemary's family could fly, and longed to fly, but were forced to remain grounded. Juniper, in her owl-skin, would sneak out of her bedroom window after everyone was asleep in order to fly on her own.

Minnie was not so lucky, nor was she brave enough to disobey. If Rosemary found out, she would have another breakdown, she could become unresponsive again. Minnie couldn't be responsible for that. And, Rosemary didn't just hate that they flew, she hated anything to do with the dragons. They terrified her, and somehow she always knew when Minnie had shifted, even if she hadn't been flying. Most days Minnie was so exhausted from caring for their mother, she didn't have the energy to shift, let alone sneak out. Even if she did, as a dragon, she was much too large. She would surely be caught. Minnie had thought many times about running away. She had inherited the lynx-skin from her mother, she could easily run miles through the forest, far enough to shift unseen. But... who would care for her mother, and help her family if she left? She couldn't put that on Juniper's shoulders, or her father's.

Thomas nudged her arm, drawing her back from her reverie.

"I came out to tell you that supper is ready. We've fed your mother and got her tucked into bed. You'd better eat before it gets cold," he said, preparing to stand.

Minnie nodded. "I'll be in soon, thanks."

Thomas stood and ruffled the unruly hair escaping her braid before going back inside. Sometimes Minnie truly wondered if she should stay. Rosemary could sometimes be volatile, she threw things, broke plates and glass cups. She'd screamed and berated Minnie more times than she could count. Oddly, she almost never behaved that way toward Juniper. Only Minnie, and always because she was dragon-bonded. Useless, her mother called her.

But when she wasn't in fits of rage, her mother doted on her, praising her healing abilities, her mastery of her other magics. She'd cheerfully teased Minnie more than once that she could heal anything, but couldn't brew a potion to save a life at all. Minnie loved her mother, she'd seen Rosemary try so hard to be a normal mother while she was growing up. Even when Juniper was little, Rosemary held herself together. But whatever damage she had sustained from that mysterious, long ago injury had changed her in the past decade, and it was exhausting.

An overwhelming desire to fly away filled her. The thought of another day caring for her mother, stuck in the village, unable to live her own life... She clamped her lips shut and choked on a sob. She loved her mother. It couldn't be helped that she required so much care, and Minnie was the best person to provide that care. Her father had to work, her sister needed to finish school. There was nothing she could do to change her Fate, so she may as well accept it.

Wiping her eyes and taking firm control of her emotions, she turned her back on the swooping birds and setting sun to enter the house.

Five

Minnie

A FTER EATING HER SUPPER and cleaning up the kitchen, Minnie was tidying the sitting room when she found a roll of thick parchment. That was unusual enough, but there was a bright gold wax seal bearing the crowned dragon of the royal family at the edge, already broken. The letter had been left unfurled on an end table. She wondered if her father had been reading it and had forgotten to put it away. Why was the royal family sending them a letter?

Curiosity got the better of her, and she unfurled the scroll. Blood drained from her face as she read, emblazoned across the top of the page in sweeping black calligraphy, Lady Jessamine Hernshaw. At first her full name, the honorific she didn't deserve, was unfamiliar. She read the line several times. Her fingers clenched around the parchment, consciously reminding herself to release her grip lest she rip the missive. With a racing heart, she read:

Lady Jessamine Hernshaw,

We have sent many invitations over the past eight years which have gone unanswered. While we understand that life is very busy, you have duties and responsibilities to attend to in the capital. It is long past time that you accepted your role, with or without a dragon by your side.

Your presence is now required in Hatherus.

You must be in attendance by the First Day of the Fifth Month. Should you fail to arrive by the appointed day, guards will be sent to fetch you, and you shall be charged with treason: Failing to obey a summons from your king and queen.

Request made by Queen Narith Davengard,
Scribed by Lady Anitra Davengard

She read it again, then a third time. This couldn't be true, she would have known had she been invited to the capital before now, right? She'd watched others leave, other dragon-bonded far less powerful than she had flown away with their dragons. They'd become guards, messengers, or joined the trade caravans that were so important to the smooth running of the country. Advisers, politicians, soldiers, teachers, elders, and healers; dragon-bonded were essential to their peoples way of life.

Minnie stared into the deepening dark of the little sitting room, her fury rising. There had to be more letters. Would they have kept them, or destroyed them? How many had been sent? Did this date all the way back to her eighteenth birthday?

Angrily, she stormed out of the room, intending to pound on her parents door to demand answers. She paused, fist raised, outside the door. No, waking her mother would not solve anything. Turning, she strode back down the hall and out the front door, letting it slam shut behind her. Fur rippled across her body as she skin-shifted into the tuft-eared form of a lynx. Claws digging into the dirt, Minnie raced down the path toward the Dragon Meadow just outside of the village.

When she reached the meadow and had enough room, Minnie called her power forth again. It rose within her, filling her body with a fiery warmth that almost burned deep in her chest. The magic swirled in and around her body as her joints pulled apart and reformed themselves into the massive shape of a dragon. She'd always wondered why it didn't hurt, how the magic was able to remove pain from a shift, but not from the healing process? Wings erupted from her back, and after releasing a jet of fire from her maw, she launched herself into the sky with strong downbeats of her wings.

Her mind whirled. Had her parents been lying to her? Why had they hidden the letters, if that's what they did? To protect her? From what? Was it because she had no dragon? What did that matter when she could become a dragon herself? And besides that, every Bonded she'd met had assured her that she must have a dragon. Minnie knew in her soul that she was connected to a dragon, no matter what Rosemary said when she was raging.

None of that should even matter, Minnie furiously told herself as she beat her wings and climbed ever higher. She had more magic, more raw power, than any other Bonded. Elder Lirance himself said so! She didn't need a dragon-bond to be useful to their kingdom. Her magic was more than enough! Doubt wormed its way into her mind, though. Was something wrong with her? Is that why her dragon chose not to be with her? Was she so powerful because of a defect, and one day she would do something dangerous? She roared in anguish, confusion swirling around her mind and clouding her thoughts.

The miles slipped away below her as she beat her wings, climbing higher, flying farther and farther from her home. But as the air around her cooled, so did her temper, sending her crashing back to a frigid reality. She had to go home. Her mother would need her. Someone surely heard the door slam, or noticed she hadn't gone to bed. More than that, Minnie needed to know about the letters, and if the missive was correct, she had no choice but to leave for the capital, and quickly. The first day of the Fifth Month, as the note said, was only two days away. The missive had threatened her with treason if she didn't arrive.

She needed to know the truth, and she intended to find out today. She turned back toward home, stretching her wings in powerful downbeats. One way or another, she wanted to know the full truth that her parents had hidden from her.

Minnie skimmed over the meadow, the long grasses rustling in the wind from her wings. She saw her sister, silver feathers bright in the moonlit sky, perched on a tree branch outside their house. Not bothering to even attempt to be silent, she back-winged not far from the front porch, calling her power in mid-air to shift her skin from dragon to humanoid. As she lost her wings and began to fall, she pulled air around her in a vortex, slowing her descent and allowing her to land softly on the stone path.

Juniper swooped down from the tree, shifting her own body to land just in front of Minnie. "Mama woke when the door slammed, and Dad saw you leaving. Are you alright?" Juniper asked, noting the frown on Minnie's face.

She shook her head. "No, I'm not alright. If they're awake, I'm getting some answers now. Let's go."

Clearly very confused, Juniper followed Minnie inside. Expecting their mother to be back in bed, Minnie was flabbergasted to see her pacing the hallway. Gone were the tottering steps. She stood upright and stable, whirling to face her daughters as they entered the house. Minnie froze.

"Mama?" she whispered, frowning.

"Jessamine! How could you storm off like that, it's the middle of the night—"

"I left an hour after sundown, that isn't the middle of the night," she interrupted, her anger returning.

"And you were flying! You know how much I hate when you go flying! How could you do this to me, what were you thinking?!" Rosemary screeched, her hands on her hips.

"Do this to— Mama, how are you this coherent? This afternoon you couldn't remember where you were when you were in your own garden!" Minnie's brows creased in confusion and anger. This was nothing like her usual temper. When she raged, Rosemary sobbed, screeched, flailed her arms, and threw things. While she shook with a fine anger, Rosemary was in control of her entire body.

Thomas appeared through the hallway from the back door, a pail of water in his hand. The second he entered the hall, Rosemary spun to face him.

"Thomas, speak to your daughter! She's been flying again, it's far too dangerous for them to be in the air, they know that, and she knows I hate that dragon-skin of hers, she's never to shift to it again. You tell her, Thomas!"

Staring at his wife, bucket in hand forgotten, Thomas stood for several tense seconds in silence. Just when Rosemary opened her mouth to speak again, he raised a hand to forestall her.

"I let her find the letter, Rosemary. That's why she was flying."

Minnie and Juniper turned stunned looks to their father. Thomas set the bucket down by the counter and slowly approached his daughters. He reached into his jacket and pulled a thick envelope from an inner pocket. He hesitated, drew in a deep breath, then handed the envelope to Minnie.

"I should have given you these years ago. Your mother told me to destroy them, but I couldn't. I'm sorry, dearest," he said in a solemn voice. Minnie took the envelope with a shaking hand. Inside, she could see folded scrolls, each of them bearing the golden crowned dragon wax seal of the royal family.

"The invitations?" she asked, not looking up.

"Yes, every one of them. Dating back to just after your eighteenth birthday," he replied. Behind him, Rosemary shrieked.

"I told you to burn those!" she cried, rushing forward in an attempt to snatch them from her daughter's hands. Thomas turned and caught her around her middle, hoisting her up and carrying her to a seat at the kitchen table. He sat her down and held her firmly by the shoulders, staring into her wild eyes.

"Rosemary, enough. Answer me truthfully. Have you been exaggerating your illness to keep her here?"

The girls gasped, both slapping hands over their mouths at nearly the same time. Rosemary sullenly stared at her husband. He shook her shoulders gently.

"You had a tremor, some mild forgetfulness, but you were energetic and perfectly able to care for yourself and our daughters until just months before Minnie came of age. Then suddenly you couldn't hold a vial, couldn't use the knife. Every time she mentioned wanting to leave, you got worse. Any time we have a letter from the capital, you get worse. Now you stand in this house screaming at her as if the past eight years of worsening health never happened. Tell me truly, have you been lying to us? Did you lie so that I would agree with you to hide it from her?" Thomas punctuated his demands with another firm shake.

Rosemary's eyes filled, and she looked away. Finally, she nodded. Minnie's vision swam, she felt her sister's strong arms brace her from behind.

Lies. So many lies, she thought through a haze. Had everything in her life so far been a lie?

Juniper led her sister to the table and sat her down. Minnie nodded her thanks, resting her head over crossed arms. She couldn't look at her mother.

Drawing a ragged breath, Rosemary said, "I couldn't stand the thought of my baby leaving me." Her words became more frantic and her voice rose to a near shriek. "She's safe here, she needs to stay here, where I can protect her. I have to protect her, I must protect my baby, please you have to understand, I must protect my baby, I can't lose another baby—"

Recognizing that her mother was approaching a complete meltdown, and wondering if this was another trick, Minnie stood and reached into a cabinet for the sedatives they kept for her. She couldn't stand watching her mother suffer, and couldn't bring herself to risk that this time, it wasn't a lie. Without a word she handed the potion to her father, who uncorked it and put it to Rosemary's mouth. She swallowed reflexively and was asleep within seconds.

Thomas scooped her up and left the room, no doubt carrying her to their bedroom. Minnie met Juniper's blue eyes. Neither knew what to say. They stared at each other in silence for several moments, until Thomas reappeared.

Their father seemed to have aged decades in the last few moments. He'd run his hands through his graying hair, causing the short strands to stand on end.

Minnie swallowed, opened her mouth to speak, but couldn't find the words and closed it again. Juniper had no such issues.

"What the fuck just happened, Daddy?" she demanded, pointing down the hall toward their mother's room.

"Watch your language," Thomas replied, almost absently. He seemed to shake himself awake. Indicating they should sit, he pulled his own chair out and took his seat. The girls exchanged another look, but also sat.

"She's right," Minnie finally found her voice. "What is going on?"

Thomas shifted in his seat. "It's difficult to explain—"

"We aren't stupid, Dad," Minnie snapped, careful to keep her voice down, though she knew the sedative would keep their mother asleep for several hours.

Thomas shook his head. "No, dearest, it's not that, it's just... it's painful. You see... We had other children before you were born. I..." He choked, and cleared his throat. "Your mother and I had two other children. A girl and a boy."

He was silent for several minutes. Finally, Minnie had to prod him into speaking. "What happened to them, Dad?"

46

A tear slipped down his cheek. "We lived in Salt-stone, with my family, in a little house near the harbor. One night, there was an explosion in one of the warehouses, and our whole street caught fire. Our little girl died, along with my parents and brothers. She was only four months old."

Her heart wrenched at the abject pain she heard in her father's broken voice.

He drew in a shuddering breath and continued. "Our son was born almost two years after she died. We were still living in Saltstone then. He was... such a lively lad," he sighed. He shook his head and wiped his eyes, drawing another ragged breath.

Minnie warred with conflicting emotions. She felt sympathy for her father, but she was impatient to hear the story, and after the secrets and lies of the evening, she was struggling to control herself.

"How did he die? And how was Mama injured?" she asked, her quiet voice firm.

Thomas shook his head. "He died on his first birthday in the same accident that hurt your mother. It's... it's too difficult to explain."

Her anger rising again, Minnie fought to control her temper. "I need to know." Her eyes were locked onto her father, but from the corner of her vision she saw Juniper nod, but remained quiet.

Her father looked up, his eyes flashing, but almost as soon as it appeared, his eyes dulled again. "Yes," he said, "You do need to know. Your mother was flying with a Bonded, he lost control and they all fell from the sky. We lost our son, and your mother suffered extensive injuries. The healers managed to save her life, but were unable to heal her mind. I can't relive the accident, please don't ask me to."

Biting back uncharacteristically rude comments, Minnie took a deep breath, searching for questions she could ask that he might answer.

She finally settled on, "Why has she forbidden me from living my life?"

"I don't think that's what she meant to do— No, wait, let me finish," Thomas added as Minnie angrily opened her mouth. "You have to understand, she lost two children in infancy, and after her accident she struggled to conceive and lost many pregnancies. She refused to stop trying, then when you were finally born she learned you were dragon-bonded and..."

Snapping her mouth shut, Minnie just stared.

"She blames the dragon-bonded, all of them. Unfairly, of course. Your mother isn't well, and she obviously took all this too far. In her mind, she's just trying to keep you safe so she doesn't lose another child."

"Why has no one told us any of this before?" Juniper asked, speaking for the first time since she'd been reprimanded.

Suddenly looking sheepish, Thomas said, "I didn't think it would be important for you to know, and it was painful for us. Any mention of telling sent your mother into one of her fits. I thought I was protecting her, and you. Clearly I was very wrong."

Minnie cleared her throat. "She hates anything to do with dragons." It wasn't a question.

Thomas slowly nodded. "I don't know that she thinks it so rationally, but yes, she does. It's been difficult for her to reconcile her anger and hurt with loving you so much. And she does love you, both of you."

"She loves me, but hates what I am."

Hands clasped in her lap, Minnie looked up at her father with tears in her eyes. Anger warred with guilt and sadness. How difficult had it been for her mother to raise and love a child that was everything she hated and feared?

Even as the thought coalesced in her mind, she berated herself. She hadn't chosen to be dragon-bonded. If not for a cruel trick of Fate, her dragon would have come for her like all the others, and she'd have left long ago... wouldn't she? She loved her mother. How could she not? She's her mother! The one who rocked her to sleep at night, sang her songs, cared for her when she was ill. Caring for Minnie had been Rosemary's entire world until the infant Juniper had been left on their doorstep.

It was hard for Minnie to imagine a different life for herself. All she knew was this village, caring for her mother, helping in the apothecary, healing the villagers, using her magic to improve their lives. Her mother certainly had no issue with her magic when she wanted hot water or a cool breeze, or when she was asked to heal everyone's cuts and scrapes, no matter how minor.

Her entire life, Minnie had wanted more, but resigned herself to accepting what she had. She had truly been happy helping in the shop, assisting her mother. But in Rosemary's twisted desire to keep her daughter safe, she'd made her a prisoner.

Angrily shoving her chair back, Minnie braced her hands on the table and leaned toward her father. Eyes closed, she slowly let out a tight breath through clenched teeth. Her eyes snapped open and she glared at her father.

"I will be leaving for the capital first thing in the morning. I cannot, will not stay here and be her slave any longer."

Nodding, Thomas slowly stood and walked around the table. He appeared wary, as if he wasn't sure what she would do or how she would react to his presence. He had lied to her, too. His wariness of her made Minnie want to forgive him for everything, but she refused, clinging to her anger. He had allowed this. He had hidden the letters. He had lied.

But he was her father...

"I understand, dearest." He carefully extended his arms, offering her an embrace. She hesitated, but couldn't resist. She allowed herself to be engulfed in his reassuring hug. A chair scraped against the stone floor, and Juniper appeared beside them, squeezing herself under his arm and wrapping arms around her sister.

"I am so sorry, my darlings," their father whispered, kissing each of their foreheads. "I have failed you both by not realizing the depth of her illness. I cannot change the past, but I will do everything I can to improve your futures."

Minnie lifted her face to look at her father. "None of us could have imagined that Mama would lie to us like that."

"No, but I should never have agreed to hide those letters or to lie to you. I should have done more to fight for you, instead of coddling Rosemary and letting her keep you caged," Thomas insisted firmly.

Juniper, looking much older than her fourteen years, broke away from them, wiping tears from her eyes. Clearing her throat, she tentatively said, "If Minnie is leaving, will I have to quit school in order to care for Mama? Dad can't spend all his time at home."

Before Minnie could protest, her father swiftly said, "Absolutely not. If your mother can behave the way she did tonight, she clearly doesn't need round the clock care. You will stay in school, and if there are any issues with your mother, we have a few friends both in the village and in other towns who we can ask for help from."

"I'd offer to take you with me to the capital," Minnie added, "but I have no idea what will happen when I get there. I may be in some serious trouble since I never showed up when I was told to."

"I'll write a letter to send with you, explaining the situation. It may help, I knew King Taurak once," Thomas added. "Now we'd all better get to bed. It's grown late and we've all had a very difficult night."

The girls did as they were bid, but once the house had grown quiet, Minnie's door opened and the silvery form of her sister entered. Her fair hair and pale skin stood out in the bright moonlight, a drastic difference from the dark features of Minnie and their parents.

"That was wild," Juniper whispered, slipping into the bed beside Minnie. The sisters lay on their sides, facing each other, just as they'd done since Juniper was old enough to sneak in.

"I'm not sure how I should feel," Juniper continued. "Mama lied to us so often. She treated us like her slaves, and you gave up so much. But... like Daddy said... she's sick."

"Whatever happened to her, it damaged her brain. I've seen the damage when I scan her with magic," Minnie replied slowly, considering her words carefully. "The parts that are damaged... maybe they are parts that tell her right from wrong. I don't know either, Juni. I'm angry, but I'm sad and afraid. I do know... I have to leave for a while. I have to answer the summons and explain."

Juniper nodded sadly. "You weren't meant to stay here, Min. You are so powerful, you should be in the capital or in Saltstone or Aprana, helping people. And you should figure out what's happened to your dragon and why they didn't come!"

Barely audible, Minnie said, "I'm afraid of so much. And I feel so guilty, leaving you and Daddy, and Mama, and the village... I'm afraid of leaving, of learning more terrifying truths, of what awaits me in Hatherus. What will they do to me for ignoring their summons for so long? And why are they commanding me to the capital? Just because they can?"

"The other girls at school say that it's time for the princes to be married," Juniper offered.

Minnie snorted. "Well then it's a waste for me to go. No prince will marry a dragon-bonded with no dragon."

"You have to have a dragon. Only the royal family can have a dragon-skin without having a dragon, and you definitely aren't related to King Taurak."

She was correct there. King Taurak was all shades of yellows, blond hair, amber eyes, and golden tanned skin. It was his line the hereditary dragon blood came from, and all three of his children were as fair as he was. Dark-featured Minnie was the feminine version of Thomas in almost every way, from their brown curls to their deep green eyes.

"Then I have a goal," Minnie replied. "I want to find my dragon the first chance I get. And... I want to see the world. Mama may get worse again, and we won't know if it's real or not, but... we can't just ignore her. We have to help her. I'll have to return to care for her so you can have your chance to find out who you are."

Juniper gripped Minnie's hand tightly. "You're the best big sister ever," she whispered.

Minnie shook her head. "I'm not the only one with questions," she said, and Juniper nodded, squeezing the hand she held. "One day, you'll discover where you came from, who your birth parents were, why you were left for us to find, and who you're meant to be. I won't let anything stop you from your Fate," Minnie assured her sister.

Six

Zavier

Z AVIER ONCE AGAIN SAT in his father's study. This
time, it was a bright morning, and he was on
the visitor's side of the desk, repeating what he had
heard in the tavern about his elder brother. He did
his best to remain impartial and just repeat the facts
as he'd heard them.

His fingers steepled together on the desk, Taurak's
eyes never left Zavier's face as he spoke. When the
prince was finished, Taurak sighed heavily and ran
his fingers through his hair, knocking the gold circlet askew. He yanked it off and dropped it on the
desk as he stood to pace before the window.

"I've tried to speak to Caddoc many times over
the past few years. He's had such an abrupt change
in his personality, and it seems he has no wish to
confide in me. I don't even always know where he
is, he often flies off to Saltstone or Aprana without
telling anyone but his guard. We only hear rumors
or if a Bonded passes along his location."

Unsure what to say, Zavier waited. He drummed his fingers against the armrest of his chair absently. He had plenty of opinions on his brother, most of them unhelpful, but he had long ago decided to not slander him to their father. He would let his actions speak, and Caddoc's, too.

Taurak turned back to his middle son, suddenly looking old and tired. Concerned, Zavier asked, "Are you feeling unwell, Father?"

"No, no, I'm fine. I haven't been sleeping very well lately, and I've had some troubling dreams. I worry some may be prophetic, but there's no way to be sure." Returning to his seat, Taurak laced his fingers again, studying his son. "I'm in fine health, and expect to live for many decades, assuming no one tries to kill me."

A morbid thought, but not unheard of, unfortunately. Taurak's father had been assassinated when Taurak was a young man, leaving him to take the throne long before he had anticipated. When the guards investigated and located the servant who had poisoned the former king, she had sworn she'd no idea that the tea she served to the king had been poisoned. Further investigation by the dragons into the servant's memories had proved her innocent, so the mastermind of the assassination had gone unpunished. Taurak was only in his sixties, the prime of life for a dragon-bonded king. Without outside interference, he could easily live and rule another one hundred years or more before there was any question of him needing to step aside.

"Caddoc is many things, but he isn't a murderer. He wouldn't want the responsibility that badly. I think you're safe from assassination, Father," Zavier laughed. "I'm already doing a large part of your job for you, I've no need to accelerate the coronation!"

The king laughed with his son. "You've no idea how much I value what you do for me, Zavier. You've certainly halved my work, allowing me to spend more time with your mother and Branton than I was able to when you were young."

Zavier bowed his head slightly, accepting the praise. Before he could form a reply, his father went on. "Now that you are home, however, I require something of you. You'll have a choice, of course, and I won't be forcing you — yet — but please keep an open mind."

"Oh Fates, what have you done, Father?" Zavier's eyes narrowed as he stared at his father. The last time Taurak had said he needed Zavier's help, he'd been sent to the Human continent of Shaesan and had nearly died twice.

"There's no danger to your life this time, relax. While I have no plans to vacate my throne anytime soon, I would like to know the next generation is settled. Not right away, of course, but at some point. Your mother has invited women to the palace to interview as her new ladies in waiting, and we'd like for you to be... open to meeting them, getting to know one or two."

Zavier stared at his father for a long moment, not quite comprehending. Finally, he said, "You invited a bunch of women... here? To meet me? With the intent of... what, interviewing them to see who would be the best queen?"

"Not quite so specifically... But yes, in a way. Some will be hired as companions and secretaries for your mother. If, while they and you are here, you happen to take a fancy to one, then yes, we will see if she has what it takes to be your wife. Your aunt has spent weeks pouring through our records for women who may be suitable. And if you don't like any of them, that's fine. Caddoc has also been summoned home, and he's to meet these women as well."

Zavier realized his mouth was hanging open, and snapped it closed. "Why the sudden interest and urgency in our love lives, Father? You said you are feeling alright, so surely there's no medical reason why we need to marry right away?"

Taurak waved his hand. "No, no, nothing like that. I promise, I'm perfectly fine, and so is your mother. We've had numerous meetings with the council members, some of them concerning you boys. Caddoc's recent refusal to meet with citizens isn't all that has them worried, he's been seen quite frequently in Lockhill with women of... ill repute. The council has warned us that our public image is beginning to suffer for it, and it would give us a boost to have one of you settle down. Show that the next generation is secure. As that coincides with your mother requiring new ladies in waiting, we're hoping to catch two birds with one stone, so to speak."

"Father, don't you think this is a little... archaic?"

Taurak sighed. "Before he died, my father had arranged a marriage for your mother and I, and it worked out very well for us."

"You fell in love with her at first sight, before you even knew she was the one you were supposed to marry!" Zavier exclaimed, throwing his hands up. "That is hardly likely to happen again!"

His father chuckled, looking a bit sheepish. "You never know, it might! We both know that your brother is unlikely to fall in love or wed someone on his own, let alone someone appropriate, so the council wanted your mother and I to take things into our own hands."

Zavier had to agree with that assessment of his brother, but demanded, "The same council that we just discussed isn't exactly doing their jobs? And what about me? Is my taste in women so bad that you need to resort to arranging things?"

"Nothing is arranged yet, son, and it's not so much your taste in women as it is how guarded you are. You don't give anyone a chance anymore, so it's very unlikely that you would meet and marry someone on your own. These women range in age, I believe they are from three different clutches. All I'm asking of you is good manners, and if anyone strikes your fancy, be charming."

Zavier struggled not to roll his eyes. All he did was charm people, usually politicians, ambassadors, or other leaders. His few attempts to approach and charm women had all led to heartbreak, anger, and in one case, near death.

Sighing, Taurak leaned toward his son. "I know you've struggled with women and your position over the years. I appreciate that you haven't taken Caddoc's tactic of sleeping with everyone that will have him, but it seems you may have gone too far in the other direction. The guards mentioned that you never bring anyone to your rooms— No, I wasn't having them report or spy on you." He held up a hand to forestall Zavier's indignant response. "The guards keep tabs for your safety, and they have been swapping stories with Cad's team. The difference was noted. When I was young, I felt much the same way you did. Why chase a woman who only wants a crown, not the man?"

Zavier could only nod. His father had concisely summed up his feelings and he felt a flush of anger and humiliation as he recalled the previous night's debacle.

Taurak waited for his response, watching his son's face intently. Zavier sighed. "I don't like it. The council is meant to advise the crown. I'm not even publicly named heir yet, I should have the right to determine my own future for a while longer. Does this mean you are making plans to officially name one of us heir?"

"Perhaps, soon. Particularly with how Caddoc has behaved in the past few years. First and foremost, it is our duty to serve the people, and the council says the people are uneasy."

Zavier sighed again. "I'll play along, for now, but don't get your hopes up. I've watched you and Mother for too long to settle for anything but a love match with the right woman."

Chuckling, his father stood and went around the desk to clap him on the shoulder. "Thank you, son. I can always count on you to do what is best for our people, even when you hate it."

"I still fail to see how marrying is best for the people, Father. What's best for our people right now is to regulate pricing on healing services, and repair the damage caused by those storms last week. I'll do it, but in exchange, will you speak to Caddoc again, and the council, too? This business of turning away people can't go on." Zavier returned the half-hug, taking comfort in his father's unwavering affection.

"Of course, I'll see to it today. Now go spend time with your mother, she's been so anxious to see you, it's a wonder she hasn't dragged you out of here yet. She'll be in her garden."

Seven

Minnie

*S*CENES AND VISIONS FLASH *across her mind's eye. Some change too quickly to be seen, some are too disjointed to make any sense at all. Still others linger, allowing her to see every detail.*

Hundreds of bodies lay on pallets across the floor of a warehouse.

A middle-aged man clutches his midsection and vomits blood.

A ship carrying shrouded corpses being towed from the harbor by two dragons and lit aflame.

A russet female dragon flares her wings and launches into the air, hundreds of males following her.

A forest green dragon perches on a mountain outcropping and roars. Behind her a golden male echoes her cry.

Another room, another man, this one grips his head with both hands and screams. He looks around with fear in his eyes. Golden eyes, eyes that roll back in his skull as he dies.

Minnie jolted upright, gasping for breath. A glance out the window told her dawn was still hours away. With a trembling hand, she reached into the drawer beside her bed, lifting out a worn journal and ink pen. Careful not to smudge, she wrote out exactly what she had seen in the dream, struggling to capture as many details as she could recall. Heaving a sigh, she recapped the pen and replaced both pen and journal in the drawer, rolled over, and went back to sleep.

The following morning, everyone woke late. Minnie dressed slowly, brushing and re-braiding her unruly hair twice to delay going out to breakfast. She'd already packed her travel bag, taking mostly books since she had no idea what she would be facing at the capital and books made her feel more comfortable. She had a little money, hopefully it would be enough to buy clothes appropriate for court, as nothing she owned would suffice.

Finally, she had no other choice. She'd heard her parents and sister make their way to the kitchen already, and she couldn't sneak out without at least saying goodbye to her father and sister. She was still unsure how she felt about her mother.

Entering the kitchen, her stomach twisted into knots. Rosemary's hair wasn't brushed and her eyes were red and puffy. She'd clearly been crying, but she appeared alert as she sat at the table. She looked up as Minnie approached.

"I'm sorry, daughter," Rosemary said in a quavering voice. "I've been so afraid..."

Unsure what to say, Minnie sat down, folding her arms on the table ahead of her. She watched her mother for several moments in silence.

Rosemary broke first, anxiously picking at her fingers. "Your father said you are leaving today. I have something for you to take with you."

That surprised Minnie into saying, "What? You're letting me go?"

Quietly, Rosemary replied, "I have no right to tell you how to live your life, not after how I've treated you."

Feeling that she was entirely correct but it would be rude to agree, Minnie waited.

"My issues are mine, and I have to find a way to cope. I've saved this for you. It was my mothers once, and now I want you to have it."

She pushed the small bundle across the table. Unwrapping the linen, Minnie looked down at the belt of silver linked chain. Feeling more confused than ever, Minnie slowly rose from her seat, walked around the table and hugged Rosemary. Her mother's fragile shoulders shook as Rosemary began to cry.

"I love you, Mama," Minnie whispered into her hair. "I love you so much, but right now, I hate you for what you've done, and I don't know what I should do about that."

Saying goodbye to her father and sister went quickly after the pain of parting with her mother. Minnie felt terrible, and every instinct she had told her to go back inside and tell her she didn't mean it, and she was sorry, and to beg for forgiveness. She kept firm hold of her emotions, challenging herself to not be a coward. It was time to go, and it was past time her mother paid for her mistakes.

The flight to Hatherus shouldn't have been a very long one. She'd heard from other Bonded that they could make the flight in just a couple of hours. It took her nearly six, she'd had to stop for a rest once and got lost along the way, but finally she saw the Spire rise ahead of her. Unsure where she should go, she circled the city twice. There were dragons sprawled along the river, and what she assumed was the palace courtyard held two more dragons being loaded with supplies.

She swooped over the courtyard. A man looked up as she neared, waving at her to wait for a moment. She hesitated, hovering. The wind from her wings was making it difficult for them to tie a tarp to a dragon's back. She hastily summoned her magic, swirling the air around her in a vortex as she shifted her skin. Her pack came loose as she shrank out from under the long coil of rope, and she caught it by the straps. Minnie fell slowly, keeping tight rein on the winds so it wouldn't affect men trying to load the dragon. They watched her with wide eyes.

"How'd you do that?" one man asked as she landed daintily on the cobbles.

"Do what?" she replied, looking around to be sure he was speaking to her.

"With the winds? I never thought of that before," the man said. He approached her, hand outstretched in greeting. She clasped it with a smile.

"Oh, um... I don't know, it just seemed like the simplest solution, and it just kind of comes to me."

The man shrugged, grinning. "Ain't that the way? I'd love to learn how you did it, if you ever feel like sharing! I'm Ned," he added.

"I'm Minnie, it's a pleasure to meet you. I was summoned to the palace, do you know where I should go?" she asked, hoping he would have some information for her.

"Sure, go inside, tell one of the guards who you are, they'll bring you to Lady Anitra, or maybe Queen Narith herself." With a wave and another smile, the man walked back to his waiting dragon, who was snorting with impatience.

Following his instructions, she climbed the short flight of steps and entered the wide double doors to the palace. A guard stood on either side of the foyer, flanking the ornate staircase.

"I was told to find Queen Narith or... I've forgotten the name, Anita, I think? I'm Minnie Hernshaw."

Before either of the men could respond, a shrill voice sounded from above. "My name is Lady Anitra Davengard," the voice said. Looking up, Minnie saw a reed-thin woman bedecked in jewels gripping the banister at the top of the stairs. Lady Anitra was glaring down at Minnie. The woman snarled, "Come with me so that I might interview you."

Minnie hurried to obey, racing up the stairs two at a time. Minnie counted two necklaces, her wrists jangled with multiple bracelets, and every finger held a glittering ring. She stood a full head taller than the ornately dressed older woman, who somehow looked down her nose as she looked up at Minnie.

"Hernshaw, you said? Oh yes, from Ocrans. I hear you have no dragon, I've never heard of such nonsense. I'm not sure why I bothered selecting you."

Minnie tried to reply, "I have a dragon, I just don't know where they are."

Lady Anitra wasn't listening. With a dismissive sniff, the woman turned on her heel and marched down the hallway. Minnie followed, annoyed, but eager to see more of the palace.

Her hopes were dashed as the woman turned into a side room almost instantly. It was a small, tidy office, only furnished with a desk and two chairs.

"Have a seat. We expected you days ago," Lady Anitra snapped as she rooted around the desk in search of something.

"The missive said I was due by the first, and that's tomorrow," Minnie replied. "I only received the note yesterday."

"That hardly matters," the woman scowled. She must have found what she was searching for as she held up a scroll to the light, and sat down while reading it. "You should know to be here early, that's common knowledge. I see here you ignored our previous summons. You never arrived to accept a job posting. You have no formal education. Add to that you claim to have no dragon? Do you even have any magic? Are you a liar? You've no reason to be here at all, do you?"

"I told you, I do have a dragon, but I don't—"

"According to reports, your magic is quite substantial, but I don't trust that information. You certainly don't look powerful. You're entirely unsuitable to be presented as a lady in waiting, I don't know why I thought you would be."

Minnie opened her mouth, but whether she intended to defend herself or snap back at the woman, she had no idea. Lady in waiting? Is that why she was here? Should she tell the woman she was wrong? Before she could make a choice, the door behind her opened and another woman spoke.

"Anitra, you were told to escort the girls to me, and allow me to speak with them," said the firm voice, with a hint of exasperation. "They are to be *my* ladies in waiting, and I will interview them. You've been told numerous times, I will not tell you again. Now go do something useful, far away from me."

Anitra stood, her mouth in a tight line. She glared daggers at the woman now standing beside Minnie's chair. Without another word, Anitra stormed off, mumbling under her breath as she left the room.

"I am sorry for the unpleasant scene," the newcomer said, extending a dainty hand to Minnie, who shook it, feeling quite confused. "Will you come with me, please?"

Without a word Minnie stood and followed her. They walked down several corridors, Minnie craning her neck to see portraits and statues. The woman led her to an office in a quiet hallway, brightly lit and filled to the brim with plants and flowers. Every surface had multiple vases or planters on it. By comparison to Anitra, this woman didn't appear like she belonged in the palace. Her clothing looked well used, a rough skirt with mud along the hem, and a faded green blouse. Like Minnie, the woman was shapely, with more curves around hip and breast.

"Please, dear, have a seat. I'm sorry, I didn't catch your name?" she apologized, taking her own seat behind a pretty wooden desk.

"Minnie, my lady. I mean, Jessamine Hernshaw," she replied in a soft voice. Already feeling very out of place, she worried that this woman would react as Anitra had.

"Ah, yes, from Ocrans. I remember your mother, the poor dear. Such a tragedy. Is she well now?"

Unsure how to answer that question without airing all their recent family drama, Minnie simply nodded.

"Good. I'm glad you decided to come to Hatherus this time," and for the first time, her voice sounded less than inviting.

"Yes, my lady, I'm sorry for that. You see, I had never actually received any of the invitations. My father wrote a letter, but I'm supposed to give it only to the king or queen..."

"Your pardon, child, I didn't introduce myself. I am Narith, the queen. May I have the letter?" Narith extended her hand. Feeling foolish and blushing furiously, Minnie dug into her pack for the letter her father had handed her before she left. Narith was silent for several minutes as she read the scroll.

"I see," she finally said, setting the paper down. "By chance, did you bring the invitation we sent you?"

Minnie opened the front flap of her pack and pulled it out, grateful she'd brought the letter for validation that she was, in fact, supposed to be there. Queen Narith's brows scrunched together as she read.

"I asked Anitra to send invitations to a handful of young women, requesting they come to the capital if they were interested in a position as a lady in waiting. I like to switch up my ladies every few years, you see. The first women who arrived had no idea why they had been asked to come, and seemed to think they had no choice. I see here that Anitra has gone above her station once again."

Unsure what to say, Minnie just looked at the queen with wide eyes. Narith continued, seemingly unaware of Minnie's discomfort. "The king and I were aware, of course, that you had not come to the capital as was customary, but there is no law that states you must. It is simply tradition. Well, that's in the past, and you've come now. Taurak and I will discuss your unique situation, and what is to be done about your missing dragon."

Minnie lowered her eyes so the queen wouldn't see the flash of anger. It always came down to the dragon, or lack of one, no matter her own power. Schooling her features, she returned her gaze to the older woman's eyes.

The queen tilted her head as she studied Minnie. "Don't misunderstand me, Minnie. I am not con-demning you, I am genuinely curious. A missing dragon is a serious matter, and it is a mystery I would very much like solved, but we will deal with that at another time. Today, you will be shown to your room so you can unpack your belongings. This afternoon you can meet the other Bonded ladies who have already arrived."

"Yes, Your Majesty," Minnie replied, her voice tight with nerves and emotion. "I'm afraid I do not have very much in the way of possessions. Could you recommend an affordable shop where I can purchase ready-made gowns? I don't want to offend by not being dressed appropriately," she hastily added as her voice broke.

Narith watched her for a long moment. With a small smile, she nodded. "You remind me a bit of myself when I was young. I had a controlling family. If I disobeyed, I was punished. My mother demanded I do everything perfectly. Magic, school, household tasks. Nothing was ever done to her satisfaction. I almost refused to marry Taurak because it pleased her so much that the former King wanted me for his son's bride. But the moment I met him I knew I loved him, and that was more important. I discovered myself when I left my family, and I think you will too. No, I don't think your family was like mine, thank the Fates, as that is not a life I want any of my people to have, but it hasn't been easy for you, has it, dear?"

Minnie bit her lip, struggling to keep the tears from falling. She had never once thought of her mother as controlling, or felt she was being abused or in any way mistreated. Not until last night. Now she felt a sense of freedom, so far from home, able to make her own choices.

Narith seemed to come to a decision. She nodded firmly, standing once again. "Come, my child. Let's go upstairs together, and we will pick out some of my old clothes for you. We look to be about the same size. I have plenty to spare, and no need for them to sit in my closet when someone can make use of them. They will be yours to keep, and we'll make sure they're ones that will suit your coloring."

Before Minnie could raise an objection, the queen had taken her arm, raised her from her seat, and led her from the room.

Eight

Zavier

C ADDOC HAD ARRIVED THAT morning and prompt-
ly received a thorough dressing down from
their father for his callous behavior of their people.
Frustrated, Caddoc was storming from the palace
when Zavier found him.

"You just got here, brother!" Zavier cried, gripping
his arm.

"And I'm leaving again. I didn't come back just to
hear Father lecture me." Caddoc angrily tried to rip
his arm from Zavier's hand and failed.

"Stay, at least a little while. Come out and spar with
me and work off some anger," Zavier had begged,
pleased when Caddoc reluctantly relented. They'd
spent two hours beating each other with training
swords. Once they'd worn the aggression out of each
other, the brothers soaked in the river before agreeing to a mid-air race.

Now Zavier reclined beside Caddoc on the peak of
the Spire of Hatherus, their long legs dangling over

the edge. It had been their favorite place to come to since they'd been old enough to shift, long before their different personalities had set them against each other.

So far they had managed to avoid any uncomfortable topics, but now they were watching dragons and their Bonded arrive and depart. Most were deliveries, the trade caravans flown between Bonded partners, or guards on patrol. Several dragons had taken flight near the palace, and may have been the women summoned by their parents. Despite Taurak's reassurance that the women were here to be ladies in waiting, Caddoc didn't appear to believe him.

"I wonder if any of these women will be good-looking, or merely acceptably bred and suitably powerful enough for the future generation," Caddoc said, his eyes on the brown dragon currently landing in the courtyard.

Zavier fought not to grimace. While a crude way to put it, Caddoc did have a point. The royal family were the only ones who could inherit dragon-skin as a shifting animal, and it was thought that the power of the parents would impact the power of the offspring. It wasn't always a guarantee that the power passed on, their uncle Beltak had two sons who weren't shifters, because his wife Anitra wasn't dragon-bonded.

"I've not given it much thought as I have no plans to pick any of them. What use do I have for a wife when I'm always traveling?" Zavier strove to keep his tone light, to make a jest of the situation.

"How many did they say they invited?"

"Seven, I think."

"And there are no men?"

"No, they're supposed to be ladies in waiting and our possible future brides, remember?" Zavier chuckled at the affronted look on his brother's face.

"That isn't what I meant, asshole," Cad snapped.

"I know what you meant, but you flew right into it. The only dragon-bonded here by royal invitation are female. I've no idea who else may be here to dance attendance upon our parents."

"Good," his brother crowed, rubbing his hands together with a gleam in his eyes. "That means less competition, it'll be easier to seduce them!"

"Think higher than your cock, brother, please," Zavier said as he rolled his eyes.

"Never, little brother. As long as it works I will let it make all my decisions for me." Caddoc stood and adjusted his jacket back into place. "Speaking of, I'll be back in time for dinner, I feel the need to visit one of my favorite ladies."

Zavier sighed. "You need to knock that shit off, Cad. Don't be late to dinner, I don't want to deal with all those women by myself."

Caddoc waved over his shoulder as he climbed back into the window of the tower roof. Zavier reclined against the peaked roof with his arms under his head, watching the clouds drift by. A gust of air blew over him as a ruby dragon circled down into the palace courtyard across the city. After more than four months spent underground in the Stoneborn city of Nagrain, something as simple as the air upon his face was enough to bring a smile to his lips. Nagrain was a beautiful city and her people made him feel quite welcome and at home, but nothing could replace his own city.

A dragon's bugle broke his reverie and he sat up to look around. Maurgen sat on his haunches by the riverbank staring across the water. As Zavier watched, Maurgen launched himself into the air with mighty beats of his golden wings.

Through their link, Zavier heard the dragon say, *"I hear something happening across the river, but I am not sure what it is."*

"I'm right behind you, don't get into trouble without me!" Zavier stood and ran across the roof, leaping into the air as high as he could and drawing on his power to shift into his Draconid, half-humanoid half-dragon form. Huge wings grew from his back and beat rapidly to carry him into the air and after his dragon partner. His scalp itched as the horns grew, and he swore under his breath as he felt his trousers rip from the long tail sprouting at the base of his spine. That was the second pair of pants he'd ruined in as many days.

Ahead of him, Maurgen had paused over a small billow of dust and dirt rising from the ground. This area had sparse trees and many natural hills interspersed with small caves and ridges. Children loved to play here, but several times a year someone had to be rescued from one of the caves. Maurgen landed beside a fresh sinkhole, dust still rising from the collapse, and looked up to find Zavier hovering overhead.

"It looks like another partial collapse, I smell animals, but I also smell people. Two for sure, but I'm not sure how long ago they were here."

"Start digging, but carefully!" Zavier landed beside his partner, who had already started shifting a large boulder out of the way. There was a cave entrance nearby that was large enough for an adult to enter if he bent over. *"If I remember right, we're directly over an underground stream, but it should be much deeper than this collapse."*

"This ground is firm now, it may be a pocket. I'm not smelling people here. Go look inside the cave."

Wordlessly, Zavier did as the dragon suggested, ducking his head and pulling his wings in tight to his shoulders. He thought about shifting back to his humanoid skin, but remembering the rip in his pants from his tail, decided against it.

The cave ceiling was low and the space tight for his wings, but he crept along slowly as it sloped downward and to the right. Ahead he heard frantic whispering and breathed a sigh of relief. *"There are children here, Maurgen."*

"Hello there, are you hurt?" Zavier called out, softly so his voice wouldn't bounce around and deafen them. After a few tense minutes and more worried mutterings, two young boys emerged, filthy but unhurt.

"We're sorry, we didn't mean to," the youngest said with a sniffle as tears fell down his cheek. The elder, most likely his brother, nodded and wiped a dirty hand over his face, smudging more dirt. Both boys stared anxiously at Zavier, their eyes flicking from his horns to his wings.

"What happened?" Zavier carefully knelt down to be on eye level with the pair.

"We tried digging a new path, we took pick axes from our Pa, and shovels. We wanted to make a hideout just for us," said the elder boy.

Maurgen's head blocked the entrance and the cave went dark, causing both young boys to let out a frightened shriek.

"Easy, boys, it's only Maurgen. Back up, you overgrown lizard. Come on, let's get out of here." He carefully backed out until he had enough room to turn around, then took the boys' hands and led them to the cave mouth. The enormous golden dragon sat on his haunches beside the fresh sinkhole, giving them his version of a reproachful look. The effect was a bit lost on the boys, who stared in awe at being so close to the huge beast.

"It seems the vibration from your pickaxes triggered a weak spot, and there wasn't enough support to keep the ground up. You're lucky you were on this side of the collapse, you could have been seriously hurt," Zavier crossed his arms and gave the wayward pair his 'stern prince face' in hopes of making an impact on them.

"Thank you for saving us," the boys replied in unison. Zavier relaxed a bit and shook his head.

"You didn't need saving, this time. But if I hear you've done something like this again, I'll box your ears. Or let Maurgen dangle you from his claws while he flies over the river!" He smiled as he said it to show he was mostly joking, but that effect was also lost on them. He shook his head. "You two run home, Maurgen will be watching from the air, so don't even think about straying! And tell your mother what happened, or I'll come tell her myself!"

That threat did work on them, and they took off without another word. Maurgen rumbled, his version of a chuckle. With a leap Maurgen took to the air, but his voice was loud and clear within Zavier's mind.

"Boys will be boys, won't they? You must hurry now or you will be late to dinner with your family and the dragon-bonded. Will any of their dragons be joining them?"

As Maurgen spoke, Zavier turned toward the city, spread his wings and also leaped into the air. *"None have arrived that I am aware of, most dragons are on the Isle preparing for the Rising. It won't be too long before you and I are there as well, and you'll get to see all the dragons!"*

Maurgen grumbled as he hovered over the city, watching the two boys return home.

Zavier landed at the entrance to the training ground and flagged down a passing soldier. "Please find General Beltak and let him know there was a collapse about two miles from the river. I'd like him to send out a patrol to scout the area, and have someone draft a message to post in the city centers letting our people know the ground in that area might be unstable."

"Yes, Your Highness, right away!" The soldier nodded briskly and ran toward the officers' quarters. Tucking his wings against his back, Zavier turned toward the palace courtyard with a sigh. Because his pants had ripped when he shifted, he'd need to return to his apartments before he shifted back. The servants would talk, as they always did when they were reminded of their prince's abilities. There was always a marked increase in women asking him for favors in return for sex anytime he was seen like this, and that infuriated him.

He also wanted to avoid reminding Caddoc of his Draconid form. Caddoc's reaction was childish, but after their mid-air battle all those years ago because of the Draconid gift, he'd done his best to not rub it in his brother's face. Despite their differences and how horribly Caddoc had been acting recently, Zavier still loved his brother and didn't want to hurt him. He spent entirely too much effort attempting to keep Caddoc happy, but some part of him still looked up to his elder brother.

As he crossed a corner of the training field, he spied his uncle, General Beltak, speaking to the soldier. Beltak gave further orders and the younger man took off to carry them out. Lifting his hand to flag his nephew, Beltak approached Zavier.

"I've sent a patrol out as you requested. Are you on your way up for the dragon-bonded dinner?" At Zavier's nod, the older man frowned. "I understand my brother doesn't want to overwhelm these girls, but it seems like my wife and I should have been invited to attend with our sons."

Fighting the urge to roll his eyes, Zavier replied as politely as he could, "As you said, Father doesn't want to overwhelm them. It's enough that these women are vying amongst themselves for a position with Mother." He wasn't sure if Beltak was aware that Taurak intended for his sons to possibly court one of these women, so best not to mention it.

Nodding, though he did not appear mollified, Beltak said, "Anitra has been hounding me for days over this dinner. She feels it is my duty to ensure none of the women are a danger to the family."

Even as he said it, Zavier knew his uncle didn't believe his own words. The dragon connection was special, and each Bonded owed their gift to the royal family's connection to the dragons. No Bonded had ever harmed the royal family in their entire history. The dragons wouldn't allow it, making it physically impossible.

"I appreciate her concern, Uncle, but isn't she the one who selected these women and invited them here?"

Beltak nodded, a sly smile crossing his features. "Aye, she did, and she did not appreciate it when I reminded her of that fact."

Zavier bit back a small chuckle. His uncle would speak up when his power hungry wife demanded more than she was due, but he never argued when he was told no. He knew his place in their world, even if she didn't. Zavier had often wondered what Beltak had seen in Anitra. He'd been told that Beltak loved her for her beauty and wit, but she was so often unpleasant to everyone that there must be more to her than he could see. She was a wonderful mother, maybe that was it?

"As my father said, we don't want to add unnecessary people to tonight's guest list and overwhelm the women. Please inform my aunt that she will be called upon to host a formal event next week, as she has expressed such interest in tonight's affair." With a firm nod to his uncle, Zavier wished him well and hurried away.

Zavier entered the back garden instead of the front courtyard, still hoping to avoid being seen. His apartments were located in a tower near the gardens, and he had a balcony so he could fly, but he feared it would draw far more attention than if he attempted to sneak in. He hesitated just outside the garden gate and listened carefully. No voices, no crunch of gravel. The tour his mother had planned to give must have ended already.

"You are going through an awful lot of effort to avoid being seen." Maurgen's lazy voice filled his mind, along with an image of the great golden dragon settling himself along the riverbank, his favorite spot to sun.

"I am, and you know damn well why."

"It's stupid. Let Caddoc be jealous."

"I'm not going to antagonize him now after I spent all day being nice to him," Zavier snapped back.

"You spend far too much time placating your brother, worrying how he will react, and catering to his feeble emotions."

Zavier sighed. There was no point arguing with the dragon, he was right, and Zavier hated it.

He unlatched the gate and hurried in, letting it close behind him with a clang. He followed the neat paths through various flowering plant beds, rose bushes, beneath trellises and past the herb garden. He was passing under a trellis of hanging vines when a low vine caught his wing-claw.

Swearing, he struggled to carefully unhook the vine from the claw. His wings flexed as the claw was freed, catching on another low vine. The more he freed himself, the more caught he became, first his wing and then his horns as well. He swore again, louder.

A crunch of gravel nearby alerted him to someone's presence. Carefully looking around, he spied a woman anxiously rubbing her hands together, watching him.

"Would you like some help, Your Highness?" she asked, stepping closer. He swallowed nervously.

"Uhh..." His brain didn't seem to want to function. He felt like he'd been struck with a hammer. Finally, he managed to say, "Ye- yes, please. Mother will have my hide if I rip her vines and I can't seem to unhook..."

"Put your hands down, bend your knees... Yes, just a little more. There." As she spoke she had approached him and reached for the vines, deftly untwisting them from around the claws of his wing joint and his horns. He half crouched as she freed him which put him at eye level of her chest, and while her dress was modestly cut and showed just the barest hint of cleavage, his imagination filled in the gaps quite easily. What in all hells was the matter with him?

"You should stay low to avoid being caught again, but you're free now," the woman said as she unwound the final vine.

Feeling all kinds of foolish for his life choices that day, Zavier hobbled the remaining few feet to open air and stood. She was only a couple inches shorter than him and met his eyes easily, a soft smile lifting her plump lips. Images of those lips wrapped around— Nope, do not finish that thought, he scolded himself.

"Thank you for your help, my lady. I should have just flown back, I was so intent on sneaking inside that I didn't even notice which path I'd taken." He sketched her a courtly bow, his wings flaring out to maintain his balance with the heavy horns atop his head.

"You're more than welcome. I've met your mother and she's quite proud of these gardens, I can well imagine what she would do if you ruined something," she gave a soft chuckle as she looked around. Her hands, now that they weren't unwinding the vines, were fiddling with the creases in her dress. Almost like she was nervous.

Zavier studied her closely. She wasn't what most people would call beautiful. She was tall for a woman, more plump than was generally acceptable among the courtiers and nobles. Her curves fascinated him, he could easily imagine tracing his hands down each one, and what a ripe handful she would be... He mentally slapped himself and tried to focus on something other than her breasts.

She wore no jewels, there were no embellishments on her gown other than simple embroidery along the scoop neck and down the wide bell sleeves. A belt of silver links was her only adornment, and based on the level of tarnish, the belt was an antique. Despite the plain gown, Zavier was unable to stop staring at her, especially her eyes. Darkest green met his gaze, with tiny golden flecks glinting in the sunlight.

He mentally shook his head and struggled to regain his composure and come back down to earth.

Most people, even those used to seeing him and his father, appeared uneasy or even afraid of their Draconid, half-humanoid form. She hadn't hesitated at all. "I.. I don't recognize you, are you new to Hatherus?"

"Yes, I arrived yesterday." A shy smile lit up her round face as she flicked her long braid over her shoulder.

"You're one of the dragon-bonded my mother invited, then. That's why you aren't surprised to see me like this," he gestured to himself, indicating the over-sized wings, horns, and thick tail curling around his feet. He was thankful that the tail was keeping his ripped pants in place, he'd embarrassed himself enough in front of this woman without losing his trousers, too.

"Yes, your mother mentioned that you and your brother had returned. I was hoping to see the Draconid form up close, but hadn't expected this," she replied with a small giggle. Her eyes had flecks of gold in them. "I— I would love to learn more about the Draconid gift and how it makes you different from us. The books aren't very clear. If you don't mind, of course," she hastily added.

He smiled back at her, running a hand through his hair and remembering just in time not to hit one of his horns and look more like a fool. "I'd love to. I wish I could right now, unfortunately, I'm going to risk being late for dinner if I don't get upstairs and change quickly." The last thing Zavier wanted to do was leave this captivating woman, which surprised him, especially after he'd been duped and used so recently. He chastised himself again, commanding his brain to focus on what was most important.

"Thank you, Your Highness." She dropped in a wobbly curtsy, clearly not used to the movement.

81

"Zavier!" His mother's voice rang from a balcony over their heads. "You have exactly twenty minutes before the dinner bell rings and you aren't even dressed!"

"Shit," he swore. "I'm so sorry, I've got to run."

"It was lovely to meet you, Your Highness!" she called as he turned from her and jumped into the air, swearing at himself for not just flying to his balcony in the first place. He must look like a first-rate idiot to her. He tucked his wings in and dropped the remaining five feet to the balcony, still swearing under his breath.

Nine

Minnie

MINNIE WATCHED ZAVIER HASTEN away with a smile. She'd spent the morning with his mother, Narith, walking the gardens and getting to know several of the other ladies that had been invited. While she was still nervous in such a large and grand place, Narith had done everything she could to make Minnie feel welcome and more at home.

Minnie had opted to wait in the gardens before the dinner began, and had heard the cursing from nearby when Zavier had become caught in the trellis vines. He certainly was handsome, and seeing him with wings and horns had done things to her low in her abdomen that she wasn't sure she should enjoy.

His eyes were a bright gold, so pale amber that they couldn't even really be called amber anymore. Messy blond hair had fallen into his eyes several times and he fussed with his hair while they spoke, brushing it around the two sets of horns. One set was curled like a ram, the other grew up and back. A thin scar ran along his sharp jaw, ending almost in the middle of his chin. She'd wanted so badly to trace that scar with her fingers when they stood together. She was almost his height, she only had to tilt her head back slightly to meet his eyes.

As she wandered back to the garden door, she reflected further on their meeting. Why had she asked him about his Draconid form? She had read every book in Lirance's collection, she knew as much as anyone could know about the rare gift. Except what it was like to have that form, she amended. Only people who had done some kind of heroic service to the Vynar of the dragons were granted a Draconid form. Lirance had said that the fact there were two Draconid, Taurak and Zavier, alive at the same time, much less from the same family, was unheard of in the history of dragonkind.

Well, maybe he would keep his promise, and she could find out what he had done to earn such a remarkable gift. Really, any excuse she could find to see him again would be fine with her.

A footman held the door open as she approached. She nodded her thanks and turned to the hallway she had been told led to the dining room where they would have their dinner. Maybe she should avoid him, instead of hoping to see him again?

And besides, she was finally out of Ocrans. Guilt rose in her as she considered not returning to her family. She could see the places she'd only read about. Vague marks on the incomplete map that hung in Lirance's house. Stories she'd heard from other Bonded as they made deliveries.

Maybe she could become a teacher? Or a healer, there was always a need for more healers, especially one who didn't need to use material and charge a fee.

"I want more chairs added, I told you this before. Four more, for my husband, my sons, and myself. Do it right away!"

"My lady, we were told quite firmly that we were not to amend the seating or change the dinner menu."

"I outrank anyone you spoke to, girl!"

The servant, who was no girl but a woman of considerable years, straightened her back. "Lady Anitra, I take my orders from Queen Narith or King Taurak, and no one else. If you have a problem, please speak to them." Before Anitra could utter a reply, the woman turned and hastened away.

Minnie ducked around a corner before Anitra could see her. The two women had come out of a kitchen doorway further down the hall and had been walking away from Minnie, but she had no desire to be scrutinized by Anitra again.

Minnie heard the older woman mumbling to herself about impertinent servants. She must have snagged a maid or footman, for Minnie heard her give the order again to add more chairs. Minnie was so involved in hiding from Anitra that she didn't hear someone approach from behind her.

"Hiding from my wife?"

Whirling to find a large, gruff warrior-like man behind her, Minnie gasped. "I'm sorry, sir—"

"No need to apologize. Sometimes I want to hide from her, too. You must be Jessamine, my sister-in-law mentioned that you and Anitra had a run-in yesterday."

Stammering, Minnie tried to say, "She welcomed me to the palace..."

"I'm sure she did. I apologize, I've forgotten my manners. I'm General Beltak, Taurak's brother. No need to curtsy, my lady," he chuckled, offering her

85

a hand up from the half-curtsy she'd begun when he introduced himself. "Anitra is a... well, she's a difficult woman to understand. I love her, and she's a wonderful mother, but she can be quite difficult to those who don't know her well."

Unsure what to say, Minnie simply nodded, then wondered if she shouldn't have, as that meant she was agreeing. Fighting not to groan at her ineptitude, Minnie asked, "Is Lady Anitra Queen Narith's assistant? Her name was signed on the summons I received."

General Beltak scratched the back of his neck as he thought. "Narith does have Anitra assist her sometimes, but she really excels at trade, it's in her blood. Anitra's family were very successful traders and merchants, with hubs across the country and connections in every major city."

"That's incredible," Minnie encouraged, but she wondered why he was telling her all of this.

"My father imposed trade levies and taxes on goods coming in from the Human continent, and not long after the Council launched an investigation into Anitra's father, Alec Sackville. Nothing could be proved, but his business was ruined by rumor. During that time, I had fallen in love with Anitra. My father disapproved, but I insisted on marrying her. I knew I wouldn't become the next king, so my choice of bride didn't matter as much as my brother's did. She was sweet, lovely, an amazing person... but she changed when Taurak inherited the crown. Apparently she hadn't known I didn't want it."

Again unsure of what to say, Minnie remained silent. After a moment, the general continued. "I suppose I'm explaining all of this to you, because she was inexplicably rude to you. Maybe... I think what I'm trying to say is, being part of the extended

royal family isn't easy, and Anitra is more complicated than she appears to be. She really is a wonderful person, if she lets you get to know her."

He trailed off. Minnie waited, but when he didn't
speak after several tense seconds, she said, "You love
her very much."

The older man nodded rapidly. "I do. I always
have. I know she's causing issues. I know she's prob-
lematic for the family, but she's my wife. I love her."

General Beltak seemed to shake himself, scrubbing at his face and readjusting his jacket. "I'm sorry, I shouldn't have laid all of that on you. It's not
proper. Please, forgive me."

"There's no need, General. If it's made you feel
better, I'm happy to have listened. I hope everything
works out well for you and your wife," Minnie assured him.

"You'd best go on then, the dinner bell will ring
soon, and I hear Narith putting Anitra in her place,
again. Enjoy your dinner, my lady."

The general hurried down the hall toward the
dining room. Minnie stood motionless, quite confused. "What just happened..." she wondered softly.

"Minnie?" One of the dragon-bonded women
called to her from down the hall. Several of the other
ladies were also waiting.

"Coming!" Minnie hastened after them, putting
her odd conversation with Beltak aside.

Ten

Zavier

Zavier's mother waited just inside his room, her hands on her hips and a scowl on her face. Narith took one look at his clothes, dirty and rumpled from the short trip to the cave, and opened her mouth to scold him, but he interrupted her.

"I know, I'm sorry Mother, I'll be ready in time, I promise!" He snatched the clothes she had laid on the bed for him, half annoyed that she had them ready as if he were a child but also grateful he wouldn't have to find something on his own.

In the washroom with the door safely closed he shifted his body back to humanoid, dunked his head in the basin of warm water someone had set out and scrubbed his face and hands. He toweled his head roughly to dry his hair, then ran fingers through the shoulder-length locks in lieu of a brush. Wishing he had time to shave and knowing someone — his Mother — would have a comment on the day's growth of stubble, he dressed quickly before returning to his room.

Queen Narith sat at his writing desk with the chair facing him, tapping her nails on the wooden desktop. She eyed the clock on the desk that showed they had less than ten minutes before the dinner bell. "You've cut it close, my son."

"There was a cave-in and trapped children, Mother," he exaggerated slightly hoping to deflect her ire. "Then I ran into some difficulty with the trellis in your garden—"

"You better not have ripped my vines! Those are difficult to cultivate!" Her mock wrath soothed him. If she could jest about her garden, then she wasn't too mad at him. She stood, appraising his clothes with a nod, but scowled as she reached his face and his unshaven cheeks. She reached up and ran a hand along the thin scar across his chin. Zavier took her hand, kissed the back, and linked his arm through hers.

"Is there any special reason you were waiting for me with my clothes all picked out, instead of letting my valet or one of the maids handle it?" Zavier asked as they crossed the room together.

Narith didn't respond right away. She stopped him with a hand to his chest just before he could open the door to leave his apartment.

"Son, I'm a bit worried about tonight. I fear I've allowed Anitra too much leniency this time, the women she has chosen... Well, there is nothing *wrong* with any of them, but none of them are who I would have chosen myself..."

Zavier gave her a questioning look, indicating she should continue. With a heavy sigh, she did. "For instance, there are two young women from Saltstone. One is from a wealthy family, but her magic

89

is minimal and she seems to feel she's entitled to be lazy because her father is a wealthy and successful merchant. The other is by all accounts a very hard worker, but she's a dullard, and has almost no magic to speak of."

Frowning, Zavier asked, "If they aren't suitable, why were they chosen?"

"I've no idea, and that's the problem. I allowed Anitra to do this and she's gone and cocked it up," his mother snarled, unusually vulgar in her irritation.

"What about the others?" As he spoke, he opened the door and led the queen through, closing and locking his door behind them. Narith lowered her voice as they traversed the halls, but continued her description of the women.

"There is a very shy girl from a tiny village in the east, one of those newer ones that sprang up in recent decades. She has some skill with herbs and minimal healing ability, but she's so quiet. She's a lovely young woman, and would make a good partner or wife to any young man, but I can't see her leading the council or hosting as Princess of Hatherus. The final girl who is completely unacceptable is from Lockhill. I strongly suspect she is freer with her favors than a candidate for future princess should be, not that I have any objection to a woman seeking her own pleasure. One of the maids told me the girl had been overheard gossiping about a pair of Nightwalker women who trained her in the seductive arts, her words, not mine."

Biting back a chuckle at his mother's thin-lipped disapproval, Zavier said, "Might want to keep that one away from Caddoc, then."

"I've already warned him, which I'm sure means he intends to monopolize her to spite me."

"Wait, Mother— I thought you invited them here to be your ladies in waiting? Why are you acting like your primary reason was choosing a princess?" Zavier narrowed his eyes at her as they traversed the hall.

"All ladies in waiting are essentially trained as if they are in consideration for the prince at all times."

"You just made that up. I've known your past ladies, and not a single one of them were princess material," he replied with a roll of his eyes.

"You were too young, so I chose ladies that were in my taste, not yours. Now it's different." His mother's firm tone implied she no longer wished to discuss her motives. Zavier shook his head, and let it go.

"So if those women are unacceptable, there are some who are?"

Nodding, Narith braced herself against her son as they descended the staircase, holding her skirts away from her feet with her free hand. At the bottom of the steps, she continued.

"Two lovely young women from Aprana, twins, in fact. Decent family, not particularly powerful or wealthy, but with good reputations. The ladies are intelligent, attractive, and mannerly. However, they have very little magical talent, and while they are capable of healing, it's not with their touch, but through good old-fashioned herbs and potions."

Zavier nodded again. Magic in the royal family was inherited, and some people claimed that the more powerful the non-royal was, the more powerful their offspring would be. However, no one had ever proved if that was true, or if power had any bearing on if a royal child was born with a bonded partner or not. Superstition made the royals lean toward powerful consorts.

"Then there's the last one. A rather powerful young woman from Ocrans. She never arrived for her placement when we summoned her before, but apparently she had family trouble. She also says that her dragon never arrived to claim her, which greatly concerns me, but ultimately is no matter to me. If she were formally educated, well connected, and not surrounded by mystery and drama, she might be a solid contender for your princess, but she's altogether disappointing in those areas. Let me tell you, though, the power on that girl! It's far more than the twins, who I had assumed would have the most power considering they are from Aprana."

His mother's favoritism of her hometown was a legendary joke amidst the family. The large town lay at the foot of the mountains and had strong ties to the Stoneborn who lived nearby. The major animal families were falcons, goats, wolves, and mountain lions, each having claimed roughly a quarter of the town for themselves. His own mother came from a family of powerful mountain lions.

"Are they felines like you, Mother?" he teased her.

"No, they're from a hawk family, but still lovely girls." Narith swatted his arm as they turned down another hallway.

"Might be for the best, we don't want to breed too closely to our own bloodline, it's not healthy," he teased her.

"You're horrible, but correct. Not to worry though, your father has checked everyone's bloodlines, and none of them are related to us. Well, not closely, the Aprana girls are cousins several generations back, as I'm from Aprana, but certainly not close enough to cause an issue."

Zavier nodded and wisely kept his mouth shut. While she may be right— and probably was, he conceded— he knew from a political standpoint it wouldn't be wise to choose either of the women from Aprana. Not because they may be distant cousins, but because his mother *was* from that town, and it could be deemed favoritism. He wondered if the woman he had met in the garden was on the list of acceptable or not.

Outside the dining room entrance they saw Anitra waiting for them. She was dressed as she usually was, in rich fabrics and more jewelry than any woman should wear. Compared to his mother, wearing an understated gown of deep blue paired with a simple sapphire necklace, earrings, and her crown, the woman looked ridiculous.

"Ah, there you are, I've told the servants to add additional seating for my family—" Anitra began, as if there had been some misunderstanding at their exclusion.

"And I've told the servants to ignore orders from you regarding the dinner this evening," Narith replied, her voice frosty. The women had never liked each other and spoke in barest civilities. "You've been told several times, this dinner is for the *royal* family to greet my new ladies in waiting and get to know them a bit." Her emphasis on their rank did not go unnoticed by Anitra, who glared daggers at mother and son.

"As I told Uncle this afternoon, you'll be hosting a formal event for our visitors and will have plenty of time to meet them. Now, if you'll excuse us, Auntie, we don't want to be late to dinner," Zavier smiled and opened the door for his mother, turning his back on his aunt.

Mother and son entered the dining room from the rear entrance seconds before the bell rang outside. Taurak gave them both a reproachful look and rested a hand on his youngest son's shoulders. Branton stood awkwardly, almost as if he wanted to hide the inches he'd grown in recent weeks. As the women were led in by footmen, Zavier saw Caddoc slip into the room from the same door he and his mother had just used. His clothes were rumpled, as if he had just picked them off the floor and put them back on. Zavier narrowed his eyes and glared at his brother. Taurak pointedly ignored his eldest son, giving all his attention to the gathering guests.

"May I present to the assembled, their royal majesties, King Taurak and Queen Narith, their royal highnesses Prince Zavier, Prince Caddoc, and Prince Branton." The majordomo called in a loud and clear voice. Each royal gave a small bow to the women, who all curtsied deeply in return. Beside him, Zavier felt Caddoc tense. Never before had the brothers been announced in anything but order of birth. It was a clear sign of how far out of favor Caddoc had fallen.

"Your Highnesses, I present to you, the ladies Adaline, Coraline, Rebecca, Jessamine, Maisey, Olivia, and Lavender."

Each of the women curtsied again as their name was called, and Zavier finally had a good look at each of them. His eyes were drawn repeatedly to the woman from the garden, standing in the middle of the others. She appeared nervous, her eyes downcast and her fingers twisted in the skirt of her gown.

"Welcome to Hatherus, we are very pleased you all came. Please, let us be seated," his father's voice rang out with a gesture toward the table. Footmen from around the room came forward to pull a chair out for each of the women. Taurak pulled out his wife's chair himself, waving off the young man who came forward to help her. They normally ate as a family at a small table within their private wing, but since today was formal they were spaced out.

His father sat at the head of the table with Lavender to one side and Maisey on the other. Beside them sat Caddoc and Branton, then Adaline and Coraline, his mother, himself, Rebecca, Olivia, and Jessamine at the foot of the table. Zavier almost offered to swap places with Jessamine, she appeared unnerved that she was singled out and furthest away from the family, but a sharp look from his father told him to leave it alone.

It was a good thing he did, as after a few minutes of polite conversation she appeared to relax. She spoke at length with her nearest neighbors, and his mother asked her opinion several times. He had noticed the way her vibrant eyes sparkled when they were out in the garden in the sunlight. Here inside, they were so dark they looked like a forest in twilight. Unlike the other girls with carefully curled and pinned hair left loose in the current fashion, Jessamine still had hers braided tight.

The first course came and went with Narith and Taurak guiding the conversation, each asking various questions about the visiting women's homes. As the ladies grew more comfortable, conversation flowed easier between them all.

Despite his stern lecture to himself to not stare, he found himself constantly watching Jessamine. She had obviously learned proper etiquette for meeting the royal family but hadn't fully mastered it, instead reverting to a casual, if nervous, manner as soon as she felt comfortable. His family wasn't strict about formality, and it was a nice feeling to have one person not bending over backward to grovel.

Since Zavier was so often away from home acting as his fathers ambassador to other nations, he was nearly always at a formal dinner or eating by himself while he read a book, there was rarely any in between. He couldn't even remember the last time he'd had a casual meal with a friend. Her friendliness intrigued him, and he found himself idly daydreaming of sharing a meal with just her, discussing a book they'd read, or the latest reports from some small town. Ruefully, he chastised himself for flights of fancy.

"Jessamine, tell me, does your mother still run the Apothecary in Ocrans?" Taurak asked as the footmen brought out the second course of the meal.

"Yes, Your Majesty, though she's had to step back a bit due to her health," Jessamine replied, her smile faltering a bit.

"She's quite clever with her herbs and potions, I do hope her health improves quickly."

"I'll pass along your compliments and well wishes, Your Majesty, she will appreciate that she is in your thoughts," the woman replied. Because he was watching so closely, Zavier noticed a tightening around her eyes and lips, as if she struggled to keep her smile in place.

Taurak continued, oblivious to the woman's discomfort. "It was such a tragedy, your mother's accident. I've always regretted that we were unable to do more for her as she recovered."

Every face turned to Jessamine, who lowered her eyes to her plate, clearly uncomfortable. Narith, after shooting her husband a stern glare, thankfully changed the subject.

"Rebecca, that is an unusual design of gown, is that the current fashion in Lockhill?"

"Oh, yes, Your Majesty," Rebecca preened, the low cut of her gown threatening to expose her chest. "Many seamstresses are drawing inspiration from

Nightwalker traditions and designs, they're quite comfortable!" The young woman turned to look down the table at Lavender, who had on one of the plainest gowns Zavier had ever seen. Not that he was an expert by any means, but it was clear that Lavender's dress, while well made, was of simple cut and cloth. Even Jessamine's gown, while plain, was of a delicate silky fabric that clung to her form.

"Lavender, where did you get your gown?" Rebecca's almost snide tone didn't fool anyone that she was belittling the simplicity of the dress.

Lavender mumbled a reply, cleared her throat, and said slightly louder, "My sister and I sewed it ourselves. We don't have much fashion in Calding…"

"I think it's beautiful, Lavender. Simplicity is the best thing to showcase the beauty of the wearer, instead of relying on adornment or fancy cuts." The sharp retort came from Jessamine, who seemed shocked that she had been so outspoken.

"And you, Jessamine? Where did your gown come from? I remember my mother wearing a gown similar to that when I was a child," Rebecca snapped back with a sneer.

"I borrowed it when I arrived. Ocrans is a small town, and we prefer to focus on our industry, and not frivolous things like fashion," Jessamine replied with a sly smile. Zavier, eyes flicking from between the two as they traded barbs, was surprised that his mother wasn't putting a stop to the sniping. He glanced at Narith and saw a soft smile as she gazed at Jessamine.

"Borrowed, from where, the homeless donation bin?" Rebecca chuckled, but she seemed to realize she had overstepped when she looked around and saw no one else was laughing with her.

"No, I gave the gown to her," Narith finally spoke, her voice cold. Zavier realized then that the gown Narith was wearing wasn't dissimilar to the style of Jessamine's, a style Narith had favored and worn in various ways for years.

Rebecca shrank in on herself as Taurak changed the subject again, asking questions of the women sitting next to him. Caddoc broke his own silence and engaged several of the ladies in a discussion of things they wanted to do while in the city, and places they had been to recently.

"Adaline and I spent several weeks in Amthryn, we were scribing for their high council," Coraline offered, gesturing to her sister.

"It's a beautiful city," Adaline agreed.

"I returned to Calding when I received the summons, but before that I was in Cliffside on the far east side of the Wildwood. They don't have a healer, so I was instructing some of their people in herbs," Lavender added.

Maisey leaned forward, "Cliffside is so unique, isn't it? How they've built their homes directly into the cliff itself? I love the sound of the ocean hitting the rocks below the dwellings. Has anyone else been?"

Everyone nodded, except Jessamine. "Oh you have to go sometime, Jessamine," Olivia exclaimed, clapping her hands together. "It's just beautiful."

"I'd like to," Jessamine replied quietly.

"What is your favorite place you've been, Jessamine?" Olivia asked.

Jessamine sat quietly for several seconds. Zavier noticed she had her hands clasped in her lap, and looked uncomfortable again.

Finally, she said, "I've not traveled anywhere. This is the first time I've left Ocrans. But Hatherus is amazing, it's been a fun experience to see a city of this size, after how small Ocrans is."

After an awkward silence, the conversation continued around them, but Zavier wasn't paying attention. Why had she never left home? What was it his mother had said about her? She was powerful, more powerful than most Bonded. So why hadn't she been assigned as a teacher, or a soldier? Had she refused?

Deep in his own thoughts he nearly missed his cue from his father to stand and begin escorting the ladies from the room. He realized he hadn't even noticed the food he'd eaten, or that they had finished several courses. He allowed himself to reach for Jessamine's arm before Branton could, and offered his other arm to Lavender. Caddoc had gleefully escorted Rebecca and Maisey out, saying in a mock-whisper that if they wanted to see the city he would happily escort them anywhere they wished to go. Branton extended an offer to escort Adaline and Coraline, who each took his arm, one requesting to see the library.

"Ladies, where shall I escort you this evening?" He asked them both, but his eyes met Jessamine's.

"Lavender, you said you enjoyed the gardens, would you care to go for a walk? Perhaps the prince or his mother would give us another tour?" Jessamine said.

Queen Narith heard them and smiled as she took her husband's arm, Olivia on the king's other side. "I'm afraid I've promised to meet with some of the musicians from the city tonight, or I would love to take you around the gardens. We will visit again for sure, I remember Lavender particularly wanted to visit the medicinal greenhouses."

"That would be lovely, Your Highness," Lavender replied in a soft voice, a smile lighting up her face. She transformed from a plain but pretty girl into a beauty with that one smile. "I think I am rather tired tonight, and I would like to go rest in my room, if that's alright with you, Prince Zavier."

"Of course, shall I escort you there?"

"Oh no, that won't be necessary, thank you," she replied with a curtsy. Zavier glanced over her head to summon a footman to show her back to her room safely.

"A walk in the gardens then, my lady?" Zavier turned his attention back to Jessamine. Another footman approached them holding two long light-weight cloaks with the royal crest embroidered on the breast. He helped her put one on, then donned the other.

"Thank you, I would like that," she grinned. Together the two left the dining room arm in arm.

Eleven

Zavier

WALKING DOWN THE LONG hallway from the dining room to the garden foyer, Zavier half turned to her. "We were sort of introduced, but perhaps we should do so again. I'm Zavier."

"Oh, of course! I go by Minnie. It's nice to officially meet you, Your Highness," she said, bobbing a quick curtsy.

"Thank you again for saving my mother's vines from my carelessness," he gave her a small half bow as they stopped by the garden door. A footman opened it for them and they stepped outside into the fading twilight.

"Not a problem at all, I'm happy to help. If I may be so bold, why had you shifted?" she asked, retaking his proffered arm and following his lead to one of the garden paths.

"Maurgen, my dragon, heard something across the river, and I met him there to see what happened. A partial shift is faster and easier within the city," he explained. "A pair of boys had been playing in one of the caves down that way, they caused a small cave in, but no one was hurt."

"That's a relief, it's good you and Maurgen were able to help them," she replied, worry clear in her voice.

He smiled at her. "I don't think they were in real danger this time, but we gave them enough of a scare that hopefully they will think twice about doing it again."

The pair strolled along quietly for several minutes, both looking around at the gardens lit by lamplight. They stopped beside one of the lamps so Minnie could examine a flower more closely, but after a moment she looked up at the lamp itself. She cocked her head and stared at the flickering ball hovering in the middle of the glass. Zavier smiled.

"It's dragon fire. My father comes down before dinner every night, usually with Mother, and lights them all for her. It's been one of their private rituals since they married."

Minnie lifted her hand toward the flame and it pulsed, flashing brightly and expanding to twice its size then shrinking again as if it hadn't happened. Zavier gave her a curious look. His mother had said she was powerful. Sensing that kind of power wasn't one of his abilities, so he had to take her word for it.

"That's a very romantic thing for your father to do. Does it not wear him out to keep the fires burning?" she asked as they resumed walking.

"They burn like this for an hour or so, then someone comes along and lights the actual wicks, so when he stops the magic the light continues. If you watch carefully when it happens, sometimes you will see the change. To properly answer the question, no, not really. He is especially gifted with fire, and he finds it calming to burn off that extra magic."

"I'm much the same way," Minnie said, looking up at him. "Fire is so calming, it's never a drain to wield it."

They continued on, discussing the flowers and layout of the garden beds. His arm tingled where it touched hers and he was acutely aware of her every movement. She stepped away from him several times to examine a plant or sniff a flower, and every time she returned she took his arm once more. It sent a thrill down his spine that he didn't understand and had never felt with someone before.

She stepped away again to the opposite side of the path to investigate a new flower bed. Zavier leaned against a lamp with his arms crossed and openly stared while he could. She was shapely, he decided, not honed to muscle and bone like the warriors, nor thickly padded like some of the wealthier women he'd interacted with. She wasn't starving herself to be thin, as some people did. As she turned back to him with that smile spread across her face, his breath caught in his chest. Her dark copper skin almost shone in the lamplight as she neared, her hands cupped together.

"Look!" She thrust her hands out to him and opened them to reveal a Luna moth. "Isn't it gorgeous?" She carefully spread her hands so the moth could fly away if it wanted to, but it sat still with its wings quivering. She awed over the beautiful creature, then brought it back to the bush she had found it in. She bent over and Zavier mentally slapped himself for admiring her ass.

Once again Minnie returned and took his arm as he pushed himself off the lamp to meet her. She looked up at him with another smile. "Please let me know if you want to go inside or do something else, I don't want to take up your entire night. It can't be much fun for you, showing a stranger around gardens you've known your whole life."

He studied her for a moment, a soft smile on his lips. Her face was open, almost transparent, any emotion she had felt that evening had been plainly visible, at least to him. "You actually mean that, don't you?"

Her smile faltered. "What do you mean? Of course I do, I don't want to be a nuisance."

He faced her fully, still staring. Not a drop of guile. She wasn't asking for anything. Either she was the world's best actress trying to throw him off the scent, or she truly had no ambition or ulterior motives. She hadn't asked him one personal or probing question since they'd been outside. Most women he had met pried incessantly into his life and demanded all his time be devoted to them, not understanding his position as the prince.

"My apologies, my lady, but people rarely ask me what I want to do."

He tried to form the words to explain further, but she interrupted him, her head tilted to the side and a knowing look on her face. "You don't have friends, do you? Someone to just... exist with, go on a walk with? Everyone wants something from you."

He let out a breath he wasn't aware he'd been holding. "That's actually accurate enough. I do have a close friend, but he's as busy as I am. Our version of 'existing' together usually involves drinks, flying, or fighting. Often surrounded by strangers or while traveling to another place."

She frowned. "That sounds incredibly lonely, Your Highness."

"Yes, it is. But I have Maurgen, so I'm never really completely alone."

She lifted a hand as if to reach for him. "But do you ever sit down and just talk to someone? Share? Vent? With someone who isn't mentally connected to you?"

He considered, but it wasn't really something he had to think about. Jarn was a great friend, but he wasn't the sharing type. "No, I guess I don't. I mean, my family, but some things just shouldn't be shared with one's mother. Actually, this is probably the most personal conversation I've ever had with someone who wasn't my family."

Her lips twitched as if she wanted to laugh, but settled on a quirky half smile, just one side of her mouth curving up. "Answer me truthfully, Prince Zavier. What do you want to do tonight? It can be anything in the world, with anyone, don't hold back."

Without thinking, almost as soon as she'd finished speaking, he had an answer for her.

"I want to spend more time with you."

Her face flushed as she smiled brightly, almost laughing in delight. "Your wish is granted, Your Highness. Might we go to the river? I enjoy walking in gardens, but I already miss the sound of water."

He took her by the arm once again and they started off in a new direction, this one leading toward the river gate.

"It'll be a bit colder near the water, are you dressed warmly enough?" Zavier asked as they skirted the edge of the garden.

"Oh yes, I'm fine, Your Highness."

"Zavier, please," he found himself saying as he lifted the latch on the heavy stone door of the wall and held it open for her.

"Thank you... Zavier." The smile she gave him as she passed made his knees weak and his stomach flip. What the hell was wrong with him, he thought, shaking himself and sternly telling his cock to calm the fuck down.

They walked down the dirt path to the river in silence. The sun was nearly set behind them and lights in the city windows began to appear as lanterns were hung. A crescent moon hung low in the sky over the tree-lined horizon. The sound of running water grew louder as they neared the river. This part of the river was slower, having rushed down from the mountains around Aprana to the plains where Hatherus sat. The city was nestled in a cradle of the river and half the city perimeter faced water, with the palace situated at the closest point to the banks.

He noticed Minnie was looking around at everything. She studied the wall behind them for a moment, then scanned the river that stretched ahead and to each side of them.

"This city is incredible," she whispered, turning around again to view the city. From here, the palace upper levels were just visible over the top of the wall, but beyond the city rose in staggered tiers toward the middle. Guard towers were situated at strategic points, raised above other buildings around them. The very center of the city housed the giant market surrounding the Spire, everything built up with more stone walls spiraling around. What wasn't visible were hidden entrances in those walls that led to underground caverns where the citizens could relocate to in an emergency.

"The original settlement was where the palace is located now, the builders built the stone walls up to protect from flooding and everyone lived within those walls," Zavier explained as they reached the bank. "As the city grew, it expanded outward, and the original settlement was rebuilt as the king's new home when he decided to leave Saltstone to the traders."

"It was smart of them to guard against flooding. The walls feel oppressive to me because they're so thick, but I imagine they are secure when the waters rise every year," Minnie replied with a shudder.

He gestured back up the bank to the wall some three hundred feet away. "The water normally doesn't rise that high, but it has happened. We mostly get flash floods when the snow melts that recede within a few days."

This had to be one of the most boring conversations he had ever had. Why couldn't he think of something more interesting to talk about? He had traveled the world, he was well educated, but all he could tell her was boring facts about a city wall?

While he berated himself, Minnie had dropped her cloak, kicked her shoes off, and hiked her skirt to her knees. He watched as she stepped into the slow-moving water, hissing at the chilly temperature.

Over her shoulder she said, "I love the water. When I was a child my father would take me to the ocean's edge to swim. He's a heron, my mother is a lynx, he thought because I inherited the lynx skin I wouldn't like the water." As she spoke she slowly stepped deeper into the river. The water was up to her knees before she stopped. Zavier stood at the edge, the toes of his boots just barely getting wet.

She turned back to look at him, curiosity in her eyes. "Do you swim?" she asked.

He nodded, "Father taught us when we were young, but it's been years since I swam for fun. If I swim now, it's training, or a quick dip to clean up."

107

"Don't you ever do anything to relax?"

"I typically read in whatever room I've been given in whichever city we're in," he replied half-heartedly.

"You never spend time in the city with other people?" she queried, cocking her head to the side.

"Not usually, no. The guards get nervous about things like too many strangers."

She nodded. "Oh, yes that makes sense, I hadn't thought of that. You said you had a friend?"

"Jarn, the guard in charge of my security team," he said. "When we have a free moment we will spar in the ring, or fly. Have a drink at night. It really depends on where we are, I get more freedom in some places than in others."

"It's probably different for you. I'm sure you're given tours and have seen almost everything in every place you've ever been, so a night by yourself must seem like paradise." She'd crossed her arms tightly, and for the first time since dinner, she wasn't smiling.

She seemed heartbroken over whatever secret thoughts she was dreaming of. Suddenly, all he wanted to do was lift her from the water and make all her dreams come true. He prayed to the Fates he hardly believed in that she was a sincere person and not a con artist. He honestly felt as if his soul would shatter if this were all a ruse. That startling thought frightened him. What was wrong with him, that he was suddenly so invested in this woman?

"You've stopped smiling. Why?" he quietly asked her.

She looked back up at him, her eyes wistful. "I'm envious of you. This is my first time away from home." She turned back to the water and knelt down to run her hands through the chilly river. Despite the solemnity of the conversation, his eyes raked over her body as the bunched material of her gown tightened over her rounded ass.

"What are you doing? Your thoughts are a jumbled mess." Maurgen's mental voice broke through and he realized he'd been staring. Again.

"You need to get over here and keep me from doing something insanely stupid," he replied to the dragon. A chuckle resonated down their mental link as Zavier felt him approaching.

She stood again, but her posture was hunched in on herself, as if she were frightened, or upset. Zavier could feel Maurgen was almost to them. "Don't be alarmed, but we're about to have a giant guest arrive," he called quietly to her. Without hesitation she turned to face the direction the dragon was approaching from.

"He's gargantuan," she said in an awed tone as the dragon approached. "I never get to use that word in a sentence, it's an amazing word, and it suits him so well... Gargantuan..." Zavier followed her gaze to see his dragon gliding in with wings spread wide, his burnished gold hide nearly brown in the rising moonlight. Maurgen was one of the larger dragons, nearly sixty feet long from the tip of his nose to the tip of his tail, with a wingspan over twice that of his body length. He circled around them in a tight curve, his wingtip slicing through the water and sending a ripple over Minnie's legs. He landed nearby and walked up to them, the ground vibrating under his mass. Minnie left the water and ran up to him with no hesitation. His head was bigger than her entire body, she looked fragile beside the behemoth.

"Hello! I'm Minnie, it's so wonderful to meet you!"

Most dragons would only speak to their own Bonded, so Zavier was readying himself to relay a message from his dragon to Minnie, but Maurgen shocked him by replying directly to her. He could still hear the dragon's words and voice in his own mind, but he sensed they were being shared with Minnie as well. Briefly, he wondered why Maurgen would choose to speak with her directly, and made a note to himself to ask later.

"It is a pleasure to meet you, little one. I call myself Maurgen."

Maurgen settled on the dry sandy bank of the river, curling himself up like a cat and creating a tent out of one wing, encasing them both. The soft sounds of the spring evening faded around them.

"Come sit beside me and be warm. You will catch chill from wading in the water," Maurgen continued after he was comfortable. *"You may rest on my leg, if you like."*

"Oh! Thank you! Actually, I can—" She interrupted herself with a wave of her hands. A wind rose up and circled her, a ring of fire appearing at her feet. As he watched, a sphere appeared around her and inside a vortex of fire churned. The swirling air grew warmer even outside the sphere. Her gown lifted and flared out. Within seconds, she was completely dry again, and she let the power fade.

Zavier was astounded, he had been told she was powerful but had no idea she could control both elemental aspects of their magic so casually. Without a word, he ducked under the wing and retrieved her shoes and cloak, returning and handing them to her. She thanked him as the wind and fire died completely and sat down on Maurgen's hind foot to put her shoes back on.

"That was quite impressive," he said, removing his cloak, tossing it over Maurgen's neck and leaning against the dragon's broad shoulder.

Twelve

Minnie

MINNIE WAS GLAD FOR the dark that hid her blush at his compliment. She had never in her life felt so flustered or wanted to show off her magic just to impress someone.

"Thanks. Fire and air came easily, I was especially lucky in that regard. Though I assume that most Bonded are able to wield our magic just as well?"

Zavier lifted his hand and snapped his fingers, setting a ball of fire on the sand nearby. He smiled, a flash of white teeth. "Once, maybe. Now most dragon-bonded are lucky to fully master one element, let alone two. While I can control and create both elements, my power is fairly minimal, and I can't heal at all."

Maurgen rumbled above them as he turned his great head around and tilted his wing to allow him to see the two. His four massive horns barely fit under his wing, even when he laid his chin on the ground. Their little nook grew warmer still with his hot breath. "*He speaks the truth, little one. His magic is weak, but his sword is strong. You, however, are not weak. I can sense your dragon through your bond, and she is not weak either.*"

Stunned, Minnie couldn't respond. He could sense her dragon? That meant she really was alive, which of course Minnie knew had to be so, but to have it confirmed… A weight lifted from her chest, but almost immediately settled again in her stomach. Why had her dragon not come, then? Did the dragon not want the bond? Was something wrong with Minnie, that she would be rejected like that?

She finally cleared her throat and tentatively asked, "Do you know who she is? My dragon?"

"*Yes. I was there for her hatching. The connection between us is faint now, but I can feel that she is eagerly waiting for you to come for her.*"

Minnie gave a wistful smile. "For me to come for her? I wish I could. I've no idea who or where she is. I've wanted to meet her for so long…"

"You've not met your dragon at all?" Zavier exclaimed.

"No. I don't know anything about her, other than that she must exist, somewhere."

"*A dragon of her power is born once in several generations, and it takes time to control that power. Until she has mastered herself, she is dangerous to everyone, even her own Bonded partner.*"

"How do you know so much about my dragon?" Minnie asked, astounded. Zavier looked confusedly between the two as Maurgen spoke.

"*All dragons know who she is.*"

The simple statement caused sudden understanding to dawn across Zavier's face. His eyes widened as he looked at her.

"Your dragon is the next Vynar," he said in wonder.

No one had ever said it out loud, though Elder Lirance and Horth had certainly hinted at it in their lessons. The Vynar was the dragon that all dragons obeyed, and the one who clutched dragons that would hatch bonded to Skinshifters. Minnie herself had suspected for years.

"I don't know for sure, since she never came for me. But it would explain why my magic is so powerful," Minnie replied quietly.

The three sat in silence for several minutes, uncomfortable. Minnie scuffed her booted foot along the dirt beneath their feet.

"What bothers you about this bond, little one?" the dragon asked her, his tone softer and more soothing than before. She thought about it, wondering if she dared express herself to someone so important as the prince and his dragon.

Zavier was watching her carefully. He stepped away from Maurgen's side and knelt in the dirt at Minnie's feet, resting a hand on her knee. She gasped and met his eyes.

"Whatever you are thinking is something that frightens you, and you feel is too horrible to say, isn't it?"

She nodded, wordless.

"If I tell you something no one else knows, would you tell me what you are thinking?"

She bit out a small laugh. "It would have to be pretty bad, the thing I'm thinking is quite selfish of me."

"This isn't something bad, really, but it is the most selfish I've ever been, and pretty out of character, some would say."

She nodded again, whispering, "I'll tell if you will."

He smiled up at her, his gold eyes shining in the light of the fire beside them. "I've never spoken of this out loud, so I'm trusting you. I know I will be my father's choice for his heir. I'm more suited to the throne than my elder brother, I'm bonded to a dragon like Father is, and I've been gifted a Draconid form. He hasn't made it public, but I'm confident that he will. And I want to be his heir, and one day, when it's time, I will be ready to be king."

Minnie watched his face as he spoke. His eyes glinted with firelight and his voice was firm. There was no waver in his words, no fear. He believed with all his heart that he was the right choice, and after meeting Caddoc that evening, she had to agree.

"But... and here's the selfish part..." Zavier continued. "I want what my parents have. I would give up anything and everything to have the love, trust, and loyalty they have with each other. They aren't just king and queen, and while they technically had an arranged marriage, they loved each other from their first meeting, before they even knew who the other was. I don't need love at first sight, but the friendship... They are never alone. They have each other, and they have each other's dragons as well as their own. I have Maurgen, but he isn't the same as having that one person who is your everything."

"That sounds incredible," Minnie whispered. "I can see how you would want that for yourself."

"I would be willing to give up my crown to have that with someone. That's my deepest secret. Will you tell me yours?"

She drew in a deep breath. "I've always dreamed of leaving Ocrans. My parents... My mother is very overprotective of us. I've cared for her for almost my entire life. She hid the invitations from your parents so I wouldn't leave home. She pretended to be more sick than she is to keep me at home. In spite of all of that, she's still my mother, and I love her..."

Minnie wiped a tear from her cheek and continued, her voice breaking slightly. "I found the latest missive commanding me to come to the capital, and it all came out that she had been lying to us. Now I'm too angry to go back home, but afraid of being on my own. As a dragon-bonded, half my soul is my dragon, but where is she? And... if my dragon really is the Vynar?"

Minnie sighed. "If my dragon is the Vynar, I might always be alone, because my dragon might always be somewhere else. I may be forced to go back home, stuck there forever and unable to see the world, experience life the way those women at dinner have. And... Well, I never really thought of it until you mentioned, but yes, I'd like to meet someone who loves me. Just not in a controlling way like my mother did. I want freedom."

Zavier lifted his hand and swiped his thumb across her cheek, wiping away another tear. "Minnie, we're strangers, I know that, but I want you to listen to me, and trust me. No one will force you to do anything you don't want to do anymore. I think you will feel a lot different when you do finally meet your dragon."

"Zavier is right, little one. Right now, you are missing half your soul. It is no shock to me that you feel such distress, or feel lost. It is not natural for Bonded partners to be separated for so long, and in the past the newest young Vynar would have come for her partner long ago."

"Then why hasn't she come?" Minnie cried, feeling desperate.

"I do not know. All I do know is that her power was unstable for a long time and she flew south to train apart from other dragons for their safety, and for hers. If she returned, I have not been made aware of it. I rarely speak to anyone on Dragon Isle anymore."

The three sat together in silence for a few minutes. Zavier nudged Minnie and she scooted over on Maurgen's leg for him to sit beside her. Minnie welcomed the warm line of his thigh pressed against hers.

"Meeting your dragon won't magically solve all your problems or make your fears and worries instantly disappear. Being with her, however, will help you feel as if you can handle anything no matter what it is," he promised, wiping another tear from her cheek.

"Is that... how you feel with Maurgen?" she hesitantly asked.

He nodded. "Yes. Maurgen came for me earlier than most dragons do, and he's been with me since I was a toddler. With him by my side, I know I will always be safe and have my best friend. Even if that friend is an over-sized lizard," he taunted the dragon.

"I had to grow so big, in order to look after you, idiot. You may appear suave to others, but I've hauled you out of enough scrapes to know better!" Both Maurgen and Zavier laughed. Minnie choked a half laugh, half cough, unsure if they were joking or not. This was nothing like she had been prepared for by Elder Lirance. She had been expecting serious and formal, not teasing and laughter. She did owe him a 'thank you' for the book on protocol he'd insisted she take. She'd read it that morning, hoping to avoid a troublesome mistake.

Still chuckling, Zavier turned back to her. "Are you feeling any better?"

She nodded. "I'm sorry for unloading and turning this into a pity party," she whispered, her voice barely audible. It wasn't like her to be this brave, she'd never even told her village friend, or even Elder

Lirance, all about her home life. Surely Lirance had an inkling, but she just never discussed it. Looking into Zavier's golden eyes, with Maurgen's half-lidded eye behind him, Minnie felt safe. They would keep her secrets and not judge her.

"No need at all to be sorry, we're all entitled to our feelings. What is spoken under the wing, stays under the wing, you have my word," the prince reassured her with a smile and a teasing nudge.

She giggled and slapped his hand away, but he had succeeded in partially lifting her black mood. She decided to put it behind her for now, be cheerful, and change the subject.

"Your mother said she had us summoned here to interview as her new ladies in waiting, but I got the feeling from the other women that there is more to it than that. Do you know something that I don't?"

He groaned. "Oh, I'm sure you can guess. Father wants us to start thinking of the next generation, and Mother is hoping that we will have a great romance in our lives."

Dumbfounded, she stared at him. "We're here as potential consorts?"

Zavier smiled and shook his head. "Mother really does want new ladies in waiting. But, if Caddoc or I happen to fall in love like she and Father, so much the better."

"You said your parents technically had an arranged marriage?" If he wasn't worried, Minnie decided not to let it bother her. Surely she wasn't a candidate anyway, not after her disastrous meeting with Anitra.

"Yeah, Grandfather had arranged it before his death. When they met, it was instant love and Father was planning ways to sneak off and marry her in secret. It took days for them to discover they were already engaged to each other, no sneaking needed. I'm sure you'll hear my father tell the full story several times while you're here, it's one of his favorites," Zavier chuckled.

"That's wonderful for them," she clapped her hands excitedly. "They're still in love?"

"Oh yes, and being the sentimental saps they are, they want the same for us. Especially as our uncle, Beltak, married a complete shrew that no one can stand. He fell in love with her beauty and insisted on marrying her. His parents, my grandparents, were reluctant because she wasn't dragon-bonded, but he said he'd marry her or no one. His two sons aren't dragon-bonded, so I think my father will wind up selecting someone for us if we don't find our own love. Caddoc has already proved in many ways he isn't capable of making good choices."

Minnie thought about telling him of her conversation with General Beltak, then decided against it. Zavier clearly had no fondness for Anitra, and she didn't want to cause any strife between nephew and uncle by relaying Beltak's defense of his wife. Besides, she reminded herself, that was all said in confidence.

"Do you think your father will choose for you, or allow you to choose?" she asked, genuinely curious. She had a few tentative friends back in Ocrans, even a few male friends, but had never felt so closely connected to anyone before meeting Zavier. She wanted him to find his 'someone,' ideally without him having to give up his crown for her. Briefly, Minnie almost wished it could be her. He was kind and caring, intelligent, handsome, and so easy to talk to and just be with.

But, she had to remind herself forcefully, he has to marry someone worthy of being princess and future queen, and that person would be expected to remain at the palace in Hatherus. Minnie clung to her new fragile hope that she might be allowed to explore the world, visit other cities and races, and experience things for herself. On top of that, she wasn't remotely worthy of being a princess.

"I'm not really sure. I know my parents trust me far more than Caddoc. If I found someone suitable, I'm sure they would approve. If I don't, and have no good arguments against a person, they will choose someone for me at some point. I've been told this doesn't have to happen right away, I think they're just preparing me for the inevitable," he sighed. "I have no contenders in mind, so as of right now, they will choose, eventually."

Minnie bit her lip, dying to ask a personal question but too afraid to be so bold. He must have read her face because he chuckled and said, "Go on, ask. We're well past embarrassment now, my lady!"

Despite his words, she flushed, but gathered her courage anyway. "Have you had any serious relationships before?"

He lowered his head for a moment, but then looked up and said, "Not really. I thought I was in love once, and she said she loved me, but she didn't want to do any of the work of being a princess, she only wanted the perks. So no, no real relationships." He ran a hand through his hair, woefully shaking his head. "And you, my lady? Do you have a lovesick fisherman or farmer back in Ocrans?"

She barked a harsh laugh. "No, not at all. For one, my mother rarely let me out of her sight for longer than it takes to run an errand. For two, everyone in that town knows everyone else's business. Especially mine. Some were too afraid of me," she scoffed. "Others wanted to worship me as a gift from the

Fates for my magic, especially since I can—" She cut herself off mid-sentence, and deflected, hoping to not reveal too much about her abilities. "If you've had no relationships, then are the rumors true? Are you innocent and chaste?" Her cheeks burned with embarrassment, but she stubbornly met his eyes, hoping to distract him from her magical gifts.

Around them, Maurgen rumbled. It took her a nervous few seconds to realize he was laughing.

Zavier's cheeks also flushed, and she was about to speak, tell him she was sorry and shouldn't be over-stepping, when he answered. "No, I'm not innocent. A, uh, a large appetite tends to run in my family, my brother is a prime example. Father has always been faithful to Mother, but to hear the servants talk, they've been caught in every room and position imaginable. And for me..." He stopped. She waited, and after a moment placed a hand on his thigh.

Dangerous ground, this conversation. Etiquette and decorum had apparently gone out the window the second Maurgen's wing descended.

"You?" she coaxed.

"Caddoc never hides his desire. His exotic tastes, vast appetites. I don't want my people to see me like that, so I keep my wants hidden. I don't have the luxury to indulge like he does, because to our people, I am their hope for a comfortable future. It should be him, but he clearly doesn't care, so I try to maintain that appearance."

She flexed her fingers on his thigh, silently begging him to continue. When he did, it was almost a whisper, as if he were confessing his darkest secrets to her. "I *want* so badly. More than that, I want to be wanted for *me*. Women who come to me only want rewards, hoping that sleeping with the prince will earn their family favor. I've had bribes, I've had married women offer themselves in exchange for a husband's promotion. I've even had young men approach me when a woman failed. I no longer entertain any notion that a woman wants me for myself, so it's... it's been a long time since... Since I was with someone in that way."

"Every woman has done that to you?" she gasped, astounded.

"Every one, in some way, only wanted the prince," he sighed. "A couple nights ago, Jarn and I were drinking in a tavern, we thought no one would notice me since we had only just arrived and no one knew we were back. But a young woman did recognize me. She successfully got me back to her apartment, but then she asked if I would help her get a better position as a healer. I hate it any time someone uses sex to try and convince me of something, but to add insult, she wanted to overcharge people for the privilege of being healed by her!"

Her nails dug into his thigh as the flash of anger seared through her. "I'm sorry," Minnie whispered. "She's a fool. They all are."

Zavier nodded in agreement. "Yes, I thought so, too. And I'm the biggest fool of all, for constantly falling for it. I'm not proud of my base urges, nor do I let those urges run my life, but I want so badly to give in to them that I allow myself to think maybe, just maybe, this woman doesn't want anything from the prince."

They lapsed into silence for a moment, listening to the river flow downstream nearby, and the soft breathing of Maurgen.

Zavier turned his head back to her, smiling again. "And you, my lady? Are you innocent?"

The question took her by surprise, though she supposed it shouldn't, she had asked him first. She was just so comfortable here with him, she trusted him in ways she couldn't understand or explain, even to herself. Deciding to damn the consequences, she forged ahead. He had shared, and they had established a trust.

"Because of my mother, I wasn't often given privacy or much free time. The only free time I had, I used to study with the Elder. Well, we had a young man, a scholar, staying in the village for a while. He was studying with Elder, too. We... got along very well," she blushed furiously.

"We started sneaking out at night to meet in the Tangled Wood, I used my lynx-skin to sneak out without being heard. He was far more experienced than I was, but I have always been a quick learner. We exchanged letters after he left, he would send them to Elder since my mother wouldn't approve. He sent me gifts that were... well, let's say my mother wouldn't approve of those, either."

"Gifts?" It was Zavier's turn to coax the truth out of her.

She turned her head away, staring at a small rock sticking out of the grass. "He was from Amthryn, a Wealdkin. He sent me... toys, he called them, that were... um, they were shaped like a man's... parts."

Zavier shifted a bit on Maurgen's leg, and she could feel him looking at her, though she refused to look up. She felt his hand under her chin lifting her face, and she opened her eyes slowly to meet his.

"Did you enjoy yourself with the toys?" he asked in a husky murmur.

"...Yes. Very much," she replied breathlessly.

Color rose on her cheeks at the admission and she noticed that Zavier was shifting uncomfortably next to her.

"I'm sorry, I shouldn't have said that, maybe I should go—" Minnie rose and anxiously turned, searching for a way out past the dragon's great head. Maurgen had his one visible eye trained on her as she panicked.

"Wait." Zavier stood and grabbed her arm, sliding his hand down to grasp hers tightly. "Please, don't run. I'm sorry I've made you so uncomfortable. It is inexcusable of me to be so forward. I swear, I'm not usually so open with someone." His shoulder-length blond hair, dark in the moonlight, had fallen over part of his face and she longed to push the locks back.

She swallowed, and stammered, "No— I'm not... I mean... I started it, and I shouldn't have been nosy. It's rude of me, and I'm sorry."

Zavier pulled her closer, wrapping an arm around her waist. He lifted his hand to gently cup her face, running his thumb over her lip. When he spoke, his voice was deep again, husky with need. "You aren't rude, you're curious. You're brave, and a bit bold. I find I very much like that about you. It's... intoxicating."

She'd never felt less brave or bold than she did at that very moment. She wanted to run. She wanted to lean into him. She wanted to disappear into a puff of smoke and pretend this conversation had never happened. Why had she said such things? What was wrong with her tonight?

His thumb slid along her lower lip, lightly tugging it down to open her mouth. She gasped a sharp intake of breath, half closing her eyes, begging herself not to lean into his touch. She should leave, but oh how she wanted to stay. Her core tightened with need at his words, and she could feel the moisture between her legs.

But she shouldn't get involved with the prince. He wasn't a casual fling, or a quick romance. But oh, how she wanted to... Her hands, wrapped around his upper arms, flexed as she warred with herself. Her lips parted, she almost leaned in... She couldn't do that to him. She couldn't be just one more woman who led him on. True, she wanted nothing from him, but it wasn't fair to either of them to get involved. She pulled away from him.

"I... I'm sorry, Your Highness. We shouldn't... I think I should return to the palace now," her whispered voice wavered as she spoke, and she struggled not to fall into his arms. Firmly berating herself, she stepped back, tugging her hand out of his grasp. Zavier straightened, his smile fading. He swallowed, ran a hand through his hair, and nodded.

"Of course, I'm sorry. Maurgen, please lift your wing." He grabbed their cloaks and offered his arm to her. After a moment's hesitation, she took it. As she touched his arm, the fire beside them went out. They walked back to the stone gate in awkward silence. Behind them Maurgen rumbled as he turned in circles, making a fresh wallow in the riverbank. As they walked through the garden, Zavier spoke, but his voice was no longer quite so warm and inviting.

"Tomorrow, a group of us are going into the city to help clean up after last week's storms, and catch up on some planting. My father has arranged for you ladies to come as well. You're all secretly being tested to see if you would be suitable as a royal consort to myself or Caddoc. Anyone who does well will be in consideration, so if you don't want that life for yourself, I suggest you do something to appear incompetent or indifferent to our people." By this time they were at the garden door to the palace. The

125

lights inside were dimly lit, only every other lantern glowed with half-shuttered light.

Minnie looked up at his tight features. She had offended him, led him on, then slammed a door in his face. He had every right to be annoyed and upset with her, though she regretted it. The frostiness in his previously warm voice was painful to hear. She opened her mouth to say something, she didn't even know what, but he interrupted her.

"I'm sorry, I was aggressive and domineering. It is unbecoming of a man, especially of a prince, to treat a woman as I have. My behavior was inexcusable." His voice was firm, but when he took a deep breath, he sounded more like his previous self. "I'm not sure what it is about you, but since I first heard you laugh in the garden this afternoon, I haven't been able to think clearly. No woman has ever affected me like this. I am ashamed of my actions."

She began to apologize, to absolve him of blame, but he raised a hand to stop her.

"I will not bother you again, my lady, if that makes you more comfortable. But if you are in need of a friend, you may always rely on me." He stepped back and bowed to her deeply, then rose and gestured for a footman to come forward out of the shadows he'd been standing in. "Good night, Minnie."

She watched him walk away and wanted to call out to him, but again had no idea what she wanted to say. Don't go? Kiss me? Take me to your room and ravish me? Her thoughts were a confused mess, and maybe he was right. She hadn't been thinking very clearly that evening either.

As she followed the footman up to her room, she thought back to the dinner they'd shared. Nervous at first, as she was sitting at the foot of the table across from the king himself, which felt like a very important position to be in, she had finally relaxed enough to enjoy the meal after the first course. Most of the other women were lovely, and Queen Narith was a delight to speak to. She had noticed Zavier watching her more than the others, and she'd struggled not to stare back at him.

Minnie entered her room, bid the footman thank you and good night, and crossed to her bed. As she flopped on the extravagant mattress, she thought of the handsome prince. She hadn't been able to see his face clearly while they were by the river, he had often been in shadow from his little fire on the ground, but when they were at the garden trellis she'd gotten a long look at his face, and again when they had stood so close in the garden by the lamps.

Without a doubt, his eyes were his best feature. She'd thought the same of Taurak and his other sons, too. They all shared the same golden eyes. Almost the same shade of Maurgen's hide, Minnie realized. And Zavier's eyes... His eyes had glinted with lust during their conversation, until she had ruined it.

Well, she had insulted him, and that was that. She had no business flirting with a prince anyway. She would go on the tour tomorrow, and either do nothing, or do something to make herself look bad so she wouldn't be considered as a lady in waiting or a marriage, no matter how much power she had.

Thirteen

Zavier

W HAT IN ALL THE hells was wrong with him today? Zavier paced in his apartment with a
glass of whiskey in his hand. Balcony to door, back
and forth. He felt Maurgen's presence in his mind
and attempted to block him out.

*"That has never worked before and isn't likely to work
now. Why don't you just talk to me about what is bothering
you, instead of all that walking?"*

"You know damn well what is bothering me," he
snapped at the dragon.

"Temper, temper."

"Oh, hush. You know what I meant."

*"Yes, I do. You want the girl. You want her more than
you've ever wanted anyone. Why is this a problem? She
wanted you, too, you know."*

That made him stop pacing. He turned toward the
window as if he could see the dragon curled up by
the cold river. *"She did?"*

"Of course she did, idiot, most women want you."

"Shut up and speak clearly, lizard!"

Maurgen chuckled down their mental link. An image of the two people standing together formed in his mind, and Zavier watched as he lifted his hand to her chin. Her lips parted. She had almost leaned into him, the movement was there in the set of her shoulders as she pulled back. Sadness and regret crossed her face as she told him she wanted to return to the palace. He hadn't seen her as clearly in person, her face had been in shadow.

"I could see you both clearly in the dark, she leaned in. I won't repeat what she was thinking, those are her own private thoughts and she probably has no idea I could hear her. But her scent changed while you were speaking. It matched yours, almost."

"Our scent? What— Oh." Zavier took another large swallow of his drink. Maurgen had smelled their lust. *"If she was interested, why did she pull back?"*

"Zavier, you took a big risk tonight, being so open with her. My instincts are telling me that this woman is important to both of us, but I'm not sure how yet. Regardless, I can't tell you why she pulled away from you, but be patient. Don't lose heart."

Zavier sat hard on the edge of his bed, his mind racing as Maurgen pulled away from their mental link. He flung himself back on the bed still fully clothed, having only divested himself of the cloak and his boots when he entered his apartment. His mind whirled, replaying every second of the evening.

Was there really something different, special, about this one woman? Had it just been too long since he'd slept with someone? He imagined other women of his acquaintance, women who had already made overtures at him since he'd returned home a few days ago. None of them moved him, as attractive as they were, and certainly not as much as Minnie had tonight.

For the first time since he had believed himself in love as a young man, he dared to dream of a future with someone. For so many years he had imagined himself alone. Taking the throne, alone. Now, he could easily see her standing by his side, hand in hand, waving to their people. She was comfortable to be around. She was intelligent, witty, humorous, and oh-so-beautiful.

As he closed his eyes, more visions came to him, but he wasn't sure if they were a dream or not. He saw Minnie with her long braid over her shoulder, wearing rough riding leathers with blood smeared across her face. Her arm lifted, fire poured from her hand straight toward him. But the fire split, going harmlessly around him and engulfing a person behind him. A person holding a lifted dagger in their right fist, poised to stab him. He rushed to Minnie as she collapsed, the fire sputtering out.

"Mine..." he whispered to himself in the dark. "Minnie... My Mina... mine."

Fourteen

Minnie

A FTER A RESTLESS NIGHT, Minnie woke determined to not dwell on Zavier and the night
before. This morning after breakfast, she and the
other women were going into the city to help the
citizens. With luck, she could be so busy helping that
she could avoid Zavier entirely.

Prince Zavier and Prince Branton met the seven
dragon-bonded women in the courtyard after their
meal. Most of the women wore casual gowns in a
sturdy style suited for working. Minnie noticed that
Zavier carefully avoided looking too long in her
direction as he explained where they were needed
that day.

"We've had some damage to the roads to the west
between here and the forest that are being repaired
as we speak, which means some of the families will
need our help today. Planting, some early harvest-
ing, cooking the community meal for that neighborhood, little things like that. These may not seem

131

like important tasks on the surface, but it is vital that we help all of our people, regardless of status."

The group set off through the streets, pausing now and then to speak to shopkeepers or citizens. When they reached the neighborhood closest to the west gate they found it empty of men, and only a few women were minding the children. The rest, they were told, were in the valley gathering rock and material to repair the roads and walls damaged by the spring storms.

A kind-faced older woman greeted them, an infant on her lap. "We appreciate you coming to help us, Your Highnesses. It's been difficult finding the time to do repairs with everything else going on. We have the kids working in the little gardens' but some of them do more harm than good." She chuckled as she bounced the infant on her knee.

Zavier returned her smile. "We're happy to help, Greta. We'll take care of everything, you just tell us where you want us today."

Greta delighted in bossing around the princes, Minne thought. She had Branton and two of the dragon-bonded go to the fields just outside the gates to plow the earth in preparation for a summer planting.

While Greta gave orders, Minnie looked around the neighborhood they were in. The houses were small but tidy, each one had little raised beds of herbs growing near the front entrances. She wandered down the path a little to get a closer look at a decoration hanging from a window, but something else caught her attention. She could hear what sounded like a small child crying. Glancing over her shoulder, she saw that some of the girls had left already, and no one was paying her any attention.

Minnie didn't want to stand out, what better way than to just not be there. She felt bad leaving the group and not helping, but from the panic in the child's cries, someone might be hurt. She hurried down the little lane, tilting her head this way and that as the street curved to be sure she was going the right way. Every Skinshifter had heightened senses to some degree, but it was all based on their animal skin. As a lynx, Minnie's hearing was excellent. It took her no time at all to track them down to a small market square several blocks from Greta's house.

A Wealdkin woman with pale green skin and what appeared to be ivy inked across her arms knelt beside a flower cart that had been converted into a stall. The crying child, almost a miniature replica of her mother, sat on a crate behind the cart, clutching a doll to her chest. The mother was anxiously looking at one of the child's bare feet.

"I'm not sure what it is, seedling, I don't know why it's swelling!"

Minnie approached, skirting around buckets of flowers that sat at the base of the stall. "Can I help? I've some knowledge of healing," she said, kneeling beside the distraught woman.

"Please! We were picking flowers in our field this morning and she was fine. Just a few minutes ago she started complaining of pain in her foot!" The Wealdkin woman sat back, giving Minnie room to examine the foot for herself. Out of the corner of her eye, Minnie saw that Zavier was approaching the stall, and other people were gathering around to see what the fuss was about.

The small green foot in her hand was quite swollen, but Minnie easily saw the two puncture wounds on the inside of the arch. She turned the foot gently, pressing below the swollen lump until a few drops of blood emerged from the punctures. The little girl cried out, burying her face into her doll's hair.

"Sorry, pet, I know it's painful," Minnie crooned to the little girl. Glancing at the mother, she said, "Look, here, I think she stepped on a snake. Some of them resemble rocks when they curl up, she may have thought she stepped on something sharp and paid no mind to it. The venom is climbing her leg."

As she spoke, they could see the swelling crawl higher, deep, angry red lines appearing across the foot, radiating from the bite.

"What will I do? Can a healer help her? I don't have any coin, how will I pay them?" The Wealdkin woman wailed, clutching her apron to her face. Behind her, Zavier stepped closer.

"I can help get her to a healer," he offered.

"There's no need," Minnie replied, sighing. Turning her attention back to the little girl's foot, she called her magic. The golden glow filled her hands, encasing the foot completely. Draining venom wasn't the same as knitting together wounds or broken bones. Those acts were a reversal of the injury, almost like turning back time so it was as if it had never happened. Draining venom required her to chase down every drop and magically cleanse it of any harm. It was tedious, but thankfully the damage was minimal and she had arrived before it had spread beyond the ankle.

As the last of the venom was neutralized and the swelling receded, Minnie closed the punctures and let the glow fade from her hands. It was true that healing required more energy than using either fire or air, or even using them together, but it was no more strenuous than a brisk walk over a short distance.

"There you are, sweetheart, how does that feel? All better?" Minnie asked the little girl with a smile.

Slowly, the girl nodded, staring down at her foot as if she couldn't believe it no longer hurt. The girl's mother sobbed again, this time in relief.

"Oh, Fates bless you, bless you, and thank you so much. How can we repay you, please? If you come at the end of the day I am sure to have sold enough flowers to give you coins," cried the mother, grasping Minnie's arm and pulling her in for a relieved hug, then gripping her daughter and holding her tightly.

"No need at all, I promise. I'm glad I could help her," Minnie said, waving off any question of payment.

"If you don't mind," Zavier said from directly behind Minnie, startling her. "I would like to buy your entire stock. My mother loves flowers and keeps fresh vases all over her office. Would you be willing to bring her some bouquets?" As he spoke, he slid several coins across the booth.

Recognition slowly crept over the Wealdkin woman's face. Abruptly she gasped, eagerly clapping her hands together.

"Oh, of course, Your Highness! Forgive my bad manners, please. I'll make the most beautiful bouquets and bring them up myself, within the hour, I promise! Please, my lady, let me—" Her hands had closed over the coins and were trying to push them onto Minnie.

Minnie firmly cut her off again, "No, I couldn't accept, please keep it for your daughter."

"What is your name?" Zavier distracted the mother again. "We could use someone to bring fresh flowers weekly, as well as help decorate for all the events my mother insists on hosting. I'd like to employ you full time, if you are agreeable. Mother hates to take flowers from her garden, but adores having them in the palace."

Her tear-streaked face crumpled again, and fresh tears fell. "That would mean the world to us, Your Highness, thank you. I'm Aspen Greenleaf, and this is my daughter Hyacinth. My talent is with flowers, I can help them grow even in deep winter. There was no need for that back home, so we came here when Hyacinth's father died."

"I'm sorry for your loss," Minnie said quietly, and Zavier murmured condolences as well.

"You're a wonder, you are," Aspen praised, gripping Minnie's arm. "We're from Marshmere, I've seen the leeches in the mushroom swamps cure snake bite, and other poisons and venoms, but of course I had none here. I hadn't even thought of snakes here!"

"I'm glad I was able to help her," Minnie replied, her smile suddenly hard to maintain. The people who had been watching were closing in, waiting for a break in the conversation.

Zavier gave Aspen directions to the garden gate entrance to the palace and told her who to ask for when she delivered the flowers.

As Aspen began making flower bouquets, Zavier took Minnie's arm and pulled her a few feet away, further from the growing crowd. "Why are so many people gathering?" he asked in a strained whisper. It occurred to her, belatedly, that they were alone in the city with no guards to protect the prince. How had that happened? Guards had followed them from the palace. Had he slipped away to follow her? Anxiously, Minnie looked around at the gathering.

Thankfully, the crowd wasn't going to be a dangerous one. Not to him, at least. She replied with a hint of doubt in her voice, "They're waiting for me. People with injuries or illnesses that they think I can heal. It's happened a few times in Ocrans when we have a large group of visitors in the city who aren't used to me."

The group had edged closer, pointing and whispering. One old woman, cradling her hand, pushed to the front of the queue. In a creaky voice the old woman said, "Please, my lady. I've broken two fingers and the medics turned me away. The price was so high I couldn't afford treatment."

Then a middle-aged man in rough work clothes, "I 'ave gash on me leg that's gone putrid, the 'erbs I was given didn't 'elp at all. I wasted me coin and now they want to chop me leg off!"

"I cannot stand up straight, my back hurts!"

"Please, my lady, my husband needs treatment for a growth on his neck. They told him at the medics that they couldn't help him, only give him pain relief until he dies! He can't die!"

Minnie could tell that Zavier was overwhelmed by the complaints almost instantly. So many people with such difficult ailments. It was more than she was used to, but years of drill with Lirance had trained her for scenarios like this one. She pushed down her fear and doubt and directed people to line up and made swift work of the easier ailments the people had brought to her. After sending away one boy who claimed he had a broken heart, correcting a curved spine, mending and curing the infection in the putrid leg and the broken fingers, she began to feel a bit overwhelmed. Zavier brought her water from a nearby well and she pushed on.

More and more arrived as she worked, but she didn't turn anyone away who truly needed help. The amount of people who repeatedly claimed a healer had refused them service due to money bothered her. A full hour passed as she worked, more people kept arriving as word spread. Finally, the last person in the square begging for healing was the woman who said her husband was dying of a growth.

"Lead me to him," Minnie told her as the rest of the crowd dispersed. The anxious woman took Minnie's hand and led her down an alley, Zavier following close behind like a shadow. They followed her to a quaint, tidy home not far from the market square. Two small children played in the fenced yard. Their mother told them to stay quiet while they went in to see their father.

Inside, a man sat slumped over in an armchair, clearly in pain and near the end of his life. Minnie rushed to him, the light filling her hands once again. She hovered her hands over his body from the top of his head down to his toes. He was riddled with clumps of diseased tissue. Sitting back on her heels, she looked up at the anxiously waiting wife.

"The growths are in his lungs and brain, as well as nodules in his neck. I'm not sure I can do anything, I've never seen anything quite like this before." Minnie closed her eyes and moved her hands back to his head, calling on her magic once more.

It was more draining this time than ever before. Even compared to piecing Old Tobias back together a few days ago, this was more difficult. Each patch of diseased tissue needed to be healed individually, and there were thousands of them in one spot. It took her achingly long minutes to completely heal and remove just one of the tumors.

Finally, Minnie wavered, then opened her eyes and lowered her hands. "I think that's done it. They shrunk until they were gone, but I'm honestly not sure if they will grow back or not, or if he will recover—"

But even as she spoke the man lifted his head, the gray pallor leaving his face. He was still rail thin, but no longer looked to be on death's doorstep. The wife gasped and covered her mouth, then ran to her husband, sobbing.

Minnie struggled to her feet until Zavier gripped her under the arm and helped her up. "Come on, before they try to pay me," Minnie whispered as she grabbed his arm to steady herself. Zavier led her to the door, unseen by the emotional couple.

On the doorstep with the door safely closed behind them, one of the children looked up and asked, "Is our daddy dead?"

Despite her fatigue, Minnie knelt down beside him. "No, sweetie, I think he will be alright. Please tell your parents that if he gets sick again to go up to the palace and have someone send for Minnie Hernshaw. I'll come back and help him again."

"Yes, my lady. Thank you," the little boy replied with wide eyes. He grabbed his brother and they ran inside, where Minnie heard more relieved sobs.

"Let's go, you look like you're about to fall over." Zavier took her arm and led her away. Minnie let herself be led, following quietly. She stumbled a few times, grateful that Zavier kept her standing. After the fourth time she tripped over her own feet, he turned to her and scooped her into his arms in a cradle carry.

"No, put me down, I can manage," she tried to insist, attempting to squirm away. He bounced her once, resettling her in his arms.

"Hush. Let me help you, you've worn yourself out. It was harder than you said, wasn't it?"

She calmed herself and relaxed into his arms as they rounded a corner. They weren't walking toward the neighborhood they'd been in earlier, she realized. They were in a quiet little park area littered with benches, climbable trees, and a small duck pond with a little stream running through it, a water source for that area of the city. He set her on a bench, ensured she was stable, then sat beside her, his hand still on her arm as if reluctant to remove it.

"He was near death. It took time to shrink the growths, yes, but I also had to repair the damage they had caused. Healing the tissue and organs isn't so difficult, but there was so much of that disease... After healing Old Tobias a few days ago, then flying here, and the people at the market, I guess I am more tired than I thought."

"Old Tobias?" Zavier gave her a curious look.

"He's a farmer in Ocrans. He had a heart attack, and fell from his hayloft. His spine was crushed from his neck to shoulders, and his skull cracked. He survived the fall, and one of the villagers found me very quickly after his accident."

"And you healed him, just like that man?" Zavier sounded impressed.

"Yes," she said softly, sighing. She'd drawn so much attention to herself today...

"What's wrong?" he asked, but he seemed to realize quickly. "Oh. You didn't want to stand out."

Minnie shook her head. "No, I didn't. But I couldn't turn them down. That little girl would have lost her foot, maybe her life. And that man, his leg was rotting off. And if we hadn't helped that woman's husband, he'd have been dead by the end of the day. I couldn't say no to them."

Zavier took her hand and squeezed it tightly. "That shows you have incredible compassion, that isn't something you should regret."

She nodded slightly. "I don't regret helping them, no matter what. I just... I had planned to stay out of sight today." She wavered, her vision suddenly growing fuzzy. Zavier caught her and leaned her against his shoulder.

"Close your eyes for a few minutes, rest. We'll walk back to Greta's and get you some food in a little while."

Minnie couldn't respond. With her head resting in the hollow between his shoulder and neck, exhaustion won out. She was asleep in seconds.

Fifteen

Zavier

T HE FATES APPEARED TO be playing a cruel joke on him, Zavier thought as she slept. He wanted a woman he was able to trust, to talk to, someone who he could be himself around. Why was it that the one woman he had met who appeared to be exactly what he needed, was the one woman who wanted nothing to do with him? Maurgen could hint that she wanted him as much as he wanted her, but that meant nothing if she wouldn't act on it in any way.

He sat in silence, watching the ducks swim around the stream and dive under the water for food. Zavier and Minnie would need to return to Greta's soon, it was nearing mid-afternoon and the work parties would be returning in due time for the evening meal. The dragon-bonded would be expected to join the neighborhood for their community potluck meal that evening as a way for the people to show their appreciation for the help given that day. Zavier was reluctant to wake Minnie, partly because he was enjoying their closeness, but mostly because of how much she had done in the past few hours. It was clear from her exhaustion that she had overextended herself.

"I had no idea she could heal," Maurgen interrupted Zavier's thoughts. He was stretched out with other dragons in the hills north of the city, the remains of several large deer between them. *"She must be one of the most powerful dragon-bonded currently alive, magically speaking. It's incredible that she can heal so much, as well as master both fire and air."*

Maurgen's voice sounded impressed, and Zavier had to agree. All dragon-bonded could breathe dragon-fire, even in their human-skin. Most of them could control one aspect of their racial magic, usually fire, and often only minimally. Controlling the air was a rarer skill, and summoning or controlling both fire and air even rarer still.

But to have mastered air, fire, and healing with such skill and power— that was unheard of in living memory, as far as he knew. Stories and records passed down from previous generations spoke of powerful dragon-bonded who possessed such power, and if memory served him, several of those had been Bonded to the Vynar of their time.

Movement at his shoulder snapped him out of his reverie. Minnie was lifting her head and rubbing a hand over her face. "I fell asleep?"

"Only for a little while, you seemed to be worn out," he reassured her.

"I'm sorry, I shouldn't take such liberties or be so familiar—"

"Shhh, Minnie. You haven't done anything wrong." He twisted on the bench until he was facing her, and held a hand out. His stomach jumped when she laid her hand on his own.

"I'm sorry for what happened last night. I'm sorry you felt you needed to push away from me, and sorry that I put you in that position in the first place."

"You don't need to apologize, I wanted it, very much. It's honestly a bit terrifying to me, just how much I wanted you, and how fast these... feelings... have arisen."

"I feel it, too," Zavier admitted.

Minnie swallowed, biting her lip. "I'm afraid..."

He took a deep breath. He should stop there, but fuck it. May as well take the shot. "I'm attracted to you, and I want nothing more than to explore this... this connection we feel. I hope you want to, as well, but regardless, I don't want you to be afraid of me."

"Zavier..." She hesitated, her eyes sliding past his face toward the stream. "I'm not sure if this is a rational fear or not. I've heard rumors from servants that your parents are looking for magically powerful Bonded for your future wife. You said last night that they were trying to match-make." She took a deep breath and looked back at him before continuing, "Maybe I'm being conceited, but I am afraid that if they find out just how powerful my magic is, they'll force me to marry you, or your brother, regardless of what I want."

Zavier cupped her face with both his hands. "I promise you, on my honor as a prince of this territory, I will not allow anyone to force you to marry me or anyone else. You will choose your own path."

She swallowed, responding in a small voice, "I believe you. I don't know why I trust you so much when I hardly know you, but I do. I believe you." He wiped a small tear from her cheek and pulled her into a hug.

"I hope you'll continue to trust me, and it would be my pleasure if you would be my friend. I'm more comfortable around you than anyone except Maurgen. And he really likes you, too." She pulled back from him and he saw a grin split her face despite the tears. She let out a chuckle.

"I like him, too. And you. Yes, of course we're friends, I just... I really wanted to... last night. But it didn't seem right, I didn't want to hurt you or get too attached to someone I shouldn't have." Minnie appeared worried again.

He felt his chest constrict at her pain and concern. My Mina, he wanted to say, itching to pull her close and kiss her. Instead, he smiled, "You are the most compassionate woman I've ever met, Minnie. If you ever decide you're willing to hurt me or get attached, you let me know, alright?"

She snorted, wiping tears away around a giggle. "You have my word, Your Highness," she laughed.

"Now, if we've got that all sorted out, we should get going back to the others." Zavier pulled her up and looped her arm through his.

"Thank you for letting me rest, I really did need that." She gave him another smile as they walked through the park.

"Of course, saving people's lives must take it out of you. And I won't tell anyone if you don't want me to, but you shouldn't be surprised if my parents already know. They've been speaking to all the village Elders and senior Bonded for years about anyone who shows enough talent or power to be of use to our country."

Minnie groaned. "Then yes, they'll know. It's never been a secret in Ocrans. It's probably the healthiest town ever, anytime someone had a complaint they came to me or my mother. She was a gifted herbalist, between us we have been able to heal most of our patients."

They turned up the final path toward Greta's house to see a small cluster of people around the old woman. Inside the largest house came sounds of women laughing as they cooked the evening meal. Another group was walking up the road through the gate, most likely the field workers or the people who had been repairing the road.

As Minnie and Zavier neared the house, a man turned from the small group. Recognition lit his face when he saw Minnie, and Zavier cursed to himself. He could feel her tense where their arms were linked and he knew she recognized him, too, as one of the people who had witnessed her healing at the market square.

"There she is! That's the one who fixed Smitt's leg, and that Wealdkin child's foot!" The group all turned and gathered around them. Zavier saw Greta heave herself off her chair and hobble inside.

"You've got to help me, I have bunions on my—"

"No, me first, I've a bad back!"

"Please, my stomach gives me fits—"

"ENOUGH!"

They all turned to see Greta standing in the doorway with her arms crossed over her chest, a wooden spoon clutched in one fist. "Settle down, now. She is not at your beck and call. The issues you are describing are common complaints that any herbalist or medic can fix, and do not require the magic of a Bonded. You leave her alone and come up here, we'll fix you right up."

The men seemed about to protest the old woman's command, but as one opened his mouth to argue, Zavier stepped forward and snorted smoke in his direction. A glare took care of the rest, and they meekly obeyed. All except one.

146

"I'm sorry, Your Highness, but please, let me explain?" The young man's voice was louder than it should be, and sounded frantic. He had been in the back of the gathering and hadn't been one of the ones demanding treatment. Zavier looked at Minnie, and at her nod stepped back. "Thank you, both of you. I've been losing my hearing for several years. People have to yell so I can hear them now, and only on one side. Please, can you help me?"

Minnie cocked her head to the side, studying the young man. He looked to be only in his late teens, Zavier thought. Minnie beckoned him closer, indicating he should kneel on the ground. Her hands began to glow with the golden light and she cupped them over his ears. Several minutes passed in which they all stood silently. Finally, the light dimmed and she stepped back.

"Can you hear me?" she asked in a quiet voice. Shock and pleasure erupted across the young man's face.

"Yes! Yes, thank you!" He leaped up and hugged Minnie, spinning her around in a circle. Zavier growled to himself and reached out to grab the youth, but Minnie's happy laugh stopped him.

"You're welcome, I'm glad I was able to do something. Go on home now, I'm sure someone is waiting for you." Minnie pushed him along down the path and he took off, waving over his shoulder as he ran.

"What was causing the hearing loss?" Zavier asked from behind her as the two of them watched the youth disappear.

"The bones of his ear had fused together and sound couldn't penetrate through them. I've no idea how or why it happens, but I've seen it twice. A young woman had near total hearing loss by the time she was grown. Her father did, too, but he... He killed himself. His wife, the girl's mother, said that he complained of ringing in his ears, and that was all he could hear for over a year. It drove him mad, and he dove off the cliff overlooking the ocean. I didn't know how to help him then, I was only twelve or so when he died. But I was able to help his daughter."

"She feels their pain," Maurgen said quietly, echoing Zavier's own thoughts.

"I do, and I don't." Her reply as she turned around surprised him, had she heard Maurgen? She must have read the confusion on his face, because she added, "I heard Maurgen."

Zavier didn't have time to dwell on how unusual it was that she heard his dragon when they weren't together and Maurgen hadn't intended to speak to her. Minnie was explaining, "I don't feel their pain exactly, but I see how such things can ruin lives. I sympathize for the ones I'm not able to help. That's one of the reasons I want to travel. It's not just to see the world, but to be able to help other people, not just my own village. The Fates have given me an amazing gift, I shouldn't be selfish with it."

Zavier frowned. "You feel like you wouldn't be allowed to travel around the country, healing people?"

"Part of it is not wanting my parents to worry," she said softly. "I'm sure the king and queen would let me go, it would be foolish to refuse to let a healer heal. But my mother... She is very unwell. And, I'm afraid of my power as much as I love it. I can help so many people... but I'm only one person."

"So you want to be everywhere, available to help anyone?"

"Yes, and that's impossible. One person can only be in so many places. And... also... to experience the world, have fun, and other selfish things..."

The sound of returning people grew louder. Zavier tugged on her arm until they stood off the road by the little fence around Greta's garden. He stepped in closer to her, probably too close. Tucking his finger under her chin, he raised her to meet his eyes. Her tilted, deep green eyes shimmered with the barest hint of tears.

"I don't think you are selfish at all. You are an incredible woman, Minnie," he whispered.

"Isn't it selfish to want to do things for myself?" she asked, her voice barely audible.

He shook his head rapidly. "Not when you give so much of yourself, and from what I've seen that's all you do, give. Sometimes you have to take what you want and damn the consequences."

He watched her eyes as they darted from his lips to his eyes and back several times. She wanted to, he didn't need his dragon's voice in his mind pushing him to lean in. Her lips parted, her tongue ran along the inside of her bottom lip as she stared at his mouth.

"Minnie..." was all Zavier had time to say before people arrived back from the fields and they were no longer alone. He stepped away from her, regretting the interruption. Together, he and Minnie rejoined the other Bonded gathering around Greta's house. Zavier was relieved to see that Greta, Lavender, Adaline and Coraline had corralled the complaining citizens around an apothecary table and were giving them various remedies. He made a note to compensate Greta for her supplies as he approached her.

He looked around to see where Minnie had gone when he noticed she was no longer by his side. She had been snagged by Olivia, the pair chopping vegetables on a table outside beside a large bubbling stewpot.

149

"You stare at her as if she is the rarest treasure, Your Highness," a gruff feminine voice said from his elbow. Looking down, he met the sharp brown eyes of Greta.

Offering her his arm to help steady the old woman, Zavier smiled. "Aren't all women the rarest of treasures, Greta?"

"Not even a little bit, rascal, and you know it!" Her vehemence made him chuckle. She was right, and he knew it. Greta had been dragon-bonded, but a tragedy killed her dragon when he was a child. Greta had been offered a position in the palace as Zavier's and then Branton's nanny. While he had been unable to spend as much time with her as he'd have liked in recent years, she still had the uncanny ability to see through him.

Of course, that could be because she had been gifted with prophetic dreams. That was the rarest skill a dragon-born could have. Taurak claimed to have them occasionally, but the only person Zavier knew who had true visions was Greta.

"You know something, don't you Greta?" Zavier asked, guiding her to the padded rocking chair her son had built for her.

"If I know something, I'm not going to tell you, scamp. You can just figure it out for yourself!"

"But Gretaaaa!" Zavier teased, drawing out the vowels of her name like a child begging for sweets.

"Oh hush. You're too big for that nonsense!" Greta swatted him, and Zavier ducked, pretending she had injured him. "You are the worst, Zavier. Now, listen to me, child."

Sensing she was about to impart something important, Zavier straightened his shoulders, then knelt beside her chair.

"There is something coming, something big, that will change your life. It's up to you whether it's for good or for ill. I can't tell you more than that, I don't know. It's a feeling I have. No, I haven't had any dreams lately, if I do I'll let you know. But there is something about that girl, Zavier. She is someone special. Maybe to you, maybe to me, I don't know. But she's someone. Keep her safe, child." She reached down and patted his cheek fondly as she spoke.

Nodding, he cupped his hand over hers, pressing his face into her palm. "I will, Greta. I promise."

Sixteen

Minnie

MINNIE FLOPPED ON HER bed later that night, too tired to even remove her clothes and get under the covers. The celebration at Greta's had lasted for hours, all the neighbors had arrived bearing more food and drink than they could possibly consume, so they'd spread the word of the feast to surrounding neighborhoods. People flocked to the little square to eat, talk, dance, and unwind after a long week of work.

But she hadn't really enjoyed herself. She'd eaten heartily, grabbed a drink, and hid in the kitchens, completely overwhelmed by the sheer number of people, and with all that had happened in the past several days. Her quiet life in Ocrans had not prepared her for the bustle of a city. Of course, she hadn't healed dozens of people in a couple hours back home, either. Fire and air magic came easily and naturally, and never drained her energy, but healing had always been different. It wasn't a physical drain, but a mental and emotional one. Fear that she would fail, let someone down, be unable to help them. She had stubbornly held onto her brave face while she worked so as not to worry any of the patients, but inside she had been roiling in doubt.

She had hoped Zavier would seek her out again, but he'd been in conversation with someone every time she'd spotted him. A few times he had looked around, and she'd wondered if he was searching for her… But then she chided herself for acting like a love-sick fool. Of course he wasn't.

She opened her eyes and was about to sit up, but the painting over her bed caught her eye. It was a flight of dragons of all different colors circling a clutch of eggs. The largest of the dragons was mid-nudge on a hatchling that had cracked its shell and poked its head out.

She knew so much about dragons in general, but almost nothing about their society, if they had one, or what they did with their day-to-day lives. She knew the Vynar was important, but beyond clutching new Bonded dragons, what did she do? Minnie knew many of the Bonded dragons spent most of their time with or near their dragon-bonded partner, like Maurgen and Zavier, and right now most of them were in Dragon Isle preparing for the Rising, but she didn't even know for sure what the Rising was.

She groaned and threw her hands over her face. How had she never pushed for answers to these questions? Always letting Elder Lirance or Horth say, it's not time, you'll learn when you're ready. Well fuck that, she thought. She had spent years of her life letting other people push her around. No more. Time to be brave.

Rolling out of bed, she went to her window. She'd noticed which balcony Zavier had flown to the day before when he had left her in the garden, and if anyone would answer questions it would be him. But though her window overlooked the garden, when she leaned out she couldn't be sure which balcony was his. They were all dark, in any case, so he was already asleep or not in his room. There wasn't anyone else... unless...

"Can you hear me?" she thought hard, searching within her mind for the soothing presence she had met last night.

"I can, little one. Are you alright?" Maurgen's deep voice wrapped around her like a warm quilt on a chilly night.

"Yes, I'm fine. I have some questions, would you be willing to answer them?"

"I will do my best," he replied. *"Will you meet me by the river? It has been lonely today while Zavier has attended to his princely duties."* The dragon's snarky tone was accompanied by a rumbling chuckle.

"Of course, I'll be right down, thank you!" Minnie squealed with excitement. She put her boots back on, grabbed her cloak from the back of the couch where she'd tossed it, and left her room. It was late enough that most of the staff were in their beds, and the lamps had been turned down to their lowest settings. She made her way downstairs to the garden door without any trouble, and was relieved that the doors weren't locked. The garden felt eerie at night when she was alone. The shadows cast by the lanterns and crescent moon played tricks on her eyes. It seemed like the plants were overgrowing, though she knew they were neatly trimmed. The great stone door took all her strength to push open,

but she managed, and left it cracked open slightly just in case it locked behind her.

Down by the riverbank, the hulking form of Maurgen could be seen curled up like a feline, with his tail wrapped around his body and wings tucked in tight. As she approached, he lifted one wing, tucked his head under, and lowered it again, creating a warm space that had her shedding her cloak in seconds.

"Hello, little friend, did you have a good day?" Maurgen asked her, nudging her gently with his nose. His muzzle was so large, and his breath so ticklish across her chest, that she let out a nervous laugh. He pushed her until she sat on his curved foreleg and tucked herself into his elbow, kicking her shoes off.

"I did, though it was tiring," she answered. *"Has Zavier told you what happened?"*

"I usually hear everything that goes on with him unless I am distracted, so yes, I know you saved the lives of several people and helped rid others of pain or suffering." His voice held a warmth that made her swell in pride at herself.

"It's my duty to help others."

"Just because you were born with power doesn't mean you must use it for others."

"Yes, I must!" The automatic reply was more forceful than she'd intended. With a jolt, she realized she had spoken aloud. *"If I didn't help others I would be the worst person alive, completely selfish! I can't allow that."*

"I know you can't. You are a good person at heart. But it's not just a duty for you. You like helping others." His voice held not a trace of doubt, and he rumbled deep in his throat. A small puff of smoke blew through his nostrils.

"You're right. I do." She settled back into his elbow and smiled. *"It's satisfying, figuring out what's wrong and fixing it. And not even just the healing, but fire and air, magical solutions for normal problems that just make lives easier if I'm around. It makes me feel wanted, needed."*

"I think it's normal for you to feel that way, but my exposure to people is limited to what Zavier sees, and no one treats him like a normal person," he grumbled. The dragon released another huff that sounded almost like a sigh. *"He is needed by literally everyone he meets, and he is always working. He's forgotten how to relax and have fun."*

"He said he spends some time with a friend, a guard? Doesn't he also see some women? He said he wasn't..." She trailed off, unsure how to phrase her query.

"Minnie, little friend, as he said to you last night, no one wants him for himself. They want the prince. All women who seek him out do so out of selfish motivation." Now anger colored the dragon's mental voice. His tone deepened and felt jagged, rough. *"Without fail, they have seduced him, he would hope that it was different that time, so he would allow it, and when they finish the women ask for a favor. Patronage of a relative, a word with the king, any number of trivial things."*

Minnie was furious that someone would treat Zavier that way. The fact that there were multiple people over the course of years... She seethed. An image flashed through her mind of herself and Zavier in bed and she blushed, hoping Maurgen hadn't seen it.

"He would enjoy that," the dragon replied, his voice softer than she had ever heard it. She groaned, closing her eyes. Of course he saw.

"You have lowered your mental shields right now, little friend, you are sharing everything with me. I am sorry, I do not mean to invade your privacy."

She sighed, replying, *"I don't think you are, Maurgen. Horth taught me how to guard myself and I'm not doing it like I should. I'm too comfortable with you, and with Zavier."* A soft smile lifted her lips as she thought of the handsome prince.

"It's alright to like him," Maurgen advised, almost hesitant.

"Well of course you would say that, he's your person." She huffed a small laugh, shaking her head. *"It's not that I don't want to like him, or be attracted to him. I don't want to hurt him. He is supposed to be choosing a bride, and I'm just... In a few weeks, I might have to return to my family. Or if I'm lucky, the king will assign me somewhere useful."* She heaved a deep sigh, idly tracing a shadow on Maurgen's hide.

"If you wanted to, Zavier could see that you stay here. Or help send you wherever you want to go."

"I couldn't ask that of him," Minnie replied, shaking her head. *"Other than wanting to search for my dragon, I don't even know where I want to go first. The world is so big and right now I feel so small."*

Maurgen shifted his wing, stretching it out and curving it around them again. *"You are small, it is incredible that so much power fits inside one little person."*

Minnie chuckled, looking down at her body. *"I am taller than most women, silly dragon. I'm only small to you!"*

She could feel a sense of pride at his size radiate from the dragon's mind, and he rumbled in his throat again. *"My point remains, little one. Your power is astounding. Zavier said you want to heal people around the world. Did you always dream of being a healer?"*

"No, not until my dragon-bonded gifts developed. Actually, when I was a little girl... I once dreamed of being a princess."

"But little girls grow up," he replied quietly.

"Yes, little girls grow up, and princesses often become queens. Princess and queen are huge responsibilities, ones that should go to someone worthy of the honor. I've done nothing with my life yet, I am certainly not worthy."

"You have saved lives with your gifts. And, you are not old, you have time to accomplish many great deeds," the dragon assured her.

She chuckled. *"My current plans do not include vying for Zavier's hand in marriage, no matter how handsome he is. But you're right, Maurgen. I'm young, and in a brand new city, getting to experience new things! If I remain positive, maybe the Fates will allow me to do the things I want to do!"*

The dragon's mental voice took on a curious lilt as he tilted his head slightly, his giant eyeball on a level with her head. *"You're always so cheerful, every flash of you I get from Zavier, you're smiling. How do you do that?"*

She regarded him for several minutes as she debated on how to answer that. Finally, she said out loud, since her thoughts had become so jumbled she wasn't sure they would make sense if she tried to share them with the dragon, "I'm not sure. Life is hard enough for so many of us, we should try to enjoy every bit of it that we can. I'm getting to experience a brand new city, see things that I've never seen before, and I was able to help people today. But... I think I have smiled more when I'm with Zavier than I normally do. He makes me want to smile..."

The dragon rumbled in his throat, the vibration against her back almost unnerving. She had never been so casual with Horth, the only dragon she'd really spent time with, but like so many things in the past two days, this just seemed right to her. She leaned back and closed her eyes.

"You said you had questions for me?" Maurgen's voice penetrated her mind before she could fall asleep and she sat up, her eyes snapping open.

"Oh! Yes, I'm sorry, I completely forgot why I bothered you in the first place," she flushed, something else she had also done far more than usual lately.

"You are no bother to me, little friend. What is it you are curious about?"

"I wanted to ask about dragons, actually. There is a painting over my bed in the palace that depicts dragons around a clutch of eggs, and it made me realize that I know almost nothing about dragons on Dragon Isle and their lives. What do you do all day? What is Dragon Isle like? What is the Thunder's Rising I keep hearing about? What other purpose does the Vynar serve? How did the Vynar get her magic? Why is it that she is so special? I have so many questions, and I guess I could—"

"Peace, little friend, I will answer your questions," Maurgen interrupted with another of his rumbling chuckles. *"How much do you know of the origins of the dragon-bonded?"*

"I know that a dragon flew north, and made a pact with a Human."

Maurgen rumbled as he carefully shifted the forelimb she wasn't laying on to a more comfortable position. *"Correct enough. I will summarize, for the full story would take hours to share, and is best done in the dragon tradition of visual memories. A female named Vyn did fly north with her mate, Laron. They endured many hardships, including the destruction of their first clutch by Humans and Skinshifters. A Human healer named Enrick helped them, and Vyn gifted him his dragon-skin. When Laron and Vyn next mated, their hatchlings Bonded to newborn Skinshifters. Enrick became the king, and Vyn became, essentially, the queen of dragons. Her mating flights became a celebration for dragonkind, the Thunder's*

Rising, as they weren't as frequent as a normal female dragon's flights."

As Maurgen fell silent, Minnie pondered his words. *"What made Vyn so powerful in the first place? Don't all dragons have magic?"*

"Yes, all dragons do have magic, but Vyn was never like other dragons. We do not know where her power came from, or why she was so strong."

"Maurgen," she said aloud, her voice barely above a whisper. "Someone mentioned the Rising is happening soon. I hope that I'll go too, since the other ladies in waiting are, so... When we go to the Rising, will that be my dragon's mating flight?" Her voice wavered despite her effort to keep calm. "And what would happen to me during her flight?"

"No, this will be Vynar Vera's flight, your dragon's mother," he soothed.

Minnie still felt a bit nauseous at the thought. A mating flight sounded so... bestial? Exhilarating and terrifying. She swallowed anxiously and asked again, "Does anything happen to the Bonded partner during a mating?"

"It varies. If the male is also bonded, sometimes the people are overwhelmed by what their dragons are doing and will mate. I've seen some take a random lover, and I've seen some be completely unaffected. It really depends entirely on the person. Do not fret, when the time comes, you will be protected if you do not wish to partake."

Well, that was... somewhat reassuring, she thought. Though knowing her luck, she'd be one of those swept up in the emotion and hormones and wind up sleeping with multiple people. Maurgen must have caught her thoughts because he chuckled again.

"You won't, you aren't casual enough for that. I've seen many mating flights between Bonded dragons, you are one

160

who is likely to hold yourself apart from sheer stubborn-ness."

She groaned. "Can't you just pretend you aren't hearing all my thoughts?" she demanded, but without rancor.

"I could, but that wouldn't be as interesting. Besides, this is a novelty, I've only ever been so close to Zavier. Your mind is fascinating to me, and while you let me I plan to enjoy this little bond we have. Most likely this will change and we will grow apart once you have met her."

Minnie decided to ignore the more concerning parts of that statement.

"Why do you speak to me so casually? Horth said that it's not common, but he never explained further. Just that he would speak to me in order to instruct me, and not to expect it from others."

"Hmm... It just feels right," Maurgen said, with a note of finality in his voice.

She debated on pushing him, but decided against it and instead asked, *"You always avoid saying my dragon's name, why?"*

"She hasn't chosen one yet. She won't, not until you and she meet. It's part of the bond, her name will come to her when you touch her for the first time," he explained. *"Rest now, little friend, dawn will come soon and we have talked for hours. Curl up and sleep, I do not trust you will find your way to your bed unharmed. I will keep you safe and warm."*

She wanted to argue and ask a dozen more questions, but he was right and she was exhausted. Her eyes closed and she was asleep within minutes, tucked safely into his elbow.

Seventeen

Zavier

"ZAVIER. ZAVIER."

The mental roar jolted him out of his sleep and he sat upright, reaching for the dagger under his pillow. He shook his head in confusion as the dragon in his head chuckled.

"Good, you're awake. Get up, you need to come to me." The damned lizard sounded smug, Zavier thought, rubbing his eyes and longing to go back to sleep. A glance out the window showed that mist from the river still covered the garden grounds. The clock read—

"Why in all hells are you waking me up so damned early?!" he snapped at his dragon as he rolled out of bed.

"Because I need your help, I can't get her back to the palace by myself, and she'll miss breakfast with your mother if she doesn't go now."

Reaching for his shoes, Zavier stopped mid-motion and nearly fell over. *"Who and what are you talking about?"*

"Minnie."

Maurgen sent an image through their link of what he was seeing at that moment. Soft light filtered through his wing membrane, highlighting Minnie curled on his forearm, her hands tucked under her chin, sound asleep.

"She wanted to talk last night. It grew late and she was tired. I promised to keep her safe and warm, so I did."

Zavier pulled his boots on and grabbed a cloak, mumbling under his breath about infatuated lizards making foolish decisions.

"You're one to talk about infatuated, oh mighty prince of the kingdom. Hurry up, my legs are asleep and I can't move her."

"I'm on my way. You could have just woken her up, you know."

"That would have been rude of me, I can't have that. You do it."

Damned reptile. Zavier navigated the halls as quietly as he could, so as not to wake anyone lucky enough to still be asleep. He had reached the first floor and was passing the kitchen entrance when he heard frantic whispers and labored breathing. He stopped to listen, concerned.

"Just arrived... need dragon-bonded... the king... people dying..." The man was bent over gasping for breath, while two servants held him up. One looked up and saw Zavier. Relief flooded his face.

"Catch your breath, I'll take you directly to my father," Zavier told the messenger. To Maurgen he said, *"I've been delayed. Wake her yourself."*

"What's happened?"

"I don't know yet, the messenger says people are dying."

The messenger caught his breath quickly and stood. "I'm better now, Your Highness."

"Come with me," Zavier held the door for him, then led the way down the hall. They were passing the garden doors just as Minnie entered, bundled in a cloak.

"Maurgen said you might need my help?" Concern filled her voice as she glanced between the two men.

"Come with us, please," Zavier nodded, offering her his arm. She took it, and they all continued to Taurak's study. Always an early riser, Taurak sat at his desk, pen in hand.

"Good morning, son, is everything alright?"

Zavier stepped aside, gesturing for the messenger to begin his report. The other man took a step forward and bowed.

"Sire, I am Lorcan, a Bonded from Saltstone. I've been sent by the Master of Trade to request assistance as quickly as possible. A ship arrived from the Human city of Adreayu on Shaesan three days ago. Every person on board took ill shortly after their departure. The first death occurred one full day after the first sign of illness, and so far there has been no one reported to recover. Hundreds of people across Saltstone have now reported ill. Symptoms included nausea, vomiting, loose bowels. The severity varies, but once they begin vomiting blood, they die within a few hours."

Zavier rapidly went over everything he knew of trade management in Saltstone. The city required all goods to be stored in warehouses for at least two full days, except for perishable goods. Most of the containers from that ship would still be within the warehouses, but some crates may have been dispersed to taverns and homes throughout the city.

164

It was even possible that dragon-bonded deliveries had already gone out to other Skinshifter towns, and even to Stoneborn or Wealdkin territory.

"Messengers have been sent this morning to any location that received a shipment from Saltstone in the past three days, but it will take some time to hear back from them all. Illness is confirmed via dragon relay in Newmere, Holvan, Cliffside, and Calding. Shipments also went to Eerla and Aprana as well as Amthryn." The messenger, standing tall with his hands behind his back as he had been trained to stand when giving his report, had tears slipping down his cheeks. "So far, there have been no confirmed cases of a dragon-bonded contracting this illness, despite so many of us having handled the same goods as others. Therefore, the Masters in Saltstone have concluded we are immune and request immediate aid."

"We will, of course, grant you aid. Is there anything that is confirmed to help this illness? Any herbs or tonics we can send?" the king asked, sitting back in his chair and stroking his chin.

"None, sire. Some pain relief has been found mildly effective, but nothing has curbed the symptoms. Those ill are unable to keep down any food or water, if they can be coaxed to eat."

"We'll begin mobilizing help. Zavier—"

"I'll go," Minnie stepped forward, pulling her hand from the prince's. "I have been trained in herb lore by my mother, and I am an accomplished healer. I may be able to find the cause and a way to save them."

Behind her, Zavier nodded. "She's the best person for it, I haven't met another healer as gifted as she is. Of the dragon-bonded currently here, Lavender, Adaline and Coraline are all talented alchemists and have the temperament for nursing. Our Master Physician is also dragon-bonded, but she is unable to heal via touch, I feel she would be better used researching if this has happened before within the royal libraries."

Taurak nodded his agreement. "Time is of the essence, so I want the women you named and yourself to be ready within the next hour. I'll have others ready themselves and more supplies to follow you later in the day. Oh, take Branton, too. He's skilled with basic healing and maybe he can learn something."

"Yes, Father." He took Minnie's arm to escort her out, but his father's voice stopped him.

"Lady Jessamine," Taurak focused his golden-eyed attention back to Minnie, his stern face softening slightly. "I heard what you did in the city yesterday. You have my thanks, both for helping our people and for exposing just how my citizens are affected by the healer's fees. While charging for the use of herbs and time is expected, no physician should charge so much that someone cannot afford basic care. I have people looking into every physician in our city, and I assure you it will be taken care of."

Minnie's bright smile lit her face as she curtsied awkwardly. "Thank you, sire, I didn't want to cause trouble for anyone, but I am very relieved that the citizens will be helped."

"You hurry on now and get ready to leave, and tell those women they're going to Saltstone, please. I'd like to speak to my son for a moment."

Minnie curtsied again and left, giving Zavier a quick smile over her shoulder as she turned the corner. Taurak noticed, and when Zavier faced his father again, he groaned at the wide grin on his father's face.

"Father—"

"You like her!" His father sounded giddy. Zavier half expected him to clap his hands and bounce in his seat like a child.

"Whether I do or don't is irrelevant—" But Taurak interrupted him again.

"She's perfect, son. Have you broached the subject with her yet?" The older man had a wide grin across his face as he leaned forward. Zavier ran a hand through his hair and sighed.

"No, Father, I haven't, because she isn't interested. She doesn't want to be a princess, let alone queen, and we won't force her."

"But son—"

"No, Father. Trust me." The two stared at each other for a long moment while Zavier fought the urge to squirm and look away. Finally, he said, "Trust me on this, Father. Don't bring it up, don't set Mother on her, and don't make any plans or a big fuss. Let me have time with her. She wants to travel, heal and help people, and most importantly, find her dragon and discover herself. Let me show her what I can offer, and that she can do that and more with me. Let me win her over. I gave her my word that no one would force her." Zavier took a deep breath before firmly adding, "I've never defied you before, but I will for her."

Taurak leaned back in his chair, studying his middle son. After a long moment, he smiled. "You were always my choice for heir, did you know that? It's written in my will, and I've made my wishes clear to the council. Caddoc isn't suited for this life, and never was."

Zavier had known. They'd never overtly spoken of it, but he'd known. Hearing it confirmed, and that his father had spoken to the council without telling

Zavier, made his chest swell. Taurak had confidence in him, trusted him.

He made to speak, but his father cut him off with a lifted hand. "I've never heard you acknowledge before today that any spouse of yours would one day be queen, nor have you ever spoken out against me. You've always been the dutiful, damned near perfect son and prince. You have my word, son, that no one will force young Minnie to do anything she doesn't wish to do. But take my advice: get that girl to fall in love with you and want to stay with you, because having her as your queen will make your job a lot easier!" The two men chuckled, the younger rather nervously, and his father continued on.

"I loved your mother from the second I first spoke to her, and was fully prepared to marry her whether she was dragon-bonded or not. The Fates were with us then, and I hope the Fates will be with you. Take care of her. I saw the way she looked at you when you weren't paying attention to her. It won't take much to steal her heart."

Zavier smiled softly. "I don't want to steal it, Father, I want to earn it. Give me time, there's no rush. I hope I'll bring you a princess and a queen." he chuckled, running his fingers through his hair. "Or she'll figure it out and kill me, then Brant can have the throne."

The king stood and walked around his desk to hug his son. "Fates be with you, and safe flight. I know you will take care of Saltstone, but let me know if you need more assistance."

Zavier returned his father's hug, then hurried out of the study. He stopped by Branton's room long enough to tell him to pack a travel bag and meet him in the courtyard as quickly as he could, and that he would explain everything then.

Back in his apartment, Zavier was throwing clothes into a pack when Maurgen spoke up.

"I see you gave in to your own feelings. That was fast."

"You shush. He wasn't going to leave it alone unless I agreed with him."

"But you didn't agree, did you? I think you vaguely threatened your father, something about not forcing her to marry you."

"You know damn well he wouldn't actually force her to marry me, he's not that kind of man."

Grumbling, Maurgen conceded his defeat. Smirking to himself, Zavier threw the pack over his shoulder and turned to leave, coming face to face with Jarn, his main guard and the only person he'd ever considered an actual friend. "I was on my way down to find you. Saddle up, we're going on a trip."

Jarn groaned, rolling his eyes as the two left the room together. "We just got here a week ago, you promised me at least a month here! I've got plans! There's a pretty lady at the tavern singing my praises!"

"Tough shit. People are dying in Saltstone, and I have to leave. Is there anyone else you want to send to protect me from pesky threats? Oh and did I mention Brant is coming, as well as some of our fair maidens?" Zavier gave his distressed friend a harsh glare.

"I fucking hate you. Let me get my shit, I'll meet you downstairs," Jarn pounded him on the shoulder and turned toward the guard wing to pack. Zavier chuckled, continuing down the spiral stairs.

Zavier took one detour, to the garden. Every morning, regardless of rain, snow, or disaster, his mother walked the garden paths. As luck would have it, Narith was just entering the foyer as he descended the final set of stairs. "Good morning, Zavier, did you sleep well— What's wrong?" She had noticed his pack and serious expression the moment he approached her.

He bent to kiss her cheek and accepted a kiss from her before replying. "There's some kind of illness in Saltstone. Father will tell you more, I have to meet the others and get going. Hopefully, we will figure it all out quickly, but based on the reports I fear that I'll be gone a while. Might even have to miss the Rising," he finished with a sigh. Maurgen roared from the courtyard across the palace.

"He's certainly not happy about that," Narith said with a shake of her head. "You fly safely, and be careful in Saltstone. If you do make it to the Rising, send word to us, please."

He nodded, "Of course, Mother. I love you and will see you again soon."

"I love you too, my son," she waved him off with a sad smile before turning for the stairs he had just descended, probably to his father's study.

Zavier exited the foyer and navigated the winding halls to the front foyer, which housed the massive front doors and main courtyard. The doors were flung wide despite the chill in the air, revealing two dragon-bonded guards anxiously strapping a rope harness across Maurgen's chest and back. Next to him, stroking his eye ridges absently, stood Minnie.

As he approached the doors, the master physician appeared at his elbow with a large leather pack in her hands. "Your Highness, I've gathered all the pain relief and anti-emetic herbs we could spare from the stores for you to take, as well as anything I thought might be useful. I've spoken to Lavender and she's quite knowledgeable about these herbs, as is Minnie. The other two ladies are well versed in potion craft, if not the herbs themselves. I'm quite sure they won't do more harm than good, and have my blessing to do as they see fit."

"High praise from you, thank you for the help, Master Marelly. Please send word by dragon if you find anything that may help us," Zavier took the pack from her with a bob of his head. The fidgety woman began to wring her hands and pull on her fingers the second the pack was out of her hands.

"Yes, of course, Your Highness. Be safe." She left as quickly as she appeared, nearly running into Branton as he walked down the staircase. Zavier waved for him to follow and set off toward his dragon.

They were stopped before they'd gone far by his uncle Beltak and aunt Anitra. As usual, the woman was covered in gemstones and baubles, despite the early hour of the morning. Not for the first time, Zavier wondered where all the valuable stones came from and how she afforded the jewelry. He pushed the thought aside for another day as his uncle greeted him.

"Is there trouble, nephew?" Beltak asked, indicating the flurry of activity beyond.

"Yes, illness in Saltstone, Father is sending a small group to render aid."

Anitra scoffed, waving a hand in dismissal. "Peasants are ill all the time. Why should royalty drop everything for them? Can't they help themselves for once?"

Zavier leveled a glare at her. "It is our duty as their sovereigns to assist when needed. Our subjects are dying, the least we can do is bring them what medicine we can and Bonded to nurse them. But then, you aren't royal, so maybe you don't understand that."

"How dare you—" Anitra began, but Zavier cut her off with a glare.

171

"I don't have time for your histrionics, Auntie," he snarled, turning to leave.

Beltak stepped away from wife, asking, "Do you need anything more? Guards, medics?"

"This illness is highly contagious and only Bonded have proved immune. Anyone else we bring is likely to become ill, and we currently have no cure. If you could arrange food, household supplies, care packages, and small pouches of gold, I would appreciate it. Send it all as soon as you are able, the families of those who have died will need the support."

"Of course, I'll get it started right away. Please let me know if there is anything else we can do."

"I'll send word. Thank you, Uncle."

Beltak nodded, and clapped him on the shoulder. Turning back to his wife, he took her roughly by the arm, loudly scolding her as they left. Zavier shook his head again, beckoned to Branton, and resumed crossing the courtyard.

While everyone going to Saltstone had their own dragon-skin, if they all flew, they'd all arrive tired. Maurgen was large enough to carry several passengers, and Zavier could carry the rest, but not with all the luggage they were taking as well. He pulled aside two of the guards known to be strong in the air and requested that they carry passengers and supplies. That would leave Jarn and one more guard unencumbered in case there was trouble. Finally, he turned to his younger brother, who eagerly stood beside Maurgen. Despite the severity of the situation, Brant appeared excited to be included.

"Brant, I want you to fly with either myself or Maurgen, I don't want you overtiring yourself on this trip. If all goes well, you can fly yourself to Dragon Isle, but don't tell Father or Mother," he winked at his little brother, who was on the verge of arguing. Branton snapped his mouth shut and nodded eagerly.

Minnie turned from her place beside Maurgen's head, "I'd like to fly myself, it's been several days since I was in the air."

Zavier shook his head, eyebrows creased in a concerned frown. "I'd prefer for you to ride; you'll be using a lot of energy and power when we arrive, and the last thing we need is you worn out from flying. The wind is from the south today, we may be fighting against it most of the way."

Minnie looked annoyed, but agreed without complaint. He promised himself there would be plenty of time for her to fly as soon as this disaster was over, and set about giving orders for who would ride with whom and where supplies should go.

Jarn turned the argument Zavier used on Minnie back on himself. "We don't need you exhausted when you have to give orders and make sense of everything in Saltstone," Jarn said, pushing Zavier toward Maurgen and indicating he should mount.

Zavier didn't have a good enough argument for that, so he wisely mounted his dragon behind Minnie and Branton without a word.

Eighteen

Zavier

W ITH A FEW POWERFUL downbeats to gain altitude, the dragons leaped to the sky one by
one. They formed a wedge formation with Maurgen in the lead, flying as straight as they could
southeast to Saltstone. Zavier checked all their
safety straps, ensuring everyone was securely attached to each other and to the saddle. The wind
was indeed pushing against them, but Maurgen
continued to climb higher until they broke out of
the current. The others followed him and everyone settled in for a lengthy flight. As the wind
whipped past, Zavier was relieved that Minnie
had, as usual, braided her hair in a tight weave
down her back.

Zavier, situated behind Minnie, who in turn was
sitting behind Branton, wished more than anything
they could speak while they flew. Not that Maurgen was ever boring company, but he didn't want
to distract the dragon from his flight. Wind rushed

by them with their speed, loud enough that it was impossible to hear anything below a shout.

Maurgen rumbled, and suddenly it was quiet. Zavier's ears popped at the rapid change. Ahead of him, Minnie turned to face him, looking smug.

"What did you just do?" Zavier asked her, leaning around to peer over her shoulder.

"I wrapped us in a bubble of air, we can breathe easily and hear ourselves without all that noise. Anyone who can control air at all should be able to do it," she replied as if it were the most obvious thing in the world. Zavier was both impressed and annoyed with how simple her explanation made it seem.

"Won't that tire you out? You're supposed to be saving your energy," Zavier questioned.

"No, fire and air have never been difficult for me, I can maintain this for hours and not feel it," Minnie replied, turning her head to look at him. She said it as a plain statement of fact, no bragging or conceit in her tone.

"Could you teach me?" Branton squirmed, attempting to look back at her. Maurgen puffed smoke from his nose in warning, which would have enveloped them but for Minnie's air bubble, and Branton stopped his wiggling.

"Of course. But don't wear yourself out, just try a few times. I'll explain how to do it, then drop mine so you know if you've done it, alright? Good, here's what you do..." While she spoke, she wrapped her arms around Branton to demonstrate. Zavier fought not to growl in his throat.

"Jealous of a teenager now?"

"Shut up and fly, lizard."

Maurgen's only reply was another smug chuckle.

"Cup your hands like this, and imagine you are holding a soap bubble, but instead of soap, it's air.

You can't see it or touch it, but you know it's there, you feel its power. Shape it around us, imagine the bubble growing until we're all inside it. Start small if you need to, but push the power until it surrounds us. Got it? Alright, I'm dropping mine now."

Wind rushed past them again and Zavier dug at his ear with the sudden return of sound. He leaned further around Minnie, bracing himself with his hands on her hips, to watch Brant. The boy held his hands before him like she'd demonstrated, shaking slightly as he concentrated. Zavier couldn't feel anything, but he saw Brant lift his head and almost look around, then bend back to his invisible bubble. A minute later Minnie rubbed her ears and gave an excited clap of her hands. Soon after, the bubble had grown to include Zavier as well. It wasn't as strong as Minnie's, based on the occasional breeze he felt when the bubble weakened, but it was still effective. He leaned forward and clapped his brother on the shoulder.

"Well done!" He praised, quite pleased with his brother's display.

"Very well done, Brant. It took me several days to make one this big!" Minnie exclaimed, squeezing his shoulders in a quick hug before dropping her hands back to her thighs. Zavier still had one hand gripping her hip; he returned his other hand to his thigh and debated whether he could get away with touching her more.

"But you said it was really easy!" Branton cried, and with his attention diverted the bubble wavered. He focused again and it grew stable once more.

"Yes I did, because that made it easier for you to do it, and it worked. You're magically stronger than you think, Brant, I can feel it. Your magic is much stronger than Zavier's," she replied, and Zavier could hear the smile in her voice. "Sustain it for a bit longer, then I'll take over again."

"How can you tell how much power someone has?" Branton asked, craning his neck to look back.

Minnie shrugged. "It's a feeling, I'm not sure how to explain. I can just sense a Bonded's magic level. Your mother said she can do it as well. It's not a common gift, but it's not that rare. It's just innate ability."

Zavier recalled that his mother had gushed about Minnie's power level before their dinner party. She'd often made comments about a person's magic, he'd never understood how she knew but had never thought to question her before. Feeling magic wasn't something he could do.

"How did you think of this?" Branton asked. "I've been reading in the library for my magic lessons and no one has mentioned doing something like this before."

"Well, I grew up near the ocean, and I love to swim. My father is a heron Skinshifter, he would take me to any body of water we could find when I was little. When I first shifted around age five we thought for sure I'd also be a heron, but turned out I was a lynx like Mother. That didn't stop me from swimming all I could, and with paws I was even better at it."

Zavier imagined a striped kitten with giant paws paddling around a bathtub and fought not to laugh. He covered with a cough and apologized for interrupting while Maurgen let out a rumbling chuckle that vibrated them all.

"I showed signs of magic around age ten, when I breathed fire over my birthday candles instead of blowing them out. I began training with the Elder, but when the weather was nice enough he would take me out for practical lessons. I figured out rather quickly that if I applied his lesson to the real world, he'd be impressed and let me go have fun for the day without my mother knowing. I also realized that wrapping air around my head meant I could breathe underwater, something I forgot to mention to him the first time I tried it, and he panicked when I didn't return from a dive!" She laughed at her memory, a blush climbing her cheeks. She turned back toward Zavier.

"Did you never find magical ways to do simple things?" she asked.

Zavier thought about it, but had to shake his head. "No, not really. My magic has always been fairly limited to creating a bit of fire, a small breeze, and not much else. I can breathe fire, of course, but magically I'm fairly useless. As a Draconid though, I'm stronger than other shifters, and can use my tail as a weapon, horns too, and of course I can fly without the full shift. And I have Maurgen."

"Which has annoyed our brother since the day you were born," Branton cackled from ahead of them.

"What do you mean?" Minnie asked in confusion.

"Our parents didn't know I was clutch born right away, not until Mother's dragon told them hours later that Vera's clutch had hatched. Clutch born royals are almost always extremely powerful. Father was clutch born, but Caddoc, who is eight years older than me, wasn't."

"So he hated you because you were clutch born?"

"I don't think he hates me, but he was always annoyed, and probably jealous. Maurgen arrived when we were only two, he refused to stay on Dragon Isle any longer, and rarely went back during my childhood. I showed magic early, though not much, and when I was fourteen Father sent me to Dragon Isle with Maurgen. He taught me to really fly, read the wind, all things a dragon needed to know to fly exceptionally well. We trained with wild dragons, and I spent weeks living as a dragon and rarely shifted back. While there, I witnessed a much smaller dragon being bullied by some of the others. I intervened, defending her, and fought the others until they left her alone. That dragon was a favorite of the Vynar, and for protecting her she granted me the Draconid gift."

"And when Zavier returned with his fancy new gift, Caddoc saw red and trashed his room, then challenged him to a fight as dragons!" exclaimed Branton.

"A fight? Why would he fight you? It wouldn't change anything!" Minnie cried, clearly irritated by the insanity.

Zavier shrugged and laid a hand on her leather-clad thigh, leaning around her to see her more clearly. "I'm not sure he even knows. Maybe he thought defeating me would make him the better dragon? Regardless, he lost. He got in one good swipe along my chin with his talon, but that was all. I'd seen mating flights, even fights to the death while with the dragons. I didn't want to hurt him, and was going easy until he clawed my face. I trapped him by the claws, and since I am bigger, he was unable to break free. We crashed into the ground together."

Minnie leaned her body back against his slightly, resting her hand on his. "That sounds horrifying. I'm glad you were alright. Didn't your parents try to stop the fight?"

"Mother did, but we weren't listening. Father was more practical, he didn't think we'd really hurt each other, so he said to let us fight it out. He tried to intervene after Cad slashed me, and the dragons attempted to separate us, but they couldn't without hurting us and they weren't willing to do that."

"That's terrible…"

Deciding it was time to change the subject, he said, "We still have a long flight, why don't you both get some rest and I'll try Minnie's little air bubble trick?"

Branton let his magic bubble fade with a slump of his shoulders, clearly more worn from the power use than he wanted to let on. While Minnie leaned forward to check on him, Zavier imagined the bubble she had described. A push of power outward and he had them safely ensconced in air. He found it wasn't too difficult to maintain, but suspected Maurgen was assisting. Another rumble confirmed his suspicions.

"Is that wise? You'll grow tired."

"I'm fine, the wind is with us now and I am strong."

Zavier looked around for the others, noting that they had staggered in their flight levels below and far to either side of Maurgen. There must be currents that he couldn't sense in this form and each dragon had found their own space.

Branton leaned forward to stretch out along Maurgen's neck. Minnie rubbed a hand along his back in a gesture reminiscent of a mother soothing her babe to sleep. Zavier was struggling to fight off another stab of jealousy, but she leaned herself back against him, tucking her head into the crook of his neck. Wordlessly he wrapped his arms around her, squeezing her tightly as she sighed.

Within a few minutes, Branton was snoring.

"Poor kid, he should have said he was getting tired," Minnie whispered back to him.

"Not a chance in hell would he admit something like that to a pretty girl. He was probably awake all night, I could smell smoke when I went to his room this morning. I bet he's been secretly practicing with fire."

"Let's hope he doesn't burn the palace down!" she giggled quietly.

"You did really well with him. His instructors have said he doesn't apply himself or pay attention, but I think they bore him," Zavier praised.

"He's naturally gifted and has good instincts. I bet they're relying on books, not practical demonstrations. I'm more than happy to show him what I know. You, too, by the way. You have more power in you than you give yourself credit for, I can feel it."

He scoffed, but didn't reply. A lock of her hair had worked itself loose when they swapped air bubbles and was tickling his nose. She'd used some kind of flowery soap that smelled intoxicating. He closed his eyes and let himself breathe in the mixture of flowers and her. She shivered, but didn't say anything.

"Maurgen said you wanted to talk to him last night," he prodded in a soft voice, daring to rest his cheek against the top of her head.

"I just had some questions about dragons, I thought he might be the best source for answers," she replied. She tilted her face back and he lifted his head, looking down into her eyes. "I heard something interesting about you today from a maid."

"Oh?"

"Mhmm. Apparently she heard it from a girl in the kitchen, who heard it from one of the upstairs maids, who was cleaning your father's library, which happens to be located adjacent to his study."

Zavier swallowed nervously, but said nothing. She smiled and continued. "She says that your father confirmed you as his heir. Is that true?"

Relieved, he nodded. "Yes, he did."

She studied his face for a moment. "Did you discuss anything else, maybe something that concerns me?"

Well, shit. Zavier swallowed again. "Nothing that I am brave enough to say out loud, no..."

"Coward," she cooed, her voice a soft, melodious purr. The velvet sound of it sent a jolt through his body.

"Yes! Self-preservation," he nervously agreed. Maurgen grumbled in his head and Zavier told him to hush.

She giggled, the stern look she'd tried to maintain crumbling away. She shifted further so she was sitting halfway facing him. He tightened his grip on her waist as she spoke. "I was told you stood against your father when he suggested you marry me."

"Of course I did, I promised that no one would force you." Never mind that he was sorely tempted to beg and plead with her to never leave him, a feeling that, frankly, terrified him as much as it thrilled him. Maurgen was right, a sentence he hated thinking. He was a besotted fool, and it had only been two days. He'd spent the entirety of the previous night at Greta's, firmly forcing himself not to seek her out.

"You did. You also said something to him about giving you time to win me over." Silence. He'd figured that part was coming and dreaded it all the same. He waited for her to continue, but she didn't speak. Finally, he did.

"I said that, yes. Partly to keep my father from getting ideas about arranging things, though it's not in his nature or mine to force someone into anything they don't want. If he thinks I am trying to win you over, he and Mother won't interfere, and I'll have more time to spend with you. You've been on my mind constantly since we met."

"Is that what you want? To spend more time with me?" she asked, again in a low, purring voice.

"Yes," he whispered back.

"And do what?"

"... Everything," he breathed along her neck, his voice gone husky with need.

She turned, sitting straight ahead for several long minutes, the only sound around them the beating of Maurgen's massive wings as they flew south. Zavier was worried he had offended her beyond repair, and was readying an apology when she moved. She twisted toward him again, shifting in such a way that he braced a hand on her hip to keep her in place as she nearly slid free of the restraints.

"Do you want to fuck me?" she asked, her dark forest eyes meeting his. He saw fear and doubt cross her face.

The vulgarity of the question shocked him, and for several long seconds he was unable to think. Desire pulsed through him, stirring his cock. Struggling to form a coherent response, he stammered, "O-of course, I-I mean, yes, I would. I think it would be incredi—"

He was cut off by one of her hands gripping the back of his neck and pulling him closer, their lips meeting. The swiftness of the maneuver left him stunned for several seconds before he snapped out of it. He deepened their kiss and squeezed his arms tighter around her midsection. His cock pressed hard against her lower back, almost pulsing with need. Her arm stayed on his neck, fingers twisting into his blond hair. He groaned softly, wishing they were anywhere but on dragon-back, or at least without his still snoring brother just inches away.

He lifted one arm to her face, cradling her cheek in his palm, and broke their kiss. He pulled back slightly, just enough to meet her eyes. He saw delight, lust, and joy dancing in the dark orbs before he descended for another kiss. When they came up for air a moment later, they were both almost panting.

"I'm not saying I want a relationship, or anything serious. I'm not what you need. I won't be allowed to stay with you. But... It's been two days since we met, and I've never been more aroused. I swear I've spent those two days with soaked panties." She sounded terrified by her admission, so he kissed her again. Breaking away, he looked ahead and saw Branton was still slumped forward, sound asleep across the dragon's neck. Safe enough, especially with Maurgen's level flying and the straps they'd tied around themselves and attached to the saddle.

He peppered small kisses across her lips and nose. "I've told you I want you, and if you want proof, reach between us and feel my need." He waited, giving her time to see if she would. After a long moment, she slid her hand behind herself and pressed her palm into his firm cock. She closed her fingers around him as much as she could through his leather trousers, her other hand gripping his thigh. He nudged her head with his until he could speak directly into her ear. "If my brother weren't here, I'd love to turn you around and have you straddle me. If we were alone, I'd worship every inch of your body until you begged for release."

"If he weren't here, I'd let you. I'm sure Maurgen wouldn't mind," she said, almost too loudly. She squeezed his cock, biting one side of her lip.

He rocked his hips against her palm, then raised his hand to cover her mouth. "You set the pace, because if you leave it to me, I'd fuck you until you screamed. I give you my word, I will never pressure you to do what you don't want to do. If you say stop, that's it, we stop. If we do this, and you walk away, that is perfectly fine. If I fall head over heels, madly in love with you, but you don't feel the same, I will survive and be just fine with that."

He took a deep breath of her flowery scented hair, and pressed a kiss to her cheek. "I warn you, that is quite likely to happen. I desperately want to make you mine in every way possible. You have consumed me. You are in charge. As far as I am concerned, you are my queen, and I am nothing but your servant eagerly awaiting your pleasure, no matter what form that may take."

She was almost panting against his palm, her fingers digging into the leather of his pants. A glance ahead confirmed Branton was still asleep, his head pressed against Maurgen's neck and arms pillowed a neck ridge, sleeping as only an exhausted teenage boy could. He pressed a kiss to her cheek, trailing down to her neck, before whispering in her ear again.

"I hope we can continue this discussion at another time, if you are agreeable. I have enjoyed this little interlude immensely, and eagerly await your invitation, if it comes. You may release me, or hold on as long as you like, just do me a favor and don't make a lot of noise. Might give him the wrong idea if he were to wake up," he jerked his head, indicating his sleeping brother. Zavier's lips curved up in a grin as he teased her.

Her eyes narrowed, glaring at him, but when he pulled his hand from her mouth she did not remove her own hand from his groin. Instead, she took that hand and guided it to her breast, and she continued to rub him through his trousers, a smirk across her face. With a groan Zavier buried his face in her neck.

It was going to be a long flight to Saltstone.

Nineteen

Minnie

M INNIE TRIED NOT TO fidget during the remainder of the flight to Saltstone. She could acutely feel every inch of Zavier behind her. Fates, she had pushed herself so far back and away from Branton, she was practically sitting in Zavier's lap. The teenager had only slept about an hour, and the second he began to move about, they had yanked their hands away from each other. For Minnie, it was a telling sign of how much they wanted each other, that they'd even been willing to touch at all with the boy so close. Zavier had a death grip on her hips, his fingers teasing under her shirt and dipping into her trouser waistband to tickle her. Every few minutes he rocked his hips against her just enough to remind her he was still firm at her lower back.

The day so far had been a whirlwind blur, starting with waking up that morning. Maurgen had nudged her awake ever so gently with his massive nose, huffing warm and slightly smoky breath over her.

She'd been disoriented at first, definitely not used to waking up after a night spent tucked into a dragon's elbow, and he'd apologized for waking her at all. After she'd clambered off his arm and found her shoes, she saw he was stiffly trying to stand and realized he hadn't moved from that position all night. She'd tried to apologize to him, but he'd told her that Zavier needed to see her right away. She'd felt a tingle up her spine and deep within her core with that statement.

Her thoughts were a jumble within her mind and she didn't know where or how to even begin sorting through them. All she knew was she had awoken this morning, for the very first time, without fear of her future. Fear that she would be forced to abandon her dreams for yet more responsibility. She had awoken in the middle of the night from an unsettling dream she couldn't quite remember, and while she settled her mind again her thoughts had focused themselves on Zavier.

He clearly wanted her. He didn't seem all that interested in his parent's wishes that he marry right away. If he was so determined to be near her, why should she argue with that? She hadn't lied to him; she wasn't worthy of being a princess, and she didn't want to give up the possibility of exploring the world.

Although, it had been absolutely thrilling to have made a difference in so many peoples lives with her gifts, and as princess she could do more of that… Plus King Taurak had commended her for her abilities! There was more she could do, if only she could be allowed to go out and see the world, help other people. If her mother didn't guilt her into returning to Ocrans…

The confusion swirled around her mind. Each possibility was tempting. Follow her lifelong dream of exploring the world, starting with finding her dragon. Or follow her currently overwhelming desire for Zavier, take the risk, and see where it leads. He wanted her. He was willing to let her take the lead, even if it meant he got hurt. But she didn't want to hurt him, she didn't want to be just another woman using him. She sighed.

She was on dragon-back for the first time. The land below her sped past, they were almost too high to make out any real features of the land other than the river below. She was finally experiencing things, and she was too bogged down in her own mind to enjoy it! Firmly, Minnie pulled her mind back to the present.

Around her, Branton and Zavier were chatting about the possible state of Saltstone, what their various plans would be if this were the situation, or if that occurred, and whether it was likely at all they would make the Thunder's Rising. She assumed they just wanted to prepare, but then she realized Zavier was asking questions to Brant on what they should do in each situation. He wasn't just making conversation, he was testing him! Even knowing that Zavier would be the heir, he was including his little brother in royal business as if he may need to know. Undeserved pride swelled within her chest at the thought.

"It's not just to include and educate him, though that is a big part of it," Maurgen interrupted her musings.

"Are you still eavesdropping in my head?"

"Stop projecting so loudly if you don't want me hearing," came the almost snappish reply. She felt instantly contrite.

189

"I'm sorry, Maurgen, that wasn't fair of me. I don't mind you hearing, truly, it's just such a new experience I keep thinking that I should mind, if that makes sense?"

"You'll get used to it. Once you meet her, you'll never truly be alone again. Zavier and I have attempted to block each other out for years, but no matter how hard we shield, we can always feel or sense the other and get flashes of what they are doing. We can build a slight distance for intimate situations, for the illusion of privacy, but we're always there."

"So you always hear what he's thinking, even during... sex?"

"Yes, but often, I will sleep, or go hunting, again, for privacy."

"... You have been hearing my thoughts this whole time, haven't you?" she asked with another sigh.

"Yes, but I give you my word, I have not repeated anything I've heard to Zavier. The connection between you and I is unusual, and I will protect your mind and secrets as I protect his."

"Thank you, Maurgen. I'm sure I will get used to it, if I— No. When I find my dragon."

"Remain positive. Zavier has mentioned to me that he wants to help you search. As a royal, it is part of his duty to protect the Vynar and her heir, so discovering what's kept you apart is vital." Maurgen's voice was firm, encouraging, and it warmed her to her toes to hear his confidence.

"It's not fair that we were kept apart, especially since it's been so damned long. I really wasn't completely sure if I even had a dragon at all, or if she were dead."

"You would know if she had died. You wouldn't have any magic, or have a dragon-skin anymore."

"What!?" Minnie gasped, her entire body going rigid. Zavier stopped what he was saying mid-sentence to check on her.

"I'm fine, sorry, it's nothing," she tried to cover for herself but Zavier seemed to know better.

"He's asking if you are truly alright. May I share with him? He knows we are speaking but not what about."

"Oh... yes, of course. I can't ask you to hide from him. Honestly, until just now, I assumed anything you knew about me, he knew."

"No, I will not betray your trust.. Shall I explain this conversation?"

"Yes, of course."

Branton had turned almost entirely around to look at the two silent dragon-bonded behind him. "What's going on with you two?"

"It's nothing, Brant, just something occurred to me I hadn't thought of before. No need to worry. Hey, let me see you create a ball of fire. Can you turn that ball into a wreath?"

She vaguely heard Maurgen somewhere in the back of her mind while she was distracting Branton. She wondered if this was what Zavier heard all the time? Why could she still hear the dragon despite him not actively speaking to her? She shored up her mental shields, but could still hear Maurgen's side of the conversation faintly.

Branton had his hands up, attempting to summon fire, so she left him to it and looked down to view the passing landscape. She thought she recognized some landmarks from visitor descriptions, but wasn't quite sure. They were flying lower now, over a swamping marshland. She knew from the map that Newmere was a relatively new town in the marsh near Saltstone, but she couldn't see it from here. Ahead of them, little more than a smudge on the horizon but rapidly growing larger, lay Saltstone.

"Got it!" In front of Branton, hovering above his spread hands, was a wobbly wreath of flickering flame. Oh yeah, the kid was powerful alright.

"We'll be there in a few minutes," Zavier said, his voice tight. Minnie almost shrank in on herself at the sound, convinced she had done something wrong. Then she realized with a jolt that he had wrapped one arm almost protectively across her midsection, his wide hand splayed across her stomach just under her breast. She decided to leave it be for now, and hoped to talk with him about it later when they had averted disaster.

Disaster might not be a strong enough word for the panic and chaos that met them when Maurgen carefully landed on a long stone pier beside a massive warehouse. Zavier climbed nimbly down Maurgen's raised foreleg and assisted Branton and Minnie to the ground, calling orders to those around them. She wasn't listening.

The first thing she noticed was the smell. She recognized salty ocean air, tar used on boats, wood, and fish. Overwhelming all of that was the scent of death. Loosened bowels, the coppery tang of blood mixed with the acrid stench of vomit. She stepped away from Maurgen, looking around. Lining the edge of the wharf in hastily sewn linen shrouds were bodies, some with blood stains near the heads. She walked slowly past them, counting until she had passed thirty corpses and hadn't even gone halfway.

A woman was sobbing ahead of her, kneeling beside a shroud being sewn, a young boy's face still in view. Tears stung Minnie's eyes and she turned away, but every direction she looked held sorrow and death. She felt someone approach behind her and turned to see Lavender, Adaline, and Coraline, all somber.

"Come on, we'd better get inside," Coraline whispered, and the others nodded. As one, they passed the grieving relatives to the main walkway, following the sounds of panic ahead of them. A frantic man waved at them from a warehouse entry wide enough to accommodate a wagon cart.

"Are you the dragon-bonded from Hatherus?" he demanded, nearly pushing a young girl out of his way in his urgency to reach them.

"We are some of them, yes. The others are behind us, what can we do to help?" Adaline asked him, attempting to soothe his frazzled nerves. The man began to ramble, so disoriented and incomprehensible that nothing he said made sense.

Minnie skirted around her companions and looked inside the warehouse. Her stomach sank and fear flooded her entire body.

The dream from several mornings ago returned to her in a flash. Bodies littered the floor of a massive warehouse, the very warehouse she was now looking at. Some were still moving, groaning in pain, but many, far too many, were still. She heard retching, and whirled to see the man who had stopped them was vomiting. Coraline was holding him without concern that she was being splattered with vomit.

"Quickly, let's get him in a bed. Someone fetch water and set it to boil!" Minnie called loudly, pointing Coraline to an empty bed nearby and meeting the gaze of a woman standing idly beside the hearth. She spied two young boys and nabbed their shirts as they tried to run past her. "You two, grab buckets and fetch water. Don't stop until I say."

"Yes, milady," the wide-eyed elder boy said, the other nodding nervously. Minnie pointed them toward buckets set just inside the door.

She turned toward the other women, but Lavender had already commandeered herself a table by the hearth where one pot had just been set on the hook. She sorted herb packets while Adaline called for flasks, mortar and pestle, and other implements she would need. They'd brought everything with them, but it was being unloaded from the dragons. A look back to the long wharf they'd landed on showed Maurgen had left and a Bonded in dragon-skin had taken his place. One pier over, Jarn was skin-shifting back to his humanoid form. The guards carried bundles toward the warehouse.

Lavender was already setting aside flasks to dip in the boiling water. A boy returned, staggering under a heavy pail, sloshing some down his pants. Water to cleanse their instruments, their hands, and the patients.

Minnie turned back toward the table. "You'll have your stuff in a few minutes. I'm going to walk around and see if I can help anyone. Yell if you need me."

The women nodded absently and waved her off. Lavender was twice as knowledgeable about herbs as Minnie was. Vaguely, she wished her mother were here, then changed her mind. She would be of more help using magic than herb lore. Minnie had memorized lists and uses of plants, but she didn't have the *feel* for alchemy. Her talents lay elsewhere.

She walked up the ramshackle aisle, confirming death in almost a dozen people before she found one still alive. The gnarled fingers of the old man reached for her as blood dribbled down his chin. Even as she knelt beside him, he turned to retch into a small bucket set beside his pallet.

"Hurts... Please..." he whispered, too weak to roll himself back to his folded cloak that served as a pillow.

"Soon, they'll bring you something soon. May I examine you with magic?" she asked in a soft voice, not wanting anyone who may be alive to get their hopes up if she couldn't help.

He tried several times to speak again, but blood filled his mouth. He nodded and spat into the bucket. One hand bracing his frail shoulder, she called the power to her and ran a glowing palm slowly down his body, searching for anything that might be causing this illness. She'd only reached his lungs, however, when he gasped once, then went still. The vision within her mind, how she saw their bodies when she scanned them, went black. A tear fell slowly down her cheek as she covered him with his blanket, pulling it over his head.

She stood, already searching for another living person. They needed to do something about these bodies before they began to rot and spread more disease. She retraced her steps to the hearth, relieved to see Adaline and Coraline had nearly a dozen small flasks of some potion or elixir ready and were working on more.

A strong voice rose over the clamor around them. "Call every Bonded left in the city, I want these bodies stacked in carts or wagons and hauled out. Get several miles away, then bathe them in dragon fire until there is nothing left. Be sure to get an identity before burning them! If there are spare ships, load them with bodies and burn those, too. Anything that is lost will be replaced or paid for, just get these bodies out of here." Zavier's firm voice reassured her that someone else would handle the important details. Minnie scooped up several of the flasks Adaline indicated were for pain and went to find a living patient.

Twenty

Minnie

THE REMAINDER OF THE morning dragged on, mentally and emotionally draining. Fewer than she hoped were still alive. Those living were so close to death, Minnie asked young men and women who had come to help to sit with them while they passed. Several had refused to let her touch them with magic, and she remembered that most of the lower class who lived in Saltstone were quite superstitious. Briefly she wished Maisey had come with them, she was from a fishing family in Saltstone and might have been able to bridge this cultural divide she was encountering. As she pulled a cover over yet another body, she sighed heavily.

"Another?" Zavier stood at the foot of the pallet, watching her. She nodded. "Any luck finding what's doing this?"

"No, they're all too sick. I hate to say it but I need— Wait, I know who I need." She whirled around, looking for the man who had met them at the warehouse door. "I don't know why I didn't think of him, I was only thinking I needed to save those closest to death first. Where in all hells is— There!" She pointed across the vast room.

The man was actually standing under his own power, clutching his stomach, speaking to a younger man. She sped over to him with Zavier on her heels.

"—the rest of the cargo needs to be moved away from the corpses, don't let it get fouled up by the death," he was saying to a younger man furiously writing in a leather-bound book. "After that's done, go to my house. My wife can show you where everything is kept. If he's alive, everything I have goes to my eldest son. When all this started I sent him home and made him stay there. If you can, find out for me before I get too sick. If he's dead, the business goes to my wife. What are you standing around for, get going, you have work to do!"

The older man groaned as the younger ran off to carry out his instructions. Clutching his stomach, he leaned over and vomited blood. Flashes of her dream sprang to her mind, and briefly both images overlapped as one.

"Sir, get back in bed, please. I'm Minnie, who are you?" She guided the weakening man to the floor, Zavier bracing him from the opposite side to stop him falling back.

"Names... Anders. Ship captain, trader. It was my ship that brought this hell to us. There..." he pointed a weakening finger out the door of the warehouse, where she could see a three-masted ship being pulled out by two slow-flying dragons. "I had them load the crew, they're all dead now. I'm the... last alive... from our... voyage."

"Captain, can you tell us if there was anything unusual about the cargo? Did anyone come aboard at your last port?" Zavier asked, masking his obvious worry with a deep, soothing tone. As he spoke, Minnie called her power and began to examine the captain, not bothering to request permission. The time for niceties had passed.

Captain Anders swallowed hard, but continued on after a labored breath. "Only stopped... one time. No new crew. No one sick. Cloth, some leather, caught some fish. Spices, all barreled. Nothing new.... No. Wait. A gift. A spiced salt, from... I don't know who. Check... ships logs. Cook opened it... final night... made salted... meat rolls.... I didn't eat... didn't get sick... until last."

The man drew in a ragged breath and went silent. He was alive, just tired. Minnie met Zavier's eyes.

"Do we know the progression yet? Who was sick first?" she asked, moving her hands further down the man's abdomen. His head, throat, heart, and lungs were all clear, though his throat appeared raw, probably from vomiting.

She expected Zavier, but the captain spoke instead. "Cook was first. Sick before we made land."

As he spoke, she moved her hands over his abdomen and gasped. Bloody holes riddled his stomach, acid leaking into his abdominal cavity. As she watched the vision in her mind, the holes grew wider as if something was eating away at the internal flesh. "I've got it," she whispered, the golden light of her hands flaring. "Stay still, please, I think I can..." She pushed the power into his abdomen, smoothing over the leaking holes and knitting the enraged organ back together. Nothing could be done about the bile in his abdomen but to wait it out. She didn't think that would kill him, but a dozen holes in his stomach certainly would.

Relief filled the captain's face as the pain faded. She sat back on her heels, releasing her hold on the magic.

"It must have been the salt. Cook used it first, and used a lot of it to season all those meat rolls, so he fell sick first. The crew ate it, but you said you didn't eat that night? I doubt the crew washed their hands all that often, so everything they touched left traces of the salt. It's not a disease…" She met Zavier's eyes again. "It's poison. Someone poisoned the salt."

Zavier hardly waited for her to finish before standing and rushing off, issuing orders as he went. She heard him calling for more hot water, soap, and anything else that could be used to cleanse everything within the warehouse, including the cargo.

"Captain, where is the salt now?" Minnie asked, shaking the exhausted man slightly to draw his attention back to her.

"Was offloaded with the rest, either in stores away from the water, or divided up and sold by now. It may have been a gift, but good salt is expensive, and we have families. Find my factor, he'll have the records," he replied, his voice and breathing already stronger. "You're a miracle, you are. I don't normally hold with magic, being the good sturgeon stock I am, but you have my thanks."

"You're welcome," she smiled down at him, wiping a drying trickle of blood from his face with the hem of her shirt. "As soon as we can, we'll get you washed up and moved away from all this. I expect quite soon Prince Zavier will have the warehouse emptied and his men tracking down everyone and everything that was touched. Thank you for fighting, your strength will save many people."

"Nah, it's not that, milady. When the crew got sick, I stayed away from fear I'd catch it. But then Cook died, we'd all been together so long, we were family. I had to be with 'em, hold their hands. I've lost 'em all now..." Fat tears leaked from the corners of his crinkled eyes and slid down weathered cheeks.

Minnie felt a tear slide down her own cheek and brushed it away. "Rest now, if you need anything, just call for us." She settled the blanket around him and stood, looking around for anyone not busy. Spying a young girl, she called her over. "Please stay near this man, keep an eye on him. If he needs something or his condition changes, find myself, or any of the Bonded right away."

"Yes, milady," the girl curtsied, rushing away to grab a chair and hauling it back to sit near the now sleeping captain.

Minnie retraced her steps to the hearth table, now covered in flasks. "I know what is causing the vomiting, they have stomach ulcers, but not normal, small ones. A poison is eating their insides and destroying the stomach. The only thing we can do is heal them magically, they would all die before any herbals took effect."

Lavender shook her head, face full of worry. "I can only heal minor things, Minnie, even a broken bone is too much for me."

"How about a cut, or a puncture?"

"No one ever taught me how, our village elder couldn't heal at all, so I had to teach myself."

Minnie nodded, adding one more thing to her ever growing list of things she'd love to do something about. She faced the twins, asking, "Can either of you heal?"

They shook their heads as one, and Coraline added, "No. Our elder could, she tried to teach us, but we couldn't even summon the power."

"Alright, stay here and make more pain relief potions, and anything that could soothe an ulcerated stomach. I mended the holes in the captain's stomach, but we have no idea what will or won't work as far as relief after. With luck, they'll recover if we can heal them fast enough. Where is Prince Branton?" Minnie finished, looking around. She hadn't seen him since they'd disembarked from Maurgen.

"He is helping a group load bodies," the dragon said at the same time Adaline replied, "I saw him with Jarn heading toward a wagon about an hour ago."

Minnie asked Lavender to accompany her and left the twins to their task. Together, the women left the warehouse in search of the young prince, running into Zavier just outside the doorway.

"There you are, good. I've given orders for anyone who is sick in the city to wash in the hottest water they can manage and scrub with soap, which is being dispersed to any who don't have access. Healthy people are to scrub anything that may have been touched. I've also ordered that anyone sick be moved to the city center. There is a large building used for meetings that we will be using as a makeshift hospital. No sense in you wearing yourself out traveling to each person when we can bring them to you."

Minnie sighed in relief. "Good, I was worried about that. Lavender and I will make our way there now. I need Branton, I want to see if he and Lavender can mend these ulcers. Is there anyone in Saltstone who can heal?" She looked about her, just realizing that they were the only Bonded on the wharf.

"Apparently most of them left for the Rising almost a week ago. The days and weeks leading up to the flight are filled with races, mock battles, and other... revelries, so the city has cleared out but for those

201

who wouldn't or couldn't leave their responsibilities yet," Zavier replied with a heavy sigh. Lavender, beside her, snorted. Minnie gave her a wide-eyed stare.

"I'm sorry, that was rude," Lavender said meekly, her eyes downcast.

"I'm just surprised you did it!" Minnie gasped, relieved to know the woman had some spirit in her. A nervous, anxiety-filled laugh threatened to escape her lips, but she bit it back. Lavender met her eyes and smiled. "Having not met my dragon yet, I've no idea what I'll be walking into at the Rising."

Lavender blushed, but seemed to be emboldened by her friend's acceptance and pushed on. "What our prince is so politely not saying is, they've gone for the mating flights. Females will often choose to fly near a Rising because so many males attend. Even dragon-bonded like us can rise in a mating flight if we choose to." A deep blush colored her cheeks, Minnie made a note to ask her about *that* again later.

"As interesting as this conversation is, we need to get going and save lives. The streets are filling with people. What's the best way for us to get to the city center?" she asked, turning her attention back to Zavier.

He pointed behind her and over her head. "That." She whirled to see Maurgen approaching in a steep dive, Branton on his back. "He'll carry you over, no need to lose strength shifting yourselves. I'll meet you as soon as I can." Before she could leave, Zavier gripped her hand and met her eyes. His own were a deep gold filled with worry. "Don't overexert yourselves. If they aren't dying right away, leave them for tomorrow, after you have rested. Consider that an order from your prince." He tried for a stern glare at her that didn't quite erase the worry from his eyes.

As Maurgen landed, Lavender walked away from Minnie and Zavier to properly introduce herself to the dragon.

Minnie smiled softly. "We'll be fine. Maurgen will know if I am overdoing it, and you can scold me later."

He gripped her shoulders with both hands, giving her a tiny shake. "Promise me you won't overdo it," he pleaded, with a voice full of distress that made her heart ache. She glanced around and saw an alleyway between buildings. Taking his hand, she pulled him to it.

"Why are you afraid, Zavier?" She asked softly, reaching up to cup his cheek.

He leaned into the caress with a sigh. "You've done so much in the past few days, and I don't know what your limits are. Maurgen showed me your conversation last night. We both worry that you would give everything you have to save just one more person, no matter what it costs you."

Minnie didn't know what to say to that, as it was very likely true. She smiled, and ran her thumb across his lips. He caught her wrist and kissed the palm of her hand. "Promise me you will take care of yourself, and rest when you need to, Minnie, please."

She pulled him in for a soft kiss, and whispered, "I promise."

"Good girl," he whispered, covering her lips with his. Minnie released an almost feral growl as she parted her lips and licked along his, raising herself on tiptoe to reach him better.

She was the first to break their kiss, leaning her forehead against his as they panted for breath. "We will continue this conversation later. I have to leave now or I won't leave at all. When I fuck you for the first time it won't be in some alleyway." Another swift kiss to his lips and she ran for Maurgen, refusing to look back or be caught by him again.

Maurgen held his leg out for her to scale. She was hardly seated before he took off, not into the air but leaping atop the nearest warehouse. He jumped from the roof into the air and snapped his wings open, gliding across the city to another sturdy roof.

"I think you broke him," Maurgen said as he landed on a thick stable roof. Horses below screamed in fright, but they were gone again before any could break free.

"Did I go too far?" Now that she wasn't caught up in the heat and passion, she was afraid of her boldness.

"He thinks you didn't go far enough, but does agree with your assessment of the location. His words, not mine. I think you're both overthinking it all, and it's a good thing I'm here to be your wing-dragon or you'd talk and worry yourselves to death."

"Did... did you just call yourself a wing-dragon?!*"*

"...shut up, you're as bad as he is," but he was chuckling inside her head. They made a final leap across an open plaza to a three-story meeting hall with open verandas. The timbers within the building groaned at the weight of the dragon, but nothing broke.

"How did you do that and not crush the building?" She asked as he carefully peered over the edge. People were scurrying out of the way so he could land in front of the meeting hall.

"Dragons have hollow bones, so we aren't as heavy as we look. We use magic from our bond-mates to generate air currents beneath our wings, making us seem lighter than we are. If we don't put our full weight down or stay too long, we can land almost anywhere solid."

Shaking her head at the creativity of a creature bonded to a man who claimed to be magically use-less, she dismounted and helped Lavender down.

Branton followed clumsily, his awkward limbs fouling his descent. Pretending not to notice his stum-
ble, she led the others inside to set up for and await
the arrival of their patients.

Twenty-One

Zavier

Z AVIER LEANED AGAINST THE brick wall in the alley for several minutes after Minnie left. Her words kept running through his head, *"When I fuck you for the first time... Fuck you for the first time... Fuck you..."* Oh, how he wished she would, and if only there wasn't a disaster around them!

"Zavier!"

He shook his head, realizing someone had been calling for him for several seconds. No time now to fantasize and daydream.

"I'm here!" He left the alley and waved down Jarn, who had just returned from disposing of bodies.

"This warehouse is almost empty, get the bodies out, but have someone identify them first if we can. Wash their hands and faces with alcohol, I think that will stop the spread. As soon as the warehouse is empty, have it scrubbed down with soap and water."

"Yes, sir," Jarn mock saluted and turned to his companions, beckoning them toward the warehouse door.

Zavier entered the warehouse again, squinting his eyes as they adjusted to the dim light inside. Adaline and Coraline worked diligently, filling potion bottles with a pale blue mixture.

"Ladies, I'm going to try and track down the salt, I'll be nearby. Jarn should be around if you need anything," he told them.

"We're nearly out of bottles, I'll go find someone to take these over to Minnie and bring us more," Coraline replied. Zavier and Coraline left the warehouse together, separating in different directions once they were outside.

"The captain told Minnie that his wife and steward have access to all his records," Maurgen told his partner.

Replying, *"Thanks,"* to his dragon, Zavier asked a dockworker for directions to Captain Anders' house. It was a short walk to a well-kept, two-story home sandwiched between near-identical houses. The only difference was the door, painted blue with a ship's wheel knocker. He rapped on the door and waited patiently. He was unsurprised to hear sobs approach before the door opened.

"Is he dead?" The crying woman asked, her apron held to her mouth.

"No, madam, your husband will live. A companion of mine healed him, and with his help she discovered what is causing this outbreak and we believe we can stop it." He was unable to go any further as the distressed woman threw her arms around him in gratitude. He hugged her awkwardly, patting her back.

"Oh, thank you, thank you. Please come in, let me get you something to drink, please—" Zavier had no choice but to follow her in as she grabbed his arm and bodily forced him inside the home. She pushed him into a chair and within seconds handed him a tankard of sharp ale.

"Thank you, madam. Is Captain Anders' steward still here? I need to speak to him to trace the— ahem, to locate some missing trade goods that could be dangerous." Berating himself for almost speaking too frankly, Zavier mentally slapped himself.

"Keep it together, idiot," Maugren said smugly. Without being asked, Maurgen sent him an image of Minnie and Branton safely inside the meeting hall, both working on patients. Jarn had allowed Branton to leave without a guard simply because there were no guards to spare. Maurgen would be protection enough, but it was still nerve-racking. Relieved, Zavier focused his attention back on the captain's wife, who was chattering away without noticing he wasn't paying attention.

Thankfully, the young man who had been speaking to Captain Anders walked up the stairs from the basement at that moment, a second young man behind him. The second man's resemblance to the captain meant this was most likely the son.

"Ahh, Your Highness. Is my master...?"

"He's healed and recovering, young sir. He should be up and about in no time," Zavier assured.

The captain's son covered his face. His mother crossed the room, wrapping her arms around her son. Zavier gestured for the steward to follow him away from the pair.

"I need to track the salt that Captain Anders received as a gift. We believe that is the source of this illness, and it's poisoned. Anyone who eats it, or even touches it, gets sick and eventually dies. It's passed from hand to hand, and from hand to mouth," Zavier explained. While he spoke, the young man was flipping through pages of his leather-bound book. Zavier was pleased to see the man had a neat, legible script that filled the pages.

"Here, Your Highness. It was divided, and shipped to these taverns in the city for a payment, some was given to loyal patrons of the captain, and others were sold out of town." He looked up, fearful at the daunting task of tracking them all down.

"Come back to the docks with me. I'll send Bonded to each location, you just need to tell them where they need to go. Come on."

It took only a matter of minutes to return to the docks and gather the dragon-bonded who weren't burning bodies and send them out across the city. Within an hour they had all returned, bearing the poisoned salt. Zavier poured it all into the original casket, which the steward had produced from the captain's office. They put that cask into another box, labeled: DO NOT OPEN: POISON on every side. The Bonded were sent out again, this time to chase down the wagon trains carrying shipments overland. Most trade was done via dragon-back, but this close to the Rising, non-perishables had been sent out by horse and wagon to avoid any more delay.

The burning group returned, loaded up the final group of bodies from the warehouse, and left again. Zavier had two helpers scrub down Captain Anders, then themselves, before helping the captain back to his own home. Of all the people who had been inside the warehouse when they arrived earlier in the day, only Captain Anders had survived.

Throughout the afternoon, as Zavier gave orders and made decisions, his thoughts constantly turned to Minnie. He hoped she was doing alright, not overextending her power, remembering to take breaks. Maurgen had gotten so fed up with him asking for updates every two minutes, the dragon had mentally roared at him that if he asked again, he was going to fly away.

Touchy lizard, he thought, knowing Maurgen was full of shit and would never leave Minnie or Branton alone and unprotected, but also knowing when he'd pushed his partner to his limits. Zavier sighed, conjuring an image of Minnie as she had looked in the alley. Sweat stained, her hair frizzing around her head and coming loose from her braid, rough work clothes rumpled from kneeling over patients. She was beautiful.

Once again shaking himself out of his reverie, Zavier set about ordering clean up for the warehouse. He sent Adaline and Coraline off with Jarn to the meeting hall with all their flasks and herbs, and continued giving orders until everything was organized and he could follow them.

Twenty-Two

Minnie

MINNIE AND HER COMPANIONS entered the meeting hall to a bustle of activity. Benches were pushed out of the middle of the room and blankets brought out of the basement. Someone had two large pots of water hovering over the hearth along one wall and was cutting cakes of soap into smaller pieces to pass around. Minnie gathered a group of anxious people around her to give them instructions.

"We will need to set up a triage of sorts, anyone vomiting blood is to be cared for first. I want more buckets of hot water ready, and some people to haul water and clean buckets between patients. Every patient needs to wash their hands when they arrive. No matter what, wash your hands after you touch a patient, and do *not* put your unwashed hands in your mouth."

She turned just as the first group of sick people entered the hall, some being held up or carried by family and friends.

"Has anyone thrown up blood?" She called out, almost relieved that no one raised their hand or spoke out. "Good, who has been sick the longest?" After a brief discussion among the patients, one young man was brought forward, having become ill the morning before. "Lay him on this table, please. Sir, I'm going to use you to show these Bonded what exactly they are looking for, then I will help you, is that alright?"

The man nodded nervously, his hands clenched into fists at his sides. Minnie called her power to her hands and hovered them over his stomach, relieved to find the same as the captain, bleeding and leaking holes devouring the organ. Feeling guilty for the moment of relief, she nodded to the others and removed her hands.

"Call on your magic and focus it to the palms of your hands. When you hover your hands over his belly, you should see an image inside your head. Lavender, you first." Minnie guided the woman on where exactly to hold her hands and waited, smiling when her friend gasped.

"I see it, there are holes everywhere!"

"Yes, that's it. Let Branton see, then watch me smooth the holes over." The two swapped places. Branton was slower to create the glow around his palms, and it wavered a bit more, but he did succeed in finding the afflicted organ. Minnie had them angle their hands off to the side so they could view the stomach without being in the way, and returned her hands to his abdomen. "I'm going to heal you now, there may be some discomfort or pain. It'll be over soon and you'll start to feel better, so please be as still as you can."

Mending the ulcerated stomach took only a few seconds, but she did slow down enough to walk them both through the process and how she did it, hoping her explanation made sense. After the young man was healed, he sat up in wonder, thanking them profusely.

By this time, other people had organized three tables in a row and had sorted the patients based on severity of symptoms. The next person to their table was an older woman. After assessing her condition, Minnie had Lavender do the healing. She was slower and more cautious, but successfully healed the wounds without any help from Minnie. Another patient came to their table, and Branton was also able to mend the bleeding ulcers. Elated and buoyed by their new ability, they went off to their own tables and the less severe patients.

Time passed slowly but steadily as people came to the meeting hall and were healed. Another dragon-bonded arrived after two hours and asked to be shown what to look for and how to heal them; she replaced Branton, who had grown pale with dark circles under his eyes. Someone sat him down near Minnie's table and made him eat and have some warm tea before he fell over. The old motherly woman who tended him wanted to take him to her home across the plaza to let him rest, but Minnie refused to let him out of her sight, painfully aware they had left without guards to protect the young prince.

"I am here. No one will hurt him. Or you." Indeed, Maurgen had found an open window and had curled up just outside it where he could watch

everything unfold within, as well as any who approached from without.

"I just want to make sure, I'd never forgive myself if he was hurt." She soothed his ruffled dignity with a mental scratch about his eye ridges and he snorted smoke outside. Smiling to herself, she waved for the next person to approach.

Hours passed. Lavender was made to sit and rest, while Branton insisted on taking her table and continuing on. The matron forced Minnie to eat, though she refused to stop healing people in between bites. The poisoned population continued to arrive by the hundreds. Such a simple thing as salt had caused all this damage. She hoped with all her heart that Zavier had managed to track down the cask of poisoned salt and that they would learn who had poisoned it to begin with. And, of course, who the target was. It didn't make sense that a ship's captain and his crew were the targets. Was it just to sow mass chaos?

Faces blurred together as she worked, and the shadows in the hall lengthened. Mentally, emotionally, she was exhausted. Her back and arms ached from her leaning over patients. She lifted her head to call for the next, and no one was there. She looked around in confusion.

The older matron hurried over to her, explaining, "I've sent them home, my dear. The rest aren't very ill, and your friends have set up a table outside with a new tonic they've developed that will mend them, as well as an herbal drink that will soothe the stomach. You've done your part now, my dear, you can rest."

In a fog of confusion, Minnie stumbled from the table to see who and what the matron was talking about. Her legs were stiff from hours of standing without moving and she realized her bladder was

screaming to be emptied. The matron took her arm
and helped steady her. "Come, child, rest first. Your
friends will be there when you're ready."

Unable to argue, Minnie allowed the older woman
to lead her to a room off the main hall where there
was a toilet, a fresh washbasin of steaming water, and
a hot meal. "Tend to your needs and eat, you can go
outside when you're done."

"Maurgen, can you see—"

*"He's fine. Zavier arrived not long after Adaline and
Coraline, Branton is with them."*

With a smile for the dragon, she did as she was
bid, groaning in pure relief as she used the toilet. She washed her hands and face, neatened her
flyaway hair back into its braid as best she could,
and scarfed down the food. Though simple fare,
the hearty soup, fresh and steaming loaf of bread
and cup of chilled milk were exactly what she was
needing after such a long day.

Refreshed, she left the room, pausing to thank the
matron graciously and offer to pay for the meal.
She was refused with a tart reminder that she had
more than earned a single hot meal. Minnie wisely
nodded and scurried to the front door.

Descending the steps of the meeting hall, she
found Adaline and Coraline still passing out small
packets of herbs, while Branton passed glass bottles
of a bright green elixir to several people. Zavier
looked up when she approached, his face lined in
worry and exhaustion that began to fade when he
saw her. Other bottles of a pale blue elixir sat in a
crate under the table.

"Did you find the salt?" she asked when she
reached his side.

"Yes, but it's been distributed already," he replied.
"We recovered it all within the city, based on the

steward's records, and have Bonded searching for what has left already. Adaline and Coraline knew of a remedy used in Aprana for ulcers, so anyone not seriously affected will heal on their own when the poison leaves their system. Healers in every town have been alerted on what to look for and how you healed them,"

"What about towns with no magical healer? If they've left already, or never had one?"

"Right now there is at least one dragon-bonded in every town, even if only an elder too old to fly to Dragon Isle, but the relay is taking time since we have to run everything through so many people or dragons to get the information. For now, don't fret. If I need to, I will contact Hatherus and send a healer to every town," Zavier ran his hands down her arms in an attempt to soothe her fears. "Dragons are speaking mind-to-mind and to their partners, we will soon know everything we need to."

Minnie was still worried, but she trusted in him to have everything under control. This was the kind of thing he had been trained for, wasn't it?

"It is, and he's right. You did your part, you saved them."

"But we lost so many, Maurgen..."

"Little one, there is no way we could have saved them all. It was poison, murder. You saved hundreds from severe illness and probable death. I watched, I saw what you saw. It was eating away at their insides."

"Exactly, if we delay now, people in other towns could die!" Her mental voice sounded full of anguish even to herself. Maurgen was silent, then Zavier took her hand and pulled her away from the table. As they left, Jarn stepped up beside Branton, ever the guardian.

Zavier led Minnie around the side of the meeting hall to the back of the building where Maurgen had moved himself after Zavier arrived. A wide grassy area surrounded by simple flower beds served as a garden, and curled in the middle lay the giant golden dragon. Maurgen watched them approach, shifting his forepaws to create a sheltered alcove for them to sit on the grass. When they were settled, he curled his head around them, blocking them from the view of anyone who may approach.

Leaning her against Maurgen's foreleg, Zavier lifted her legs into his lap, removed her shoes, and began rubbing a foot with each hand. They sat in silence for several minutes as he worked the tension from the balls of her feet, until she let out a long sigh and closed her eyes. Smiling, he released one foot and focused all his attention on the other, working away the knots in her arch and toes before rolling her trouser leg up and beginning on her calf muscles.

"Thank you," she whispered, eyes still closed but a small smile lifting her lips.

"Feeling a bit less panicked?" Zavier asked as he worked a tense muscle in her lower leg.

"A little bit, yes," she replied truthfully.

"If it makes you feel better, Aprana has a skilled healer, Eerla only had three mild cases and they've already treated them with the herbals the twins recommended." He moved to her other leg, kneading the tight muscles in her calf. "We haven't heard from Amthyrn yet, but they have some very skilled healers, I'm sure they will be fine. Just in case, the Bonded sent to them is carrying treatments."

Relief filled her. "That does make me feel better. I should have trusted that you would think of everything. That feels incredible, by the way," she added.

Zavier chuckled, "I don't always think of everything, so it's good that you were worried. In this case,

I had others helping me and a whole network of Bonded to do the relay. I just had to give orders and be their figurehead. Without you, this day would not have ended so positively."

She shook her head, "No, Lavender and Branton did amazing. Someone would have figured it out. Adaline and Coraline would have, they had the ulcer recipe."

"Minnie, there were only a handful of Bonded left in the city, and that one healer who barely knew what she was doing. Everyone else is at the Rising. If that was deliberate, it was a stroke of pure genius. If it was a coincidence, whoever did this got very lucky." He ran his hands down her calves, absently stroking them now that the muscles were relaxed.

"For tonight, you need to just rest and recover. We will know more in the morning. I have people out doing my dirty work for me, delegating like a proper leader should, and I intend to make certain you have eaten and slept."

She eyed him with a sly smirk, asking, "I've already eaten, so do you know where we will be staying the night?"

He snorted. "Of course I do, it's all arranged with an innkeeper not far from here. There are several official royal residences, but the one that's ready is stuffy and I dislike staying there," he added, waving his hand vaguely behind him.

"I kept my promise, you know. I didn't overexert myself."

His smile was almost feral as he lifted her legs off his lap and scooted closer to her. "I know, Maurgen kept me informed." He hovered just a few inches from her lips and she nearly asked why he was hesitating when it occurred to her: he was doing as he'd promised. He wasn't pushing. He was waiting for her to come to him. She shoved him back into Maurgen's chest and lifted herself to kneel with a leg on either side of his. A lock of wheat-colored hair had fallen across his face, as she brushed it away she leaned over to kiss his forehead.

His hands slid up her thighs and over her hips to rest on either side of her ribcage, thumbs brushing tantalizingly under her breasts. She peppered kisses down the bridge of his nose and across a cheek, avoiding his lips no matter how he tried to turn to catch hers. She grinned as he growled in frustration and knelt down further to lick a wet line down his neck. His fingers tensed, digging into her ribs as he groaned.

"You are a delightful little cock tease, did you know that?" he grunted, half lifting his hips in an attempt to grind against her. In response, she nibbled his earlobe and slid down, resting her core against the thick bulge in his trousers. She moaned into his ear at the contact, grinding against him. Zavier swore, throwing his head back and closing his eyes, sliding his hands down to grip her ass.

"Maurgen, is there anyone around?" she asked, sitting back and running her hands up the hard planes of Zavier's chest.

"Yes, but not very close. You'd have to be very quiet," the dragon replied, lifting his head and extending it around the corner of the building to scout. She swore. Too eager to stop now, she asked the dragon to cover them with a wing and warn her if anyone approached.

The dragon lifted his leg over their heads and rolled to his side, facing away from them, and draped a wing over them, completely blocking them from view. She knew he would feel everything and it was only an illusion of privacy, but it was more than enough for her at that moment.

Confused, Zavier opened his mouth, but she silenced him with a kiss before sliding down his body to pull the laces of his trousers loose. She had the flaps open before he fully realized what she was doing. She nudged him to lean back against the dragon, and wiggled his trousers down a few inches until she had completely freed his cock from the confining leather. Putting a finger to her lips to indicate he should be quiet, she wrapped her hand around his firm length and stroked slowly.

With a muffled groan he let his head fall back, one of his hands reaching almost desperately for her. She ignored him and stroked again, sliding her hand over the weeping tip and back down, spreading his seed over his shaft. He caught his breath and whispered her name, eyes wild as they met hers. She gave a feral smile.

"How's this for a cock tease?" she whispered, an almost sultry husk to her voice. She tightened her grip and made another pass over the bulging head and back with slow and even strokes.

"Incredible..." he breathed, hips jerking as if begging her to increase her speed. She refused, slowly and steadily working her hand over him. His breathing became more labored as his cock wept seed. "Please, Mina—"

She took him in her mouth, sliding her hands to grip him by his hips and dig her nails into his flesh. His cock slid to the back of her throat and she forced herself to breathe through her nose evenly or risk gagging. He swore fiercely, a hand wrapping itself in her long braid. She bobbed her head, keeping him as deep as she could tolerate, only lifting a few inches before letting him slide back down her throat. His grip tightened.

"Mina... If you keep going—" She raked her teeth gently over his flesh and wrapped her tongue around him, coming all the way off with a wet pop before engulfing him again and pressing her nose into his groin. His groan was long and ragged. "Fuck, Mina, stop or I'll come down your throat."

She growled and sucked hard, bobbing up and down repeatedly, her tongue suctioned to him. His hand clenched, pulling her braid. He began panting her new nickname, begging, whether for her to stop or continue she didn't know. She certainly had no plans to stop. She could taste fresh seed at the back of her tongue that made her moan around him.

"Mina, Mina I'm about to—" She sucked him down hard, almost slamming him into the back of her throat and he groaned loudly, hips arched and fist jerking her hair almost painfully. She froze with him buried to the hilt within her mouth and let his seed slide down her throat. He flexed his hips under her so she moved again, slowly licking up and down and sucking hard to pull every bit she could from him and swallow it down. When he collapsed back and his grip on her hair loosened, she gave another long swipe of her tongue before sitting up. She wiped her mouth with the back of her hand and met his eyes.

"Am I still a cock tease?" she whispered with a smirk.

He gave a weak chuckle. "If I said yes, would you promise to do that again?" She leaned over him and lightly kissed his lips. He tried to pull her in closer, but she resisted with a hand to his chest.

"We need to go before we're caught here. Someone was making more noise than he should have been," she teased.

"At least let me—" he started to say, but she silenced him with a hand to his lips.

"I fully intend to ride you long and hard tonight, as well as take you up on that offer to worship me like a queen, but not here. I want walls, a bed, and most of all, a door that locks. I'd prefer somewhere without neighbors, but I'll make do." Her voice was husky and thick with need, she could see he was already hardening again from her words. "Get dressed and take me to our room, Your Highness."

Twenty-Three

Minnie

THE PAIR EMERGED FROM their gold-shaded hiding spot to oncoming darkness. Murmurs of voices from the city center nearby meant people were still picking up their remedies. Zavier took her hand and led her around the building opposite the way they'd come and down a side road she hadn't even seen. After several minutes, they turned down a new street and entered a quieter area of the city. Fewer people passed them, though she saw several half-wild cats scurry under bushes. Businesses had given way to houses, spaced apart by lush gardens. This was a wealthier neighborhood, she decided, admiring the well maintained lawns and stone walkways.

"I thought you said we were staying with an innkeeper you knew?" Minnie asked quietly, not wanting to disturb the serene peace of the neighborhood.

"I did, but I had a better idea," he replied with a sly smile.

"So where are you taking me?" she exclaimed, pulling on her hand to stop him. He turned and cupped her cheek in his hand.

"You said you wanted somewhere without neighbors. If you've changed your mind, I'm happy to take you to the inn," he murmured, meeting her eyes. They stood in shadow, so she couldn't see the true gold of his eyes, but she did see the sincerity. He would take them back, and not complain if she had changed her mind. She shook her head.

"No, I don't want to go back." He leaned down to kiss her, a gentle meeting of lips that felt almost reverential. When they parted, he took her hand and looped it through his arm, leading her on. They came to another side road leading up a winding path to a two-story stone house set on a hill, surrounded by stone walls and thick trees. The place looked and felt ancient but was clean and well maintained. Beyond, the city sprawled out around them past the walls. "What is this place?"

"It belongs to the royal family. It used to be the official residence, but someone decided to move closer to the city center and made it fancier for visiting diplomats," he said, reaching for a rock on the ground. Below it, hidden in a hole, sat a brass key. "This is the house my parents stay in when they come, and I've always preferred it too, but we don't keep it staffed. There will be no one here but us."

He kept the key when he unlocked the door and led her inside, closing and locking the door behind them. Inside was just as tidy as the outside; someone had clearly been in to clean regularly. He led her by the hand through the foyer and down a short hallway to a dining room, but continued through to the kitchen on the other side. He absently waved a hand at the lanterns about the room and dragon-fire flared to life.

"I'm not sure if there will be anything left in the cupboards, but I can go over to the inn and get us some food," he said, dropping her hand as he began to search the cupboards. She turned to check the ice chest but found it was warm, the ice had been removed.

"Some old hardtack and jerky that I'm not brave enough to eat. What are you in the mood for? You need to eat again to keep up your strength after today," Zavier returned from the cupboard and ran his hands up her arms. She met his golden eyes with a smile.

"I'm really not very hungry... I was fed back at the meeting house before I came outside."

He shook his head, "You used too much energy today healing those people. If you don't eat more, and then rest, you may not feel well tomorrow. I've seen Bonded make themselves ill by not taking care of their energy levels." His eyes were filled with genuine concern that absolutely ripped her heart to shreds.

"Alright, I'll eat. Don't go to any elaborate trouble on my account, though," she added, wagging her finger at him. He grabbed her finger and kissed it, not breaking eye contact with her.

"I won't. I'll be back very soon." He leaned in and gently kissed her lips, almost as if he were afraid she would push him away. "There's a bath upstairs, why don't you go up and relax?" She nodded. Yes, a bath did sound delightful.

He showed her where the stairs were and gave directions to the best bathing room, because of course there was more than one. Even after several days in a literal palace, the place felt opulent, especially when she thought of her little home in Ocrans. Minnie lit the lamps up the stairs and climbed to the second floor. Stopping at a window, she saw Zavier hurry down the winding path. For a moment, she wondered if he planned to return. Doubt flickered through her mind and she huddled in on herself. Had she gone too far earlier, when they hid together beside Maurgen? Would the dragon hear her concerns?

"Of course I hear them, and you're being ridiculous."

"I am?"

"You are. Go take your bath, he'll be back soon."

She didn't reply further, instead she turned down the hallway to the furthest room on the right, just as Zavier had suggested. Opening the door, she used her magic to light the lamps and gasped. A massive four-poster bed hung with curtains dominated the room, thick blankets that appeared to be fairly fresh folded at the foot of the mattress. Several chests lay scattered around the room, as well as a chest of drawers, a wardrobe, and a vanity with a gilt-framed mirror. To the side of the hearth, a small hallway led down a short flight of steps to the bathing room. She lit candles with dragon-fire as she entered.

They hadn't brought their packs with them, so as she stripped off her clothes she folded and placed them on the counter beside a stack of towels. Thankfully, she'd managed to avoid anyone throwing up on her, but all her clothes reeked of blood and illness. She wrinkled her nose. Oh well, at least she could clean her hair and body. And wash her boots, apparently she had stepped in something and they were splattered. She grabbed the oldest looking towel, filled a basin from the pump in the sink, and scrubbed the filth. Tossing the towel to the corner, her boots under the sink, she turned around to examine the bathtub.

It was massive. Steps led up to the tub for easier entry and there were benches spaced around the tub itself for her to sit down. She had to use a pump to fill the tub, and her own magic to heat the water, but neither took very long. She found she could easily stretch out her legs and have foot room to spare, unlike their little tub at home. Most people in Ocrans bathed in the sea, and used a laundry basin in the winter, barely large enough to sit down in, let alone stretch. She decided she could easily get used to such luxuries.

With a towel behind her neck and arms draped over the rim of the tub, candlelight flickering around her and near scalding water to soak in, she wasn't surprised that she nearly fell asleep. She sat up and reached for a bar of a woodsy scented soap and small cloth and began to scrub herself.

She was just rinsing her hair a second time when she heard the door close downstairs. She froze, water dripping everywhere, and listened hard.

"It's Zavier, you're safe. I'm about to land nearby and I have your packs with me."

Blowing out a relieved breath, she gathered up her hair and twisted to wring out the extra water, knotting it on top of her head. She pulled the plug of the tub and climbed out, grabbing several towels. She scrunched one towel into her curls to soak away the water, then twisted the mass into a rough knot on top of her head. She'd just tucked the end of the second towel under itself around her chest when she heard footsteps climbing the stairs.

"I hope fish is alright, it's freshly caught and nicely spiced. Not salted!" She could hear him in the other room setting things down on a dresser. A door opened and there was movement as something was dragged across the floor. She debated getting dressed... but she really wanted fresh clothes now that Maurgen had them so close, and the aroma of food was suddenly too much. Her stomach gurgled loudly. Fuck it, she thought, reminding herself that she was done hiding. She climbed the short stairs to the bedroom.

He'd pulled a table and two chairs into the room and set them before the hearth, which was now blazing merrily. Their packs leaned against the foot of the bed, and Zavier ladled soup into two bowls. Mugs of cider accompanied fresh bread, two plates of fish, and assorted vegetables. "Where did you get all this?" She asked in wonder. He didn't look up as he answered, pulling another jug of cider from the basket he carried.

"I flew over to the tavern we were supposed to stay at. They had more than enough food for all of us, so they packed us a basket. There should be butter in here too, and salt they assured me was safe, plus enough for breakfast tomorrow morning." After he'd set everything on the table, he turned and looked up at her. His eyes grew wide, raking over her body from the damp, tangled curls piled in a messy knot atop her head, across her towel covered bosom, and down to the long expanse of copper leg. The towel had been wrapped around her, but it barely covered her ass because her torso was so long.

"I'm really too tall for a woman..." she said, gripping the towel between her breasts and self-consciously tugging the bottom down. He stepped over to her and pulled her hands away, bringing them to his lips and kissing her fingers.

"You aren't too anything, except maybe too perfect for words." He kissed her forehead, and as he continued speaking, pressed kisses across her cheeks and lips. "Too beautiful. Too kind. Too compassionate. Too damned good for any mortal man." She wrapped her arms around his neck to kiss him deeper, nipping at his lips with a smile.

He finally broke away with a groan into her damp hair. "We have to eat. Let me get you a robe or something before I rip that towel off of you." He crossed to the wardrobe and pulled out a thin dressing gown decorated with embroidered roses. He held it up so she could slip her arms through the sleeves and wrap it tight across her chest. When he turned back to their table, she shimmied out of the towel and tossed it to a corner, quickly tying the sash of the robe tight so she wouldn't flash.

He pulled her chair out and she thanked him as she sat. They ate quickly and quietly, only saying things such as "pass the bread" for several minutes; however, their eyes met constantly. Lust flickered in his eyes as he watched her lick a dollop of butter from her fingertips. She smiled and did it again.

"Did you hear any news while you were out?" She asked, eager to know before either of them became too distracted.

Zavier took a deep breath, his light-hearted mood fading. "No sickness in Amthryn, it seems they had some kind of problem and didn't actually open the salt shipment until after our message got to them. There were two more deaths here, people living alone who were sick and no one knew. I issued an order for all citizens to check on their neighbors."

"That's not terrible. I feel like we saw over a thousand people today, but I know that can't be right."

"You've underestimated," he replied, heaving another sigh. "One of the women helping at the meeting house thought to record the names of everyone

229

who came in today. There were one thousand and ninety four total who came in for healing."

Her mouth dropped open. She stared for several long seconds before she realized what she was doing, and snapped her mouth shut. Over one thousand people ill, plus hundreds who had died, many of whom were currently unidentified. She felt tears stinging at her eyes and looked down. So many loved ones.

Zavier came to her side, kneeling beside her chair and pulling her around to face him. "There is nothing more we could have done. Without you, this would have continued to spread until the poison either infected or killed everyone, or became so thin it was no longer dangerous. Only the Fates know which would have happened, or if anyone would have survived. But you figured it out, Minnie. You saved them."

She nodded, but didn't answer for a long moment. The only thing she wanted to say was something completely selfish. Seconds ticked by, agonizingly slow. She couldn't stand it. Almost too softly to hear, she whispered, "I loved when you called me 'Mina.' I don't even know why you did, but it made me feel wonderful."

He leaned into her, breathing the fresh flowery scent along her skin. "It's how I've thought of you in my mind since the first night we met, though I have zero right to think of you that way. I've longed to take you in my arms and call you mine, ever since I saw you standing up to your knees in the river."

She interrupted him with a kiss. He rose higher on his knees, pressing into her with a low groan. His arms snaked around her waist to pull her close. Minnie lifted her hands to his neck, twisting her fingers into his hair. She felt the tie to her robe loosen and begin to slip down her shoulders, but it didn't matter. Breathless, she broke the kiss and tried to push him backward. She wanted to pin him to the wooden floor, but he firmly stopped her.

"Please believe me when I say I want nothing more than to continue this, but I also want to bathe, and we both need to sleep. Especially you, your cheeks are still pale."

She growled and tried to resume kissing him, but he held her arms in her lap. "Please, Mina. I said I wouldn't ask for anything, but will you let me wash up and then hold you tonight? Will you rest?"

Damn him and his logical concern for her health and well-being. Truth be told, she was as exhausted as she was aroused. With a shock, she realized that she had healed at least one third, possibly as many as half of the people who had come to them today. No wonder she was tired, she was lucky to still be standing.

"Oh, of course. You go wash, I'll clean up our dinner mess. I'm sorry for being so pushy—"

"Never apologize for wanting me, my Mina. The Fates know I want you, but I'd never forgive myself for letting something happen to you." His golden eyes shone in the firelight, once again full of concern for her health.

She smiled and nudged him to get moving. "Go on, you smell. I'll be waiting for you." Zavier leaned down for one last lingering kiss before leaving for the bathing room.

After tidying the table and stacking dishes, Minnie shook out the blankets and laid one over the bed, plumped up pillows, combed out and braided her hair, and changed from the robe to a light cotton nightshirt. By the time she was dressed, Zavier had returned from his bath wearing nothing but low-slung pants. His skin glowed in the firelight, and she had to resist the urge to cross the room to him and run her hands down the planes of his chest. He gave her a heated look that she was sure matched her own. Taking a deep breath, she doused the magic keeping the lanterns burning, and climbed into the bed. Zavier had lit a real fire in the hearth, and before he joined her in bed he had put the grate up to keep the fire from escaping.

Zavier lay stiffly beside her, as if he wasn't sure if he was allowed to snuggle up to her. Minnie decided to be brave once again and rolled toward him, resting her head on his chest and curling an arm around him. He slid an arm under her, kissing the top of her head.

They lay together for several minutes, but a burning desire wouldn't leave Minnie's mind. She clenched her thighs together and tried counting dragons, she tried listing herbs. Finally, she couldn't stand it. Pushing up on her arms, she looked up at Zavier, surprised to see he was still awake too.

"Everything alright, Mina?" he asked quietly.

"No... not really..." She hesitated, suddenly doubtful again. Maurgen grumbled in her head, calling her a coward, so she mentally gathered herself. "I... I want you too badly, I can't sleep. Will you... please touch me?"

A look of pain mixed with desire crossed his face, and she knew he was debating with himself about making her sleep or doing as she asked. She leaned into him, kissing his chin scar, whispering, "I can do it myself, if you don't want to—"

With a growl, he rolled her on to her back, running a hand up her thigh. She hadn't put on undergarments, so there was nothing to bar his searching fingers from finding her moist heat. She eagerly spread her thighs, clenching her fingers in the bedding in anticipation. He stroked a single digit through her center, teasing the bundle of nerves at her apex. His golden eyes glinted and almost seemed to glow as he watched her face.

So slowly she almost cried at the torture, he slid one finger into her, groaning alongside her at the feeling. She was wet and eager, but so damned tight around him. After several slow strokes, he added another finger, curling them up against her walls. She threw her head back and gasped for breath around a moan. Using his thumb to rub small circles over her clit, he increased his pace with his hand until she cried out as she climaxed. He slowed, drawing out her pleasure until she begged him to stop.

With a gentle kiss, Zavier left to wash his hands and fetch a damp rag that he used to clean her up. Without a word, he helped adjust her shirt back down around her hips, climbed back into bed, and wrapped his arms around her.

They were asleep within minutes.

Twenty-Four

Zavier

B RIGHT SUNLIGHT STREAMED ACROSS their bed, slowly waking Zavier. He rolled away from the window, burying his face in Minnie's upper back, loose strands of her braided hair tickling his nose. This felt right, waking up beside her. What magic had she weaved around him, that he'd fallen for her so completely in just a matter of days? He slipped an arm around her waist to hold her close to him, releasing a contented sigh.

He'd bathed in record time the night before, eager to curl up beside her. She had surprised him by begging for him to touch her. He'd given in, unable to say no to her for long, and the sounds of her pleasure had filled his dreams all night.

"Are you finally awake?" Maurgen demanded. An image flash showed Maurgen flying low over the swampy land to the west of Saltstone in pursuit of a deer. A burst of flame, a swift crunch of jaws, and the deer was dead.

"Not really. Has there been any change in the city?"

"Zahite says that Jarn said there was nothing to report. No new sickness, but the Bonded sent after the shipments have all returned bearing the salt. We must still discover who did this, but we are no longer required here. City officials have begun delivering the assistance packages Beltak arranged on your order."

"That's all very good to hear!"

"Vera is close to mating. If you want to make it to the Rising on time, we need to go today."

The very idea of soaring across the ocean with Minnie in his arms brought a smile to his lips. Unfortunately, they'd still need to contend with his little brother. Zavier had promised to let him fly to Dragon Isle on his own, but if they had to get there quickly, he may not have the strength to keep up.

Putting the problem aside for now, he questioned Maurgen, *"Do you plan to fly in the mating?"*

"No, not this time. For what may be Vera's final flight, we have decided we will not give Oranth too much competition. He has been her mate since the tragedy, we will not disturb that."

"Yet she doesn't declare the mating off limits? She lets others fly?"

"Of course. If Oranth weren't worthy of her, someone else would catch her instead, and that would improve our bloodlines. Anyway, I've been with you two-legs for too long. The idea of mating with my mother is odd after so much time with you."

There was a gentle chiding in that thought, despite it being entirely Maurgen's decision to stay full time near Zavier. Many dragon partners visited only occasionally and chose to remain on Dragon Isle. They didn't see familial relationships the same way, so it wasn't entirely uncommon for hatchlings to fly in their mothers' or siblings' mating flights.

"I will be conserving my strength. Minnie's dragon is well past the age when dragons fly to mate, and I suspect that when she and Minnie finally meet, it will trigger her mating lust in full force. I intend for no one but myself to sire her clutches."

That surprised Zavier, and he took a long minute to think it over. Maurgen wasn't wrong. Wild dragon females mated around their fifth year, and every few years after that. Bonded dragons wouldn't mate until their partner had reached sexual maturity. To his knowledge, no dragon had ever failed to find their partner in childhood, but it was safe to assume that she wouldn't mate without the bond between them being completed.

"Do you know where she is? Why she didn't find Minnie like she should have?"

Maurgen's mental voice sounded thicker, muffled as if he were mentally eating as well as physically. *"I know nothing for sure. I reached out to some dragons that remembered me, and there are rumors. That she is still south of Dragon Isle, that she flew to the far north of the Stone Mountains, and even that she's flown to the Human continent of Shaesan. All we know for sure is that no one has seen Vera's heir in many years. But I do know she is waiting for Minnie. She has to be. It's our nature."*

Zavier's heart ached for the un-Bonded pair. *"Then let's find them so they can be together. We're getting up. Nothing else will distract us, we must find her."*

Running a hand up Minnie's arm, he quietly whispered her name. "Minnie, wake up. We're going to Dragon Isle today." She grumbled in her sleep and turned toward him, but didn't open her eyes. "Come on, beautiful, it's time to wake up."

Twenty-Five

Minnie

D REAMLIKE VISIONS FILLED HER mind.

A dragon screamed overhead. She looked up and saw the russet female leading dozens of males in a mating flight. The land shifted, crossing the vast lake and over a barren, geyser-filled valley between mountain ranges. Across a strip of ocean to an island surrounded by waves. A steel building guarded by Humans sat in the middle of a compound of smaller buildings. The steel frame shook as a terrified roar penetrated the still morning air.

"Help me. You're the only one who can save me."

She woke with a startled gasp. Zavier hovered over her, his disheveled hair falling into his worried eyes.

"You wouldn't wake up, is everything alright?" He lifted a hand to her face and stroked his thumb over her cheek.

Shaking her head, Minnie struggled to remember everything from the dream. This one was unlike any she'd had before. "My bag, I need my bag. The journal. Help me find it?" She tore at the covers, trying to untangle herself from the blanket.

"Slow down, we'll get it. Will you tell me what's going on?" Zavier left the bed and picked up her pack, placing it on the bed for her. She snatched at it, yanking the leather ties and only succeeding in tightening them further. She growled in frustration.

"Here, let me, please," he gently moved her hands from the pack and untied it easily. Minnie took a deep breath, steadying herself.

"Sometimes, not very often, I have dreams that are real. Become real, I mean. A few days ago, the day I came to Hatherus, I saw a vision of the warehouse, and the captain vomiting. I watched his ship being towed to sea and set on fire. I write down every dream I have and what I see, just in case they start coming true."

Zavier handed her the small leather bound-book without a word. Thumbing through the pages to the latest entries, she read them to herself quickly.

"I had one dream while in Hatherus that I thought was just a dream, but I wrote it down anyway. Now I'm not so sure. I've been seeing a dark green dragon a lot lately. Look at this," she leaned into him to show him the book, pointing to the entry from several mornings ago. "A green dragon and a gold dragon. Actually... I think the gold dragon was Maurgen. He certainly looked big enough. A russet dragon... I don't know who that would be."

"Vera."

"Vera, probably," Zavier and Maurgen said at the same time. "Especially as you say she was seen flying a lot of males. Who is this?" He touched the page just below a sentence that read, "Golden eyed man dies, possible head injury?"

Minnie closed her eyes and conjured the image as best she could remember. She knew the man wasn't Zavier, but she wasn't sure who... The only other man she'd seen with eyes similar to him had been his father, Taurak, but his eyes were much darker, more brown with gold. Zavier's were so unique...

She looked up and met those golden eyes. "I think... it might have been... Caddoc. His eyes are also gold, aren't they? Darker than yours, more like your father's, but still fairly gold?"

Zavier was nodding. "Yes, I'd say so. You only met him that first night, didn't you?"

"Yes, but I didn't really study his face. I think it might be him," she finished softly, worried.

"How accurate are your visions?" He rubbed his hands up her arms in an attempt to comfort them both.

"It's hit or miss, to be honest. Sometimes everything comes true, sometimes it happens in a way I don't expect." She drew in a deep breath and huffed it out. "And sometimes it's completely wrong, like it was a warning of what could come. There's never any way of knowing which way it will go."

Zavier nodded again. "Greta has said the same, that she's never sure what might actually happen. So, we don't panic over what could be nothing. Half of this vision came true yesterday. There could be more to come. What did you see this morning?"

She tilted her head as she thought, half closing her eyes to concentrate. "The mating flight, that same russet dragon. But then the land seemed to... move. Not like an earthquake, more like how you see it when you're flying across, but sped up. I saw mountains, then a huge flat area with water spouts and steam. More mountains, then it gets fuzzy, almost like there is fog or it's too far away."

Zavier wrote everything she said down as she spoke, for which she was grateful. She gripped her own hands to stop their trembling. "I was in the middle of the ocean, but then there was an island. Very bare, almost like the island was dead or dying. A tall building made of gray metal, nothing like what we build here. There was a roar, a dragon I think, and the building shook. I heard a voice begging for me to help her."

Zavier met her eyes. Outside, they heard Maurgen rumble as he stretched his wings. *"We need to go. Now."*

"He's right. We need to get you to the dragons. If that green dragon you saw is yours, it sounds like she's in trouble." He paused, then cupped her cheek and met her eyes. "We will find her. I swear it." Zavier kissed her lightly, then stepped away to pick up their bags. He pulled clothes from the pack and handed them to her. Taking them on reflex, Minnie frowned.

"Do we really think that's my dragon?" she asked.

"It would make sense," Maurgen said as Zavier pulled a tunic over his bare chest. *"I was telling Zavier, I found a dragon on the Isle that remembered me. Dragon memories are sparse when we aren't with our Humans. No one can remember the last time your dragon was on the Isle. It was assumed she flew to find you, but we know that obviously isn't what happened."*

Too stunned to reply, Minnie dressed in fresh travel clothes and repacked her rucksack. "We'll eat in the air, let's get over to the inn," Zavier said, fully dressed now. He scooped up the basket that had held their food. There was a rustle and thump from outside as they descended the stairs and left through the front door, Zavier locking it again behind them. Maurgen waited impatiently, tucked as tightly as he could get between buildings. A tree half leaned over from where his rump pushed against it, the ground groaning in effort not to release the roots.

Minnie clambered aboard Maurgen, gripping the ridge in front of her as she settled into the hollow at his shoulders. Zavier expertly climbed up behind her. Maurgen sprang from the ground, his rear claws digging furrows in the dirt. He glided across part of the city, to the large empty square in front of the meeting hall from the night before.

Zavier leaped to the ground calling orders, leaving Minnie to scramble down after. Within a couple of minutes, every Bonded who had accompanied them to Saltstone had gathered around their prince.

"Maurgen says Vera is likely to rise tonight or tomorrow morning. From this moment on, you are all dismissed to enjoy the Thunder's Rising and festivities in whatever capacity you wish. Safe flight!" Around him the guards cheered, several rubbing their hands together with eager anticipation of what was to come. Jarn, the only one to not cheer, stepped into Zavier for a whispered conversation.

"Min, will you fly with us? We're going to stick together across the sea's strong air current," Adaline asked her, indicating her sister and Lavender. "You've not been to Dragon Isle before, have you?"

"No, I haven't been before," she replied "I've promised to fly with Prince Zavier today, but thank you for the offer."

"Alright, we'll have breakfast and then be off," Coraline replied, nodding back toward the busy common room inside the inn. She leaned in to whisper something to her sister.

Adaline shook her head, whispering loud enough for Minnie to hear, "Nothing official, but he hasn't taken his eyes off of her since we arrived. Anyone can see he's crazy about..."

Minnie frowned as they left. Lavender, who hadn't followed right away, reached out and took her hand. "I think they're just curious. Prince Zavier has never shown such interest in any woman before, and some of the girls had hoped they were being chosen as a bride. But don't fret about those two, they aren't vicious like those other girls were."

"Lavender..." Minnie began, unsure what she should say. She couldn't confirm something that wasn't true, but she couldn't bring herself to deny her growing feelings for Zavier.

"Enjoy yourself, Min. We'll see you on Dragon Isle!"

As Lavender went inside, Minnie turned to look for Zavier and Branton. They stood beside Maurgen, talking.

"We need to fly quickly, and I don't know that you have the strength to keep up this time," Zavier was saying to his irritated brother.

"You promised, Zave. I am more than old enough, you can't baby me forever. I'm flying on my own." The teenager had a stubborn set to his shoulders that made him look more like his father than any son had a right to look.

Minnie hesitated. She had no business involving herself, but at a mental nudge from Maurgen she stepped up. "Let him fly, we will be with him. If he falters, one of us can catch him. Truth be told, if the current is as strong as I've heard, I may need to be rescued. I haven't had a lot of long distance practice."

Branton turned hopeful eyes to Zavier, who looked almost annoyed with Minnie. However, he capitulated and nodded his agreement. Branton let out a whoop.

"There are too many of us here to all shift, so we need to spread out. Get your pack, then load up on Maurgen and he'll take you outside the city," Zavier instructed. Branton raced back to his room to grab his belongings.

From the corner of her eye, Minnie saw Jarn and the other guards disappearing into the inn. Frowning, she said to Zavier, "You've ditched your bodyguards again, I thought they were supposed to always be with you?"

Zavier nodded. "They usually are, but we are usually in foreign territory, too. Truthfully, he was pissed that I disappeared without letting him know where I was last night. The only reason he's allowing Branton and I to fly on our own today is that I pulled rank on him, and we're going somewhere completely safe from assassins. I also pointed out that if we're hurt, we have you with us. In his mind, after what you did yesterday, you can heal anything."

Her eyes wide in surprise, Minnie wasn't sure what to say to that. The guards trusted her that much? Should she insist that a guard come with them anyway? What if something did happen and she failed to protect or heal one of the princes? What if—

"Here, let me have your pack and I'll rig the straps to Maurgen's chest. He'll carry our things for us to lessen the load on you," Zavier held a hand out to Minnie for her bag. Startled, she handed it to him, and shook off the nagging doubt that filled her.

"That's awfully sweet of him to volunteer. Thank you, Maurgen," she teased, rubbing the bridge of Maurgen's nose.

"You're most welcome," the dragon replied, nuzzling against her. Unfortunately, he was so large even the slightest nudge knocked her off balance and she stumbled into Zavier. He caught her around her

243

waist and steadied her with strong arms. She looked up into his bright golden eyes. Fragments of memory from the previous evening flew through her mind. His face, every time he looked at her, filled with heat. Lust, desire, yes, but something more. He looked at her like she was his entire world, and it showed in his eyes. As she gazed up at him, she felt the same emotion fill her own. He was rapidly becoming everything to her.

Branton reappeared at that moment with his rucksack and a handful of toast. Zavier steadied her on her feet and took the bags. He strung them together between Maurgen's front legs, tight to his chest. Minnie and Branton climbed to his back, both slow and almost hesitant to hurt the giant beast. Zavier followed easily, instructing them to hold on to each other and the ridge of Maurgen's neck. The dragon leaped into the air.

They flew south and east toward the coast, crossing over Trader's Bay and the skeletal remains of several ships that had been set ablaze yesterday. They landed again as soon as they had enough solid ground and free space for several massive dragons. Everyone disembarked as soon as Maurgen had settled onto the ground.

"Now Brant, we won't be able to speak in the air, so if you need help tell Maurgen, he'll be listening. Don't act tough and stubborn, you won't win any points with us or Father if you wear yourself out crossing the sea!" Zavier reminded his brother.

Branton rolled his eyes. "I promise to ask for help if I get tired. Can we go now?"

"That goes for you, too." Maurgen reminded Minnie softly.

244

"Oh don't worry, I'll ask if I need help. My longest flight was from Ocrans to Hatherus." She sounded nervous even to herself.

"Yes, we can go now," Zavier sighed and shook his head, but he was smiling at his little brother.

"Time to shift!" Branton crowed, running away from the others to open space. It took him several long seconds, but his body began the shift with wings erupting from his back. Bronze hide replaced his tanned skin, arms and legs becoming muscled paws tipped in dagger-like claws. He let out a roar as he settled his new shape, stretching out his wings and neck. He was much smaller than Maurgen, still ungainly with youth.

Minnie walked away from them as well, reaching within herself for the familiar power. The process was faster, almost seamless as she grew in size and changed her skin. Stretching out her muscles and reacquainting herself with the much larger form, she looked back at Zavier.

He had shifted as well, his golden body nearly the same size as Maurgen. His left side faced Minnie and she saw that the long chin scar was much more prominent now than when he was humanoid. It stretched along the edge of his jaw, clearly marking where Caddoc had caught him with his claws during their fight.

Maurgen touched the minds of the others to ensure they were ready to go, and led them all into the air. Minnie stayed safely behind him, trusting his instincts and flight knowledge. They climbed for several minutes, much higher than she had ever been on her own, until they found an air current flowing in the direction they wanted. By the time they settled in for distance flying, they had passed the cliffs that marked the entrance to Trader's Bay.

In the distance to the east, she could see the small island reefs that dotted the coastline.

Ahead of them lay hundreds of miles of open ocean. Beyond that, Dragon Isle. She'd studied the only map in the Elder's house back in Ocrans. There had been one in Taurak's office in Hatherus, but she hadn't had the time to really look at it. She had seen, however, that Dragon Isle was no island.

"Why is it called Dragon Isle?" she asked Maurgen as they flew.

"That's how we want it. If people think it's small, they won't be interested in it," came the reply, as if that were the most obvious answer ever.

"But it's partly drawn on the maps, even incomplete it's huge!"

"The only people capable of mapping the continent are dragon-bonded, and every one of them has agreed to keep the true size hidden from the general populace. It's worried that people would get greedy and want to take land from the dragons, and get killed in the attempt."

"That's why the whole continent isn't mapped?" she asked.

"Partly. There's an old magic at work that prevents anything south of Titan Lake from being drawn out. It's also nearly impossible to even see the shape of the land from high in the air because of the weather. Parts of the continent are always covered in storm clouds, others have constant volcanic ash in the air."

Minnie fell silent thinking all that over. She hoped she would get a chance to explore while she was on Dragon Isle, which brought her right back to worrying about her vision from that morning.

"Do Bonded partners always match? Like you and Zavier being gold?"

"No, not always. There's some theory that the powerful are matched, or that those who are matched have a Fat-

ed mate somewhere in the world, but it's not something anyone has ever proved," he explained. He projected images to her of other Bonded pairs, showing that out of hundreds, only a few dozen matched their partners.

"What's interesting to me is that the Bonded pair usually share a feature as well as their color. Like Zavier and I share golden eyes as well as my hide and his hair. Another pair, Malcolm and Syrsil, are almost the same earth-brown of his skin. And to head off your next question, Syrsil is female, we aren't always bonded by gender or sexual preference."

They fell silent as Minnie thought all that over. She wondered if she would match her partner, then realized, if the deep green dragon of her vision was her partner, then she was the same shade as Minnie's eyes were. Worry for the unknown dragon filled her again.

Twenty-Six

Zavier

Z AVIER FLEW BEHIND MINNIE and Branton in order to keep an eye on them both. So far Branton flew well, using the tricks he had been taught over the previous winter to save his strength. Minnie didn't seem to know much more than the basics of long distance flight and he resolved to teach her as soon as there was time. He wished he could speak to her while they flew; relaying conversation through Maurgen would be rather awkward.

Hours passed. Branton began to falter in the air but stubbornly continued on. Zavier was about to say something through Maurgen when the bigger dragon suddenly dipped down and slowed until he was below Brant. With precise movements of his wings, Maurgen lifted himself until he was just under Brant and the boy could rest on his back. Ripples danced down his exhausted body as he shifted his skin back to his humanoid form.

"He's fine, he'll sleep and be well rested when we arrive," Maurgen assured his partner. Zavier sent his gratitude down their mental link.

With Branton safe, Zavier soared closer to Minnie. She looked over at him, and he swore there was a smile on her draconic face. She had more angled cheekbones, and her two horns had more of a spiral than most other females. She dove for the sea below them, wings pinned along her back. Zavier followed her. Above them, Maurgen slowed his speed and looped back, careful not to dislodge his passenger. *"Continue on, we won't be far behind. I think she wants to see the ocean up close."*

"Be careful of the sea creatures, some are big enough in this part of the water to cause some damage even to us," Maurgen warned as he resumed his flight.

Zavier gave him a mental salute and refocused his attention on Minnie. She was nearing the water now, and he admired the contrast of her dark green hide against the deep blue of the sea. He flew alongside her and they both dragged their paws through the water. She chuffed, a sound suspiciously like a laugh. They played in the water as they flew, splashing each other back and forth.

Twenty-Seven

Minnie

MINNIE DESPERATELY WANTED TO dive into the water and swim, but Maurgen's cautious warning about sea monsters kept her airborne. Movement from the corner of her eye made her back-wing to a halt, hovering over the water. Sleek bodies leaped out below them, their gray hides glistening in the sunlight. Huffing a sigh of relief that they were only dolphins, she resumed her flight, climbing higher. She waited until Zavier was nearby and they were high enough that he would have time to react, then pulled her power around her and let her skin shift back to her humanoid body. As she began to fall, she gathered the winds around her to slow her descent and lessen the impact as Zavier caught her on his back.

He wasn't as wide or stocky as Maurgen. She found she fit a bit easier in the hollow between neck and back as she settled into her place. She thumped him on the neck twice to indicate she was safe. He changed his flight angle to gain altitude again and resume their flight to Dragon Isle. Minnie stretched along his neck and wrapped her arms around him, content to watch the ocean pass as they flew. Much like when she was in his arms, she felt safe and secure on his back.

Time passed quickly on the massive oceanic air current, and by afternoon the horizon had darkened to the towering cliffs that encompassed Dragon Isle.

"How was the coastline formed? It's completely sheer!" Minnie asked Maurgen as they neared the cliffs.

"Ancient dragons carved it from the rock of the earth using their magic and claws. We didn't want anyone able to land here by ship. The only way to reach Dragon Isle is by air."

"That's amazing..."

Maurgen and Zavier flew side by side as they approached land. Minnie leaned dangerously over Zavier's shoulder trying to see everything on the ground. They were whizzing along so quickly it was all a blur. The setting sun glinted on a body of water so large she thought it was the ocean again, and she wondered if her eyes were playing tricks on her.

"Your eyes are fine, that is Titan Lake."

"Titan Lake is aptly named!" she said to Maurgen, in complete awe.

"It is, though most of us refer to this area as the Caldera. The first dragon-bonded to try and map the island gave places names, but other than the lakes and Hatchery we rarely use them."

"Hatchery?"

"The image you saw in your bedroom in Hatherus. The Hatchery is the volcano that Vyn and her mate hollowed out for her second clutch, and where all dragon-bonded clutches are hatched." He sounded almost distracted

251

and Minnie saw he was craning his head about as they flew.

"Looking for someone?"

"Just seeing who is here, it's been a very long time since I've returned."

There were dragons everywhere. There was over a mile of cleared land mixed with sandy beach stretching away from the water's edge, before the jungle took over again. Thousands of dragons sprawled in the dying sunlight, basking on baked rocks, swimming in the water, or flying aerial acrobatics overhead. From this distance, she couldn't see a single humanoid shape.

"I'm sure there is someone still on two legs down below, but for the most part the Bonded remain as dragons while here." Maurgen had picked up on her thoughts again, preemptively answering another question. Minnie smiled to herself.

Zavier spiraled down toward a clearing in the jungle, well away from the hubbub at the lake shore. Maurgen followed, both taking care not to descend too quickly and dislodge their untethered passengers.

"We could have just shifted in the air and flown ourselves again," she grumbled.

Maurgen rumbled a laugh. *"Zavier said no, he was worried Branton wouldn't make the shift."*

She snorted. Protective older brother was a cute look on him, but he did take it a bit far sometimes.

Despite their caution, it didn't take long to descend and land in the clearing. Branton launched himself off of Maurgen before the dragon had even settled his wings. The instant the boy touched ground, Maurgen took off again, flying toward the lake.

252

Zavier tilted his shoulder for Minnie to slide to the jungle floor. She landed on squishy moss-like ground covered in leaves and stumbled on the uneven turf. Zavier's strong arms caught her from behind. He'd shifted to his Draconid form, with his golden wings spread out behind him.

"Thanks," she breathed, caught off guard by the swiftness of his transformation.

Oblivious to the pair, Branton looked around the clearing. To one side was a small cave half hidden in trees and trailing vines, and nearby lay a well-worn path in the direction of the lake.

"There are little shelters all around the forest, for anyone who chooses to sleep as a humanoid, or for..." Zavier cleared his throat, looking away from Minnie. He did not remove his arms from hers, instead he squeezed her gently as he looked to Branton.

"So long as you don't pick a fight with anyone, don't join a mating flight, and stay in contact with Maurgen, you can shift and go. Don't get into trouble, Father would murder me."

The younger prince whooped and jumped in the air, pumping his fist. He shifted to his bronze dragon form with far less effort than he had used this morning. Within seconds of shifting, he flew into the air toward the lake. Other than the sounds of the jungle around them, Minnie and Zavier stood together in silence.

Zavier squeezed her closer and nuzzled his nose into her braided hair. Minnie leaned her head back against his shoulder with a sigh. "I'd love nothing more than to hide away somewhere. However, we need to go find Vera and ask about your dragon."

Nodding, she turned in his arms. "Let's go." The words were barely out of her mouth when Zavier scooped her up in a cradle carry. Wings beating powerfully, he jumped upward and took to the air. She wondered if he even realized he was using air magic to make themselves lighter, or if it was something he did instinctively.

They found Vera only a few minutes later, stretched out on a rocky outcropping. Her russet muzzle was graying with age, but her yellow eyes were clear and bright as she watched them approach. Her mate lay below her, his dark brown hide almost blending with the darkening rock around them. Zavier landed them nearby and carefully lowered Minnie. Hand in hand, they walked up to the dragon pair and bowed low.

"Greetings, Vynar. I am Prince Zavier, bonded to Maurgen," he called to her in a loud, clear voice.

"Greetings, my child. I remember you well. Who is it you have brought with you, and why does she come before me in human-skin, not dragon?" Her voice felt rich and velvety smooth in her mind, Minnie thought, not unlike how Horth and Maurgen sounded, but with a distinctly feminine tone.

Zavier swept a hand toward Minnie with another small bow. "We have only just arrived, and came straight here to introduce ourselves."

"Greetings, Vynar," Minnie struggled to keep fear from her voice. "My name is Minnie, and I think that I am bonded to your daughter, the next Vynar. We've come to ask you where she is."

The old female sat up, staring at them. Confusion and a bit of fear radiated from her. *"What do you mean, 'where she is?' She told me she was leaving here to find you. She never arrived?"*

"No, Vynar, she's never come for me," Minnie confirmed sadly.

The mental roar of the mother's anguish became real as she finished speaking. A great jet of flame erupted from Vera's mouth into the air above them.

When she settled back to her position, she once again had control of her voice. *"When my daughter hatched, she conjured flames that filled the hatching cavern and the surrounding hallways. My mate was killed, and my Bonded, Caryn, was caught in the blast. She was injured so badly we were unable to fully heal her, and she remains in a great deal of pain to this day. The dragon elders feared that until my daughter's power was under control, she might kill herself and me, leaving us without a Vynar. For the safety of all, my daughter was taken to a secluded place by other dragons and their Bonded to be trained."*

A deep sense of sorrow filled Minnie as they listened, and she knew that whatever else Vera felt, she deeply regretted all that had transpired. Maurgen had said dragons typically weren't very maternal, but it seemed things were different when it came to the Vynar and her heir.

Vera continued her story after a long pause. *"She returned after nearly a decade. Our history tells us that sometimes the power collides with a dragon's natural abilities in those that are particularly strong and it can be difficult to master, but almost ten years was unheard of. Not long after she returned, she decided to fly north to find her Bonded. We have not seen her since."*

Minnie and Zavier shared a stunned look. Before they could say anything, Vera spoke again. *"I am ashamed to say, it has escaped my attention that so many years have passed between then and now."*

The earth-colored male next to her lifted his head to touch his nose to hers. His mental voice sounded gruff when he spoke to them. *"It is not uncommon for Bonded dragons to stay away, or not speak to us for long*

*periods of time. Maurgen is one such example. A drag-
on's memory is a fickle thing, and while the Vynar holds
our history's memory within her, the everyday events
tend to be forgotten."*

Minnie bit her tongue. Her dragon had been
missing for over fifteen years and—

"Are you really telling us that she has been missing for seventeen years and no one thought to
check on her?!" Zavier had no issue giving voice
to his anger, Minnie was relieved to note, and
apparently was better at rapid math than she was.

The two dragons shared what she could only
describe as a chagrined look. Minnie swore vi-
olently and turned away from them, storming
across the pebbled beach. She didn't care that she
was being rude. She heard Zavier call for her and
ignored him. Letting her anger flow through her,
she shifted her body while moving and took to the
air without pausing. Her wings carried her over
the jungle, back toward the clearing they'd landed
in not long ago, and the relative peace it offered.
She landed roughly, shifting back again.

Strong arms wrapped around her once more
and she looked into the golden eyes of Zavier.
Anger still simmered in his features, but they
softened as he held her close.

"We'll find her. Can you sense anything now
that you're on Dragon Isle? There's old magic
here that might help you focus on your dragon."

She closed her eyes. With her shields down, she
felt the buzz of dragon magic all around her. At
her back, Zavier vibrated with immense rage that
was almost too distracting for her to ignore. One
by one she blocked out everything around her,
searching for something that felt...

There. A tiny thread of power wrapped around her heart. She tried to follow the thread, untangle it, but it was wrapped in and around, knotted, completely tangled and twisted within her core being. That must be her, Minnie thought.

The thread of power pulsed as Minnie mentally touched it, sent her own power down the line. There was a roar in her mind and Minnie stumbled, physically knocked off guard by the pain she felt.

Blood.

Slashes to her hide.

Holes in her wings.

Chains clamped to her legs, threaded through wounds in her wings, wrapped around her neck.

Worst of all, siphons placed around her, draining her magic from her body, rendering her incapable of moving or freeing herself.

So many years. So many escape attempts failed. Human wizards gleefully rubbing their hands together as they harnessed her power for their own uses.

"Help... me."

Minnie whirled around to face Zavier, tears sliding down her cheeks as she gasped for air. "We have to go. She's trapped!"

Twenty-Eight

Zavier

As Minnie told him what she had felt, Zavier frantically tried to decide what to do. They obviously had to find and rescue her dragon. Minnie was certainly not going alone, but if he and Maurgen went with her, who would keep an eye on Branton until Jarn and the others arrived?

Maurgen appeared above them, wind blowing across them as he hovered. Zavier pulled Minnie to the side to give the dragon space to land. She was gasping for breath, dangerously close to hyperventilating.

"I can hear her. She's so weak, doesn't know where she is, she's in so much pain—"

"Mina. You have to take deep breaths. Stop talking and just breathe with me." Zavier gave her a small shake of her shoulders to grab her attention. Staring into her eyes, he took in a deep breath, encouraging her to do the same. They held it for a few seconds, released, and repeated until she was calmer.

"There. We will find her, you have my word. I just need to—"

Maurgen snorted at the pair, turning his wedge-shaped head to face them. *"Branton will be fine here. I've asked a friend to keep track of him, so let the boy have some freedom. Now get on, we're leaving."* He crouched down as low as he could and offered his shoulder to the pair. Zavier helped Minnie onto the dragon's back before she could react. Within seconds of Zavier settling into position, Maurgen launched into the air.

Zavier held on tightly to Minnie, who had a death grip on the ridge ahead of her. The hollow between Maurgen's shoulder blades snugly fit the two riders, but they had to clench their legs tight to remain fixed without ropes to hold them in place. Making note to rig flying straps for them in the morning, Zavier wrapped his arms around Minnie and held on to the ridge as well.

"Did you get a sense of which direction she's in?" Maurgen asked as he leveled off. He'd set a course to fly directly over Titan Lake, but they could see storm clouds ahead of them. Below, dragons were gathering around the rocky outcropping where Vera lay.

Minnie mentally shook herself and did her best to get her thoughts in order and to stop panicking. Zavier had wrapped air around them when they took off, so she replied to Maurgen out loud as well as internally to include him in the conversation. It would be so much easier, she thought, if they could all speak mentally.

"I'm not completely sure, all I can feel is her pain. I'll try again."

She closed her eyes, trusting Zavier to keep her in place, and reached down the thread of power. It was easier this time, the dragon seemed to almost meet her halfway.

"I need to see what happened to you. Show me how you were captured," she thought, desperately hoping the dragon could respond.

There were no words, but images flashed through her mind again.

Half a dozen young male dragons chasing her, pinning her to the ground, urging her to rise in a mating flight. Someone saving her. She flew away, leaving the lake and everyone else behind. Vera catching up to her at the Hatchery as the moon rose. Saying goodbye to her mother, eager to find her Bonded partner.

She stood on a peninsula of land overlooking the ocean. Far behind her lay the giant volcano that housed the Hatchery. Ahead of her, miles and miles of open ocean, and somewhere to the north would be her life mate, the other half of her soul. She dove off the cliff, free falling until just before she hit water and spread her wings, pulling up and dragging paws through the rough waves. She soared over the dark sea without a single concern, nothing could possibly harm her. She was the most powerful dragon alive, she finally had her freedom from her teachers and her mother and she was on her way to find her soulmate. Everything was well in her world.

Pain pierced her side. Before she could react, her wing crumpled, the joint shattered. She fell into the water, roaring her fury. She wrapped the winds around her, creating an air pocket that lifted her from the waves. Blood dripped down her foreleg from the harpoon lodged in her shoulder. Something round flew past, barely missing her, and she knew it was another of the objects that had broken her wing. Flame erupted from her maw as she searched for her attackers.

A Human ship readied another cannonball and fired, hitting her squarely in the chest. She fell again. This time the Human magicians on board caught her before she could enter the water, using their magic to drag her to them. They tethered her to the ship and changed their course, sailing due east.

Minnie opened her eyes and wiped away tears.

"Did you see?" she whispered.

"Yes, and I know where she started her flight. The only thing we can do is trust that instinct will guide you to her once we get to the ocean." Maurgen's voice sounded rough and full of emotion. *"Settle in. It's several hours flight across the forest and Mist Lake, I'll have to stop there for a rest."* They began climbing higher to avoid the oncoming storm, and though the air was warm enough, Minnie shivered.

"Cold?" Zavier asked, leaning into her and rubbing her arms.

She shook her head, but rested her head against his chest. "Afraid. Confused. So much has gone wrong in so short a time... Although, I suppose it's more accurate to say things haven't been right since... well. Ever."

Zavier squeezed her and rested his cheek on hers. "It's certainly very complicated. I can't believe none of the dragons thought to check in with her. She's their next Vynar, for Fate's sake, how did they all manage to forget about her?"

Maurgen huffed beneath them, his angry thoughts reaching their minds. *"Dragons tend to be very 'out of sight, out of mind' and only deal with what is in front of them. We live so long that time moves oddly, especially for those that never leave Dragon Isle. Wild dragons not remember what they do not see daily."*

"That's no excuse," Zavier growled back. The rumble in his chest sent a zing through Minnie.

"No, it isn't. It's a failing, especially among the Bonded and more intelligent dragons, Vera in particular. I assure

you both, I will have things to say to Vera when all is resolved."

They flew on in silence for several minutes. Minnie sat as if frozen. She was too afraid to reach out to her dragon, worried she would tax all her strength and cause her harm. She didn't know what to do, what to say, or even what to think. Zavier's arms were securing her in more ways than one. She felt like she would fly away, breaking into a thousand pieces.

"Is there anything I can do?" Zavier asked her, murmuring quietly into her ear.

Nodding, she begged, "Please keep me distracted?"

There were plenty of ways he would like to distract her, but he hardly thought now was an appropriate time to spin her around and ravish her like he wanted to. Instead, he searched his mind for something he could talk about that might keep her mind quiet for a couple of hours until they landed for the night.

"Do you know much about the Fates?"

Minnie shook her head, adding, "Not really, theology wasn't something my educators were concerned with, I guess."

Pitching his voice low, he began telling the stories in a half-song tone, just as he had been taught them as a child when his mother tucked him in at night. As Zavier spoke, Minnie sat and listened to his melodic voice. She did her best to sink into the repetitive beat of Maurgen's wings, the soothing tone and rhythmic rumble of Zavier's voice.

Twenty-Nine

Zavier

T IME PASSED WITH AGONIZING slowness. They had out-flown the storm and avoided the air currents that flowed toward the impending deluge, so they reached the far western bank of Titan Lake within a few hours. The sun had long since set, and while the moon had risen, even their keen eyesight did them little good in the weak light of an almost empty moon. Maurgen landed them on the shore with a grunt, his wings twitching as he lowered himself to the ground.

"We should have waited until morning," Minnie cried as she rushed around to his head and cupped his massive cheek. "You're exhausted, you haven't strained a muscle have you?"

"No, I will be fine, I just need to rest. I will hunt quickly, and sleep. That will restore my strength." Maurgen replied, nuzzling his nose into her chest. Zavier undid the knots holding their baggage, noting that Branton's had already been removed. He must

have grabbed them while they visited Vera, Zavier thought. Maurgen leaped into the air with strong downbeats of his wings and glided over the forest.

Minnie turned to face Zavier. "I'll go catch us something for our dinner, we didn't bring anything more than a few meat rolls."

Before he could formulate a reply, her skin rippled and fur sprouted all over her body. She shrank down into a crouch, a feline with wide paws and tufted ears taking her place. She rubbed against his leg and nipped a hand before running off into the dense wooded area surrounding this portion of the lake. Zavier slung their bags to his back and began to follow her, when Maurgen reappeared over his head carrying a small deer.

Maurgen stretched out on the firm earth to eat his meal. The night was muggy, the sound of insects filled the air. Instead of setting up a camp near the dragon, Zavier searched for a suitable place to build a shelter. He discovered a massive fallen tree, part of its interior rotted out but the shell of the tree was still firm. Using his fire breath, Zavier cleared out any debris and insects from the small shelter. More of the interior burned away, but what was left seemed solid and, more importantly, secure. Digging through their packs, he found a bedroll and thin blanket in each. He spread out the rolls, then pinned one of the blankets to the entryway using a rock and some sticks as nails.

He had noticed thick, lush grasses growing around the lake shore, so Zavier gathered several armfuls and piled them inside one of the blankets to form a long pillow for them to share. Satisfied he had built a decent little shelter for the night, he set about finding kindling for a fire. Yes, they could create one with no fuel needed, but that would vanish when they slept. A breath of fire on real wood would burn all night and not use any of their energy.

Minnie returned less than an hour later carrying two rabbits. Zavier watched in awe and slight horror as she skinned, gutted, and cubed the meat as if it were an everyday occurrence. Well, for her it may well be, he chided himself. Most of the time he was fed well by servants and chefs. Even when they traveled, rations were provided for them, and they rarely had to hunt simply because travel by dragon was so much faster than by land. If he did hunt, he often just ate in dragon form, giving in to his baser urges and instincts.

Using two long sticks stripped of their twigs and bark to spit the meat, Minnie held them over their fire, turning occasionally, until they were ready to eat.

"If it weren't so dark I'd love to find some kind of vegetable to go with this, but it's still tasty," she said, nibbling on a cube of meat. Zavier enthusiastically agreed as he devoured his portion. When they were finished, they wrapped the remaining meat in large leaves and placed them near the fire under a rock to save for breakfast.

Through the trees, Zavier saw Maurgen was deeply asleep, his entire body gone limp. No sign of the deer remained.

"Should we leave him alone like that?" Minnie wondered as they turned toward their shelter.

"There aren't many predators on this continent, and none that would take on a dragon, sleeping or not. If there's danger, he'll wake up, or we'll wake him. I plan to keep watch while you and he rest, anyway," Zavier soothed her fear, lifting the curtain to their little nook inside the fallen tree.

She gave a small squeal in surprise at the cozy space, but after only a second to admire the nook, she turned around to scold him. "You can't stay up all night, you need to rest. Let me keep watch, and I can sleep while we fly tomorrow."

Smiling, he rubbed his hands down her arms and took her hands. "Not a chance, my lady. Maurgen will need you to reach your dragon and get directions. I'll have time to rest while we fly."

She started to argue again, but he silenced her with a finger to her lips. He lowered his head, nuzzling his nose against hers in a silent request for permission. She lifted her head to his and kissed him, sliding her hands under his shirt and up his back to pull him close. A low groan escaped her as his hand fisted itself in her hair beneath the braid.

Breaking the kiss with a wicked smile, she bent to unlace and remove her boots, tossing them aside. His eyes firmly fixed on her hands as she lifted the hem of her shirt over her head, dropping it near the boots. She ran her hands back up his chest, lifting his own shirt as she went.

Raking his pectoral muscles with her nails, she whispered, "We're completely alone for the very first time."

He cleared his throat, stammering out, "Y-yes, we are..."

She tugged his shirt up until he lifted his arms and she could remove it, dropping it near her own. His tanned skin gleamed in the light of a hovering fire globe above them.

"Are you sure you don't want to go to sleep? You've had an exhausting and stressful few days..." Zavier whispered, running his hands up her arms and down her back. His fingers slipped under the edge of the breastband she still wore.

"I'm quite sure." She nudged him downward with a firm press of hands on his shoulders until he was kneeling on the pallet he'd made. She pushed him again, forcing him to lean back on his hands with his legs straight ahead of him. She straddled his thighs, bringing her bound breasts within inches of his face. He sat forward to wrap his arms around her.

"Take the band off," she commanded in a hoarse whisper.

Fingers trembling, he unhooked the fastenings. As soon as the final hook was released, the band snapped free of his hand and fell to their laps, forgotten. Zavier cupped her waist almost reverently, slipping his thumbs under the curve of breast. His thoughts were an incoherent mess of desire, the only thought clear enough to him was to wonder how a simple breastband had contained them so thoroughly.

As he watched, she ran her hands down her chest, tweaking the dark nipples with a slight gasp. Zavier fought the urge to bury his face in her chest and allow himself to suffocate. His hands squeezed her ribcage with the effort of restraining himself. Minnie lowered her hands to his arms and with a smug smile, guided his hands higher to cup her breasts. He groaned as they filled his palms and overflowed the sides.

Minnie pressed his hands closer together, creating a mound of dark copper flesh. He swallowed, hands trembling against her body. Slowly she leaned forward, until a nipple was just grazing his lip.

"Zavier…"

"Mm?"

"Lick them."

Restraint flew out the window. With a growl he mounded her breasts together and took them in his mouth, swirling his tongue over the peaks and suckling hard. He switched between the pair, licking one, nipping the other. He licked and nibbled, biting almost to the point of pain, slowly caressing the sensitive area with the flat of his tongue then flicking the pebbled nipple with the tip. He buried his face in her cleavage with a deep groan of desire.

Minnie pushed him back, scooting herself off his lap. For a moment he panicked, afraid he had hurt or scared her. Relief filled him as she stood to remove her leather trousers and panties. She knelt beside him before he could get a good look at her, tugging the laces to his trousers. Lifting his hips, he helped her wiggle them down, both laughing nervously as his cock sprang free.

She straddled him again, hovering over his aching cock with a teasing smile. "Can I tell you a secret?" she murmured as his hands traced over her ass.

"Of course," he replied, attempting to focus his attention on her face and not the red imprint of his teeth around her nipple.

"I've fantasized about riding this cock since the first time I saw you in the garden. Every time we've been together, I imagine holding you, stroking you, sucking you down my throat. It's not what a proper young lady is meant to think of—"

"Fuck that," he grunted, gripping the back of her neck. "I don't give a shit how someone thinks you should behave. I want you, all of you, any way I can have you."

She kissed him so hard their teeth clacked together. With a muffled laugh they parted, Minnie resting her forehead on his. She lifted her hips, grazing her wet slit over his cock. With each stroke he came closer and closer to entering her, driving him wild with want. She was completely in control of him.

268

With a shove to his shoulders she laid him down on the pallet, his hands holding on to her thighs.

She braced her hands on his chest, rocked forward, and caught her breath as the head of his cock prodded her entrance. So slowly he thought he was going to lose his mind, she lowered herself down to engulf the head. She stopped, as if she were adjusting to the feeling.

"Want to know another secret?"

He looked up from where they were joined to meet her green eyes and nodded. "I may have only slept with one man, but I've used those toys he sent me almost every night since. So if you're worried you'll hurt me or something... Don't."

Before he could even process her words completely she had sat back with enough force that it tore a grunt from him. Warm, wet ecstasy. She leaned forward, lifting herself almost to the point of him falling out of her before slamming back down with a guttural groan. She found a rhythm, rising and falling with loud slaps as her plump ass hit his thighs. The sound was exquisite, but not as arousing as the pure ecstasy coming from her mouth.

She slowed her movements to a more rolling, grinding motion. Her nails dug into his chest. He slid a hand around to rub the bundle of nerves between her thighs. She arched her back, sitting upright.

"You're so fucking beautiful," he rasped out.

She looked down at him, her hips never stopping their dance over his, and as their eyes met, she cried out in orgasm. He continued a circular motion, pressing her into him as hard as he could to draw out her pleasure. She collapsed forward, panting.

Within seconds he had her flipped over and lying below him. He pulled her legs up and over his shoulders, plunging back into her with a groan. Sweat glistened across their bodies in the firelight, and he thought she had never looked more beautiful than she did right now. With every thrust into her, her breasts wobbled. The image would be burned into his mind for the rest of his life. He put his thumb back on her nerve center to stroke her to another climax. Gratification filled him as she screamed her pleasure again after only a few minutes. He slowed to appreciate the view of her eyes closed as she caught her breath.

When she opened her eyes and gave him that little smile of hers, he lost all control. He thrust as deep as he could before exploding inside her, shaking with the force of his orgasm. She cried out, reaching for him. He leaned down, bracing himself with hands on either side of her head to kiss her. He pressed himself as close as he could get without suffocating her, still twitching with the aftermath of his climax.

She nuzzled his face, kissing him repeatedly. "That was incredible," she whispered.

Breathless and speechless, Zavier could only nod. Incredible, that was the very word he'd used the day before, and one of many words he could think of to describe what they'd done, and her. She was incredible, amazing, clever, compassionate, gorgeous, and so much more. He rolled to her side and propped himself up on his elbow to look down at her.

He pressed a kiss to her lips, then said, "A few days ago, I thought you were one of the prettiest women I'd ever seen. Yesterday, watching everything you did, I knew you were the most clever, most beautiful, the wildest, most passionate woman I've ever known. Tonight... tonight you managed to look even more... Just more. You're exquisite, Mina."

Tears filled her eyes. He cupped her cheek and she nuzzled into him as the tears fell. "You shouldn't say such things to me," she whispered.

"Why not? They're all true," he asked.

She sniffed and smiled weakly. "The way you speak to me... you make it hard for me to remember that I shouldn't want you. I forget that I want to see the world, and not be trapped forever in one place, even a place as lovely as the palace is."

Zavier chuckled, kissing her nose. "Do you really think that's what your life would be like if we were together? You'd sit in Hatherus all the time?"

Her smile faded, replaced by a frown. "Yes, that's what the servants said... The consort is to host balls and events, and of course produce the next heir."

He shook his head, running fingers along her cheek. "You could do those things, if you wanted to. But remember, I'm a diplomat and ambassador, my father is in excellent health and has no plans to step down. I travel constantly, to every corner of this continent and sometimes farther. I could show you the whole world," his voice faded to a whisper against her ear.

"Is... is this you asking me?" she timidly asked as he nibbled her earlobe.

"Do you want me to ask?"

"We've only known each other a few days," she replied truthfully.

He leaned back a bit and smiled. "Then I am just making a comment about how much freedom to travel my princess would have." His features turned serious. "We need to get cleaned up. I don't have any water bottles, so we'll have to walk to the lake."

She stretched before rolling over and getting to her knees. He stood and offered her a hand, helping her up when her knees wobbled beneath her. Hand in hand they walked to the water's edge. The balmy night had kept the water warm enough to be comfortable as they stepped into the shallows and scooped water over themselves.

Remaining as quiet as they could to not disturb Maurgen, still snoring nearby, they returned to the little shelter. They each pulled out sleeping clothes, hanging their travel clothes to air out overnight, and dressed for bed.

Snuggled together, Zavier couldn't help but worry that he had pushed her too far. She was draped over his chest, her breathing already shallow, but he had to know.

"Mina," he whispered, half hoping she would respond and half hoping she wouldn't.

"Hmm?" she mumbled, not opening her eyes.

"Am I pushing you?"

Minnie sat up to look at him, rubbing her eyes. After a moment, she said, "No, you aren't. I wanted this. I wanted it days ago, and I wanted it yesterday. If anything, I think I'm pushing you..."

"You aren't," he interrupted hastily. "I wanted you from the beginning."

She smiled up at him, cupping his cheek in her hand. "Don't fret, Zavier, you have kept your promise not to push me. You could almost be a little more pushy, I might start to feel awkward if I'm doing all the instigating," she teased, kissing his lips lightly.

"If you're sure..." he fretted, but she stopped him with another kiss.

"I am. Now, shut up and go to sleep, we have a dragon to save tomorrow."

"Mmm, yes, my lady," he growled, tucking her back under his chin. Zavier watched the firelight from outside play across the walls of their bower as Minnie's breathing evened out and deepened. Squeezing her close, he gave in to the nagging wish he'd had for days. In a soft voice, barely audible, he whispered, "My Mina, my love, my princess."

Thirty

Minnie

M AURGEN WOKE THEM THE following morning with an earsplitting roar. Jolting upright, Minnie and Zavier exchanged worried glances, but Maurgen's voice in their heads soothed them in seconds.

"Sorry about that, just having a bath. I've found my breakfast, once you've eaten we can leave."

Stretching, Minnie flopped backward on the bedroll. Surprisingly, she'd slept soundly all night, and she suspected Zavier had too, judging by the rested but guilty look on his face. He leaned over her and gently kissed her good morning.

"Is he always this cheerful in the morning?" she asked as Maurgen let out another bellow.

Smiling, he said, "He enjoys Dragon Isle, and he could be putting up a false front to not worry us, but most likely it's the promise of action when we find your dragon. The pride of a dragon runs deep, and daring to imprison one? Many people will die for that insult."

She should probably be concerned about impending violence, but honestly, she agreed with Maurgen.

As they changed into their travel clothes, Minnie reached her thoughts toward her dragon, hoping to feel her again. Searing pain filled her mind, accompanied by a hazy image of a dark green dragon. Injuries still covered her body, as well as the siphons that drained her magic.

"Is that... my partner?"

"Yes, yes I'm Minnie. We're coming to find you, is there anything else you can tell me about where you might be?"

"Humans, not shifters. It's warm, and I hear a volcano erupting almost every day."

"Every day? We're on our way, please hold on just a bit longer. We're coming."

Minnie slowly pulled away from her, wincing again at the pain the dragon was in. Zavier gathered their bedclothes and shook out their makeshift pillow. He looked up as she cleared her throat.

"Did you speak to her?" he asked.

"I did, but my knowledge of the world is limited, so I'm hoping you know where this is. I saw an almost barren island in the vision, dead trees and sparse vegetation. She says she hears a volcano erupting almost every day, and it's very hot. The people are all Human, no shifters at all."

Thirty-One

Zavier

Z AVIER FURROWED HIS BROWS, thinking. He idly
folded a blanket, his eyes unfocused. "I think
there are some Humans on Balvin Island, but that
volcano is dormant. Shaesan has a volcano near
the southern coast, but it isn't active. Besides, they
wouldn't take her anywhere near other people,
someone would hear and the Human leadership as
a whole would certainly object to injuring a dragon."

"In the first vision I saw, they went east after they
stole her."

"East..." A map filled his mind, the one over his
father's desk. Beautifully drawn and colored in wa-
tercolor paints, it was the most complete map of
their continent and surrounding islands one could
have without using Human magic to map the land.
He'd been to most of the places on the map, placing
little tacks when he went somewhere new, but one
island was deemed too dangerous to visit right now.
In his great-grandfather's time it had been a lush

jungle forest, but the volcano had awoken again and had destroyed everything on the island.

"Yeah, I think I do know. The island is left off of most maps because no one can live there, and it changes so often there's little point in drawing it. We call it Inferno, the whole island is molten rock, fire, and dead vegetation. The Humans must have found a way to shield themselves from the heat and lava."

They finished packing quickly, throwing everything into the bags without bothering to fold the rest. Zavier scooped up the leaf-wrapped chunks of meat they'd buried the night before, taking half for himself and handing the rest to Minnie.

Maurgen fanned his wings dry on the lake beach, looking much better than the previous night. He lowered his head to accept pats and a caress of the small horn that grew on top of his nose.

"I agree with Zavier that Inferno sounds like the place. I've flown over it before. Dragons enjoy it there, but people cannot survive the interior without magical help."

"Will we be able to get through whatever magic they have protecting her?" Minnie wondered.

"I hope so. We will figure that out when we arrive. Get on and settle in, it's a very long flight, and we will be backtracking a bit."

They did as he said, climbing up his shoulder to the hollow space between ridges. After another stretch, Maurgen leaped into the air, seeking out a current he could ride.

Thirty-Two

Minnie

INNIE KEPT THEIR WALL of air tight around them, grateful she could maintain the small magic with no effort. She felt Zavier resting his head on her shoulder and assumed he was sleeping, she didn't want to turn and disturb him. Time passed much slower than it had the day before without him to tell her a story.

She wanted desperately to reach out to her dragon again, but feared it might weaken or distract her.

"Never," came a soft reply within her mind. The tone was distinctly more feminine than Maurgen's deep rumble. Instead of underground caves as she'd imagined with male dragons, she felt like she was in a deep forest.

"Now that I have heard you, you are giving me strength. Our bond grows as he brings you closer," the dragon continued.

"If I had come to Dragon Isle sooner, would that have awoken our bond?"

"Yes. For a normal bond pairing, contact is needed, but I am all dragons, as my mother is. My mother— is she well?"

"Vera? Yes, we saw her yesterday just before she rose to mate. She was upset to learn you were missing."

"She didn't realize I was gone, did she? Her memory is long, but only when she wishes it to be."

She sounded both heartbroken and accepting of that notion, as if there was nothing that could be done to change the fact.

"They all thought you were with me. I didn't come sooner... It's a long story. I wasn't allowed, and didn't know I should. I'm sorry, I'm so sorry I've failed you. I'm coming for you now, and we will never be apart again."

"Good. We have much to learn of each other. I am eager to know you, and to finally have a name."

"How do you get your name?"

"I'll know it when we meet, and you'll be the first person I speak my name to. I must rest now, before they come back. Fly swiftly."

Hours passed. Minnie reviewed everything she knew about dragons with Maurgen's help. Zavier took over the air shield, and she set him to practicing other little magics that were the foundations for stronger abilities. The sun was past the zenith and beginning its downward descent when Maurgen began a shallow dive for the ground. They were near the cliff-edge coastline, the jungle a green mass behind them.

"We'll eat, and rest for an hour, then fly across the channel. It shouldn't be too far, but we don't know where on the island she is. You'll need to focus as we get closer, you should be able to feel her and guide me to her." Maurgen landed and deposited them on the ground beside several large boulders, then took off again, swooping over a ridge and down into a shallow valley filled with herd animals.

Zavier and Minnie dug out some of their travel rations and snacked on them while foraging around. They found some edible berries and nuts, but nothing particularly substantial. While pushing through a group of bushes, Zavier nearly fell into a little creek, soaking one of his boots.

While he dried his boot and sock, Minnie turned over rocks looking for crayfish and other edibles. She came up empty, but Zavier called to get her attention, pointing toward a wild chicken fluttering away. She scrambled up the creek bank and ran after it, snatching the bird by the wings. After a deft twist of the poultry's neck, Minnie directed Zavier to start a fire and find rocks they could use for cooking the meat while she plucked and prepped the bird.

By the time Maurgen returned from his hunting trip, Minnie had the meat laid out on thin rock slabs to bake. Maurgen hastened the cooking by blowing a thin jet of flame over the chicken until it was cooked through. Zavier and Minnie ate their chicken quickly, washed their hands in the little creek. They separated into different areas of the woods to take care of bodily functions before they remounted Maurgen and left.

Once again in the air, Minnie ahead of Zavier with his arms wrapped around her, Maurgen flew low over the ocean swells. His broad wings beat rhythmically and steadily toward a hazy smudge. Their first glimpse of the island known as Inferno appeared misleading: green trees and overgrown bushes grew not far from the sandy beach they soared over. The greenery didn't last long, and Minnie sucked in a breath as the vegetation grew scarce. Charred skeletal remains of once towering trees rose beneath them, their branches reaching toward Maurgen's wings almost like claws.

Further inland, they flew over a small river of lava flowing down from the mountain above. Maurgen flew them higher and out of the range of the acrid stench of burning earth.

"Focus now, Minnie. Where is she?" Maurgen asked her as they neared the rocky beach.

Minnie reached out to her dragon again, *"We're almost there. I need to know where you are!"* She didn't hear a verbal response, but she did feel a tug within her chest, pulling her toward the southeastern side of the island. Zavier leaned around her, pulling the leg straps to their limits as he peered over Maurgen's side at the passing carnage.

"The whole island has burned from the eruptions and fires breaking out. Just feel how hot it is," he said, wiping sweat from his brow. Minnie didn't respond, she focused on the line tugging in her chest. It grew sharper as they flew, pulling her straight ahead. She was just about to warn Maurgen to slow down when the feeling changed. Now the line was tugging *behind* her.

"Maurgen! Turn back, we've passed it!"

He turned on a wingtip, all three scanning the ground. They couldn't see anything out of the ordinary, so Maurgen circled lower. Within Minnie, the tugging feeling made her almost nauseous as it changed direction.

"Underground?" Minnie asked as she searched the area for a possible cave entrance.

"Maybe, or maybe spelled invisible. Unlike our magic in Virankan, which are all elemental in nature, the Humans can do all kinds of things we can't," Zavier replied. Maurgen rumbled, back-winged and swung his tail below him. The massive spiked tail collided with something with a mighty thunk.

"That wasn't a magical shield. That was a building! Hold on tight," Maurgen swung around again. Minnie gasped, clinging to the ridge in front of her as she almost lost her seat. She tightened her thighs around his body and felt Zavier doing the same behind her, wrapping an arm around her to hold onto the ridge as well.

After two more slams with his tail into the building, they heard a crumbling noise. Maurgen lowered himself slowly until he was able to land on the invisible building's rooftop. He felt around with a clawed paw for the damage he'd done, then began digging at it. A hole appeared where they could see inside the building below them.

"Only the outside is spelled. Climb down, go find her. Be careful, someone will have heard. I'll guard out here and wait until you say I can cause some more trouble or you need a distraction."

They didn't argue. Zavier went first, sliding down Maurgen's foreleg and lowering himself until his feet touched ground. Sliding down the limb to stand on Maurgen's foot wasn't so bad, but lowering herself to empty air twisted her stomach. She fought not to summon her magic as she released Maurgen's foot, and was grateful to Zavier for catching her. Together, they lowered themselves into the hole, entering a sparsely furnished bedroom. No personal items sat on the dresser, and the bed looked as if it hadn't been slept in recently.

"Living quarters for the Humans? Can you sense her?" Zavier asked, placing his hand on her lower back. In his other hand, he held his sword. Wishing she had a weapon and knew how to fight, Minnie gestured down and to the right.

"She's below us, but I'm not sure how far."

Zavier led her out of the room, moving his hand to grip her own tightly. They spotted stairs and hurried toward them, but stopped when they heard voices approaching from below.

"Earthquake? Did the roof collapse? The volcano's already erupted today, hasn't it?" A man's voice asked.

"That was no volcano," a woman replied. "Something hit the building, and multiple times!"

"The sound came from this way," A second man, his voice much deeper, agreed. Zavier and Minnie had just enough time to duck into a room near the stairway and close the door almost all the way shut before the three emerged. Led by a short, round woman, they hurried to the end of the hall and the damaged room. Minnie heard gasps and startled exclamations.

"We can't sneak out, they'll see us, we'll have to fight them," Zavier said softly with a sigh.

"No, wait," Minnie whispered back as she stopped him from opening the door. "Maurgen?" she spoke aloud, so Zavier would hear the plan. "Rip the ceiling off that room, then fly away, keep them distracted."

Zavier grinned at her as the dragon's claws audibly ripped into the building again and the trio of Humans screamed. The dragon-bonded pair stayed hidden long enough to ensure the Humans weren't going to run back down the hall, then slipped out and down the stairs. Behind them, they heard the mages readying a spell to hurl at Maurgen.

"He'll move, right?" Minnie asked, breathless as they hurried down the steps.

"Yeah, but he'll stay close enough that they think they can hit him. Don't be shocked if he roasts them, though," he replied with a shrug.

She paused, a stricken look on her face. "Zavier... I don't know if I can... I mean, I've never... I'm a healer!"

He turned back to her, climbing the steps until he was on eye level with her. "If you can't hurt someone, that's alright. It's not something that is easily done. But Minnie, we are rescuing a dragon— *your* dragon— from people who have been hurting her, torturing her." He lifted his hand to cup her cheek, wiping away a lone tear. "People are going to die today. If you can't do it, that's fine, but you'll need to stay out of our way. I will defend you and the dragons to my last breath, killing whoever I need to in order to protect you and save your dragon."

Minnie nodded, swallowing roughly. "I understand, it's just... No, of course, you're right."

Zavier studied her a moment longer. The furrow of his brows and thin set of his lips showed his concern, and Minnie's stomach twisted. She had been so focused on the knowledge that she was meeting her dragon today, it had completely escaped her what they were doing. They could die here. There was no question of leaving without her dragon, but suddenly she wasn't as eager as before. The thought of him or Maurgen being hurt...

We will be fine, little one. Those Humans are dead. I've found an underground entrance large enough for me, I'm coming. Zavier is right. People will die. Protect yourselves, and I will do the same.

A smile lit Zavier's face. "Maurgen is confident. Whatever you've thought of, he doesn't seem worried at all."

"Let's go, before he does it all himself," she urged, nudging him to turn him around and continue down the stairs.

Every landing held a door, but the little magical tug on Minnie told her to continue down until they reached the very bottom floor. They must be underground by now, as the building above hadn't been very tall when they'd landed on the invisible roof. There was a large metal door, and the tug told her they needed to pass through the door to get to the dragons. In the distance they could hear the crunch of massive claws on stone.

Zavier pushed against the door without any success in moving it. He examined the hinges, muttering to himself about possibly removing them. Minnie frowned. The door itself was metal, probably steel, but the wall it was attached to...

"Well that's almost too easy..." she mumbled, stepping forward. "Stand back, Zavier."

She placed her hands on the wall, calling fire to her palms. Within seconds the wall fell away, burning rapidly beyond her hands. Wooden studs held up the frame of the wall and door, but thin wood pulp sheeting had been used as the wall itself.

As the wall burned away, Zavier whistled behind her. "Clever," he praised.

"I've no idea why they'd use a metal door but wooden walls, it doesn't seem very well thought out. Anyway, it helps us," Minnie shrugged, and moved her palms to burn away another section.

Thirty-Three

Minnie

ONCE ENOUGH OF THE wall had burned away, Minnie summoned air to put the fires out and they clambered through the hole, careful of still glowing embers. The other side was starkly different from the smooth walls of the stairwell. They stood in a dimly lit cave, rough walls on either side leading in a gentle slope downward.

Ahead, the sounds of panicked shouting grew louder as they neared. The tight hall opened to a cavern hundreds of feet across and deep. Maurgen filled the other side, his golden hide spotted with blood. He let out a roar and a long tongue of flame that bounced harmlessly off the Humans' magical shields.

Lifting his sword and drawing his dagger, Zavier charged toward the battle with a cry of rage. Frozen, Minnie watched him engage a man wielding a sword with flames dancing down the blade. They moved so quickly she had trouble fully seeing what they were doing, their swords a blur of movement. Beyond, Maurgen shook his head with a Human dangling from his closed jaws, snapping the Human's back with a loud crack.

A vibrating groan from her left snapped her back to attention. A green dragon almost identical to her own dragon form lay pinned to the floor with chains. Three Humans had their hands raised, black haze surrounding them as they chanted a spell. For a long moment, Minnie was rooted to the spot, frozen with fear and indecision.

More guards poured in from the far side of the cavern, coming to aid their cohorts. Zavier had dispatched his opponent and turned to face the new arrivals. Maurgen slammed his tail down in front of them, giving Zavier time to shift his body to his stronger, faster Draconid form. Wings flaring, he rushed forward again with his sword raised. The trapped dragon shuddered in pain as fresh blood flowed from her wounds. Minnie's fists clenched.

They could handle the guards. Minnie needed to disrupt the mages and find a way to free her dragon. She stalked toward them, raising her hands to chest height. A gust of wind blew ahead of her, whipping their long cloaks around their legs. One man looked over, startled.

As she neared, she could see dozens of wounds and hundreds of scars along the dragon's hide, some still healing, others thick and darker green than the rest of her. Her wings were in tatters, dripping blood. Rage filled Minnie at the sight of such cruelty.

Never in her life had she used her magic to fight, or even to hunt. She'd killed animals of course, but always with a weapon, or claw and fang. Now as the rage filled her and she screamed in fury, fire poured from her palms toward the two men. Wind lifted the fire and swirled around them. The fiery vortex she'd once used to dry her clothes encompassed the men. She ripped the oxygen from their throats and they gaped at her as flame licked up their clothing, unable to draw breath to scream. One tried to step closer to her but was pushed back by the wall of air surrounding him. The heat washed over Minnie and the acrid stench of burnt flesh and hair nearly gagged her. The three Humans collapsed, burnt beyond recognition. Slowly, she dropped her hands and released the magic.

Heavy iron chains were welded to thick rings in the floor. There was no sign of a padlock or any way to release the chains. She circled toward the dragon's horned head, examining every point where she was shackled. Almost without realizing, she stood before the dim eye of her dragon.

"Little one..."

Minnie reached out a hand to caress the dragon's muzzle, carefully avoiding a thin wound that leaked blood. As she touched the dragon, a sense of completeness overwhelmed her and she fell to her knees with a choked sob.

"We are together, little one. I know who you are, Jessamine, and I know who I am. I am Zeniyah, and I am yours, as you are mine."

Power swirled between the two of them. Minnie gasped, struggling to contain the suddenly overwhelming amount of magic within her. She focused it down her arm and through the hand touching her dragon, into Zeniyah, to heal her wounds. They were too numerous to fathom, internal damage from being beaten and poisoned to keep her weak and unable to use any of her magic. Minnie pushed all the power they had through their link to heal every major injury. The only areas she avoided were the shredded wings that still had iron chains running through them and the banded collar around her neck.

Minnie opened her eyes, not realizing she had closed them because of how clearly she could see and feel Zeniyah. A huge, vivid green eye stared at her, lid half closed as the magic swirled through her ravaged body. Zeniyah groaned in discomfort at the rapid healing, but breathed a vast sigh of relief. Through their connection, Minnie felt the dragon's pain faded to almost nothing, the first time she was nearly pain-free in seventeen years.

"The chains are iron, I am so weak I cannot break them," Zeniyah told her, rolling her eye to indicate the chained rings on either side of her. Minnie stood, a bit unsteady on her feet. Zavier approached, his blade covered in blood and favoring one leg. He wiped the blade on a nearby body and sheathed it.

"Maurgen took care of most of them for me, kind of ruined all my fun. I caught a blade on my thigh but it's not deep, it can wait until later." He faced the bound dragon, and bowed deeply, his hand over his heart. "It is an honor to meet you, I am only sorry the circumstances aren't better. I am Zavier."

"Please tell him I appreciate him coming for me, and the honor is mine," Zeniyah said to Minnie, her voice sounding almost shy.

"She says the honor is hers, and she appreciates you coming to save her." Minnie turned back to her dragon, running a hand over her eye ridges and scratching between the two curved horns. "You can speak to him directly, if you want, I don't mind. Maurgen, the great gold beast over there, speaks to me constantly."

From the corner of her eye Minnie caught movement. As she turned toward the motion, a man behind Zavier raised a dagger over his head. Her voice caught in her throat as she raised an arm, as if to stop the man. A confused, concerned look crossed Zavier's face.

Almost without thinking, Minnie called her fire and sent it searing toward the assailant. Zavier's eyes widened as the fire split, skirting him and wrapping around the assailant. The man dropped the dagger as he began to scream. Minnie forced the fire down the shocked man's throat, roasting him from the inside out.

As the man collapsed, Zavier rushed to Minnie, concern in his eyes.

"Are you alright?" he asked, hurrying to her side.

A wave of nausea flooded her, but she felt no remorse for the man's death. Like the men who were hurting Zeniyah, he had tried to kill someone she cared about. She nodded. "Yes, I'm fine."

"You're sure?"

She nodded again. "He would have killed you, Zavier. I'm just... it's all a bit overwhelming."

Maurgen approached, and Minnie was astounded at how large he was compared to Zeniyah. Granted she was still trapped on the floor, but he was easily twice her size. Rage filled her again. Zeniyah had been in captivity so long, had it stunted her growth?

Maurgen lowered his head to Zeniyah and touched noses with her. Then, far more delicately than she would have thought possible, he blew a tiny jet of flame over the iron ring, concentrating the fire on one spot until the iron was red hot. He hooked a claw through and yanked, breaking apart the iron. He went around and repeated the process until all the chains were free.

Zavier took one heavy chain in his hands and flew up, dragging it behind him and carefully threading it back through the wing joint to release Zeniyah. She groaned in pain and fought not to move as the chains were removed from her body. Minnie placed her palms on the dragon again and called back the healing magic, smoothing over the wing wounds. The edges of the beautiful wings were still in tatters, but the main sail, joints, and bones were all intact and healed. Scars covered her body, and nothing would be able to remove them. The only thing that remained trapping her was the collar around her neck that somehow bound her power and siphoned her magic away.

Minnie investigated it carefully. There was no lock, and while it was made of metal, it wasn't any she recognized. Spikes dug into the dragon's thick neck, keeping the collar in place. It almost looked...

"Were you full grown when they took you? Or did you grow into this?" Minnie gasped, anger filling her voice.

"I grew. It hurts when I move, and they can send shocks through it to keep me still."

"How will we remove it?" Zavier wondered, hovering in the air over the dragon's back to see the collar from above. "I'm sure it can be melted, but that would hurt her as well."

Maurgen, standing behind Minnie on the lookout for any approaching Humans, snorted. *"Is it laced with Dragonsbane?"*

"What in the Hells is Dragonsbane?" Zavier snapped as he landed beside Minnie.

"It's an ore, very rarely found in some volcanic areas. When mixed with one herb in particular, it poisons dragons, suppressing our strength and magic."

291

"And why have I never heard of Dragonsbane before?"

"Well, we don't really advertise how to kill us, now do we."

"Sometimes, I hate you, you oversized pain in my ass lizard... How do we nullify it?"

While Maurgen and Zavier bickered, Minnie carefully climbed Zeniyah's shoulder to examine the collar again. She thought there was a seam along the top, but it was hard to tell because the ring dug into Zeniyah's flesh.

"You may have to just melt it. One more pain is nothing for a lifetime of freedom," Zeniyah's sad voice filled her mind again. Minnie mentally reached for her, wishing she could wrap the dragon and protect her always.

"Absolutely not. Obviously we can't leave it, but there has to be a way other than melting it and hurting you. Do you remember them putting it on? Did it snap on?"

"Yes, I think it snapped on, it certainly couldn't go over my horns... I do still have horns, don't I?" The sudden concern in the dragon's voice was almost amusing and a nervous chuckle burst from Minnie's mouth.

"Yes, you still have your horns, and they're beautiful. If it snapped on, it has to snap off."

"Someone is coming," Maurgen said, turning his eyes to the small entrance Zavier and Minnie had used. Zavier pulled his sword and moved to stand beside Maurgen.

"Peace. I am not your enemy," said a small, timid voice. Hands up and splayed out, a teenage boy emerged from the hall. "I'm Damian, I was sent here by my father to learn all I could from the mages about dragons. My father wants to make dragons into a weapon for his army."

"Who is your father, and how does all that make you not our enemy?" Zavier demanded, blade raised.

"I have been lying to them about dragons, giving them wrong information. Dragons aren't a tool to use or weaponize. My father is one of the advisers for the Human king."

"Do you know how to remove this collar?" Minnie called to him from Zeniyah's back.

"It requires magic to unlock. Please, if you let me approach, I can unlock it."

"If you try anything or hurt any of us..." Zavier brandished his weapon, a clear threat.

"I understand. You have my word, I want to help."

Zavier and Maurgen stepped apart, forcing the boy to walk between them to approach Zeniyah. Minnie, perched in the hollow between ridges, watched him warily. Zeniyah turned her head slightly to watch him.

"I remember him. He spoke out against hurting me, and they beat him for it."

"That may be, but we can't trust anyone here, no matter how innocent they seem. He could be a distraction."

Minnie was sickened at how quickly she had become mistrustful. Her quiet life in Ocrans seemed like a hundred years ago, instead of scarcely a week. The politics she had been thrown into, the illness in Saltstone, Humans torturing a dragon and stealing its magic, it almost seemed surreal. Days ago her biggest worry had been if her mother would worsen, or that she would be stuck in Ocrans forever caring for her.

The young man, Damian, carefully approached Zeniyah. Maurgen rumbled a threat but didn't move. Zavier followed closely, almost stepping on his heels when the youth stopped beside the dragon's shoulder.

"I'll need to climb up, is that alright?" Damian looked from Zeniyah to Minnie. Zeniyah rumbled assent so Minnie granted him permission. She scooted herself back to give him room, but kept her hands ready to summon fire if she needed to.

Damian climbed the shoulder awkwardly, reaching just high enough to place his hand on the top of the Dragonsbane collar. Runes she hadn't seen before began to glow with a white light. Zeniyah groaned, twitching her head and flexing her claws in pain. Minnie was about to tell him to stop when the thick metal band split apart, falling away from her neck and leaving behind deep wounds and ragged scar tissue.

Choking back a sob, Minnie laid her hands on the dragon and once again called her magic. The golden light filled her and smoothed the punctures, but nothing would fix the deep scar that ran the circumference of her neck. Damian slid down the dragon's forearm as Zeniyah sat up completely, shaking her head and twisting to look around her. Slipping back into the hollow between Zeniyah's neck ridges, Minnie wrapped her arms around the dragon's neck, tears sliding down her face and onto the scarred hide. Craning her neck to see Minnie, Zeniyah crooned low in her throat.

On the ground, Zavier asked, "Are there any more guards or mages we should be concerned about?"

"I don't think there is anyone left alive in the building. Two guards went out on patrol earlier, but I think you've got all the rest here."

"Why so few people, if they are trying to steal dragon magic?" Zavier questioned, indicating the broken collar.

"My father said that not all the advisers were on board with using the dragons this way. Many of them think that we are becoming too reliant on magic, and there's a push to stop using it as much. My father and the Head Mage came up with this plan, but they had to be selective on who they sent here. If the wrong people found out, there would be trouble."

"No shit," Zavier snorted. Behind him, Maurgen growled. "Didn't your genius father think of what would happen when the dragons realized what you have done to Zeniyah?"

Damian shrugged. "Honestly, I doubt he did. He tends to be rather short sighted. When he told me I was to come here and learn so I could take over, I told him this whole plan was horrible. We'd be lucky if the dragons didn't kill us all."

"You're right. Also, attacking the dragons could be seen as an act of war with Virankan and the Skinshifters, considering our link to them is what gave my family the throne."

Minnie slid to the ground beside the men as Damian lost all color in his face. "I never thought of it like that, so I know my father hasn't. My king doesn't want war, he doesn't even know this is going on. When my father first brought it up, the king was furious and turned him down right away. I'm not sure what else my father is planning, but I want no part in a war. I'll do whatever you want me to do to prove that."

"For now, we need to get out of this cave" Minnie firmly told them, putting a stop to the discussion. "Do Humans have magical transport, or do you only travel by ship?"

"Magic, creating portals between one place and another. The only times they've used a ship were when they were trying to capture a dragon."

"Or succeeding," Maurgen snarled with a snap of his teeth. He was crouched beside Zeniyah as if protecting her from anything that could come near.

"There aren't other dragons here, are there?" Minnie asked, looking around as if she'd missed seeing another trapped beast.

"No, they tried to capture another one, but the dragon died. Only... Zeniyah, was it? Only Zeniyah was held here. I have no idea if there are others in Shaesan." Damian replied.

"Well then, that means we need to go now, before others arrive and wonder what the Hells happened. Maurgen, lead the way out, please," she gestured toward the exit. Zeniyah rose stiffly, holding her wings out awkwardly as she began to hobble toward the passage. Within a few steps, she was able to fold her wings back and begin walking a bit more normally. Minnie placed a hand on her foreleg, lending what support she could to her dragon, wondering if she would be strong enough to fly.

"I will be able to fly, a dragon can always fly," Zeniyah replied, indignant.

"It's not a mark against you as a dragon, dearest. You've been here a long time, you're malnourished and your wings are damaged..."

"A dragon can always fly," came the short reply in a very firm tone.

"Don't nag, she's right. We can always fly. Our wings only help and guide us, it's our magic that lifts us, and she has that to spare now that the collar is off. Can't you feel it?" Maurgen's soothing voice chastised her. Feeling foolish and a bit overwhelmed, Minnie used her magic to reach out around her. Zavier was the same

muted hum he had been since she'd met him. Maurgen was a brilliant halo of untapped energy pulsing in golden waves. Zeniyah had been non-existent at first, thanks to the collar stealing her magic. With it off, even though it had only been a few minutes, she vibrated with power.

Now that she was focusing on the magic, Minnie could feel the raw power coursing through her own body, far more than she'd ever felt before. It occurred to her that she had used an incredible amount to heal Zeniyah, but she wasn't at all tired.

"Soon we will have all the time we need to learn about each other. There isn't a lot to me because I've not lived my life as I should have. However, I am the most powerful dragon to ever hatch, according to Vera and our history. I could fly us all to the Hatchery or to Hatherus without feeling any exhaustion. Physically I am weak, for now. But magically, I am still very strong." Zeniyah turned her head to look back at her mate, a strange look in her eye that Minnie couldn't quite read.

Thirty-Four

Minnie

I T WAS A SHORT journey through an enlarged cave tunnel back to the surface. The exit was tucked into a deep gully facing south with a rocky overhang hiding the opening from above. Both dragons had to crouch to avoid scraping their heads and wings on the roof. The air was hazy with smoke from the volcano to the north, which partially occluded the sun overhead. Nevertheless, Zeniyah lifted her head to bask in the faint rays. Anger filled Minnie once again, and she wondered how many reminders there would be. She would not be letting this go. As reluctant as she had been to take Human life an hour ago, now she craved vengeance for her beloved dragon.

"Maurgen," Minnie began out loud. "Is there anything alive on this island?"

"If the boy is correct, there may still be a couple Human guards, but I saw and smelled no signs of animal life."

As furious as she was, she didn't quite have it in her to suggest Zeniyah hunt and eat the Humans. If they were attacked, maybe, but not like this.

"I have the strength to fly back to Dragon Isle, if that is what concerns you," Zeniyah said, and judging by the way Zavier turned his head to face her when she spoke, she had included him as well.

"I don't think we should return to Dragon Isle..." Two dragons and two men stared at her, waiting for her to continue. "Zavier and Damian raised valid points. If some of the Humans are trying to raise an army, and draining dragon magic to do it, we need to go to Hatherus to tell King Taurak."

"I have attempted to reach Taurak from here, but he does not hear me. I would need his dragon, Alyss, to relay the message. It is the same for Narith and her Faladrik."

Minnie frowned, tilting her head in confusion as she studied him.

"You can't speak to any of the other dragon-bonded?"

"No," Zavier replied. "Most dragons are unable to speak to anyone but their own bonded mate, or to another dragon. In some cases a dragon can speak to someone close to their partner, or someone physically close, like when Maurgen flew Brant, but he wouldn't be able to speak to Brant now."

"That's odd..."

"What, that Maurgen speaks to you?"

"Yes, and not just him, Horth too. Is it because of Zeniyah? Because she is the next Vynar?"

Damian, who had been standing quietly beside Zavier attempting to not draw attention to himself, went pale and gasped. "Vynar? Like, queen?"

Feeling snide, Minnie gave him a sly smile. "Oh, didn't we mention? Your idiot father had the next ruler of all dragonkind kidnapped and tortured."

Turning away muttering to himself, Damian found a rock to sit on and braced his arms on his knees, tucking his head down. She thought she heard him repeating, "We're all gonna die," but as he wasn't currently a danger to them, she ignored him in favor of their current issue.

"To answer your question as best as I can, yes, the dragons are probably speaking to you so freely because of Zeniyah. Maurgen has always been odd, so I didn't think too much of it when he spoke to you," Zavier explained.

Minnie waved it off. "Back to the current problem. We need to alert your father. If war is coming, he needs to know, and the Human king as well. If there is no way to tell him telepathically, we need to return to Hatherus right away. And he," she pointed at Damian, clutching his head and still muttering, "has to come with us."

Nodding, Zavier said, "I can't think of another way to tell Father, unless our young friend knows something. Damian?" Zavier turned, prodding the panicked man with his boot.

"Yes, what? I'm sorry?" Hair disheveled and eyes wide, Damian looked up at them.

"Know another way to tell King Taurak what your father has done?" Minnie summed up.

"Oh, um. I'm not very good at portals, I don't think I could make one big enough for dragons to pass through."

Zavier furrowed his brow in thought. "If I described the palace, could you get yourself there? But no, how would we know you did it, I can't risk losing you until you've spoken to Father..."

Damian cleared his throat. "A portal would open a doorway of sorts between here and there. If you can describe it clearly enough, I can open it, and you'll see where I go. You could go through too, and return before I close it."

Minnie shook her head, ready to refuse entirely, but Zeniyah spoke up. She had crouched behind Minnie, her eyes darting back and forth as they hashed out their ideas.

"I know you don't trust him, and you have very little reason to, but I do. I think sending him to King Taurak is the best plan for now. It would take at least a day to fly to Hatherus, and time may be of the essence."

She saw Zavier nod. "I don't like it, but I think Zeniyah is right. Father needs to know. I won't go through if I don't recognize the location, the worst thing he could do is trap me in Hatherus."

No, Minnie thought, the worst thing he could do was kill them all, but she held her tongue. Instead, she nodded her ascent, and Damian set to work. He strode over to the wall of the cave they'd exited and traced a huge oval with his hands. He muttered several short phrases and wrote runes she didn't recognize into the oval. After a moment the surface began to shimmer.

"Alright. Tell me where to open the portal, be as clear as you can."

Zavier thought for a moment, looking up at the sky at the deepening twilight that was falling around them. "Large double doors, made of dark brown wood, diamond window panels. A black marble porch with four steps leading down to a garden. There are rose bushes bracketing the porch. On either side, wrought iron lanterns with small dragons on top."

As he spoke, the image began to form. Damian must have had more talent than she'd given him credit for because not only did she recognize the garden doors at the palace, but they watched the doors open and Zavier's parents walk out arm in arm.

Sweat beading on his forehead, Damian gestured toward the portal. "I think it's big enough that we can step through together, I assume you'd have issues with going first or second."

Zavier exchanged a brief look with Minnie, then nodded. Taking the younger man's arm, the pair stepped through the portal together, with Zavier having to duck and turn almost sideways to fit his wings. Nervously, Minnie paced back and forth, watching as the two men spoke to the startled couple on the steps. She couldn't hear what was said, but Zavier's gestures seemed to speak volumes as he summarized their trip and rescue of Zeniyah.

Two guards appeared behind the king and queen to take custody of Damian, but she saw that they treated him kindly, not roughly or threatening him. Zavier kissed his mother before turning back to the portal and stepping through. She breathed a huge sigh of relief once he was back on firm ground and the portal closed behind him.

"All taken care of?" she asked, stepping closer and half lifting her hands to his before she realized what she was doing.

"I gave Father the highlights, hopefully Damian will be honorable and tell them the rest. Regardless, he knows what the Humans have done here, and will take some action before we get there." Zavier took her hands, drawing her flush against him with a devilish grin. "There is nothing else we can do until Father's spies have reported back to us, which will be days at the earliest."

He wrapped an arm around her waist and threaded fingers through her hair at the base of her neck, invitation clear. She smiled. Despite the previous evening, he was still asking permission and waiting for her to make a move. She leaned in to kiss him, wrapping her own arms around his middle.

A snort of smoke over their heads broke them apart after only a few minutes. Maurgen looked down at them and snorted again.

"We still need to leave this island, or have the two of you forgotten that Human mages could arrive at any moment and discover we rescued their magic source?"

Unwilling to admit that she had, in fact, forgotten that very important detail, Minnie scrambled away from Zavier and retreated to her dragon. Zeniyah hummed and nuzzled her.

"I don't know what that feeling is, but when you did that with him, it made you feel good, and I felt good. I like it very much." Zeniyah's voice was much softer in her mind, almost a mental whisper.

"It's called a kiss, and that feeling is... well. It's complicated, is what it is."

"We need to return to Dragon Isle, before going to Hatherus."

"Won't that be unnecessary flying, though? We need to get to the capital to pursue the Humans for what they've done to you."

"That is true, but vengeance will have to wait. Now that my magic and I are free, I will need to rise to mate soon. Especially if you and the prince continue doing... whatever the complicated feeling was."

"Ohh..." Minnie turned away from the two males to hide her flush. Of course, Zeniyah should have risen to mate years ago. Adult dragons in the wild rose by age five, Maurgen had said, and while bonded female dragons wouldn't mature until their rider did, both Minnie and Zeniyah had been fully mature for years.

"I could easily rise anywhere, so long as there is one male, but as I am the next Vynnar, once Vera passes the power to me, my clutches will create future bonded dragons, I must have the best male possible to sire my hatchlings."

"Yes, of course. You're right, I hadn't thought of that. Alright, that's what we'll do, then. The dragons ought to still be at Titan Lake, Vera only rose yesterday."

Hoping her features were under control, Minnie turned back to Zavier and Maurgen, who appeared to have conferred between themselves.

"Since Hatherus is warned, we should go to Dragon Isle. You said we ought to have a couple days?"

Zavier nodded. "Yes, that's what Father guessed. And without the dragon-bonded as an aerial cavalry, we couldn't take an army to the Humans with any speed anyway, so we really can't do anything until the dragons return from the Rising."

"There is to be another Rising," Maurgen said to them all. As all eyes turned toward him, he added, *"I scent it on you, Zeniyah. You must rise soon, or your instinct will take over and do it for you."*

Minnie moved to climb onto Zeniyah's back, but Zavier stopped her. "I think you should fly yourself, or with me. Let's not overburden Zeniyah until she's had a proper meal and regained her strength, no matter how confident you are in your magic," he finished with a stern look at the dragon female. She snorted, but dipped her head.

"I'll fly myself, it's a short trip across the water," Minnie agreed. She didn't want to admit it, but she had been quite sore after their long flight from Saltstone across the ocean. The only way she would grow stronger is to fly more, especially now that she could fly with Zeniyah.

Zavier and Minnie stepped away from the dragons to give themselves room to shift. The familiar tingling magic felt different now, more raw and wilder than any other time she'd shifted. Assuming it had to do with Zeniyah's power, Minnie let it flow through her and tried not to be afraid of the sudden rush of desire that flashed through her midsection.

"I'm sorry, Maurgen was right. We must hurry." Zeniyah's voice felt soothing within her mind, despite the chaos they were both feeling. With a jolt, Minnie remembered what Lavender had said about females at the Rising, and how sometimes the dragon-bonded women had also risen to mate. Shaking that thought away, she concentrated on changing her skin to her dragon form. The world shifted around her as she grew, and she fanned out her wings for balance. Not far away, Zavier did the same, rearing on his haunches to release a bellow. Maurgen and Zeniyah replied in kind. As one, they all launched themselves into the air, blasting dirt and rocks away with the powerful strokes of their wings.

The group set their course for the narrow strait between Inferno and Dragon Isle, much the same path they had taken earlier that day. The sun hung low over the horizon as they winged across the water. Maurgen and Zavier hung back behind the females, letting them lead the way at their own pace. Minnie warily watched Zeniyah for any signs of weakness, but she didn't seem to struggle at all. She thought she saw something from the corner of her eye below her, but when she looked, it was gone.

The wind made whistling sounds as it rushed over the holes in Zeniyah's wings, and Minnie wondered again how she was able to fly with such extensive damage. The thought must have been louder in her mind than she intended, for Zeniyah answered her.

305

"It's all about the magic. That's what lifts us, we just use our wings to steer and for some extra speed. Wild dragons don't understand that, they are too instinctual, but the bonded ones have a better understanding of how our magic works within us."

"Being bound to a person increases the dragon's intelligence, doesn't it?"

"Yes," Maurgen and Zeniyah both answered, but Zeniyah continued. *"Wild dragons are simple creatures, ruled by instinct alone. They don't have a language that you would understand, we speak in images and feelings."*

They settled back into flight for another few moments, but something below them caught Minnie's eye again. Rearing back in midair, she flapped slowly as she peered down. The waves rolled below her undisturbed.

"What is it?" Maurgen asked as he hovered beside her.

"I swear I saw something, but it's gone again. I must be losing my mind," she replied sheepishly. She was about to resume her flight, but motion below the waves stilled her again.

A black, winged creature with only two legs erupted from the water. It flew below them, squawking in fright and releasing a jet of steaming water in their direction. Its oddly scaled hide glistened with water droplets as it spun in air and dove below the sea.

"What was that?!" Minnie roared both physically and mentally. Zeniyah and Zavier had noticed they weren't following and turned back for them.

"It's a sea dragon," Zeniyah replied. *"They're distantly related to us, though they aren't particularly intelligent. Dragon-lore says there are snowy, mountain, and forest dragons, too."*

"No one has seen them in centuries," Maurgen added, studying the water below. *"Stories of monsters in the*

306

sea, yes, though it's usually hydra or kraken. These dragons avoid anything humanoid."

Maurgen lost interest in the creature, flexing his wings to climb higher above the sea. Minnie looked to Zeniyah, then back to the water. She wished there was a way to speak to them, but she'd felt nothing from the sea dragon's mind. Mentally shrugging, she also turned away and resumed flying.

They flew on in silence until the cliffs of Dragon Isle came into view. The dragons insisted they land and allow Zeniyah to hunt, and for the Bonded to get some rest, which Minnie thought was Maurgen's way of insisting Zeniyah rest as well. They landed near the spot they'd had lunch earlier that day. With a sigh for sore shoulder muscles, Minnie shifted to her humanoid body and looked around.

"Zavier, when you looked around earlier, did you see a pool in the creek?" she asked as he returned to his normal body as well.

"I didn't, but I can help you look while they hunt," he replied, striding over to her. He was looking a bit worse for wear after two days of travel and the fighting he had done. His hair was disheveled and he had blood smeared on one side of his face that she hadn't noticed earlier.

"We could both use a wash and to soak our clothes." They began walking toward the creek they'd found earlier, but were stopped almost at once by Zeniyah's voice in their minds.

"About half a mile east from where you are now is a hot spring. It is in the forest, there will be a massive redwood tree, and just beyond it is a sinkhole. Below is a cave system with a hot spring at the bottom. We will bring you something to eat once we have caught it."

The pair shared a glance and grinned. "I don't even care how she knows it's there, let's go!" Minnie laughed and began walking toward the trees.

She'd gone only a dozen steps when she realized Zavier wasn't with her, but as she turned to look for him she was scooped into his arms. Minnie wrapped her arms around his neck as he flew them toward the forest. She took the time while he concentrated on finding the landmarks described to them to examine his horns and wings. Like all male dragons, he had four horns, two rams horns grew out and circled his ears, while two long spiraled ones grew between those straight up and back. They were all a darker gold, almost a deep bronze, than the wings that flexed behind him. As he set to gliding over the treetops, she noticed a burn scar on the joint just below the claw tip.

"What happened to your wing?" she quietly asked.

He seemed confused at first, "What? Where? Oh, the joint?"

"Yes, the joint, how many injuries have you had?" she asked, a bit exasperated.

"More than are visible, the healers don't usually leave scars," he replied, and she felt a bit foolish because of course, she should know that better than most. "That happened in the Fuman country, we didn't have a healer with us so it healed on its own. One of their magicians hit me with lightning, but thankfully it didn't do any damage to the joint itself."

"Why were Fumans attacking you?"

He was quiet for a moment as he maneuvered them between trees and closer to the ground. She wondered if he was debating how to answer. He still hesitated after they'd landed and he sat her back on her feet, though he didn't remove his hands from her hips. Finally, in a voice so soft she almost didn't hear, he said, "It was an assassination attempt. The second one, and the one that came closest to succeeding."

Minnie wrapped her arms around his waist and hugged him tightly. "How long ago was this?"

"Almost two years ago. I was trying to establish trade with specific merchants, with their king's blessing, but there are some factions within the Fuman population who consider Skinshifters to be abominations, claiming we shouldn't exist and we're unnatural, the result of Humans mating with animals. It's all complete bullshit, of course, but there's no arguing with them. Father thinks that it was one of those same factions that killed my grandfather."

"Your father didn't go to war with them?" she demanded, wondering what in the Hells Taurak had been thinking.

Zavier shook his head. "He was furious, of course. The king has been trying to track down any other members of that group. Jarn and Maurgen killed the ones that attacked me. We can't punish every Human because of one group."

Minnie looked up, meeting his gold eyes. How had this man become so important to her in such a short time, that the very thought someone had tried to kill him long before they met made her want to sob?

"I'm alright, Mina," he murmured, pulling her close and tucking his head into her hair. "The shock knocked me out, but I had the guards with me. I promise, I'm fine. I won't be traveling without a healer ever again."

"Promise?" she asked with a shaky breath.

"I promise, my love, I promise," he whispered, so softly she wasn't sure she'd heard him correctly.

Thirty-Five

Zavier

Z ENIYAH HAD GIVEN VERY good directions, Zavier thought. The sinkhole was an old one, overgrown and sloping gently down. At the bottom, just as Zeniyah had described, was a small cave entrance, just large enough for them to enter if they stooped. Zavier, back in his regular form, led the way, holding a small ball of fire ahead of him to light the passage. They had to crouch for a dozen feet before the narrow passage opened to a larger chamber. Ahead was another path that continued on a downward slope. The chamber was large enough for them to stand comfortably, and no water dripped from the walls or ceiling.

With a ball of her own fire hovering over her head, Minnie explored the second path that led further down, winding back and forth. Soon they could hear the plop-plop sound of water dripping onto water and rock.

310

The passage opened to an underground spring, stalactites hanging from the ceiling over the water. Kneeling at the edge, Minnie ran a hand through the water and gasped at the warmth. She grinned up at Zavier.

"It's lovely and warm. We can scrub ourselves and the clothes, and lay them out to dry outside," she said, standing again. They didn't speak further as they stripped off their clothes, dropping them carelessly to the floor, and stepped into the water. Zavier watched as Minnie ran fingers through her loosened braid to untangle and spread the mass of curls around her before dunking under the water to thoroughly wet her hair.

Zavier scrubbed himself as well, just as eager to be clean again and wishing he'd thought to pack a shaving kit. He hissed as he carelessly touched his injured thigh. He'd forgotten about it after the fight, but now it ached as the water irritated the wound.

Minnie looked up at his hiss. "Why didn't you say it was that bad?" she scolded, approaching him. She pushed him backward until he was mostly out of the water and she could clearly see the wound. It still seeped blood, not terribly deep, but at least nine inches long on the outside of his thigh and curving from buttock to knee.

"It didn't hurt, truthfully I forgot it was there," he replied, attempting to politely shield his manhood from her even as it grew larger as she touched him.

"Hold still while I fix it," she grumbled, giving him a wry look. Calling her power to her, the golden light filled her palm and she smoothed it over his leg. Within seconds the injury was gone, leaving only a thin dabble of blood on his thigh.

"Thank you," he said as he ran a hand along her arm. He tugged gently and she stepped into him, wrapping an arm around his waist, pressing herself into his chest.

"Thank you, for fighting for Zeniyah and helping me rescue her," Minnie whispered.

"I'm not sure you needed the help. You handled yourself well. Are you alright?" He traced a finger down her cheek, a tender gesture meant to soothe and reassure.

"I think I am," she twisted her face into a grimace, remembering. "I didn't want to hurt anyone, but when I saw what they had done to her, and that man attacking from behind you... death was too kind, and their deaths didn't take long enough."

Zavier chuckled and kissed her cheek. "My bloodthirsty little healer."

She snorted. "Vengeful maybe, and hopefully not too bloodthirsty."

The pair scrubbed all their clothes in the warm water and had retraced their steps to the open cavern when Maurgen touched their minds. *"We have found a herd of deer and are eating our fill, we shall return with something for you very soon."*

After their soak and scrub in the warm spring water, the dragon-bonded met their partners on the rocky cliff above their cave hideaway. They'd wrapped blankets around themselves to protect delicate parts from branches and rocks as they scrambled up the steep path. The small mountain— if one could even call it that, after the mountains Zavier had seen to the north— rose higher than the trees, giving them a wonderful view of the treetops spread around them.

They gathered kindling for a fire and roasted the meat over a spit, the tantalizing aroma causing their stomachs to rumble loudly. Maurgen belched a satisfied reply when Minnie's stomach gurgled, wafting the coppery tang of blood over them.

"You could at least turn the other way, you damned lizard!" Zavier snarled, waving his hand before his face to clear the air. Beside him, Minnie coughed and held her nose.

"Whoops," the golden dragon replied, not sounding one bit contrite.

"He only had one small doe," Zeniyah added. She was using her claw to dig in the back of her mouth. She let out a *chirrup* sound as a chunk of bone popped loose and fell to the ground. *"Thank the Fates, that would have bothered me for hours."*

"I ate this morning, I was merely keeping you company while you ate," Maurgen replied as if defending his lack of appetite. The two dragons continued to bicker softly between them.

"If we stay here for the night and leave early in the morning, we'll be back to where the dragons had gathered by mid-morning, maybe close to noon. What will happen then? Can a dragon rise to mate at will, or will her body decide when it's time?" Minnie asked, poking a stick into the heart of the fire.

"A little of both. Wild dragons run entirely on instinct. Vynar and the bonded dragons usually choose when it's time. I'm quite surprised she's never risen, even instinctively," Zavier replied.

"Because we were un-Bonded for so long, my body did try to rise once. It was just before I left to fly north. I was being harassed by a group of young males who wouldn't take my refusal. A golden male came to my defense—"

"Wait, was that you?" Minnie interrupted, pointing at Zavier. "You said you rescued a young female that was important to Vera. Did you save Zeniyah?"

Zavier studied the dragon as if seeing her for the first time. "You may be right. I only caught a brief

313

glimpse, she left so quickly after I started fighting the males, but she was a green dragon, and quite small."

"I was always small. I do remember a golden dragon saved me, but as you say, I flew to my mother, and then to the coast to find Minnie, and became trapped." Zeniyah lowered her head, gently touching her muzzle to Zavier's forehead. *"Thank you, young prince, for rescuing me back then and again today. You truly show the same compassion that your ancestor did."*

Zavier bowed his head and crossed a hand over his heart. "I did what any rational man would do then, and today. You are most welcome," he bowed again.

"If you were not already Draconid, I would gift it to you for all you've done for me."

"Vera granted me that gift for saving you. She said I had done a service to all dragon-kind. I thought she was being overly generous, but now I understand," he replied, smiling up at her.

"What will happen when Zeniyah rises?" Minnie asked again, still poking the fire.

"Most likely, being around so many males will send my instincts into chaos, and I will rise whether I am ready to or not. The emotions may be overwhelming for you, Minnie, so it is best if you are somewhere safe, as you may not be aware of what is going on around you."

"I'll be there to protect her," Zavier added.

"You both should seclude yourselves in the forest or in a cave," Maurgen chimed in. *"I fully intend to be the male to catch Zeniyah, and when we mate you will feel the emotions as well, Zavier. As you are already involved, and your desires have been feeding into us, the release will be explosive. You, yourselves, are likely to mate again when we do."*

Minnie and Zavier exchanged looks. "Did you know that?" she asked.

Slowly, he nodded. "It was explained to me a long time ago, but I've never felt it myself. Maurgen joined a few wild matings, but I wasn't that affected."

"You will be this time," Maurgen replied. Zavier looked at him expectantly. *"Mating with a Bonded dragon is a more powerful experience than chasing a wild one. You and Minnie are already connected, that will give me an extra edge tomorrow. I will catch her."*

"You seem quite confident in yourself. Maybe I don't want you to catch me. Perhaps there is another male who is stronger and faster than you are. One more clever, who will outsmart me in the air." Zeniyah sounded peeved, though she gave the dragon-bonded a solemn wink with the eye facing them, which Maurgen couldn't see.

Maurgen snorted. *"I am the cleverest, largest, strongest, and fastest male. Is there a reason you do not want me to sire your clutch?"* he demanded to know.

A strange guffaw sound came from Zeniyah, the dragon's version of a laugh. *"As with every male before you, you must earn your place as my mate, and I will not make it easy on you out of gratitude for saving me!"*

Minnie hid a laugh from the dragon pair as Maurgen, offended that she would think he expected special treatment, continued to snipe at her.

"It's almost like she hasn't been imprisoned for most of her life..." Minnie whispered to Zavier.

"She remembers, but the memories will be hazy, almost unreal. Now that you are together, she'll begin to retain stronger memories. Be grateful for this, it will heal her and she won't be so traumatized. One day, she may not remember at all."

"I hope she does forget the pain. I know I won't..."

"They've become fast friends," Zavier said as he scooted closer to Minnie and turned the roasting meat again. He wanted to try and clear the shadow of worry from her face.

"I'm glad she's comfortable with us. I wonder how much of that is because I'm so comfortable with you both?"

"Probably quite a bit. You'll both share emotions and some memories, more now that you're together. About her mating flight... I have no doubt Maurgen will catch her. I want to... I mean, if you don't want to have sex again, I don't expect—"

Minnie snorted. "Not want to? Last night was amazing, I can only dream how amazing it will be when fueled by dragon emotions. I'm nervous about the unknown, but not about sleeping with you!"

Relieved, Zavier nodded. "We should take a long soak in the spring water before we leave, it will help you not be sore."

A curious look crossed Minnie's face. "Should we just stay here? The dragons can fly on without us, and we can catch up later. I don't want to part from Zeniyah, but if we'd be safer here, should we stay?"

Zavier considered for a moment. Finally, he shook his head. "I don't think so, but let's ask the experts. Maurgen! Hey! LIZARD BREATH!" The shout took both dragons by surprise, so involved were they in their back and forth argument.

What do you need, idiot?" Maurgen growled, a puff of smoke escaping his nostrils.

"If Minnie and I stayed here, would that have a negative effect on either of you during the flight?"

"No, distance doesn't matter once the bond has been established. Most female dragons return to the Isle alone to mate. You could safely stay here and meet up with us the day after." Zeniyah replied. She nudged Minnie with her snout. *"I would miss you, and regret parting so soon after we finally found each other, but this is a safe location.*

It might be for the best if we go ahead. If this one lives up to his claims, it promises to be a very exciting flight."

Maurgen snorted again. *"We could leave tonight, if you're so eager. I don't need any more preparation in order to catch you."*

Zeniyah stared at him for several minutes, her green cat-like eyes locked onto his golden ones. Without looking away, she said to Minnie, *"If it is alright with you, I think I'd like to take him up on that offer. A night flight amongst the stars, especially to the south where the storms rage, would be a good challenge for this cocky male."*

Minnie giggled quietly, and rubbed the side of Zeniyah's head. "Of course, dearest. I hate to be separated from you so soon, but I do think it's for the best if we wait here. But be safe, if you are planning to fly into a storm..."

Zeniyah finally looked away from Maurgen to nuzzle her great head into Minnie's chest. *"It is the duty of the female to test the mettle of the males who want to mate with her. It is even more important for me as the future Vynar, my clutches will birth more dragon-bonded. I will be safe, I promise you."*

She rumbled softly deep in her chest, almost a purr. Lowering her head, nearly the size of Minnie's whole body, Zeniyah pressed her forehead to Minnie's. Zavier's chest felt tight and his eyes burned with unshed tears at the sight of the pair finally together. Maurgen nudged his shoulder, sharing in the emotion.

"Thank you, little one," Zeniyah said, making the low purr growl again. Minnie wrapped her arms around the dragon's head and hugged her tight. Zavier thought he saw a glow radiate from the pair, but with the setting sun behind them, he couldn't

be sure. After they parted, the green dragon faced Zavier. *"Take care of my Bonded, young prince."*

"I will. You have my word," Zavier replied, bowing his head again.

Zeniyah stood and stretched her wings wide, flexing them. Maurgen followed suit, quivering in anticipation. With a mighty shove of her rear legs Zeniyah took to the sky, Maurgen a mere half-second behind her. Showered by dirt and debris, the two Bonded laughed and swept themselves off.

"At least they didn't ruin the fire," Minnie said, knocking a twig off the top of the roasting meat and turning it again.

"For creatures so majestic and magnificent, they really are oversized lizards, aren't they?" Zavier added, pointing to the flying pair as they cavorted in the air. Maurgen appeared to be practicing his catch technique while Zeniyah evaded him.

"More like oversized children," she chuckled. Abruptly, she stood and brushed herself off. "I'm going to go down and search the forest for some edible greens, eggs, anything that we can add to this meal. I'm not eating just meat again!"

After they had eaten, Zavier and Minnie carried their clothes to a short, sprawling tree just outside the cave entrance and spread them across the branches to dry. They'd discarded their blankets and Minnie appeared selfconscious, the lines of her body tense, and she constantly looked around her as if searching for people. Zavier found himself staring unabashedly at her, especially when she bent to pick up more of their clothes to drape over the branch. She turned and caught him staring, her face and upper chest flushing red. Zavier smiled an apology.

"Don't be embarrassed. I'm sorry I've made you uncomfortable," Zavier said softly. "I'm surprised it's taken you this long to catch me, I find myself staring at you quite often."

Still flushed and awkwardly standing with her hands almost covering herself, she shook her head. "No, I'm not uncomfortable.... Well I am, but not by you. I'm just not used to being unclothed outside." Squaring her shoulders, she brazenly sauntered to where he leaned against the cliff wall beside the cave.

He watched her approach, not bothering to disguise his lust for her. Her curves seemed to glow as the sunlight shined on her copper skin. Her nipples puckered in the soft breeze. Zavier bit back a groan as he watched them peak.

She traced a hand up his stomach and over his chest. She cleared her throat as if she were searching for the words. Zavier stayed silent, letting her have her way. After a moment, she asked, "You stare at me?"

She didn't understand, he thought. How could he explain to her just how much she had changed his life? How completely he belonged to her? He'd told her to set their pace and he would follow, then last night she'd said he could stand to be a little more pushy...

He leaned forward, gripping her plump ass in both his hands and pulling her roughly into him. She gasped at the sudden movement and the hard length pressed between their stomachs.

He growled into her ear, "I've watched you like a hawk watches its prey since the moment we met. I can't keep my eyes from you. You're the most captivatingly beautiful woman I've ever met. Of course I stare at you. I'm going to soak up every moment of you while I can."

Before this is over, he thought, bending slightly to kiss her lips. Where most of their kisses had been fueled by an almost desperate passion, he let this be gentle, drawing out the kiss and putting every bit of love he felt for her into the effort. He ran one hand along her back until he reached the nape of her neck, fisting his fingers into her loose curls. He realized then that he'd not seen her hair down before, she always wore it braided or twisted in a bun. An image of her above him, glorious curls haloing her head as she rode him, filled his mind.

With a groan he pulled back from her lips, pressing his forehead to hers. "I don't know what spell you've woven around me, my Mina, but please don't release me any time soon," he whispered as he stared into her eyes.

He watched as doubt and fear filled her eyes. He ran a thumb over her cheek as a tear fell, wiping it away. "What is it, my love? What's wrong?" he begged to know.

She tilted her head, nuzzling into his hand. In a soft voice, she asked, "Love? You called me that earlier, and said it last night, too, didn't you?"

He hesitated for only a second before nodding. "I did. And... I do."

A single tear slid down her cheek and he wiped it away at once. He was afraid he had ruined everything. He should have kept his mouth shut. What kind of idiot was he that he would just blurt out—

"I love you," she whispered, breaking through his mental tirade. "I've been trapped my entire life, in that house, that village, with my family. I feel like you've freed me. You make me feel like I'm strong enough to do anything I want—"

"You are strong enough," he interrupted, but she shushed him and continued.

"Shh. You've helped me become who I was meant to be. And on top of all that, as if I didn't already love you enough, you saved Zeniyah, risking yourself and Maurgen to do it. And before you say anything, yes, I know you would have risked yourselves for any dragon, just as I would, and that just makes me love you both all the more. I feel like you and I have been bound together since that first day under the trellis. This... this desire, this pull we feel, it's so wild, so freeing. I love you, Zavier."

Zavier captured her lips once again, cupping her face with both his hands. Desire surged through him. He knew that if he didn't pull away from her, he might disgrace himself across her stomach. Breaking the kiss, he lifted her up, wrapping her legs around his middle. She squealed and gripped his neck. He gave thanks to the Fates for her height as he spun them around and pressed her against the cliff wall. Bracing her with his hips, he mounded her breasts together, drawing the nipples into his mouth with a long suckle. She fisted her fingers into his hair and clutched him to her, grinding her hips against his stomach.

He slid a hand down her body, finding her wet and eager as he slid two fingers inside her. She clenched around his fingers with a shuddering moan. He swore under his breath, pushing a third finger inside her. Fates above, she was ready for him. It took more strength than he wanted to admit to keep himself from plunging his cock into her right away. Instead, he pinched her clit and nipped a breast at the same time, drawing a surprise gasp from her. A feral grin on his lips, he lowered her down until her feet touched the ground, then fell to his knees before her. He lifted one of her legs over his shoulder, burying his face between her thick thighs.

Her delicious taste and smell engulfed him, and he devoured her with long laps of his tongue. His fingers dug into her ass, holding her close. Above him, she panted and moaned with each flick of his tongue, her hips twitching frantically. He speared her with two fingers, curling them against her inner walls. She came apart, screaming her orgasm as her climax covered his mouth. He eagerly licked her clean, slowly pumping his fingers within her. He could feel her quiver, the hand tightening in his hair. He added a third finger and thrust deep as he suckled her clit, pulling another orgasm from her. He continued until she pulled him away, begging him to give her a moment.

He stood, picking her up under her thighs and once again wrapping her legs around his hips. He couldn't wait, not even as long as it would take to go inside to the smooth cave floor. He lifted her, carefully lined himself up, and thrust within her with a desperate groan. Minnie threw her head back against the cliff, clutching his shoulders and allowing him room to set a furious pace. He knew he wouldn't last very long, but he wanted one more thing before they were finished.

"Mina, touch yourself. I want to feel you come around my cock," he panted, adjusting them to give her room between their bodies. The new angle hit deeper. She pinched her clit, rubbing furious circles where they were joined. Panting for breath, she said, "Zavier... I want to spend forever with you!" She screamed as she climaxed, her entire body convulsing with the force of her orgasm.

Zavier thrust twice more before his climax crested and he spilled himself inside her, pressing her hard against the stone. Gasping for air and rapidly losing strength in his legs, he lowered her carefully to the ground, suddenly mindful of her bare skin along the rocky cliff face. He turned her to brush dirt and loose stones from her skin but she resisted, wrapping her arms around his middle instead. He kissed her forehead and embraced her tightly.

"Mina... did you mean it?" He asked haltingly, nervous of the answer. "Do you want to stay with me?"

She looked up at him, a soft smile on her lips. "I do mean it. I've been thinking about it since last night. For days, really, but especially after last night. If you can promise me that I won't be trapped in the palace, then yes. I want to be with you forever."

"But... Mina," he hesitated, afraid to make her think too hard about her words. He took a deep breath. "One day, I will become king. My father says it's in his will and he's told the council. I want you by my side in every way. I want you as my queen, but *only* if that is what you want."

She smiled her quirky little smile up at him. "I know. I'm not worthy of being a princess now, but I'll do everything to be worthy of you and your people. Especially if it means I get to be with you."

"You are already worthy, my love, in every way." He cut off her reply with another soul-shattering kiss.

Thirty-Six

Zeniyah

Z ENIYAH FELT THE PULSE of magic and desire race up her spine. She shivered, her wings flaring. Soon.

They were gathered on the edge of the great Caldera. Every Vynar going back to Vyn had risen here. Hundreds of females rose every year, using the turbulent winds over the lake to weed out the weak from the strong.

"Fly swift, fly strong, fly safe, daughter," came the ancient voice of her mother from atop her ledge. Zeniyah looked up at her and snorted smoke. It was time.

Without warning, she leaped into the air. Her first downstroke propelled her higher than it should have, boosted by her own magical command of the air around her. Below her, dozens of males followed into the sky with various degrees of speed.

She flew hard to the south. She had never understood why, but there were constant storms over this part of the lake. Most females did not risk it, it was as easy for her to be struck by lightning as it was for the males. She was not most females. She was their future, and she needed the strongest male possible to sire her clutches.

The top contender, Maurgen, slid below her and flicked his tail at her. He was taunting her, challenging her to out-fly him. He was cocky, but strong, and powerful. Zeniyah desired Maurgen as much as Minnie desired Zavier.

She soared higher, into the storm clouds. The air around her crackled as the lightning gathered. Only a male finely attuned to his magic would be able to sense the incoming bolt and be able to avoid it the way she did. As the strike ripped across the sky, the males around her scattered. All but four.

She dove, folding her wings and slipping between two males. One tried to grab her and missed. She fell toward the lake, glancing over her shoulder as the males followed. One was close, he had used his smaller size to turn quicker in midair than the lumbering giants above him. She would just see how fast he was...

At the very last moment before she hit the water, she spread her wings and summoned a blast of air to lift her higher. Wind whistled through the gaps in her wing sail, but her magic was strong, With a satisfied rumble, she soared ever higher. A splash behind her signaled one of the males had failed to make the turn.

Another bolt of lightning zinged across the sky near her. A male screamed, one wing crumpled. He fell several hundred feet before he was able to catch himself. The singed smell of burnt flesh wafted to her. Two down, two to go.

Zeniyah rose even higher, dodging lightning strikes and the two remaining males. One was Maurgen, the other a wild blue dragon not much smaller than the giant gold dragon. The blue male had countless battle scars, proving he was the victor in many fights with other males and probably numerous mating flights as well. He would give Maurgen a good challenge to prove his worth.

She slowed her pace, allowing the blue to fly close enough to almost touch wingtips. With a coy glance toward Maurgen, she flipped in the air, swiping the blue with her tail. He growled and lunged toward her, making a wild grab with his spread front claws. The blue caught her on the thigh, raking a deep trench down the muscle. Zeniyah screamed, righted herself in the air and blasted fire toward the male.

Maurgen bellowed his fury. Instead of attempting to separate them or catch Zeniyah himself, Maurgen grappled with the wild male. He caught the male by a hind leg, crawling up the blue's body. The weight was too much for the blue to keep them in the air, and his wings crumpled. Maurgen allowed them to fall, sinking his claws into the male's wings at the shoulder joint. With a fierce bugle, Maurgen clamped his jaws around the blue male's jugular and wrenched, ripping his throat out.

Releasing the blue, Maurgen hovered, watching the dying male fall to the lake depths below. Above, Zeniyah crooned a taunt to him. Could he catch her, or was he too tired to fly after all that fighting?

Bellowing again, Maurgen flew after her. Blood dripped freely from his jaws and her thigh, though neither noticed as the rain finally began to pour from the clouds around them. Higher and higher they flew, with Zeniyah remaining just out of reach of Maurgen the whole time. The pair broke out of the clouds above the storms into silence, the only sound their own beating wings and labored breathing. Zeniyah looked over her shoulder to Maurgen, but was surprised that he wasn't right behind her.

He wrapped his wings around her, engulfing her much smaller frame, fouling her wings. They began to fall, tumbling end over end, wrapped in Maurgen's glistening golden wings. He twined his neck and tail about her, growling low, an almost soothing sound. "*Mine*," he said, as he claimed her miles above the stormy lake.

Thirty-Seven

Minnie

RATIONAL THOUGHT HAD LEFT them. Power flowed through Zavier and Minnie. Flames erupted around the cave and wind swirled through, uncontrolled. Sleek and sweating, the pair were as wrapped in each other as their dragons were. With so much magic in their bodies, Zavier struggled to maintain his humanoid shape.

"Shift," Minnie panted as she rode his cock. "I want to see your wings spread above me."

Growling, Zavier rolled them over, crawling to his hands and knees. Head down, he allowed the magic free reign of his body, gasping in relief as he shifted to the Draconid shape the dragons had gifted him so long ago. Minnie reached up, allowing herself the pleasure of caressing his horns. Taking them firmly in both hands, she guided his head between her thighs. She shrieked in delight as he ate her to climax.

Sated, she released her grip on his horns. Zavier took both her hands and placed them over her head, holding her wrists in one of his own large hands. She hooked a leg around his ass as he sunk into her wet heat. Wings flaring wide and his tail thrashing, he pounded into her, both of them grunting at the force of his thrusts.

"Touch yourself, come again," he panted, unable to touch her while he held her arms and braced himself. He let up long enough for her to get one hand free, but kept the other restrained. She slipped her hand to her clit, already close to climax. Within seconds, the cave echoed with her screams of pleasure as another orgasm took her.

Releasing her, Zavier rose higher on his knees, pulling out of her. "Flip over," he commanded, assisting her as she struggled with weakened legs to her hands and knees. Reverently, Zavier caressed her rounded ass, slapping one cheek with a fierce growl. She gasped, turning back to look over her shoulder, but there was no reproach in her eyes, only lust.

Zavier fisted a hand in her untamed curls, pushing her head down and lifting her ass. He ground his cock against her slit and puckered hole. "I'll fuck you there another time," he promised. Unable to get the right angle, he released her hair and shifted the hand to her hip. Minnie groaned in eager anticipation, face down, as she tried to grind back against him. Taking her ass in both his large hands, he stilled her, lined himself up, and pushed in to the hilt.

They both screamed in pleasure. Zavier lost any restraint he had left, pounding into her without mercy. Another orgasm overtook Minnie, her body shaking as the climax wracked her. Zavier grunted as he came inside her, his wings flexing.

Beneath him, Minnie felt a surge of magic rising deep within her body. The magic pulsed at her center, and in her mind she saw an image of Maurgen and Zeniyah on the lake shore, wrapped in a mating embrace. Pulling away from Zavier she turned, pushing him down until he lay flat on his back, wings spread beneath him. The magic pulsed within her again. She wrapped her hand around his cock and directed the magic to flow from her to him. He hardened again with an almost pained grunt.

Straddling him, she impaled herself on his cock with a fluid rocking of her hips. She danced and teased over him as the magic built to near boiling point. Beneath her, Zavier grit his teeth in effort not to climax. His fingers dug into her hips. Unable to resist, he thrust up into her, taking charge and setting a faster, harder rhythm.

The magic erupted around them, bringing them both to another screaming climax. As she quivered above him, Minnie felt itchy, almost painful sensations at her shoulder blades, her lower back, and on her head. Beneath her, Zavier gasped, his eyes wide.

Emerald wings spread on either side of her body. Her head felt heavier, and reaching up she discovered two long horns similar to Zeniyah's. From the base of her spine grew the long, serpentine tail in the same emerald color as her hide.

Panting, Zavier sat up, lifting her clumsily and helping her stand. Around them the fire and wind died away, leaving only the non-magical campfire they'd made earlier in the evening. Silently, Zavier ran a hand over one wing.

"Zeniyah must have done this just before she left. Remember, she touched her forehead to yours? Vera did that when she gave me the Draconid gift... I wonder if she knew she had done it? She's not Vynar yet, she shouldn't be able to do that."

Staring at their winged shadows, Minnie had no answer. In the back of her mind, she heard Horth's deep voice. Every time he'd ever greeted her, he had said, "Greetings, little Draconid." When she'd asked why, he said it was just a feeling he had.

"He was right..." Minnie whispered, flaring her wings.

"He?"

"Horth, the dragon bonded to Elder Lirance, from my village." Minnie stretched her wings wide, then folded them against her back. Controlling them seemed to be instinctive, as easy as flying was in her dragon-skin. "Every time I saw him, he called me 'little Draconid' and just said that he had a feeling. I wonder if Lirance had a vision? Or is it dragon instinct?"

Zavier wrapped her in his arms, folding his wings around hers. "You can ask him the next time you see him. Meanwhile, let's go soak in the hot spring. There are some very interesting things I'd like to do to you now that you have some wings of your own."

Thirty-Eight

Minnie

S OFT LIGHT FILTERED THROUGH the leaves above and down the short passage into the cave. Birds twittered their morning song. Minnie stretched, muscles aching from her unaccustomed exercise the past few days. She felt twinges on her back and wondered how scratched up she was from their tryst against the rock wall outside the previous night. Or on the cave floor. Or on the rough ledge in the hot springs cavern. Or early that morning against the tree in front of the cave... Not to mention, shifting as a Draconid for the first time. Ruefully, she shook her head. She had plenty of reasons to be sore this morning.

Beside her, Zavier sighed and snuggled closer to her. A thought toward the dragons told her they were both deeply asleep. It was quite comforting to be so alone, with no one but Zavier around for miles.

She put an arm under her head, sliding the other under Zavier. Combing her fingers through his hair, she admired the morning light on his golden features. The man had no right to be that attractive.

Her mind wandered to all that had happened since she'd left home. It was hard to believe it had only been a week. Guilt gnawed at her stomach; she hadn't thought of her family in days. Was her mother alright? Were her father and sister struggling with her mother?

She pushed those thoughts aside angrily. She'd given enough of her life in service to her mother, this was her time to do as she pleased.

Minnie shifted to the side and sat up, carefully sliding her arm from under Zavier's head. He protested, one eye opening slightly to glare at her. She threw her leg over his waist and straddled him, resting her hands on his chest. She grinned down at him, her wild and unruly hair falling into her face. She grimaced and lifted her hands to start braiding her hair, but Zavier stopped her.

"No, don't," he said, grabbing her arm. "I've been wanting to see your hair free while you ride me. I hadn't realized until last night just how beautiful it is."

She scoffed. "It's a damned pain, and always a mess. That's why I keep it braided, it's just easier."

"It's beautiful no matter what, but like this…" He rolled beneath her so she rested on his hips, and arched up into her, proving how much he liked the view above him.

She ground her hips into his, but hissed and sat back almost immediately. "What is it?" Zavier asked, sitting up and reaching for her.

"Oh no, it's nothing," she replied quickly.

Zavier frowned. "It's not nothing, what's wrong? Did I do something?"

"No, no of course not." She leaned forward to kiss him but he held her back with a hand to her shoulder. He gave her a shrewd look. "Mina, are you hurt?" he asked, his eyes flicking down.

She blushed, and nodded slowly. "It's nothing, I promise. I'm just a bit sore from all our uh… vigor," she smiled. "My lower abdomen is aching, too. I've lost track of time recently but I should be due to start my, um… my cycle."

Her cheeks burned, but Zavier leaned in and kissed her lightly on the nose.

"You need to soak in the springs for a little while, that will help you feel better. Go on down and I'll get our clothes off the branches and find some breakfast."

Zavier stood and hauled her upright. He turned her toward the path to the spring, gave her a slight push to send her on her way, and patted her backside as she began walking. Laughing, she did as she was told.

She floated, her eyes closed and her head resting on a rocky ledge she'd swept clean. The spring was only a few feet deep in this section, but it dropped drastically not far away. She was careful to stay where it was fairly shallow.

Her stomach twisted with a sudden ache and she cursed. It was unlike her to forget about her monthly courses, but of course it would begin while she was all alone with a gorgeous man. She wondered if she'd packed sanitary rags in her rush to leave Hatherus for Saltstone.

From down the corridor she heard whistling as Zavier approached. She sat up, crossing her legs and sitting on the floor of the pool with just her head above water.

"Feeling any better?" he asked as he came around the corner. He held her dry clothes in his hands, along with a large leaf, flat like a tray.

"I am, thank you. I wish we had a hot spring like this back at home," she replied.

He sat her clothes on a dry ledge and came closer to her, draping his legs over the edge of the pool. On the leaf were several fruits, already peeled and cubed.

"Where did you find these?" she exclaimed, rising to her knees and hastily grabbing for the makeshift plate.

He chuckled and handed it to her. "I flew around a bit, we must have missed them in the dark last night. There's a whole grove of them not far away."

She greedily ate them up, groaning in delight at the juicy tang on her tongue. Her venture to find something other than meat for dinner the night before had ended in failure.

"These are incredible," she said, popping the last piece into her mouth.

"There are plenty more, we can stock up before we leave."

"I wish we didn't have to go back so soon," Minnie sighed. Going back to Hatherus would be overwhelming after so much time in solitude. There was sure to be a big furor over Zeniyah's rescue and Minnie's new gift.

Zavier cupped her chin, turning her face toward his and meeting her eye. "I would stay here with you forever, if I could. Unfortunately, we have to return. My father needs our report on the Humas' treatment of Zeniyah, and I need to follow up on whoever poisoned a city full of my people."

335

She nodded, ashamed she had forgotten. "Of course, you're right. I'm ready when you are. Will we meet up with the dragons?"

He nodded as he released her chin. "I'm sure they'll catch up to us. They fly faster than we do, especially with Zeniyah's magic to boost them. That's probably something you can do, come to think of it. I worry you would tire yourself though, you aren't a very strong flier, yet."

Minnie gave a sad smile. "No, I've not had very much practice before this week. I'll grow stronger, though. And now I can fly as a Draconid, too, you'll have to teach me the nuances of that!"

She rose from the water, slicking away the droplets with her hands. He watched her hungrily, admiring her curves from top to bottom. His gaze made her feel beautiful and powerful. He handed her clothes to her and she dressed quickly. He pulled something from his pocket.

"Take this, too," he said as he handed it to her.

"Did you make a sanitary napkin?" she asked, examining the folded strip of cloth in her hands that looked suspiciously like the hem of his cloak.

He flushed, but nodded. "I wasn't sure if you had anything, but I didn't want you to worry about arriving in Hatherus with bloody pants. Oh, and I saw this when I was getting the fruit, I recognized it from my lessons on medicinals. I couldn't find anything for pregnancy, something we really ought to have discussed before we let ourselves get so carried away. The medics at the palace will have anything you need, though, if it comes up." Zavier dug into the pocket of his trousers and pulled a small rolled up bit of cloth. Unrolling it revealed several leaves from a plant Minnie knew helped with cramping.

Usually it was made into tea, but in a pinch it could be chewed and sucked on.

As Minnie stared from the leaves to the wad of cloth in her hands, she felt the tears prick her eyes. Why was she crying now, she wondered to herself as she knuckled her eyes. The man had risked his and his dragon's life to save Zeniyah and she was crying over such a simple gesture?

Zavier took her hand, a frantically worried look on his face. "Mina, what is it? Please don't cry, love, I'm sorry! I'm not sure what I've done, but I'm so sorry. Are the plants wrong? I thought they were for pain? Will the cloth not work? Please, dearest, how can I help you?"

As he rambled on, his voice took on a more panicked tone that made Minnie giggle through her tears. She looked up, wiping her eyes again. "You're amazing, Zavier. I think... I think I'm just shocked at how it feels to be taken care of, after having been the one to take care of my family for so long."

Zavier frowned, idly tracing his hands over her arms. "No one cared for you if you were sick? No one brought you a hot water bottle for cramps? Or made you tea? Father taught us to do all that for Mother almost as soon as we could walk."

"Mama was ill a lot of the time, and my father would if he were home, but he spent most of the day fishing or selling fish, or making trades for fish, then when he got home he'd be exhausted. There were days that he would take a half day and he and my sister would take over with Mama and let me rest or study with Elder Lirance. I never wanted to be a nuisance to them, so I cared for myself."

Zavier's eyebrows creased as he leaned into her. One arm wrapped around her waist and the other cupped the back of her head. His grip was rougher than he had ever touched her, barring their drag-on-induced frenzy the night before. She gasped as he crushed his lips to hers in a fierce kiss before wrenching away.

In a voice so low it was almost a growl, he said, "I will take care of you in every way for the rest of my life. You have claimed every bit of my heart and whatever soul Maurgen doesn't own. Everything I am is yours, and I will spend my life proving that if you will let me. Not even my crown is more important to me than you are now. I would give up the throne if you asked that of me."

Minnie sucked in a breath, stunned. She didn't want that of him! She was opening her mouth to reply, but he cut her off.

"No, don't speak." His commanding tone, so unlike his usually soft demeanor, kept her quiet. "You need to hear this, my Mina, and understand that I mean every word. I am yours as long as my heart beats. I know you would never ask me to give up my crown or my people, but I would do it. I would take you to every corner of our world, known and unknown, if that would make you happy. I decided days ago that I would marry you, or no one at all, for no one could ever possibly measure up to you in my heart. I know you said you wanted to stay with me forever while in the heat of passion, but I want you to be completely certain. If you decide you could be happy as my queen, I am begging you to marry me."

He kissed her lips again, gently this time. Resting his forehead against hers, he closed his eyes. Minnie watched his eyelids flutter and saw a small tear in the corner of one eye. She slid a hand between their bodies to wipe the tear, and he leaned his face into her palm.

"Do not say anything now, my love," he whispered, the commanding voice gone. He sounded almost afraid, she thought with a wrench to her heart. "I do not need an answer yet, not until you are ready. I simply want you to know the full extent of my feelings for you. Maurgen feels the same. We would burn our world to the ground if you asked it of us."

"I would never..." she whispered, stroking his cheek with her thumb.

"I know, but maybe you should. You ask for nothing, yet you give everything of yourself to others. When we get home, I will have to be the prince again, and I may not see you as much as I want. You will be free to live your life, explore our world as you dreamed when you arrived, and you'll have your Zeniyah with you. You are Draconid now, you are free to go anywhere you want to, no one can gainsay you. I will not let my love for you keep you caged, when you were born to be free."

"Zavier..." She kissed him, raising on tiptoe to be on even footing with him. The force of her kiss pushed him back into the stone wall of the cave and he let out a small grunt, then chuckled. Time slipped by unnoticed as they kissed and caressed each other. There was no pressure from either to remove their clothes, this wasn't about pleasure or passion. They sought the reassuring touch of each other in the confines of their secluded cave, no one around them for miles and no expectations or responsibilities.

Eventually, the pair made their way back down the pathway. In silence they packed their meager belongings. Before she skinshifted, Minnie tucked the folded cloth between her legs just in case. She didn't know if her courses would start while she was a dragon. If they did, would the cloth even help? Better safe than sorry.

They stood hand in hand just outside their little cave for several minutes, watching birds flit around them. Minnie was reminded of how she'd watched the birds outside her home the night her entire world had changed. She had seen so much, and yet...

She looked at Zavier. He was in profile, a soft smile on his lips as he watched two small blackbirds chase each other. She was still afraid, she realized. Not of being trapped, not by him. Never by him. No.

She was afraid she would also burn the world down for him.

Thirty-Nine

Minnie

T HE DRAGONS CAUGHT UP with them only a few miles from the coast of Dragon Isle, a couple hours after they'd started flying. Branton had been left behind to learn from the dragons the same way Zavier had when he was that age, under the watchful care of a friend of Maurgen's. Minnie, sore in places she couldn't even name, gratefully accepted Maurgen's offer to ferry her the rest of the way home. She released her hold on her dragon-skin as Maurgen swooped below to catch her. Moments later, he performed a similar maneuver with Zavier. Wrapped safely in Zavier's arms, she let herself fall asleep.

When Zavier woke her up, they were within sight of the Spire of Hatherus, the city sprawled out below it. People moved around, going about their normal daily activities with no idea of what had occurred beyond their small corner of the world. Zeniyah passed them, eagerly scanning the city below. Despite the damage to her wings and scars covering her hide, she glowed with a sense of peace that wasn't there before she rose to mate. Whatever bond was forged between the mated pair, it seemed to agree with her.

Maurgen circled down to land in the courtyard of the palace. Minnie looked up at the beautiful but imposing building with almost as much trepidation as she'd felt when she first arrived. But as Zavier slid to the ground and lifted his arms to catch her, his reassuring smile allayed some of her worry. He clasped her hand and led her up the steps and through the double doors. He refused to relinquish her hand as they entered his father's study several moments later.

"You're back!" Taurak rose from his wingback chair, eagerly circling the desk. He first gave a small bow to Minnie, taking her hand and kissing the air above it, then turning to clasp his son's forearm. Zavier grinned, pulling his father into a one armed hug. Feeling awkward, Minnie hovered nearby, her hand still wrapped in Zavier's.

"We just arrived. Did Damian tell you everything?" Zavier responded, pulling away from his father. He indicated a seat for Minnie, pulled another chair over from the fireplace and sat beside her, resting his hand on her knee. Minnie wondered if he should be so obvious in front of his father. Her eyes darted from father to son, but Taurak seemed not to notice her nerves. He sat back in his own chair and pulled several sheets of parchment from a stack.

"I think he did, he was remarkably willing to speak to me, considering what his father is likely to do when he finds out. Let's see..."

"I got the impression he was honorable, but maybe a bit young and misguided," Zavier interjected as his father scanned his notes.

"Yes, that's the feeling I had as well. I'll be recommending him to the Human king when this is over. I've got... A group of mages and Human guards numbering somewhere between ten and fifteen captured a green female dragon roughly seventeen years ago. They performed magical experiments on her to siphon her magic, and they used sharp objects as well as magic to harm her, leading to severe scarring, both physical and emotional. She also was poisoned with a substance he was not willing to name, as it is private to the dragons? Can you tell me more about that?"

Minnie cleared her throat. Zavier gave her a surprised look, and nodded, indicating she was free to speak. "Zeniyah is my dragon. I healed her after we freed her from her chains. She had extensive internal damage, as well as the external damage mentioned in the report. It's clear they used their magic to harm her in ways that would not kill her right away. Their aim was to keep her weak. The poison is called Dragonsbane, according to Zeniyah and Maurgen. It's a mineral that is found on Dragon Isle and the Inferno, only near active volcanoes. In its natural state, it causes hallucinations, but when it's smelted and refined with a specific herb, it can be deadly. They would not tell us the herb, however."

Zavier nodded along as she spoke, adding when she fell silent, "Maurgen said that Dragonsbane hadn't been seen by the dragons for hundreds of years, it had nearly faded from their memories. Clearly it was written down and remembered by the Humans, or somehow rediscovered on their own."

Taurak nodded, looking pensive. "They may have a supply handed down through the ages. Some of the history books mention the dragons terrorizing Humans. They left us alone because we are seen as animals in their eyes, kindred spirits. It's similar with the Wealdkin, Nightwalkers, and Stoneborn, we are all connected to nature more closely than the Humans are, and the dragons seem to honor that."

The trio fell silent for a moment as Taurak perused his notes again. Unsure what to say, Minnie glanced at Zavier. She was surprised to find he was watching her with a small smile. He squeezed her thigh in what she thought was a reassuring gesture.

Taurak looked up again. "I've not heard back from my people on the ground in the Human lands, but I expect reports by the end of the day, perhaps tomorrow at the latest. As the dragons have given us such gifts, we cannot let this assault on them go. Has Vera been told?"

"Yes," Zavier said, turning back to face his father. "Zeniyah returned to the dragons and told them everything. For now, the dragons will not act. Zeniyah feels it is unfair to penalize the entire Human race for what may be the actions of only a few. Vera was all set to burn them all."

"It's good she talked them down, let me get the information as to who is responsible. I'll have Alyss reassure Vera that we will handle this matter, and if it goes deeper than we think, they can certainly plan their own attack. Not that we can really tell the dragons what to do!" Taurak chuckled, and put the parchment aside.

"Have you learned anything else about the poisoned salt?" Zavier asked, his eyes creased in a frown.

"Ah, yes. Well, no, not really, but we do have some information that might lead us in the right direction." Taurak pulled another sheet of parchment out, this one much more crinkled and dirty.

"So the salt arrived on the ship *Lady Clara* along with other non-perishable supplies. Over half the crew were already sick, several close to death. Two days later it had spread across the warehouse district and into the city itself. Minnie," here the king turned a smile to her, "was correct that simply washing their hands would have prevented the spread, or limited it greatly. We think we have recovered all the salt, and issued warnings to every village and outpost to be on the lookout for symptoms."

"None of the crew survived, except for the captain, correct?" Zavier said, turning back to Minnie in query.

She nodded. "Captain Anders was the last alive, though he mentioned a factor that would have the records."

"I spoke to the factor, he helped us track down all the distributed salt in the city and which wagons carried it out," Zavier added. "He said the salt had been a gift to the captain, but not who had given it to him. I'm not sure if they forgot to write it down, didn't want anyone to know, or if they were lying. I didn't think to ask at the time who gave it to Anders." He shook his head, clearly berating himself for the oversight.

"We can send someone back to interview the captain, or to bring him here," Taurak said, making a note on a fresh sheet of paper. "We need information on the supplier. I cannot imagine that it's accidental, so what was the purpose, and who was the target?"

None of them had an answer to those questions.

Zavier cleared his throat. "I can add another question, was the timing incidental, or purposeful? Poisoning a few thousand people is impressive enough, but that it was done as most of the dragon-bonded have left the country? That tells me they are knowledgeable about our customs, and that they knew Bonded would be immune."

"Well that part isn't much of a stretch, drag-on-bonded are immune to almost all poisons and illnesses," Minnie interjected. The men both stared at her. "What?" she nervously asked.

Father and son looked back at each other, to Minnie, then back again. It would have been comical if Minnie hadn't been so worried about their reactions.

"My father was poisoned, assassinated. I never connected... I've known my entire life that we are supposed to be immune, but somehow it never occurred to me that my father should not have died from poison..." Taurak replied softly.

"He wasn't Bonded, is that the difference?" Zavier asked.

Minnie shook her head. "From what I understand, that isn't supposed to matter, it's the dragon skinshifting part that makes dragon-bonded immune, because dragons are immune to poisons..." Her eyes grew wide and she stared at Zavier. "Immune except for one..."

"Grandfather was killed by Dragonsbane," Zavier snarled.

"Someone used Dragonsbane," Taurak said at the same time.

Minnie nodded. "The only poison I've ever heard of that can harm any dragon would be Dragonsbane, so clearly someone knew about it."

"I'll have the scribes check the library, both here and at the healer's school. There must be mention somewhere," Taurak said, slamming his fist on the desk.

"Have them search for a cure or antidote while they're at it," Zavier added. "It would help if the dragons would tell us what that mysterious herb is that's mixed in to make it so deadly."

"It's not that we won't tell you, it's that we do not have a name for it, or know what you call it," Zeniyah said. She was curled up with Maurgen in the hills outside of town.

"Show it to me?" Minnie asked. An image filled her mind of a purple colored flower with yellow-tinged, serrated leaves.

"The entire plant is poisonous, different parts for different races. For it to affect a dragon, they must use the entire plant, including the root. Fresh is best, but dried will work."

"The Humans had this plant?" As Minnie spoke to Zeniyah, she scrambled to take paper and a pen from the king, mumbling an apology. Rapidly she sketched out the details of the image in her mind.

"Yes, but they had the dried plant, I think because they didn't want to risk killing me. Vera said that the dragons eradicated it from the Isle, but no dragon has been to the Human continent in centuries, so some may have cultivated it."

Minnie took a deep breath. "Zeniyah says this is the plant, I don't recognize it myself."

"Would your mother know?" Zavier asked, taking the drawing from her.

She hesitated for only a second. "She should, she knows every plant used in alchemy, but to be truthful, I'm not sure what she knows and doesn't know these days. She lied to me for so long... but we can send it to her and ask."

"Would you take it to her yourself?" Taurak asked, but Zavier cut him off with a firm,

"No."

Taurak and Minnie stared at him, one incredulous and one grateful. Zavier explained, "She doesn't fly quickly, I'll send one of the messengers." He gave her a swift glance, silently begging her not to argue.

"Very well. I'll have one of the scribes make copies and get it sent to Rosemary Hernshaw, and check the libraries," the king replied, thankfully letting it go.

"Sire, have you heard of Marshmere leeches?" Minnie asked, a curious look on her face.

"I have not, why do you ask?"

She shook her head. "It may not work, but Marshmere leeches have been imbued with the Wealdkin healing magic over the centuries. The Wealdkin woman I helped mentioned that it was used to draw poison or venom from a body. If we have some, that is something worth trying. If there is time…" she trailed off.

"I'll add that to my list of things for people to look into, thank you. Now, the two of you are excused. You'll want to clean up and dress, Narith has a dinner planned and you are not allowed to skip it, either of you. Minnie is being honored by the crown for her part in saving our people."

Mouth agape, Minnie struggled to find a response, but she was saved by Taurak, who continued speaking in a far softer tone. "Narith said you didn't arrive with much, so she's had gowns commissioned for you, as well as footwear, jewelry, and other accessories women need for formal occasions. I believe she also had day wear and travel clothes made up. She said she had offered you her own gowns and you only accepted three."

Tears welled in her eyes, and ashamed, she looked down at the floor. "I'm sorry she's gone to so much trouble for me."

Taurak scoffed. "My dear girl, why should you be sorry? I read the letter your father sent, and I vividly remember the day your mother was injured. If anything, we are the ones to be sorry, we didn't follow up with your family to ensure all was well, particularly after we received word that you were dragon-bonded. I should have, I knew she had developed a fear of dragons. We let you down, and we will do what we can to remedy that, and in this case, the least we can do is provide you with suitable clothes for your visit."

"But sire," Minnie cried softly, looking up as tears fell. "The queen gave me her old gowns, that's more than enough. Mama always said I had no business coming here, that I wouldn't be of use. She'll expect me to return home to care for her…" she whispered. Suddenly all her old fears had resurfaced.

Zavier took her hand, but kept silent.

Taurak cleared his throat, meeting her eyes with a gentle but stern glare. "Young lady, you are a hero to our people. You are incredibly powerful, and I can only imagine how much more so now that you have found your Zeniyah. Who, I might add, is the next Vynar. You and she are two of the most important souls in this court, and no one will be sending you anywhere. You are your own person, young Minnie. I would be honored to have you remain in Hatherus, lending us your power and support if you wish, but you are free to go wherever and do whatever you want to. Normal rules simply do not apply to the Bonded of the Vynar," he finished with a small chuckle.

Minnie stared at him, a tear slipping down her face. "I don't have to leave? The other dragon-bonded said they were assigned jobs…"

"The other dragon-bonded aren't you," Taurak said, more gentle than before. "Even if you weren't bonded to Zeniyah, your power grants you more leeway than most. I'd have asked you to teach the younglings magic, or perhaps to become an ambassador like Zavier here, or so many other things, but no, you would not have been sent away in disgrace. You're far too valuable for that."

"Plus," Zavier added, glancing between her and his father. "Zeniyah granted you the Draconid gift. You are now one of only three living Draconid."

Tuarak beamed, nearly bouncing in his seat with his excitement. "Did she? That's incredible. Your power will have grown, and our people will know when they see you as a Draconid that you are an amazing young woman, Minnie."

She'd heard from Zavier many times over the previous days how skilled, clever, intelligent, beautiful, incredible she was. She was finally beginning to believe that he truly meant all those things, and valued her for herself, not for the service she provided. But to hear it from another, especially the king of her people? It was too much. Fat tears rolled down her eyes.

Zavier left his seat and knelt before her on the rich carpet. "Minnie, love, please."

She buried her face in her hands, struggling to breathe through her choked sobs. She tried several times to speak, but the words had no sound. Zavier pulled her up and wrapped his arms around her, hugging and rocking her as he stroked her hair. She was vaguely aware of the two men speaking, but she couldn't hear their words over the roar in her ears.

She had her freedom, she had oblique permission to go anywhere, do anything, and be anyone she wished. Guilt gnawed at her, knowing she should return to her family and help care for her mother, even as the desire to stay in Hatherus with Zavier swept over her, pushing aside the guilt.

That only made her feel worse.

Forty

Zavier

Z AVIER SAT IN HIS father's massive chair with Minnie curled on his lap. He'd given the briefest explanation to his father as he requested privacy. Taurak was only too happy to escape, closing the door behind him.

Stroking Minnie's hair and gently rocking her, Zavier whispered words of love and encouragement, despite knowing she probably couldn't hear him over her own sobs. As she began to calm, he reminded her over and over that she was safe and free to do what she wanted.

When her sobs had become sniffles, the violent shaking had slackened to the occasional twitch, Zavier reached into the drawer of the desk for the pile of clean handkerchiefs his father kept there. He used one to mop at her face, ignoring her pleas to let her do it herself and for him not to look at her.

"Shush. I don't care how much snot comes out of your pretty little nose, I still love you. Now hold still." She fought him, but he was able to dry her eyes and wipe up her face, folding the handkerchief and holding it to her nose and demanding she blow. She struggled with a laugh, and took the hankie from him to do it herself, but she did blow her nose, albeit more softly than she probably needed to.

"Do you want to tell me why that made you fall apart?" he asked softly, taking the wet hankie from her and tossing it on the floor nearby.

Hiccuping, she drew in a shallow breath, then another. Finally, she said, "I think... I'm a bit overwhelmed by how... How accepting you and your parents have been, and how much freedom I have now... I expected to be told what I would do, and I wouldn't have a choice. If I had to go home, then fine, I'd go. If I was assigned somewhere, then it wasn't my fault if I didn't go back, and I wouldn't feel so guilty."

He waited for her to continue. When she didn't, he gently asked, "And do you want to go back?"

She shook her head. "I love my family, and I do miss them, but no. I don't want to return to Ocrans. Even if that means my father and sister have a harder life. It's so selfish of me, I can't even believe I said it... but there it is. I don't want to go back. Ever."

Hugging her tight, Zavier whispered, "You don't have to go back. And you don't need to feel guilty about that, Mina. We'll find someone to help your family, a nurse who can help your mother."

"We can't afford that, Zavier, and I can't let you pay for it," she began, but he shushed her.

"Stop it, this is nothing. Like Father said, when your mother was injured, we should have kept an eye on her and not let her illness get this bad. I'm told she was injured at a royal event, and by a royal guard, it's the royal family's job to help her and we failed. Let me do this."

After a moment, she nodded. "But I want to earn the money to pay for the nurse. Please, let me do at least that."

"Mina, my love, you've already earned that and more. You saved thousands of lives, remember? Did you not think you'd be rewarded for that?"

"But... I didn't do it to be rewarded..."

"Of course not, and that's why you will be, silly girl. Now come on, we need to get you cleaned up and down to Mother so she can dress you. She's always lamented having three sons, she really wanted a daughter to play dress up with."

Ignoring her protests, Zavier stood and carried her to the door. She glared, but turned the handle for him, giggling as he bounced her higher for a better grip. He carried her across the palace, not to the room she had been assigned to on her previous stay, but up to the family level. He finally set her down outside a carved wooden door at the end of the hall.

"I asked the staff to move your things here, it's a more comfortable room," he explained as he opened the door for her.

"The last room was more than comfortable, why did... you..." She trailed off as she looked around her new space.

Every inch of the room had been freshly scrubbed and there were new linens on the bed. Her new clothes that his mother had ordered were already hanging in the closet. The windows and door to the balcony were thrown wide, giving a view of the garden and river.

Whereas her previous room had been charmingly furnished in simple but well-worn furniture, everything in this room was carved and new. As she neared the bed, she traced dragons up the posts, and more dragons in flight flew along the headboard. Wordless, she turned back to Zavier.

"This room is yours, as long as you remain in Hatherus. I felt it was the best one for you."

She looked around again, still stunned. "When did you arrange all of this?" she asked in a quiet voice.

"Before we left this morning I had Maurgen bespeak Alyss and Faladrik. They passed on my request to my parents, and Mother was all too happy to set this up. She likes you, you know."

Shaking her head, Minnie traced the door of the wardrobe. "I didn't know... in fact, I was pretty sure she tolerated me and nothing more, I've been such trouble for her."

Zavier crossed the room and drew her into his arms. "You aren't any trouble to anyone. Not here. Go take a bath, there will be a lady's maid in to help you, she's been assigned to you, so don't give her a hard time, she's following orders. Mother will be expecting you down in her dressing room once you're finished bathing."

"I suppose I have no choice but to attend this dinner?" she asked, the fear clear in her voice.

"I'm afraid not, dearest. Like Father said, you're being honored as a hero. It would be rude to skip, not to mention a bit awkward for the rest of us. It shouldn't be too bad, though. Good food, entertainment, a few speeches, and probably dancing afterward, but we can leave when the dancing starts if you want," he teased.

Kissing her forehead, Zavier reluctantly left. What he hadn't mentioned was his room was right next door to hers, so it was a short walk down the hall to his apartment. He bathed quickly, happily scrubbing days of travel wear and grime from his skin and scalp. Soaking in the hot springs had been nice, but nothing beat a good scrub with soap!

He stood at his wardrobe selecting clothes for the evening when there was a knock on the door. Ensuring the towel wrapped around his waist was firmly in place, he called, "Enter."

His mother appeared, a paper-wrapped bundle in her arms. "Good, you aren't dressed. I had this made for you, it will match Minnie's gown for tonight. Wear it with black pants and boots, you'll compliment her without drawing too much attention."

Smiling, he crossed the room and took the small bundle, lying it on the bed to unwrap. Embellishments and a circlet of gold set with a single emerald sat atop the folded garments. Setting the circlet aside, he found there were two additional items, a lightweight, long-sleeved shirt in black, and a vest. The shirt had no adornment, not even buttons, instead tying closed at the back of the neck.

The vest, however, was of a deep green with gold embroidery. The stitching and thread used were so fine, he had to bring the vest to his face to see the stitches clearly, despite his excellent eyesight. Brown and green thread formed the background of several bushes along the waist, with golden flowers dotted throughout. Along the lapel were more of the flowers, and a small bunch graced the pocket on his chest as well. He ran a finger over the embroidery. Setting the clothes down, he reached for the adornments.

The circlet was one he had seen before, an heirloom of the crown that was kept in one of the treasury vaults. He lifted the other piece, realizing it was a set of epaulets. He recognized the curved gold embellished with chains looped on the sides, but the flowers wired on were a new addition. They were the same simple blossoms that were embroidered on the vest. Setting the epaulets down, he looked at his mother for explanation.

She smiled, sitting down on the edge of the bed. "I had them commissioned the day before you left for Saltstone. A bit presumptuous of me, perhaps, but I had a gut feeling, and your father had one of his dreams. I knew she would be important to you."

He traced the golden flower on the epaulet, dropping his hand once again to the vest and its embroidery. He finally recognized the flowers that covered the fine cloth and adornments: jessamine flowers.

"Has she said yes?" Narith asked, watching him closely.

He looked back and gave her a soft smile and a quick shake of his head. "No, Mother, she hasn't, but then, I haven't really properly asked her."

"And why not?" she demanded with a huff.

"It's not the right time, Mama," he replied softly. He took a deep breath, and added, "She has to accept and want to be queen. If it were just me... It would be different, I think, if it were just me. I need her to be ready to lead an entire country by my side. Then I can ask her," he finished, almost to himself.

Narith shook her head, but smiled at her son as she stood. "You do make your life more difficult, don't you, my son. Couldn't have chosen one of the easier women?"

"Of course not, Mother. Speaking of, did Caddoc choose?"

"No," she replied, huffing. "He and one of the ladies disappeared, we thought they went to the Rising, but reports have them in Lockhill. I didn't have much hope for him anyway. Now, get dressed, I'm going to help Minnie. I'll see you at dinner."

Forty-One

Minnie

M INNIE POLITELY REFUSED ASSISTANCE in the bathing room, opting to scrub herself in privacy. She did allow the woman to help her dress, the added layers for a formal court gown being far more than the simple underthings and breastbands she was used to.

She was wearing the silkiest, softest, and lightest piece of underwear she'd ever owned. Her curves were barely contained within the slip of fabric, and Christine, the maid, warned her not to bend over unless she absolutely had to. The breastband was designed to plump her already well-endowed chest and push her breasts together. A thin slip of a dress went over, which Christine said was to hide the lines of the underthings.

Clad in a thin, black silk robe, Minnie was instructed to sit in a chair beside the balcony doors so the maid could work on her unruly hair. There was a knock, and Christine's gasp of surprise as she opened the door made Minnie turn to see who had entered. Her eyes widened and she hastily stood to curtsy as Queen Narith breezed past the maid with a polite nod of thanks.

"Your Majesty, I'm so sorry, I thought I was supposed to meet you downstairs!" Minnie cried, curtsying lower.

"None of that, my dear, no curtsying or apologizing. I decided to come to you, as you've more than enough to worry about this evening. Christine dear, be a love and let the footman in, he is carrying Minnie's dress and accessories." Narith sailed across the room as if she were floating on air, Minnie noticed with envy.

Christine vanished, returning seconds later cradling a long garment bag with another carefully wrapped package balanced on top. She winked at Minnie as she draped everything over the bed and returned to her side.

"Your Majesty, I was about to do her hair, but I'd love your opinion. I feel we should leave her hair down, perhaps braid a few small bits and pin them back to hold the tiara. Her hair is incredible, she'll make quite the impression."

Narith nodded, turning Minnie to the mirror.. "Yes, I think that would be best. Did you find the mixture I had delivered earlier? A stylist friend of mine told me it does wonders for curls, no frizz at all."

"Yes, my lady!" Christine hurried away, returning seconds later with a small pot. She unwrapped the towel from Minnie's head and massaged the mysterious mixture into her hair before Minnie could offer any objections. Not that she would, taming the frizz had been a minor life goal of hers, she thought wryly.

"This is a lot of preparation for such a small person," Zeniyah said to her. Minnie could feel the dragon as a subtle presence in her mind, comforting and steady.

"I'm afraid," she whispered back. *"I've read books on royal protocol, but nothing about a formal banquet or being the recipient of an honor. What if I make a mistake?"*

"Then someone will cover for you and everyone will pretend it didn't happen," Maurgen answered smoothly when Zeniyah had no reply. *"Listen to what Narith says to you now, and stick close to her or Zavier. Someone will guide you in what to do tonight. Beyond that, just be yourself. You have a natural instinct for this."*

Narith was watching her in the mirror with a knowing smile on her lips. "Reassuring remarks from Zeniyah?" she asked in a low voice.

"Maurgen, too," Minnie replied. She didn't miss the look of surprise on Narith's face, nor how it shifted to a satisfied smirk.

"You'll be just fine tonight. Be yourself."

Minnie gave a slightly unhinged chuckle. "That's what Maurgen said. Trouble is, I'm not sure I know who I really am anymore," she added in an undertone, so softly she wasn't sure Narith would hear.

She did, though, and laid a comforting hand on her shoulder. With a silent look, the queen sent Christine across the room, giving an illusion of privacy.

"You are Jessamine, bonded to Zeniyah. You are dragon-bonded. You are a hero to our people." As she spoke, she ran her fingers through Minnie's hair, separating out curls and re-twisting them together. She scrunched more of the mixture into the curls, creating a halo around Minnie's head unlike anything she'd ever managed on her own.

"You are Minnie, daughter of Thomas and Rosemary, and no matter what else you feel about them right now, they love you, and I know you love them. Your parents have shaped you to be the caring, selfless person that you are. Yes, you are selfless, my dear, no matter what else you may think of yourself. Your healing gifts alone make you unique, but you have not hesitated to share that gift with everyone, no matter the cost to yourself."

Minnie frowned, feeling the need to argue, but a stern look from the queen kept her silent.

"You are many people, and still discovering yourself. In many ways, we all are. There. What do you think?"

Minnie shifted her focus from Narith back to her hair, amazed that she hadn't realized the queen had been braiding and twisting curls into a half up-do. Tendrils framed her face while the rest were neatly pinned in a braided coronet at the top of her head. Christine appeared beside the queen holding a tiara. Narith took it and expertly pinned it in place, standing back with a flourish. Minnie gasped.

Burnished gold filigree framed four emerald gemstones the size of her thumbnail, and a fifth, the center stone, was twice the size of the others. Small diamonds circled the largest emerald and lay scattered across the filigree. The entire piece sat neatly on her head, framed by the wealth of curls.

"Your Majesty... I shouldn't... Are you sure it's alright for me to wear this?" Minnie breathed, lifting a hand to touch but stopping herself mid-motion.

"Of course it is, or I wouldn't have given it to you. It's yours to keep, at least while you're attending functions in Hatherus," Narith replied. With a gesture to Christine, the maid turned Minnie and began applying powders and kohl to her features.

"Keep, oh no, Your Majes—"

Another stern glare and she silenced herself.

"The tiara was mine, and now it's yours. Traditionally, it has been passed down from mother to daughter within the royal family, or sometimes to a granddaughter, but it pleases me to give it to you. There are earrings and a necklace to match, of course, no ensemble is complete without accessories." Narith chatted away as she busied herself behind Christine, out of Minnie's line of sight. It only took a few moments for Christine to highlight Minnie's features and step back, satisfied.

"Stand up, my lady, it's time to put the dress on," Christine said, taking Minnie's arm. She led her to the bed and deftly removed the robe. Before she could become self-conscious, Christine had Minnie raise her arms and carefully lowered a dark green chiffon dress over her head. The material flowed everywhere, diaphanous and light. Only the layers kept the gown from being completely see-through. Laced tightly at the back, her arms were completely bare, as the sleeves were nothing more than falls of fabric off her shoulders. Narith handed Christine a burnished gold belt that fit just under her bust, cinching her waist. The fall of the dress accentuated the curve of her waist and hip, though the thigh-high slit concerned her in several ways.

The final touch was a pair of golden epaulets that Christine pinned to her shoulders, with chains dangling in loops on either side. The dark gold filigree matched her tiara and belt, though she noticed small flowers had been attached with wire, and recently, she thought. Approaching the mirror to get a better view, she recognized with a jolt that they were jessamine flowers.

She looked up in the mirror and met Narith's pleased look. She didn't recognize herself. Her wayward curls were tamed into a halo around her head, the perfect frame for the tiara. Her gown was, without doubt, the loveliest she had ever seen or imagined. She felt beautiful, almost ethereal. She looked like a princess. She almost felt like one.

"I had them commissioned after you healed those people, the day you went to Greta's," she said, her voice extremely smug. "I had a feeling we would have a good excuse for you to wear them. I'll have them welded on properly another time, it was an experience just getting the flowers crafted!"

Stunned and close to tears, Minnie wasn't sure what to say. She turned to find Christine holding a pair of simple slippers in the same green as the gown. Kneeling, the maid helped her step into the shoes, rearranged the folds of the gown to her liking, and nodded final approval.

"Thank you, Christine, that will be all for now." Dismissed, the young maid scurried from the room, quietly closing the door behind her.

"Your Majesty," Minnie began, unsure how she was to adequately express her gratitude and unworthiness.

"My dearest child," Narith interrupted, waving her to silence. "If it takes me a year, I will break you of this deference. You are our family, now and forever."

Minnie could feel the stunned look on her face, and panic rose within her. "But, I haven't—"

"Oh, sweetheart." Narith pulled her into a hug, careful not to rumple Minnie's gown or muss her hair. "I know you haven't, and that's alright. Whether you and he come to an agreement or not, that doesn't matter, not to me. I decided the day you arrived that you were something special, and if you

363

will allow, I wish to consider you one of my own children. No, dearest, I do not want to replace your mother, no one ever could! You and I are much alike— it's true!" Narith gave a small giggle at the incredulous look on Minnie's face, a sound that didn't quite match the serene manner of the queen.

Narith continued, "When I first came here, I was afraid of my own shadow. It took years before I came into myself. Let me guide you, and make your way easier than mine was."

All Minnie could do was nod, folding herself back into the comforting embrace of the queen.

Forty-Two

Minnie

MINNIE WAITED IN AN antechamber of the massive dining hall, hands sweating. She was trying not to fidget with her dress and cause creases. Narith had escorted her here and told her to wait while she scurried off to get herself dressed, promising she would return in time to give Minnie a rundown of what to expect inside. Minnie had paced back and forth for several minutes, only stopping when she'd noticed an older woman watching her from across the room. The woman stood in shadow, hiding her face.

"Ah, here you are, my dear girl," a jovial voice boomed out, startling Minnie so she almost let out a small screech. She managed to contain the noise, looking up to find King Taurak approaching. Hastily she curtsied, but she was only halfway through before he took her by the elbows and lifted her.

"None of that, sweet girl, you are family now!" He kissed her lightly on each cheek, giving her a paternal smile of reassurance. "You look exquisite, I can see my wife's impeccable taste at work!"

Flustered, Minnie nodded. "Yes, Your Majesty, she gave me everything, and helped me dress. I'm so honored to have her favor," Minnie stammered.

Taurak released her and stepped back, sweeping her a courtly bow. "We are honored to have you grace our halls, my lady. If there is anything else we can do for you, after all you have done for us, please do not hesitate to ask."

As he stood, she heard a scoff from beyond him. The older woman she had seen was glaring at them with her arms firmly crossed over her chest. Taurak turned and gave her a withering look.

"Is there something caught in your throat, dear sister?" The words were polite, but the tone expressed clearly that he did not much care for this woman. At his words, Minnie recognized who the woman was: Anitra, the woman who had been rude to her and said she had no right to be here.

Many things had changed since then, the biggest among them that Minnie had found her dragon. Zeniyah roared in her mind as the memories played out. Beyond the palace walls she could hear the angry bellow of several dragons.

"I cannot believe you would stoop to bowing to a commoner," the woman sneered, glaring daggers at Minnie.

"And I cannot believe you would be so rude to our esteemed guest, Anitra," Taurak began. He was interrupted by the arrival of several men in the uniform of the royal guard. The older man, Minnie remembered, was General Beltak, the king's brother and Anitra's husband. She assumed the two other men, who looked like younger versions of Beltak, were their sons.

"Anitra," Beltak sighed, taking his wife's arm. "We spoke of this." There was firm reprimand in his tone, and the grip on her arm appeared to be painfully tight, though she gave no indication she noticed.

"No, husband," she snapped. "You spoke of this and I sat there. She is common and unimportant. Yet another no one who seeks to marry a prince and become queen."

Beltak growled, dragging his wife away. Their two sons gave anxious looks of apology to their king and pressed themselves against the wall as if hoping to disappear.

"I'm sorry about her," Taurak began, but Minnie shook her head.

"No, sire, it's not your place to apologize on her behalf. Nor is it her husband's." Feeling far more bold than she had just moments before, probably because Zeniyah continued to rage in her head, she continued. "She was rude to me from the beginning, I think she's just a miserable person. I don't need to prove myself to her."

"You've proved yourself to me, and that is more than enough." Her stomach gave a strange flutter as Zavier's voice reached her ears. He used his 'prince voice,' and loudly enough that she knew Anitra must be within hearing distance, but his eyes were locked on hers.

Zavier descended the small staircase so rapidly, she barely had time to see that he was wearing a shade of green similar to her gown. The vest was tightly laced across his slim chest, over a black shirt with billowy sleeves cinched tight at the wrist. His pants, also black, were tucked into shiny black leather boots. Instead of appearing monochromatic, the dark contrast, coupled with a circlet and epaulets that matched hers, set off his golden hair and eyes and deepened his golden-tanned skin to a shade almost as dark as her own.

He took her hand and lifted it to his lips, his eyes never leaving hers. "Good evening, my love," Zavier whispered, brushing his lips across her knuckles. "You look ravishing." His eyes darkened as they raked over her body before meeting her own eyes again.

She looked him up and down, slowly, lingering on the snugness of his trousers and vest. She let the heat pool into her own eyes, and gave him a small half smile. Zavier licked his lips, almost nervously, as he stared at her mouth.

Leaning forward, he whispered into her ear, "You know what that smile does to me."

Before she could reply, Taurak cleared his throat. Blushing deeply, she stepped away, mortified that she had forgotten the king— Zavier's father!— was standing right next to them.

"Narith should be— ah, here is my beautiful wife!" The queen descended the steps, taking her husband's hand and giving him a graceful twirl at the bottom. They were also matched, Minnie realized, in a gown and vest of deep bronze with black accents.

A door that Minnie hadn't noticed before opened behind Zavier. She nodded for him to look, as his elder brother Caddoc entered the antechamber.

"Son! I had no idea you were returning," Taurak exclaimed, clapping his eldest on the shoulder.

"Mother sent word that I should attend. I apologize for my tardiness," he replied absently as he fiddled with the cuffs of his shirt. His own clothes were a bit rumpled, but clean. His formal vest was a simple bronze much like his father's, a color that offset the highlights in his golden hair.

Narith and Taurak stepped aside as Caddoc approached, his hand outstretched to clasp Zavier's.

"I heard you had some excitement. I'm glad you're unharmed," he said in an undertone. While the tone almost hinted at sarcasm, Minnie felt the words were actually sincere. The way Caddoc gripped Zavier's arm implied that he had been worried for his younger brother's wellbeing.

Before they could say more, a bell rang from inside the banquet room. Narith gasped, and turned to Minnie.

"I nearly forgot! You'll go in last, on Taurak's arm. He will seat you, and you won't need to worry about anything else until after the second course. We will announce when you should stand and approach, Zavier will take your arm and lead you up, presenting you to Taurak. He'll say a few words, then you can sit back down. Nothing to worry about!"

Nervous again, Minnie nodded. Zavier took his mother's arm, and Taurak came to Minnie's side to take hers.

"Just breathe," the king whispered to her as the double doors opened.

Forty-Three

Minnie

THEY WALKED DOWN THE long aisle arm in arm with every eye on them. Minnie felt her knees weaken, but the reassuring pat of King Taurak's hand on her arm bolstered her. Zavier had escorted his mother, and they stood together with Caddoc at the head table, waiting. She locked eyes with Zavier, his serene smile grounding her. She could do this. It didn't matter that everyone was staring. It didn't matter what they thought of her.

The first course flew by in a blur. She was seated at a table between Zavier and Caddoc and given water and wine to drink. The tables were set in an oval, with gaps between each table and a wide open area in the middle. She had been told that at the end of the meal, the tables would be pushed back further to allow more room for dancing. During the meal several musicians grouped in the middle, playing peaceful music at a volume just loud enough to be heard without drowning out the conversation.

The second course was served, a savory soup. Despite the delicious aroma rising from the dish, Minnie took tiny sips from her spoon. Her eyes flicked back and forth from the high table at the top of the oval where Taurak and Narith sat, to the table directly across from her. The king's sister-in-law glared at Minnie, not eating her own meal.

Finally, after the third time Zavier asked if she was alright, she pointed it out to him.

"Oh, ignore her, she's a bitter old hag," Zavier replied.

"But why does she hate me so much? She was dismissive from the moment I arrived in Hatherus," Minnie whispered.

Zavier shrugged. "Who can tell? She thinks she's better than anyone else, maybe she hates seeing you succeed."

Resolved to ignore the woman, since no one else seemed to be paying her any attention, she took a sip of her wine.

As the servants cleared the table of the soups and prepared to bring out the next course, butterflies began to flap in her stomach again. Zavier slid a hand under the table cloth and rested it on her thigh, giving her a reassuring squeeze.

Taurak rose from the head table. He didn't need to tap a glass or even clear his throat. The second he stood, the room fell silent.

"Thank you all for attending us here this evening. We are honored to have you as our guests." He paused as the gathered gave a small round of applause. As Minnie looked around, she spotted the other dragon-bonded women who had been summoned when she was. A wave of guilt washed over her, she wasn't the only person who had gone to Saltstone, and—

"Tonight, we gather to give our gratitude to the brave Bonded who raced to the aid of Saltstone during the recent crisis. We are eternally thankful to Lady Coraline, Lady Adaline, and Lady Lavender, each of whom were instrumental in creating healing and pain relieving elixirs, as well as lending their magical skills in mending the afflicted. To each of them, we bestow a sizable dowry should they wish to marry, as well as a permanent offer of employment here at the palace in whatever capacity suits their skills."

As Taurak spoke, each of the three dragon-bonded women were escorted to the head table. They each curtsied, received a bow and a kiss on the forehead from the king and queen, then were escorted back. As the women returned to their table, Minnie saw that Anitra glared at the retreating trio. Well, Minnie thought, at least she was being equal opportunity with her disdain.

"We also want to thank our son, Branton, who is currently on Dragon Isle, for his part in healing the ill and rendering aid. Further thanks to our son Zavier, and our brother Beltak, for their rapid response in mobilizing guards and treatment for Saltstone. Without your quick thinking and leadership, more lives would have been lost."

Beltak and Zavier both rose from their seats and made small bows toward the head table as the assembled clapped for them. Minnie took a deep breath. Here it comes, she thought.

"Finally," Taurak's voice softened, and he cleared his throat. "Without the incredible healing skills and power of one woman, this story would have had a more tragic ending. We wish to thank Lady Jessamine for her tenacious pursuit of the cause of this illness, and her amazing use of magic to cure those poisoned."

Zavier stood, a hand under her arm to lift her. She rose on shaky knees and followed him. As she approached the table, Narith rose as well, taking her husband's arm. Together, they bowed to Minnie. She curtsied in return.

Standing again, Taurak continued. "In gratitude for Lady Jessamine's actions, we bestow upon her a dowry, should she choose to marry. She is also granted a position upon the royal council, as it was her actions within our own city that led to the exposure of a corrupt system of neglect that had been long overlooked by ourselves."

She gasped, stunned by his words. Taurak's kind and gentle face, and Zavier's broad grin beside her, soothed her nerves. She nodded, lowering her head again in a grateful bow.

"Finally," Narith added, as her husband gestured her forward. "As the Bonded partner to Zeniyah, the future Vynar of dragons, Minnie is to be considered a part of our family and an official royal ambassador from this moment forward."

As the assembled behind her began to clap and cheer, Minnie turned shocked eyes to Zavier. He grinned, his eyes glittering with mirth. Taking her arm, he leaned closer as they walked back to their table to say, "It looks like they will have you in the family with or without my help!"

The pair took their seats, and the third course was served. Finding herself suddenly ravenous now that the little ceremony was over, Minnie ate everything on her plate, even daring to steal a bit of Zavier's while he told Caddoc a story.

After the main course was finished and the plates cleared away, a round of sparkling wine was brought out. Each table was served by the wife of a high ranking official, and Minnie saw that Anitra served the king and queen's table as well as the princes' table. She carried a tray with crystal goblets, silently holding it low enough for each person to take a glass. As the final glass was distributed and the women returned to their seats with their own goblets, Taurak rose again.

"We drink a toast to the souls reclaimed by the Fates in Saltstone and elsewhere this past week. May Doraiz guide them to a peaceful afterlife."

As one, the assembled lifted their glasses in toast and took a long drink. The sparkling wine tickled her nose, and had a tangy, almost medicinal smell. She let the wine touch her lips, but didn't drink, she'd had enough already with her dinner. Beside her, Caddoc noticed her full glass, and indicated they swap. He took hers, winked slyly, saluted her with it, and drained the contents.

Minnie had turned back to ask Zavier a question when there was a crash beside her. Caddoc collapsed across the table, clutching his throat while his lips turned blue. A scream from across the room turned Minnie to the head table. Taurak and Narith were also struggling, mouths gaping as if desperate for air. Overhead, dragons bellowed.

The entire dining hall erupted into chaos. More people screamed. Guards swarmed in with their swords drawn. Beltak barked orders, but Minnie didn't hear any of it. Beside her, Zavier clutched his chest, his lips beginning to turn blue. He collapsed on the floor beside his chair.

"They aren't breathing!" Zeniyah roared in her head. Images of her and Maurgen launching themselves from the hills flashed across her mind. *"The dragons cannot hear their riders, their magic has been*

severed, almost as if they are dead. The dragons will go wild if we cannot mend the connection!"

Fear filled Minnie's heart. Wild dragons could destroy the city. *"Without air they'll die in just a few min— Air!"* She hoisted Caddoc upright. He clutched at her arms as she dragged him around the table and let him collapse on the floor beside Zavier.

Zeniyah pushed her power through their bond into Minnie, who took the power and shaped it. Using Zeniyah's near limitless reserves of energy, she imaged rivers of air. The river flowed from her mouth and split into four separate streams. She pushed the air into their lungs, matching the ebb and flow to her own breathing. Color returned to their faces as the precious oxygen filled their lungs. Taurak and Narith slowly came round their table, their eyes locked on Minnie. Taurak tried to speak, but he was unable to form words.

Beltak's shouted orders finally penetrated her mind as everything came back into focus. Guards locked the doors, keeping the guests in their seats. Anyone who had access to the wine was being interrogated by Jarn in the corner, two guards stood flanking him with their swords drawn.

Dragons bellowed as they landed in the courtyard outside. Zeniyah and Zahite loudly reassured Alyss and Faladrik. Maurgen, Minnie could hear, was desperately trying to reach Zavier. Time seemed to be moving in odd increments as Minnie breathed, slow and steady.

Anitra's shrill voice reached her. Minnie was so focused on breathing for the four royals, it took her several long seconds for the words to make sense.

"She's murdering them! She's woven some kind of spell, look at her! They're dying! She'll kill the entire family, she's a murderer, someone stop her!"

Zavier slowly sat up, his eyes locked on Anitra. His expression had changed from panic and fear to pure rage.

Zeniyah roared again as a loud thump sounded overhead. *"I'm here. I'll breathe for them, search their bodies for the cause!"*

Minnie gratefully allowed her dragon's presence to fill her, letting Zeniyah take control of the air magic. She knelt beside Zavier and Caddoc, golden light filling her hands. She scanned one and then the other, but found nothing amiss within their chests. She was searching Zavier again when Zeniyah spoke. *"I'm going to pause the breathing for him. You need to see what is happening when we aren't helping him."* Before Minnie could object, Zeniyah must have released the magic, for Zavier soundlessly gasped again and touched his chest. Quickly she hovered the golden light. His lungs weren't moving at all but she couldn't see a cause!

"If there is nothing wrong, why are the lungs frozen?" Minnie cried to Zeniyah as they resumed breathing for Zavier. He clutched her hand, a tear running down his cheek.

Zeniyah didn't answer. She pulled away from Minnie mentally, but retained control of the magical air flow. Minnie tentatively reached to Zeniyah and Maurgen and heard them conferring with the other dragons. She scanned the room again, hoping someone had figured something out in the past few minutes.

Caddoc had crawled to his parents and hugged his mother. Taurak was still standing, but he was being held up by Beltak, who signaled to a servant to attend them. Zavier wiped at Minnie's face and she realized she, too, was crying.

376

Turning back to him, she pulled him into her arms. "Don't you dare die," she whispered, kissing the top of his head.

Taking her hand, Zavier wiped away another tear. Struggling to keep her composure, Minnie leaned in once more. "When we get out of this, I'm never leaving you. You'll be stuck with me as your princess and queen, so I hope you meant it!"

Afraid that his reaction, whether it be joy or anger, would just distract her, she stood and carefully walked to Beltak and Taurak.

As she approached, she heard a soft voice in her mind. *"I am Alyss, the king's dragon. I have seen this before. Taurak's father died the very same way. He was unable to breathe, and the strain caused his heart to give out before he could suffocate."*

Realization dawned on her then, just as it had earlier in the king's study, and she once again felt like an idiot. Dragon-bonded were immune to all poisons, except one.

"Beltak!"

The commander whirled to face her, his hand going for his dagger. "Are there any Marshmere leeches anywhere in the city?" she cried, rushing up to him. Beside them, Taurak nodded vigorously, pointing to her.

"Marshmere—"

"Leeches, yes, can we send someone to look?"

"I have them!" A voice behind Beltak cut through their frenzied conversation. Jarn approached, a latched box in his hand.

"Before dinner this was brought from the healer's school at the king's request. I have no idea what it's for, but I was told to keep them nearby."

"Oh, thank the Fates," Minnie breathed, snatching the box from his hands. She fumbled with the latch briefly but was able to get it open. Grimacing, she lifted two wiggly creatures from the box. "I've no idea where would be best, but I'm gonna go with logic. If your lungs are affected and you drank poison, let's put them on your chest."

Taurak already had his shirt partially undone and took one of the dark blue leeches from her hand. Without hesitation he let it attach to his skin. The other followed seconds later. As she turned to the others, they already had their shirts unbuttoned, or in Narith's case, the bodice of her gown tugged low enough to give access.

"I've no idea if this will help, but it can't hurt," she mumbled as she attached several of the slimy creatures to Zavier, then turned to Caddoc. She was pleased to see that their chests were rising and falling in time with her own, and gave thanks to Zeniyah for her support.

As she attached the final leech and closed the box lid, she turned back to Taurak. "Any change?" she asked, hopeful.

He shrugged, indicating he was unable to try while Zeniyah and Minnie breathed for him. Nodding, she told Zeniyah to cut Taurak's river of air off. He gasped, tried to suck in a deep breath, then frantically shook his head.

"A little longer, I guess," she said quietly.

"My lady, you were told to stay in your seat until you've been cleared," Jarn's strong voice behind her made Minnie turn. Anitra was approaching them, pointing a long, bony finger at Minnie.

"I am the sister-in-law of the king, I am above your investigation!" she shrieked, slapping a hand in Jarn's direction. "That creature tried to kill the royal family and you're letting her near them?" She whirled on her husband, hands on her hips.

"Anitra, you must sit down until Jarn and the guards have searched and interviewed you," Beltak tried to soothe his wife, but she was having none of it.

"I refuse to be searched! I am your wife, they cannot touch me!"

"My lady," Minnie said, her eyes narrowed at the older woman. "If you have nothing to hide, there is no reason they cannot search you. I'm sure the only reason they want to is because you are the one who served both the high table and the princes."

"You bitch! How dare you accuse me of poisoning my family!"

She was ramping up for a new tirade, but was cut off by Taurak's coughing behind Minnie. She turned in time to see him draw a deep breath out of sync with her own.

Forty-Four

Zavier

Z AVIER TOOK A GASPING breath, then coughed loudly.

"Thank the Fates," Minnie breathed.

Narith began to cough, then Caddoc. Zavier grabbed Minnie around the waist, clutching her to his chest in a spine-crushing hug. Minnie encircled him with her arms, tucking her head under his chin. "You saved our lives. You're incredible," he whispered, kissing the top of her head.

"No, it wasn't me," Minnie tried to pull back to look at him. "Zeniyah directed the magic, and Jarn had the leeches, and your father issued the order to have them here just in case..."

"That is so like you, my love. You save us all with your quick thinking, then give credit to everyone else," Zavier smiled, leaning down to kiss her again.

"Almost not quick enough. I should have realized far sooner, we were just—" Minnie began to reply, but a shrill voice interrupted her.

"She is the one you should all be looking at! She is trying to kill you all to take over the kingdom!"

Anitra was still going at it, and her accusations were becoming more ridiculous, Zavier thought. Minnie tilted her head, a look of sheer annoyance on her pretty face.

"If I intended to kill them, why did I force them to breathe?" she asked in the most sickeningly sweet voice Zavier had ever heard. Well, at least she was taking credit for saving them! "Besides, I wouldn't need to resort to poison to kill someone. I could suck the air from their bodies or roast them alive."

"Maybe that's what you did! And those disgusting creatures haven't done anything at all!" Anitra screamed, pointing again at Minnie, who sighed and rolled her eyes.

Taurak had had enough. "Beltak, restrain your wife, or step aside and let others do so."

There was a moments quiet as Beltak took a firm grip on Anitra's arm, whispering furiously into her ear. Feeling a tap on his arm, Zavier looked back at Minnie. She lifted the box in her hands, indicating the leeches still attached to Zavier's chest. She went around to each of them, gently detaching the bloodsuckers and plopping them back in the box.

"Sire," another guard joined their group. "We've spoken to the servants who readied the wine. Each of them said no one was alone with the bottles, and no one tampered with any of the drinks. The wine was in full view of at least three servants at all times until it was brought onto the main floor by the wives."

Anitra scoffed. "You can't seriously believe the word of mere servants. Clearly one of them must have added the poison."

Zavier gave her a wry smile. "Just a moment ago you were accusing Minnie of trying to kill us with her magic. Now you're sure it's poison? Are you feeling alright, auntie?"

Stammering, Anitra tried several times to form a reply, but she was cut off as the room darkened. A dragon roared just outside the banquet hall. Zavier glanced over his shoulder to see Maurgen pressed against the window, peering in with one large eye.

"Alyss witnessed the former king's death. The symptoms match. Whoever did it will smell strongly of Dragonsbane."

"Do any of you know what it even smells like?"

"I do," Zeniyah replied quietly, and Zavier mentally kicked himself. Of course she would know, he thought ruefully.

"Alyss may recognize it as well, but only Zeniyah will know for sure," Maurgen added.

"Father, your dragon has told mine that our symptoms match those that killed Grandfather. They are certain they will be able to smell the poison on the assassin, and suggest we line everyone up outside for them to investigate."

Taurak gave his son a lingering look that Zavier matched. His father could tell he had left things out, and he silently begged his father to trust him. He didn't want to mention that it was Minnie's dragon alone who knew what to smell for, especially within hearing distance of Anitra.

Unfortunately, Minnie wasn't in position to see the look. She said, "They can compare the scent on the four of you to whoever put the poison in the wine."

Anitra jumped at that. "You've been all over all of them, now you suggest this! You're trying to cover up the fact that you'll smell like poison! You did use poison, and you're trying to pin it on someone else!"

"Lady, what is wrong with you?" Minnie snapped. Zavier lifted a hand behind her back to stop his father interrupting. He'd longed to go off on Anitra, but watching Minnie lose her temper was just as good.

"They almost *died*," she shrieked, gesturing behind her to the royals. "Someone tried to kill the entire royal family, and possibly me too, because Caddoc drank my wine and he collapsed first! You're so damned busy blaming me, but why would I want them dead?"

Anitra glared, wrenching her arm from her husbands and planting her fists on her hips. "You've clearly been fucking the prince. If you kill the family then have his baby, you'd be the regent for the next ruler of our country."

Everyone blinked at her for several very long seconds. That was the most convoluted, ridiculous—

Minnie laughed. "My timing sucks then, since I am currently bleeding away any possibility of a pregnancy. Beyond that, Zavier has made it abundantly clear he wants me as his princess. King Taurak flat out told Zavier he should marry me. Why would I want to be regent, when I could quite easily be queen?"

The little group fell to silence. Zavier could see wide grins on the faces of his parents, while Beltak looked nervously between his wife and Minnie.

"I think we should just move this outside and let the dragons sniff out who the culprit is. It's quite clear to everyone using their intelligence that Minnie wasn't our attempted assassin." Zavier's tone was dry.

Turning to look about the room, he realized that Jarn had already begun shepherding the assembled guests through the doors, with guards stationed every few feet. Weapons were no longer drawn, and everyone moved along without any sense of fear or panic.

Beltak took his wife's arm again, pushing her ahead of him. The family followed, Caddoc and Taurak talking quietly between themselves. There was something just not right about Anitra's behavior. She was often irrational and erratic, but tonight she seemed unhinged.

The dragons crouched together on the wide end of the courtyard.

Taurak and Narith crossed the cobbles and allowed the dragons to take a deep breath of their scent for comparison, then retreated back to the doorway. One by one the guests passed under their noses, some daring to reach out and pat one of them as they did so. As each person was cleared, they were released to go home. The celebration was clearly over.

After every guest had been deemed innocent and escorted out of the palace, Beltak dragged his wife to the waiting beasts. Maurgen rumbled deep in his throat.

"I smell the Dragonsbane on them both," he told Zavier, whiffling over the couple. *"It is strongest on him,"* he added.

"You're sure?"

"Of course I am."

Zavier stepped closer to his parents and leaned in. "Maurgen says—"

"So does Alyss," Taurak interrupted.

"And Faladrik," added Narith.

"Beltak was holding me up..." mused Taurak as he watched his brother. "If Minnie would have the scent because she hugged you, the same applies to Beltak."

"And he touched Anitra. Does that mean they're both innocent?" Narith asked.

"Or both guilty," said Zavier quietly. His parents looked at him. "She's accusing anyone and everyone. Is she protecting him?"

Taurak, a troubled look on his face, shook his head. "I refuse to think my brother tried to kill me, us. With all of us dead, and Branton underage, he would be regent. I know my brother. He never wanted to be king or to have any of that responsibility."

Caddoc, having heard his father's reply, chimed in. "As another son who has no wish to be the king or have that much responsibility, I agree with Father." Zavier turned surprised eyes on his brother. "Oh, I know I've given you a hard time, Zavier, but you are infinitely more suitable than I am, in every way. It's part of being a big brother to be a pain in your ass."

Pushing that aside to deal with another time, Zavier said, "If not Beltak, why is she acting this way? Has she finally gone completely insane?"

As they watched, Alyss lowered her head until she was eye to eye with the couple. She nudged Beltak with her snout, backing him up several paces, then turned her attention onto Anitra. The giant eye roved over the woman who was fidgeting with her skirts.

"Alyss says she remembers that smell on Anitra when my father died," Taurak breathed.

Drawing a deep breath, Zavier called for the couple to return. He held up a hand for Beltak to step aside, away from his wife.

Taurak stepped forward, and Zavier backed away, letting his father handle this very delicate issue. This was miles outside of Zavier's experiences. He reached out for Minnie, who had been quietly waiting nearby. She wrapped an arm around his waist, he pulled her in and tucked her under his chin.

"Anitra Davengard. The dragons tell us that you smell of the poison used to attempt to kill us."

Fear flicked across her face. Zavier only saw it because he was watching her face closely for any changes. Almost instantly she pulled herself together, changing her features to an incredulous look. "That is preposterous."

"The dragons also say that the same scent was on you the night my father was killed. I find that to be an important detail, as my brother was with me in another city the night our father was killed, so I know he had nothing to do with the king's death."

"I have no reason to kill anyone," she scoffed, but Zavier heard the fear in her voice now.

Taurak narrowed his eyes. "Our father never made it public knowledge that I was his heir. You had married Beltak only a few months prior to his death. This family has long joked that you only married him for the position, but now I am wondering if that's actually true."

Zavier shifted his focus from Anitra to her husband. Beltak wore a pained expression. His demands that he be allowed to marry Anitra were almost as legendary as Taurak's instant love connection to Narith. Beltak had fallen in love with the woman's beauty, and refused to consider another match. Her family had been well connected prior to the investigation that ruined her family's businesses, and Beltak had insisted that her trade knowledge would be valuable as his wife.

"Annie," Beltak whispered, reaching a hand toward his wife. "Tell me it's not true."

"Of course not, they're liars, just trying to turn you against—" As one, the dragons in the courtyard bellowed. Faladrik and Alyss shot flames into the sky.

As the dragons settled, Beltak met Taurak's eyes. Zavier caught the look, saw his father nod. Beltak reached into his pocket for a small case, and shook a capsule into his palm. While his wife spoke, he popped the capsule in and clapped his hand over her mouth. Zavier knew what he had done, and approved.

"What are you doing?" she hissed through several hoarse coughs after he'd removed his hand.

"Shut up," he hissed. Turning to his brother, Beltak saluted. "Sire, I have given the suspect one of the truth capsules we received from the Wealdkin. It should take effect in just a moment and you will be able to ask her questions and receive honest answers."

Taurak nodded, his solemn face creased in worry.

Several tense moments passed. Clearing his throat, Taurak asked, "Anitra, did you kill my father, the previous king?"

Unsurprisingly, Zavier thought, she refused to speak. The capsule contained powdered mushrooms enchanted by the Wealdkin that would force only truth to be spoken, but they could not force one to actually speak.

Minnie shifted beside him. He was about to ask if she was alright, but he didn't get the chance. She waved a hand toward Anitra. A ring of fire roared to life around the woman. As the family watched, the ring shrank until the flames were inches from Anitra's ornate gown.

"Speak, or I set you on fire," said Minnie, without any expression at all.

Zavier looked to his father, wondering if they should put a stop to this. Taurak shook his head.

"I ask again. Did you kill my father?"

As they watched, the fire crept closer. A gust of wind blew past them and sent the fire into Anitra. She screamed, but as she tried to turn away, more fire appeared.

"No!"

"No, what?" Taurak asked. The wind blew again.

Screaming and waving her hands, Anitra cried, "My father did it!"

"Your father was in Lockhill at the time of my father's death. Explain!"

"Stop, stop!" she shrieked, batting at the flames uselessly with her hands. Minnie gestured again and the breeze died, but the flames remained close to Anitra. "My father wanted him dead, and for me to be queen. He sent me a vial of something. I poured it into the king's tea when a servant wasn't looking."

"Why?" Beltak demanded, his face tight.

"My father wanted revenge, it was the king's fault that his business was destroyed."

"Did you try to kill us tonight?" Zavier asked.

"Yes!"

"Why?"

"I was blackmailed!" Anitra sobbed. Minnie allowed the flames to die down a bit, giving her several inches on every side.

"Explain what you mean," Taurak insisted. Anitra took several deep, gasping breaths. For a moment she looked like she wanted to refuse, but when Minnie lifted a hand again, she began to speak.

"The son of the man who sold my father the poison somehow found out that I helped kill the king.

He told me that he would keep my secret if I gave him information on the family in exchange."

"What kind of information?" Taurak demanded.

"Your schedules, likes and dislikes, who you supported, who you hated, he wanted to know everything. He asked questions constantly, I never knew why he wanted to know. He just said that it was all for a greater plan, but that it was best if I didn't know."

"Did you also poison the people in Saltstone?" Minnie gasped, speaking for the first time in several minutes.

"No, I had nothing to do with that." Zavier wanted to disbelieve her, but the Wealdkin truth capsule wouldn't allow her to lie.

"Do you know the man's name?" Taurak asked.

"No. Just that he is Human, and a powerful mage."

Zavier and Taurak exchanged looks. Behind his wife, Beltak had silent tears streaming down his gruff face.

Zavier quietly asked, his voice harsh, "Why did you try to kill Minnie?"

"That bitch," Anitra spat. "She's just like Narith, she doesn't deserve to marry a prince."

The family exchanged looks. "That seems like a pretty pathetic reason to kill someone," Taurak said. "You've hated Narith since you met her. Why?"

Once again, Anitra tried not to answer. As the fire rose and licked at her gown, she screamed. "She took everything that should have been mine! I should have been queen! I should have had the powerful sons!"

"So you're jealous and bitter, and for that you betrayed your family?" Narith demanded.

"You deserve death, and so does that bitch. She's young, powerful, and has the prince wrapped around her finger. I see it happening all over again, another woman coming in to take what should have been mine."

The family fell silent. Minnie allowed the fire to dwindle to almost nothing.

"Your husband loves you," Minnie whispered. "Beltak defended your behavior, he told me he loved you despite how you treated others and how you behaved... Why would you betray him like that?"

Anitra clamped her mouth shut. She tried to leave the fire circle, but Minnie waved her hand and it flared back to life.

Sighing, Anitra turned back to them. "He should have become the king so that I could be his queen."

"You did all of this because he gave up the throne." Caddoc spoke, a shocked expression on his face. "You really tried to kill us all because you didn't become queen."

"The mage swore that if I killed you all, Beltak would be made king and I could finally be queen." Anitra sighed again, apparently giving up the fight to keep her secrets. "In the beginning, he threatened to expose me for poisoning the king. After a few years, he offered me gold, jewels, new gowns, all the things that I expected Beltak to give me. I played it off as my father's remaining wealth. In exchange for the material, he asked me to help him poison other people he wanted to be rid of. When the mage asked me to poison you all, he said it was time for the royals to die, but he wouldn't tell me why he wants you all dead. He sent the poison, and I put it in the wine. He sent more than enough, so I put some in Minnie's drink, too."

"What about Branton?" Narith breathed, her hand flying to her mouth as her eyes widened.

"The second he returns to the capital, someone will kill him," Anitra replied. She almost looked remorseful. "The mage threatened my sons if I didn't poison all of you. He promised me I'd be queen, but he never said anything about who would inherit after us, so I'm not sure if he would have hurt them or not. I couldn't take the chance that he would hurt my boys, or tell someone what I've done."

"This Human sent you the Dragonsbane?" Zavier asked.

"Yes. I was told to give it to you all tonight. I don't know why, or what he plans, or where he got the Dragonsbane."

After several long, tense moments, Taurak quietly spoke. "Anitra Davengard, you have disgraced this family, committed numerous acts of treason, and attempted the assassination of your king, your queen, and two of your princes. Have you any final words before you are put to death?"

"Death? You can't—"

She got no further, though. A sword appeared in her chest. Behind her, Beltak removed the blade and watched her fall to the ground.

Forty-Five

Zavier

T HAT EVENING, THE FAMILY met in the king's study. Beltak had excused himself to his quarters. He had tried to tender his resignation as commander of the guards, but Taurak had refused, though he did give the man some much needed time off.

Taurak, Narith, Caddoc, Zavier and Minnie were seated on sofas and armchairs, discussing the events of the evening. They'd run through every moment for the second time, when Narith called a halt.

"If we go over it again, we may go insane. Tomorrow is another day," she said, resting a hand on her husband's arm. "The last thing I want to say on the subject is a heartfelt thank you to Minnie. I was truly afraid we would die, but your quick thinking saved us all."

Blushing, Minnie shook her head. "Zeniyah helped, it wasn't just me alone."

"But it was your quick thinking," Caddoc said from his corner of the room. He had been quiet though most of the discussion, something that unnerved Zavier. Cad was never quiet or sedate, and he hadn't heard his brother laugh once all night. "Your quick thinking to give us air, something well over a dozen other people in the room could have done. You also remembered the leeches. You kept your head and didn't panic. You saved us, and we are all grateful."

The family looked at Caddoc with stunned expressions. Minnie finally smiled and nodded acceptance. Caddoc took a sip of his whiskey —from Taurak's private stock, from an unopened, sealed bottle— before he spoke again. "I want to apologize to the family. My behavior has been reprehensible, and I am well aware that I have caused more work and grief for you all. I had got it into my head that Father wanted me as king, and would choose me because I am eldest. Like Uncle, I have never wanted it, and instead of speaking to you as a man, I behaved like a spoiled child. You have my sincere apologies, and a promise that I will do better in the future."

Zavier clapped his brother on the shoulder. "I knew you couldn't be all terrible, brother," he exclaimed cheerfully, offering his glass in a toast.

"I wish you had spoken to me, son, but I am glad that we have the truth now. I only wish it hadn't taken a near death for us all to be a family again," Taurak added, giving his eldest a pointed glance.

"You're right. I am sure tomorrow will be busy for you with all the aftermath, but when you are free, I would love to speak with you, and reconnect. And you, Mother, of course. I will atone for my behavior, and I also want to explain my sudden change, but not now. For tonight, if you don't mind, I think I'll go to my room," Caddoc drained his glass and stood, offering a bow to his parents. They all wished him a good night and he left.

"I think we will retire as well," Taurak said, after a shared look with his wife. "Cad was correct, tomorrow will be busy." Narith agreed, they all exchanged pleasantries and embraces before his parents left as well.

Zavier turned to Minnie with a soft smile. "Shall I escort you to your room, my lady?"

She took his proffered hand and allowed him to escort her out of the study. They walked in silence. Zavier had spent the past several hours ranging from shock, disbelief, anger, relief, and gratitude, then repeating the cycle all over again.

As he had knelt on the dining hall floor and stared up at the beautiful face of the woman he loved, all he could think of was, it wasn't fair. It wasn't fair that all they got was one week together, one single week full of turmoil and danger. He hadn't been concerned about his own death, but for her to watch him almost die was unacceptable.

Outside her door, Zavier raised her hand to kiss her wrist. "Thank you," he said softly.

She smiled at him, the cute little half smile she had that always made his heart flutter. "I couldn't let you die."

"I'm glad you didn't, it would be very hard to make you my princess if I were in my grave," he teased. Reaching around her, he opened her door and bowed. She took his hand and backed into the room, pulling him along after her. As he entered, he nudged the door closed behind him.

"Stay with me tonight. I don't want to be alone," she whispered, wrapping her arms around his midsection.

"Of course, my love," he replied, returning the embrace.

They slowly undressed their finery, carefully setting their gold adornments on the vanity and draping their formal clothes for cleaning. Neither could
figure out how her hair was pinned, so after removing the tiara, they left the braids in, though Minnie
did wash her face and take care of her personal
needs in the bathing room. Clad in nothing but skin,
the pair slid beneath the silk covers, curled into one
another.

The following several days were busy for all of
them. Minnie had been asked to go to every healer
and clinic in the city to inspect their credentials and
ensure no one overcharged for their services. Zavier spent countless hours with his father and their
council attempting to discern who had kidnapped
Zeniyah and tried to kill the royals. So far, they
had no answers. The initial group of Skinshifters
who had been sent to Shaesan as spies returned.
They had been unable to gain entry to the capital city safely, and were denied an audience with
the Human king. New plans were being made, and
everyone was on high alert for any further attempts
on the royal family's lives.

Four days after the banquet, Minnie returned to
the palace from yet another clinic tour to find her
parents and sister standing in the foyer. Stunned,
she froze in the doorway with her mouth agape.
Sitting on the stairs beyond her parents was Zavier.

"How?" she breathed, finally shaking herself out of
her shock.

"We came on dragon-back," Rosemary whispered.
She was pale, her hands clenched tightly around
Thomas's arm.

"I sent them a letter, asking if they would come,
and if they'd be willing to fly here. I thought you'd
want to see them without having to go back to

Ocrans," Zavier explained as he approached her. Taking her hands in his, he leaned in and whispered, "I know you wanted to tell them all that has happened."

Minnie, tears filling her eyes, stared at her mother. "You flew? On a dragon?"

"I took a very, very strong sedative first, but yes. We wanted to see you. I wanted to see you... I wanted to apologize again, and make sure you were alright. We'd heard some rumors about you from the Bonded making deliveries," Rosemary explained.

Minnie stepped away from Zavier with slow, cautious steps. As she neared her mother, Rosemary opened her arms to hug Minnie. That broke the tension. Minnie rushed into her mother's warm embrace, swiftly joined by Thomas and Juniper. As the family held each other, they laughed and cried together. They were escorted to a private sitting room where Minnie and Zavier told them of their adventures since Minnie had come to Hatherus.

That evening at dinner, Zavier surprised them all by standing and pulling Minnie from her seat. "It's sure to go down as family legend with how many times I've asked, so hopefully this will be the last time. Now that we aren't dying or overly emotional, I want to ask you something very important. Minnie, my love, will you be my princess and future queen?"

Unable to speak without laughing, Minnie nodded, wrapping her arms around Zavier's neck and kissing him. As they parted, he pulled a ring from his pocket and slipped it on her finger.

Plans were set in motion to hold the wedding in one month, invitations were sent to every village, town, outpost, city, and territory, inviting the dignitaries that were expected of a formal royal wedding.

Hundreds of people would attend to view Minnie being officially crowned as Zavier's Princess.

At Zavier's insistence, though, they held a small, informal wedding ceremony in the gardens of the palace, attended by just their family and friends. Branton returned from Dragon Isle, escorted by Caddoc, who had gone to fetch him. If Zavier noticed that Brant had spent most of the evening admiring Juniper, he hadn't mentioned. Minnie had noticed though, and made a note to keep an eye on the pair.

Caddoc seemed to have genuinely turned over a new leaf, or his previous behavior had all been a complete act. He was gentlemanly, kept his flirting to a minimum, and had been seen about the city itself helping their citizens. Minnie had even heard from the council (several members of which had been replaced by Taurak) that Caddoc was leading a project to build several brand new clinics situated across the city. Each one would be staffed by a rotating group of volunteer healers and would be completely free of charge.

Minnie stood on the balcony of the room they now shared, watching as palace servants scurried around the garden. In a few hours she would stand in front of every important person on their continent and be officially proclaimed princess. Her belly fluttered with nerves.

She heard Zavier rustle the sheets behind her, then his soft footsteps as he approached her. Zavier wrapped his arms around her waist from behind, resting his chin on her shoulder.

"You're up early, couldn't sleep?"

"No, not really... I had another dream." Minnie turned to face him and met his eyes. "It was more fragmented, there were a lot of flashes. I saw a

Nightwalker woman and Wealdkin man, and what might have been forest dragons. I saw Caddoc with a Nightwalker woman. Then I saw Branton and Juniper, but I'm not sure if it was just a memory from the wedding. I saw myself holding a baby—"

"A baby?" he gasped, looking down at her midsection with wide eyes.

"Relax, I've been taking an herbal mix. We still haven't had that conversation, and we really need to do that one of these days. I was older, anyway, but yes, there was a baby. Keep in mind, these visions aren't always accurate. And I hope they aren't..."

"Why, what else did you see?"

"I saw the man again, the one who looked like you, but not. It wasn't Caddoc like we thought. I can't believe I didn't see it before. It's Branton, an older, adult Branton. He was clutching his head, blood dripping from his eyes, nose, and mouth. Someone might try to kill your little brother."

www.ingramcontent.com/pod-product-compliance
Ingram Content Group UK Ltd.
Pitfield, Milton Keynes, MK11 3LW, UK
UKHW040628151224
452011UK00006B/3